APOCALYPSE 2060

APOCALYPSE 2060

MICHAEL DANFORTH

iUniverse

APOCALYPSE 2060

iUniverse books may be ordered through booksellers or by contacting:

iUniverse
1663 Liberty Drive
Bloomington, IN 47403
www.iuniverse.com
844-349-9409

ISBN: 978-1-6632-2907-6 (sc)
ISBN: 978-1-6632-2908-3 (e)

Library of Congress Control Number: 2021919229

Print information available on the last page.

iUniverse rev. date: 09/17/2021

I dedicate this book to my loving mother,
I know she is enveloped in God's love.

Thank you to my brother, without your support and
encouragement, I could not have accomplished this book.

This book is written to help bring my dad and others to "Salvation".

CONTENTS

CHAPTER 1

MEET THE CHRISTLINKS

John received the data and then let his training and DNA guide his deliberate movements; gently he squeezed the trigger and BAM! Dead center. "Nice shot." Said Mike, John's spotter. "You've been great all day." John, "No, we've been great all day. At this distance, without your help I couldn't hit the broadside of a barn." Mike, "Well, all the other snipers along this ridge are probably getting the same numbers from their spotters as you do, they should, there correct, and they hit a good percentage, but you hit bullseyes all day every day. You're the best." John, "Let's just keep practicing hard and get better every day." The two were becoming quick friends since being partnered together by base command. Mike, "I can't wait for Nationals. Our numbers stack up against the best in the corps." John, "Just keep feeding me those right numbers and we can't lose." Mike, "You can count on me buddy; better start practicing your acceptance salute," said Mike laughing, as both knew medal winners in the military do not give acceptance speeches. They packed their gear and started walking back to the barracks. As they turned the corner John saw the General's staff car blocking his path, a couple of butterflies started fluttering in his gut. A stately figure exited from the back, "C'mon son, we are on a schedule." The couple of butterflies turned into a swarm zoomin' around his insides.

He was always excited to be around his father; but now, growing older he also wanted to be...good...or better. John, "I'll see ya tomorrow, Mike, take care." In the car, fearing bad news, John asked, "What's so important dad?" Luke, "I thought you would know something. Grandpa, (Luke's grandfather, John's great-grandfather), must be up to something. I got a direct order from General Mitchell for us to be at pops house at 12: 00 sharp." John was just relieved to hear grandpa was ok. So, for the next hour they cheerfully entertained each other with stories, questions, and comments. Near the end of the ride Luke asked the standard dad question, "How's school going?" "All A's," was the casual reply. Luke, "Competitions?" John, "Very good in the master sniper division. Our scores would do well even in the older age groups." Luke, "Well, you're representing your peers, and many others; so, do not be slack in effort. I know you won't;" and then quickly added, "I'm proud of you son." Wow! John didn't expect that. He hadn't done anything spectacular. Luke, "Any kind of hand-to-hand combat?" John, "No. Never interested me." Dad didn't make any kind of indication of anything about that, good or bad, no clues. But even at his young age John sensed that dad was o.k., but also was a little displeased, disappointed. Just in time the chauffeur pulled into Grandpa Matthew's driveway.

Luke knocked on the door and they walked through the familiar entrance. Grandpa Matthew was standing at the kitchen table, he put a puzzle piece in place, high fived his wife and turned to greet his kids. "How you doing boys?" He said with a grin, tug of an arm and a friendly slap on the back. Luke, "What's the emergency? General Mitchell said I had to bring John here for a pre-scheduled drill, news to me. Do you know anything about it?" Mat, "I just wanted to see my great-grandson, that's all. Is that a crime?" Luke took a closer look at his grandpa. Was dementia setting in? Luke, "Grandpa, it's a terse time in the world, and I may be required by it." Mat, "Don't get your sensitive feathers ruffled. I know what's going on and your importance to it. But what I have brought you here for far supersedes that." said Matt in a huff. "I'm waiting for some other people to arrive before I release the facts. Now, go to the garage and get the green chair, you may have to look long and hard for it." Luke gave Mat a "way to go "look and went to the garage, except there is no green chair; Mat wanted some alone time with John. Mat, "John, this is it! I'm going to tell them everything! When they all get here, we will all team together for the good of the many." John, "Great! I'll support you anyway I can. I know my friend Angelo is waiting patiently to begin our task." Mat, "I believe you and he will be formidable partners." "Unbeatable!" Said John, like it was already proven. Mat's heart swelled with pride; a small lump lodged in his throat. Luke came in and noticed a mist in Mat's eye. Luke, "You all right Pops?" Matthew eased down into his chair. "I'm o.k. What about you?" Luke, "I'm fine." Mat, "Well, we'll see in a few minutes." Luke, "What does that mean, something grand?" Mat," That's right. Something grand is about to happen." Mat looked at the door, nothing. He shot a quick glance at the T.V. screen, nothing. He was hoping UKBA would make a perfectly timed entrance full filling his "something grand prediction."

Mat, "Make yourself comfortable, the boys will be here directly." John's elders gathered in the kitchen; enjoying the togetherness, pretending Sarah's puzzle was the most important thing. John slumped down into the couch. They were waiting on his uncles, Mat's two brothers, who are military elite, and his grand dad, (Luke's father,) Mark, who is on Mars. John assumes Mark will be left out of the meeting. John wandered how the meeting would unfold. Something dynamic was sure to happen, he thought. Only he and great-grandfather Mat know of the world changing, history changing, future changing information that Mat is going to share with his family today. Perhaps the event could be seen coming, but nobody knew for sure. Now, it is for sure, it is real, and nothing will be the same.

Then alas! To John alone, and his mentor/decipheresses, a different and equally incredible mystery has been revealed to them only. The magnitude

3

of this next bit of revelation is also incalculable. And John believes he is the only one destined to teach it. Whenever he and his most humble mentor, the decipheress, decipher its total meaning; their original plan was to share it with all mankind, but now, only after understanding the first chapter, they are not so sure that would be wise. What information they have so far, if credible, like Mat's announcement, will change everything. It will cause shock, confusion, and division. World economies, religions, and other foundations will shatter. John slouched deeper into the comfy sofa. He momentarily became tired, so the couch pulled him in like quicksand. He just wanted to rest his eyes for five minutes. His mind drifted off to the strange occurrence when he received the ancient scroll.

It was summer break from school and John was with grandpa Mat in Jerusalem, he didn't know why. He was young. But he remembers grandpa, him and their two-armed guards getting out of their cool staff car and stepping into a hot dusty area of loudness and men moving around and shouting. At first it seemed out of control to him but as the group walked toward the "beautiful gate" it became apparent that the edge of crazy was the norm for this location. John looked over to his left and about 20 yards away on the other side of the gate opening was an old tramp. He was surrounded by a half-dozen well-dressed men, prince attire it looked like to John, that was shoving and cursing the tramp wildly. The sage had an ancient scroll in his hand, but his abusers did not seem concerned about it, they were busy trying to shew him away. Strangely, John could see the man motioning to him to come over to him. Some things are unexplainable. John felt an urge to go to him, with danger in plain view. Just then several people came from within the gate and moved toward grandpa. They were dressed entirely in black, and you could only see their eyes. Grandpa stepped toward them, and they started to speak, low tones and to John it even sounded friendly, like they knew each other. Being occupied they didn't notice as John walked towards the disturbance. The old-timer continued to wave him over, as John got closer his motions became more energetic. Until John was right there, and the yellers were startled and stepped back. John was surprised himself that such an angry mob would just step aside, especially for such a young boy, but they did. John moved close to the wrinkled and battered old man. He weakly started to hand the manuscript to John, but the closest adversary reached out to snatch it; immediately something like a fireworks sparkler came out of the old man's fingertips. He didn't do it when he could have protected himself, but John wasn't going to over think the situation, the scroll was meant for him. Just then Mat and the guards came over. Mat and the sage spoke some kind of jibberish and then Mat slowly reached for the scroll; and like the scribe before he got an electrifying NO! Mat, "John, this manuscript is of some importance, and it is meant for your soul possession. Take it." John did with the man's blessing. "We have safe storage materials in the car. Take this home and keep it safe from intrusion and corruption." As Mat took John's free hand and they walked back to the car John turned and looked back over his shoulder, the angry mob and the prophet was gone, just like that, no trace.

John occasionally would get out the ancient scroll to inspect it; but it was delicate, very brittle! And in an unknowable text. So, he just kept it in a safe environment. However, after the event that Mat is going to tell family members today happened; very soon after that, John took the scroll to one of his archeology professors at the military academy he is attending. One that can decipher that style of text and more importantly he is a humble man of God that John knows he can trust to keep everything between the two of them. One day not long ago, after the decipheress had decoded a small section of the scroll, he came to John with a chilling attitude. Decipheress, "I dare you! How can you bring me these blasphemies? Oh, woe is me!" John, "I told you the truth, you know the strange circumstance of how I received the scroll. What did it say?" Decipheress, "Lord, Hear my pleas for your forgiveness. I wash my hands of this request, making me free and clean from events and spirits. Young John, I believe this scroll to be a document from the beginning, that's what it declares. I stopped decoding it when it broke my heart. You read it and then choose for yourself if you wish to continue and I will do your bidding, I am free and clean." Later, John did tell him to continue deciphering the scroll. At the time the decipheress didn't know about John and Mat's encounter with Angelo and UKBA. Now John is a natural born learner, it was easy for him to memorize the first few pages of such an important document word for word and this is it; but there's another strange fact. Decipheress, "There's another strange fact about this document. It is so ancient and intriguing I wanted to know more about it, so I took a small corner piece to be analyzed and dated. The results are scary." Scary? Thought John, he hadn't heard that word since about first grade, and now this confident investigator is using it. John, "How's that?" Decipheress, "There are NO results. Over and over again, 12 times in all, different equipment and different scientist get the same results, NO info on the read outs. No information can be gathered from the pieces of scroll. It is like it does not exist. I've seen a lot but that's scary." John was told that, and then he read the Beginning of maybe the most ancient dictation ever.

It begins like this:

For Man's Understanding and Wisdom: Before the beginning. Before the beginning means nothing! Nothing! Nothing existed. Before the beginning there was only emptiness, a blank…zero. No warmth or light from the sun, no Earth to stand on, no mass, energy, or gravity. No ideas, dreams, or imaginations. No history, present, or future, no life, no death. NOTHING!! Just an empty blank void of nothingness. Then the most phenomenal event to EVER happen, happened! Out of this nothingness GOD WILLED HIMSELF INTO EXISTENCE!! That is how GOD came to be. GOD created himself. Through his Supernatural will power and determination HE became the first and original creation. Never to be duplicated, copied, or equaled. A supernatural spirit that is the planner, designer, creator, owner, director, judge, and Master of all things. All.

Everything is his possessions to do with as HE wishes. He doesn't have to get permission to act, isn't required to give explanations, and moves at HIS own speed and discretion. Anything that you can imagine, concrete or abstract, visible or invisible, real or imaginary, good or evil, originated with the "Most High Authority." He calls himself the great "I AM."

John heard a knock on the door and moved toward the hallway/kitchen. He overheard his dad explaining and apologizing about an incident in which he disobeyed a direct order, bringing shame and a serious black mark on an otherwise spectacular flight record. Luke also heard the knock and moved to the door to avoid his need of forgiveness, at least that's what he thought. But just as he reached for the doorknob ole' grandpa shot him a good zinger. Mat, "By the way sonny, those two men of brass who issued the return to base orders you disobeyed … the generals from the pentagon that showed great patience and mercy to your career, that's them coming through the door...HA.HA..HA" Mat busted out laughing. Luke, "Oh that's cold grandpa, really cold." He opened the door and in walked new E.A.A.C. Secretary of War, Fuller; and the new E.A.A.C. Supreme Commander Roy. Mat, "Great to see you boys, thanks for being on time." Roy, "We were ordered here by the high office." Fuller, "Yes, very unusual for us to be out of place during such a tense time in the world. What's the issue and, (in a curious tone), how DID you arrange orders for us to meet at your house?" Mat, "Well now that you are here let's not worry about it." Said Mat as he tried to hush hush their method of involvement. "Step into the den and get comfortable." Sarah, being the most perfect wife and hostess known to mankind had plenty of comfort goodies to share. Luke gave a last effort "Hail Mary" trying to redeem himself to his family elders and military superiors. Luke," Sirs, again I would like to apologize for my misconduct. My head is now screwed on straight and ready for action." The T.V. crackled, saving Luke from more self-condemnation. It was Mark from Mars! Unreal! Mark," Hello everybody, what a pleasant surprise. My bosses don't do favors, how did you manage this?" Fuller, in an official tone, "How did you manage this, Matthew. It is a security measure and I give clearance for every major event; this never came across my desk. Explain yourself." Mat, "You will soon understand, but I guarantee this will be the most sensational meeting you'll ever attend." Fuller squared his shoulders and stepped back. Mark, speaking through the T.V. "I don't know Dad, your talk about the birds and bees was pretty sensational!" The jr. high kids were starting to laugh when they heard, "Hey, hey, hey!" shouted Mat with all his might. "Quit clowning around. I will say again, for all family members, this is a meeting in which critical information that has global ramifications will be distributed," so, again with all his strength to emphasize his conviction, "shut up and heed what your told." Mark from Mars, "I'm, sorry Dad, I know we all are, (they nodded in agreement,) I've never seen you so emotional or upset with us. What's up?" Luke, "Grandpa, we were pulled off some top-secret assignments. What can be so important?" Looking at John Mat took a deep breath. "OK John this is it. John knows everything there is to know." Luke, firmly, "My son knows what. I don't like it when my son knows something before me." Mat, raising his hands up as if to stop traffic, "Let's get some facts straight first." Mat, grinning ear to ear, said," Sonny, tell the group what I did last week." John, "Sure." "Grandpa beat out over 200 contestants in the Regional Chess Championships at the complex. He's now club Master." John pointed to a medium size trophy on the mantle. A series of congratulatory remarks came from around the room. Mat continued, "Now have you ever know me to be a storyteller, exaggerator, or just to plain lie?" "Oh, those are fighten words!" said Luke in his fake western drawl as he leaped out of his chair, drawing snickers from the others. Fuller," Everybody knows you're a man of integrity. Where's this going, get to the point." Mat continued at his chosen pace. "Also, would you agree that over a period of time one thing that was thought to be true and beyond the need or possibility for correction, but, due to new information, indeed was found to be false, and that new discoveries are constantly being made. Roy, "Of course, I agree with Fuller…get to the point." John, "Just tell them grandpa, they've got to hear it." Luke, "Hear what, and why do you know things that I don't." John, "Oh, I know it all, and it is really neat." said John giggling. Mat stumbled with his speech, so John jumped up and got the tape in the dresser drawer that were given to them by UKBA. John held it up and had a silent glare to him as he circled the room, eye to eye each with each individual as he did so. He spoke, "This is a hologram tape showing an encounter Grandpa and I had with an ALIEN species! John stopped for a second expecting some comments, but nothing was said so he continued in quick succession. "It happened after the 4th of July fireworks. This tape tells how and why two alien species are heading to Earth, for very different reasons. I made a new friend and grandpa met the representative of a friendly alien planet. Watch this tape that Ultimate King Bee Angelo made; it explains very well his viewpoint of the situation." The five-star generals, world manipulators, looked at Mat with disgust on their faces, only out of respect for their eldest blood brother, and military legend, did they sit silent, thus, agreeing to watch a tape of such outlandish proclamations. After an hour of award-winning documentary about Bees, Maulks, good vs. evil, protection-destruction, fleets of spaceships coming to Earth. Two different Gods? And the kicker was the story about how Bee families from another planet "adopt" families and such on Earth as their own kin. The very familiar group watched with intense concentration. The presentation was just a replay of what Mat and John heard and saw when they met UKBA and his son Angelo. The presentation was better than Hollywood professional; its 4th dimension allowed viewers to feel they were present and involved within the video. It is futuristic alien technology. At the end, the solemn information left everyone in silence, even Mat, although he has watched it many times. Oldest son Mark was the first to react.

Mark, "Grandpa, this is a lot to absorb. I know you and John are not fabricators, but this is hard to grab hold of." Mat, "So you won't help us combat the coming evil?" Mark, "I do support you, but I'm on Mars, what can I do?" Mat, "Thanks son." He said flatly. Support from Mark? Mat didn't hear any commitment in Mark's voice; not like when he said "I do" when he got married; or when he said "I will" when asked if he would be the first man to colonize Mars. Mat turned to the others, "And what about you?" Roy, "I need more time to analyze this, it could be an elaborate hoax to penetrate our security. There are some issues I must research before I am on board. I will contact you soon." Fuller, "I agree with Roy. Besides, the best thing I can do is prepare our boys for war, that's what I'm all about." In closed thought Mat agreed. Fuller, "With this information in mind I will plan a strategy and organize the coalition. This will be for all the marbles; mistakes cannot be made." UKBA, listening from above, liked Fuller's spirit, he knew Commander Bo also would applaud it. Mat, "That's fine boys. I just wanted to give you a heads up on what's really going on; inform you of the powers involved. Well, now I know I can count on you when the time comes. Go do your jobs and we'll band together when called upon." As soon as Roy and Fuller pulled out of the driveway, leaving Mat, Luke, and young John in the den, the T.V. snapped on; of course, it was UKBA.!

"Hello everybody. Mat, that's about as good as we could have hoped for. As we discussed earlier it was better to test their faith and belief without seeing me. Excuse me Luke, I am UKBA. Our race, commanded by our most high supreme creator, sent me to fore warn you of the beast that is coming to devour you. Believe me, you desperately need our help. Your relatives have yet to comprehend the depths of the beast's evil desires. He is greatly advanced and highly motivated to wreak havoc upon Earth and all its inhabitants. His success will be the human race's hell! It will take our two species working together, and the holy grace and mercy from the most high above for us to withstand the fury of the dragon." Luke was slouched down in his chair, speechless. "Looookeeeee here John!" grinned Mat. "We finally found a way to keep your dad quiet!" They both laughed and Luke perked up a little bit. UKBA, "I am arranging a few events that may help our cause. Stay alert and again I will contact you. Luke, I will make a personal meeting with you to discuss matters. The second time will be more comfortable than the first. May God bless you all with Peace and Joy. Goodbye for now." The T.V. went back to regular programming. Mat, "Thanks for your help, John. I've been in many life and death situations when it was required that I act with courage…and I always did; but saying this crap to you guys scared me frozen, doesn't make sense." Mat softly slid into his favorite chair, wiping the mist from his eyes. John went to his most special person. John, "You did fine grandpa. It is over now, and everything got said. You put the truth out there and everybody will respond accordingly, I'm positive of it." John sure is wise beyond his years, thought Mat. "Yes, I know you are right, but I must go to bed. I am emotionally drained, but it was worth it; this has been a good day." Luke, "Hey, John can you wait in the car for a few minutes while I talk to grandpa; it's personal. "At least Luke didn't use the green chair in the garage trick. "Sure dad." John slid across the leather interior and his thoughts immediately went to the old man and the ancient scroll.

UUMM. The last word that was decoded turned out to be "Time." What did it mean? His phone rang and eerily it was the decipheress. "My young friend, I am in a frenzy! I have barely eaten or slept since I have received this scroll. My mind is being twisted. This new revelation may change your daily activities and decisions, it may change everything about you. I am sending it to you to read; until you catch up to me, if you can. Take care of yourself, I will call later to discuss matters. Goodbye." John started to read: He calls himself the great "I AM."

Time had yet to be defined or measured and will be an inconsistent and unreliable standard for the overlapping futures of God's plan; but for a while the great "I AM" marveled in his own glories. All energies, forces, principalities, authorities, natural and un-natural laws swirled within his "KLUZ." God's essence manifested many many spirits, each with its own unique and strong personality. Some became dominant, a triad acted as one. This harmonious interaction gives the holy of holies his most satisfaction. Then, as today, an honest, meaningful, relationship is what HE most desires. To HIM, a close personal relationship is much more important than deeds or sacrifices. Therefore, in his wisdom, and for his own pleasure, God decided to create another life, to experience existence with. The "I AM's "nature is primarily righteousness, justice, truth, and all the moralistic qualities they encompass. So, with all HIS glories willing and eager to share their nature, God said, "Let us make an image in our likeness and this chosen image. The spirits within God's KLUZ were in harmonious agreement with the decision, therefore, God said, "My word shall come forth!" With just a spoken word, a thought, and the blink of a spirit eye, the Father created the first Son. As everything else of origin, the first son sprang from the Father's essence. The Son inherited the Father's nature. His light was not as immense nor as bright as the Father's; he was only a child. After the creation the Father said this to the Son,

"I am your Father and you are my son. I created you, you are mine. Your purpose is to amuse me. Your adventures will bring me pleasures. Together we will sense the essentials. You will learn from my teachings and examples. I will provide challenges and opportunities for you. There will be problems and obstacles that your own "Orb" must overcome. In time you will become independent and will make your own way. But always remember this: I love you unconditionally; you will never be alone; and I will never be far away. I am well pleased with my design. Your name is Love." This is the first Father-Son relationship, a perfect model for any dad to mimic.

WOW! Thought John, this book is way out there! How can the Decipheress get so involved with it? How can we know if it's true or just a fascinating story. John was smart enough to know that he really didn't know that much; and maybe this 80 year old ancient histories professor might know more than he does; still, this is much different than anything else he has ever heard. John looked out the window towards the front door.

I know there are some critical issues going on, he thought, but what can be the problem now? The critical issue was John.

Mat," What's on your mind son?" asked the warrior/philosopher. Luke. "It's John. You know the Christlinks have always been leaders, real competitors, more aggressive than most, but John seems to be lacking those qualities. I don't know what to do about it, how do I bring him around?" Mat gruffly retorted back, "Now wait a minute sonny. You have been justifiably busy with your duties; thus, I have spent a lot of quality time with young John, and I can speak clearly of his abilities. He is a true Christlink through and through." Luke persisted, "But, grandfather, he didn't even try to qualify for the base combat skills tournament. Forget about competing against the best in the corps, like you, dad, and I did. He didn't even sign up for the U.F.C. bouts!" His voice was almost at a screech. Mat, "Luke, Luke, settle down son. Those tournaments are for awards and trophies, bragging rights. Believe me truly, John has much more substance than that. He doesn't base his self-worth on meaningless accomplishments." "Jjeezzz!" said Luke as he bounced onto the couch and jumped right back up. "Well grandpa, I remember you winning the gold medal at Nationals and the Wwwhooole family showed up to the celebration. It seemed pretty important to you then." Mat answered quickly, "Oh, it was fantastic! I loved the jubilation. It was incredibly important to me at the time, very meaningful. I'm just like you, but son, John is like neither one of us. He has a higher calling. One day I believe he will be put to the ultimate test and his magnitude will burst forth." Luke silently looked at the floor and then with a sparkle in his eye said, "I have trust in your judgement; I just hope I'm around when John shows his stuff." Mat, "Ya, me to!" They both chuckled and when they got to the door Luke turned and said, "Pops, you know you are John's whole world. And you have been a tremendous help in raising him, I was gone a lot… you have made him a son to be proud of. Sleep well tonight sir." Mat was glad Luke was out the door…so he wouldn't see his tears of joy.

John returned to the academy to continue his skills training and schoolwork. He is working to be a Master Sniper. He and his teammate, Michael, had progressed faster than any other team in camp history. They were much better than their age-group peers and just last week trounced the defending and previously unbeaten state champs. Next up were regionals and the buddies were seeded # 1! Mike and John had been spending many hours together and were becoming close friends. They had many similarities. Both were from famous military families. Like John's, Mike's heritage is filled with military gusto; some family member awarded the medal of valor in every war. Mike confided in his friend John his determination to continue the family tradition but was fearful of failure. While listening to Mike's personal dilemmas about varied topics Luke would offer encouraging words, advice, or verses of scriptures. Luke would speak of God's unconditional love for all mankind and the forgiveness of all sins.

One day, on their way to target practice, they stopped at a restroom to relieve themselves. "We're gonna crush regionals, and I can't wait for nationals!" said a gleeful Mike. 'We're shooten better than ever!" Luke, "Right. Just keep giving me those accurate readings and we can't be stopped!" Mike, 'Do you think we'll see combat duty?" Luke, "Yes I do. They always want the best out front, that's us!" They combined a laugh with a high-five and turned to leave. First there was a large shadow, then four big marine goons walked in, blocking the door. Three approached them as the fourth guarded the door. The Sargent at the door called out, "do it now, it's all clear." "Hey, what's going on?" asked John politely.

"Get out of here creeper, unless you want some of the same." was the angry response. "He should get it to, their probably lovers." Said a different big, angry person. "No, NO! I don't do anything; I just want to be left alone to serve my country." Mike had retreated to the back corner of the room. John turned to see him scared and a little bit shaky.

See, Mike was having difficulty figuring out his proper gender. He was an excellent soldier. High marks in every category and national qualifier in the Master Sniper Division. But most soldiers "decided" long ago to only look at one small slice of that pie instead of the whole pizza, and they hated that slice. John, "Guys this is wrong. Let me show you some biblical verses." "Shut up you punk! No way are we letten' this fag serve with us." John was running out of patience, "You dumbass! He's the best shot in the corps, him and me. He'll probably save your butt someday." Then the third bully, the biggest, "No, in real combat he'll drop his rag and run for hills. We're not taking the chance for it to get that far; he's not going to embarrasses anybody or put good men in harm's way. This time even the nurses won't be able to help him." This time, thought John? He remembered four-five months ago Mike was laid up due to a motorcycle accident. Mike said he was lucky not to be hurt worse; John now stupidly realizes that Mike was covering up. It wasn't a motorcycle accident; it was the first of maybe many beatings Mike has suffered; refusing to quit despite the pain and humility, because the pain of losing family respect is greater than the pain from broken ribs. "Look," said Luke, getting broad in a fighter's stance, "Mike is just as worthy as everybody else; you thick heads are just too asinine to know it. Now step aside and let us pass." "Quit talking and get the job done!" yelled the Sargent from the door. John tried to walk past them but was met with a crushing blow to his jaw, felling him down to one knee. But he instantly jumped up and yelled, "Alright, you were warned. I was put on this Earth to kick evil's ass and I'm starting with you."

John was about to find out, that just like every other first born male Christlink throughout history, that he was a (bad ass!) in hand-to-hand combat. John jumped toward the bums and jammed a pointy three finger dagger into the biggest one's Adam's apple; clutching his throat and gasping for air he dropped like a demolished building. But the guy to John's left smacked him in his temple, causing John to bend over trying to re-gain his senses. Then the third dude dropped a wrestler's elbow square into

15

John's spine. He fell to the floor rolling in pain. It didn't look good for John. Then, bursting from the corner Mike ran to the closest guy and jumped kicked him! After an expert landing Mike twirled around and landed a mighty roundhouse kick to the middle one. His nose splattered blood everywhere and he was out cold! But then Mike got hammered from behind, luckily John got up in time to side wind that guy from behind, action was fast and furious, until everybody kind of backed away from each other. The two hulks on the right, Mike and John, a few feet to the left. They glanced at each other with a look of immense loyalty, winked, then and it was on, this time the good guys initiated the fight, and it wasn't even close! John was a mini-Mike Tyson, left-right-left, all hard connectors. His counter didn't even get to throw a punch! John's lightening quick moves had the dude on the floor with glazed eyes, barely able to hold himself up on all fours! Mike was more of a Bruce Lee: a hard thump to the punk's chest from a flying frontal kick then an expertly executed roundhouse sent the guy reeling all the to the front door where the Sargent caught him in his arms. The Sargent dropped him, looked at his dead beat co-horts, and walked away. The stiff-necked beaten losers got up and clumsily followed. Mike and John composed themselves and shook hands. "Thanks for being there for me," said Mike, as he was catching his breath. "No, I need to thank YOU for being there. A lot of guys would have looked the other way, you didn't, thanks again" Mike," Did you really mean those things you said about me, that I'm worth just as much as everybody else?" John, "Mike, you are O.K. with me, no matter what." Mike smiled, seemed serene, and said "Come on, let's go rip that shooting range apart." They exited to a beautiful blue sky. A good friendship had just been solidified; going through "tuff" times together can do that.

After another good practice Mike and John was walking back to their barracks and as they turned the corner there again was a military staff car. This time an imposing figure exited from the back. He produced a document which turned out to be orders for John to report to the Decipheress, who also happens to be a Colonel. Decipheress, "I am informing you that I am taking a sabbatical, the military is allowing me time off to study the scroll." This surprised John. "Is it really that important?" quizzed John. "Decipheress, "John, one day you will understand what you have stumbled upon; or that, it is what you are destined for. I strongly encourage you to read the scroll as I will privately send the decoded parts to you; to you only. You may never see me again; take heed of the scroll; heads up, I hope you believe in U.F.O's. Take care John." With that he was whisked away like the black plaque had blown in, and John was escorted back to his room. Of course, John had to immediately start reading. Previously, God had just created a son; his name was Love.

As with all young yearlings Love was full of energy, mischief, and questions. He brought tremendous Joy to the Supreme Holy Father. However, as Love mature it became obvious that he needed more than just the interaction with the Father. Like the youth of today his horizons and boundaries needed expanded. Now most cosmologist think the universe is the result of an undesigned accident they call the "big bang." When a previous universe collapsed upon itself to the point where all matter was compressed to the size of a single atom. Theocratical physicist call it a "singularity". Until the time when it's force of gravity can no longer contain the natural repulsive energies within the nucleus and bang! The famous big bang! An explosion so big there are not enough zeros to calculate its power and energy. It caused all the stuff of the universe to speed away from each other, filling up the emptiness of the cosmos. Scientific observations confirm that it is still expanding. Theory states that one day it will stop expanding, become static, shrink, form another singularity, and then bang! Another big bang. Supposedly it has happened many times before. This sacred scroll states here and now that man's big bang theory is like camel dung. This holy scripture states an absolute truth. God made the universe, not an accidental explosion. God structured it as a giant playground for Son Love, and to reveal His power and glory. Again, a wonderous creation is manifested from the Father's essence with just a thought and nod. In its ever-changing totality it was created in an instant by the S.H.F.

As Love frolicked about in his new backyard he experienced new sensations, a different and better kind of fun. It was a completely higher level of excitement. The Father was truly astonished at the wide variety and vast number of "games" Love invented. His creative abilities are amazing! On kazillions of planets he played his favorite game...a game He named Evolution. On these planets he would arrange environmental conditions conducive for spawning organic life; and most did just that, spawn life. His favorite planet, for reasons we do not know why, is called "Earth." Life forms on other planets were faster and better than Earth in generating life, but Love loved Earth more than all the others combined. We do know why. But even on Earth life forms eventually developed. In the primordial soup of Earth's oceans chemistry brought amino acids together to form proteins and over time one-celled organism adapted and morphed into higher complex self-aware creatures. Some became beings with a higher intelligence than the others. Different organisms navigated the oceans, flew in the air, and inhabited the land. One species began to worship nature and other powerful controlling forces.

God-child Love was spending more time to himself, the wonders of the universe and his game of evolution was leaving the Father behind in 2nd place. The Son's knowledge and reasoning of the strategic complexities and interactions of the Father's masterpiece was ever increasing. God was pleased with the Son's growing maturity but missed the close relationship He had with the only other life in the realm. Therefore, in His common wisdom, God chose to create more living beings, for own satisfaction.

John thought, "Well, there was nothing, and then God, then Son Love, us humans must be next. But a knock on the door interrupted his thinking. Dad Luke was on the other side of the peep hole. "Come on in." said John, surprised by the visit. Luke slowly eyeballed the interior, "Has this place been scanned?" John, "No dad, your bug team hasn't been here."

Luke motioned John to walk to his secure staff car. As soon as they hit the seat Luke exploded, "I had a meeting with UKBA! Oh, it was fantastic… an alien! He said to pick you and grandpa up to go on a mission. You know how I like mission's son!" John peered at his usually military stoic dad, and superior officer, acting like an excited grade school kid on the last day of school; UKBA had swept him off his feet!

Luke, "He didn't give me many details, but I think I understand his eye now, is that weird or what?" John, "His size is hard to get used to, but you can tell he's smart!" Luke, "Yes." Said Luke in a very somber tone. "I can't believe this is really happening."

The two sat in silence until they pulled into Mat's driveway. Before the car was fully stopped Mat was grappling for the door. "What took you slow pokes so long?' I talked to UKBA 2 hours ago. (Actually 45 minutes ago.) Luke, "do you know what's going on?" Mat, "Do you? C'mon, we can't be late." Luke, "We won't be." They made it Arlington Park and walked to the specific pond, then each individual was gently pulled up, lifted up through the air and before you could say Giant Alien Bubble Bee, they were in a U.F.O. spacecraft and UKBA was fluttering in front of them. UKBA, "Hello, my friends. Praise to the Father for your safe occurrence." This is now Luke's third meeting with UKBA and he felt comfortable enough to state opinions.

Luke, "Thank you for including me; but it wasn't the video or grandpa's words that convinced me of this reality; no, it was my faith in my son's convictions that reassured me." UKBA, "Yes, faith may be the critical factor to the victory over the coming evil. Faith in the supreme holy creator. Here is what is going on. A divided Earth cannot withstand the fury of the Red Beast. Because of this we together will circumvent the Earth to meet key military, diplomatic and religious leaders. Also, many environmental, social, and economic "movers and shakers" will be contacted." The purpose is to personally invite these influential leaders to a general conference meeting to discuss the common problem before us. At this meeting I will show myself, explain the circumstances, and garner their support for our common defense. To help Mat convince those we approach I will be in stealth mode and will insert a mental suggestion into their sub-cortex directing that person to attend the conference." John, always the inquisitor, "well if you can fool them into coming to a meeting then why just not tell them to join our side to fight the coming invader?" UKBA, "There's a big difference between agreeing to come to a meeting and agreeing to go to war. Plus, also, this "mental insertion" is brand new to our species, I will be the first to use it. I.. I "UKBA, for the first time, looked jittery. It must be the weight of lying that has him upset, thought John. "It's O.K. my friend. Just getting all those guys in one location will be a miracle." he said jokingly, trying to ease the world leader's personal delima. UKBA, somewhat in a defensive tone now, "Well, we have concluded that after many centuries of observations that once a human gets an idea into their head it is almost impossible to change that mind. One of our analysists put it this way: At times, humans can just be bat crazy.! Then his eye did change color! Mat, "Let's just hope for the best." UKBA, "One of our first stops will be for Roy and uller. "Mat, "Oh, I can't wait to see the look on their faces when they see you!" John, "Can't be any funnier than dads." chided in John. Luke, "Can you guys let that go?" "No, it's to funny!"

So, for the next three months a 12-man team composed of BEEs and Humans, made an effort to recruit world leaders for the hope of survival. Due to Mat's legendary military career, successful political persuasions and his splendid direction of the N.A.S.A. program; those accomplishments gave Mat an "in" to every invitation; but mostly it was UKBA's mental insertions that was wildly efficient in securing a 100% commitment from every one approached. Not once was there an adversarial confrontation, not even from the pagan tribal leaders of the Middle East and African Continent. During the infrequent down time the two families got to know each other better. UKBA and Matthew was like two long lost brothers that had finally found each other. Angelo # 15 and John talked of similar teenage things. Sports, games, heroes, other facets of growing up; except Angelo has no concept of females, romance, or sex. The group had memorized their roles and rehearsed dozens of possible scenarios and how to react positively in each one. As they travelled the magnitude of the times crept up on them like a destructive glacier. Such a small group of people trying to solve such a massive problem. They were the beginning.

Mat, Luke, and John could feel the love that their "Adoptive" family showered upon them. More evidence that everything in the scroll is all true. The trip ended. UKBA, "This has been good. We gave our best effort. It is out of our hands." John thought, O.K. we get it, now we sit back and wait and hope everybody shows up for the historical conference.

Once John got back to the base he couldn't wait to read more from the scroll. He thought there was some correlation between the ancient story and today's world events; but John just wanted to know what went on in early Earth, if it is true. John carefully opened the scroll, expecting to read about humans.

But this scroll tells the intertwined histories of three worlds, and the Gods that created them. John continued to read expecting to learn about humans, but he was wrong:

First, God created an army of a fixed number of spiritual beings He called Angels. They were to sing and give worship and praise to God and Love. They were also messengers, and doers of tasks and request. Angels were spirits, not flesh, and with one exception, lived forever. Next, He created a more powerful Angel he called Guardian Angels. They were to protect lesser life forms from the evil that the Father is going to let loose to roam the interior and exterior. Then He made an even more forceful "Arc" Angel. They were to do real physical and spiritual combat with evil spirits and demons. This evil presence is determined to corrupt the goodness of the Father's creations. The Arc and Guardian Angels are instrumental to Earth's History. Next, the Holy One created 72 Wise Elders. They occupied the inner circle, which is the middle of the glorious city, which is in the center of the heavenly kingdom. Great understanding and discernment were attributed to the Elders. They were to discuss, laugh, fellowship, and live alongside the King. They were to provide the close interpersonal relationship the He cherishes. Then, much to his own pleasure, He created two more son's. Immediately they gave Him pleasure and amusement, just as Love had. He also felt a sense of Pride from His accomplishment and said to himself, "This is a special emotion, Pride; I will allow my creatures to accomplish things and thus feel Proud, but they must, all they have to do, is to credit me, either publicly or privately between ourselves, for all their achievements and gifts I bestow upon them and their families." This became a Godly statute.

The new Sons were the happiness of the kingdom. The 2nd oldest was named "Joy" and the youngest "Peace." The Most High gave them the same first speech He gave Love. Finally, a very special moment, with all of creation surrounding the Golden Throne, the Father went about creating His most special heart piece. It was a spirit with a different nature and appearance. (She!) was the only one that shone with the beautiful radiance of the rainbow colors, and other light that humans can not perceive. All the other creations only had differing degrees of white light. Her aura lit up the entire court! Her glory is only surpassed by the high authority. She is considered most special by the Father and He was closer to her than any other. This is what He first said to her, "My name is the Great I AM. Your name is Sophia. I AM is your creator and Master. I AM made you to be My companion, to complement Me. We will watch, contemplate and then discuss matters before us. Together we will enjoy my Son's activities. We will share the amusement they provide. There folly will be a constant source of entertainment and will bring us much laughter, (as He laughs out loud now!) Together we will experience the magnitude of living. In the future you may suggest, I will decide. I adorned you with more power and authority than all the others, except me. We are the only two with a

"KLUZ." The others will either have an "Orb" or a "Soul." Ours will be a union of total satisfaction. You may now speak."

Sophia, in a prone position, lifted her head to speak. "Oh glorious Master. There is no one before you. There is no one like you. I offer you praise and worship. I give thanks for bringing me into reality. The radiance you adorned me with is spectacular. I appreciate your thoughtfulness. I will strive to meet all your expectations; my greatest desire is to please you. Oh, Holy One, I feel the awesome powers and authority you ordered for me. I am well aware of my robust abilities. There are few limits. I will always use my wisdom and volition to dutifully serve my Master. Yes indeed, our reign will be dominated by ecstasy."

S.H.F. "Your obedience has pleased me. Come with Me to the farthest reaches of My light, where I've not given anyone else knowledge of My favorite paradise. We must become one, it will be "the way." Sophia was ecstatic. She has the thrill of intimacy and romance all at first sight." Sophia, "Master, I am tingling from your care." The Master took her and their KLUZ'S mingled to the inner core. The vibrations from their passionate, almost violent embrace shattered and cracked space itself; the fabric of matter ripped apart at the seams. Their efforts causing cataclysmic eruptions of cosmic radiation to pass through the vastness of space in wave like ripples. Scientist today can detect these ripples and concluded that they are left-over static from the big bang; but really it is the result of the intimacy between the Two Most High Authorities.

At this time the S.H.F. did not tell His most special one, "Sophia", that within her "KLUZ" was a slither of darkness. This darkness is the opposite of good and light. The Creator designed her that way so His companion might have a slight difference of opinion, a slighted perspective different than His. Knowing her variation and diversity will spur and excite His thoughts and imagination. He wanted a lively partner nearly equal to Himself, to engage in lively exchanges, not a boring robotic duplicate. From Sophia He got all that and much much more. For now, He did not want a rebellious adversary, but knew in the future she would become a concern, challenge, and then a problem. But the Father dictates to the future, it does not control Him.

John did not know what to think of the information he was reading. Bizarre scenarios went through John's head. Am I in the scroll? Will it save my life? And the more realistic question, "When should I tell my dad about this strange tale." He reached for the phone to get some confirmation from the Decipheress, but it rang first, he picked it up and it WAS the Decipheress. "I was just getting...but then the Decipheress furiously cut him off. He spoke quickly, in a panicked hush tone, "John, "Listen hard, I do not have much time. You must finish the scroll Heed th" Then John heard something that sounded like a small explosion in the background and then the sounds became muffled..Uum aggh helll and then there was no sound. John yelled out over the line, but it was clear something bad had happened to his confidant. John felt somewhat lost and confused. Is his friend going to be all right? What is so valued in the scroll that people wanted to kidnap the Decipheress? He called the police to report the incedent; and then John had to read further; he was going to find out what was so special. So, he continued reading.

Watching Love play his game of "Evolution" completely entertained GOD and Sophia. His antics and fool's play in the enormous universe was very funny to them. Sophia commented, "What pleasure do your Son's bring our "KLUZ." We should make more. "I will consider it." Said the Father flatly. "For now, I have a present for Son Love. He is maturing rapidly and is ready for more responsibility. Sit in with me while I make a proposal to him." Sophia, "Yes, thank you for including me. The anticipation is very exciting." Love was escorted to the Golden Throne by his Angel friends and knelt on one knee. S.H.F. "# 1 Son, I am well pleased with your growth and maturity. Before My very eyes, too quick to blink, you have grown into a young adult. At the time of your creation I told you I would provide opportunities for you. Here is one now if you chose to accept the challenge. Personally, I have found that designing, making, and caring for living beings to be the most rewarding. I think now you may be ready for that kind of commitment and dedication."

With passion in his voice Love asks, "Father, are you allowing me to create and sustain my own life?" "Yes, my adorable Son." For a moment they admired each other, each becoming brighter through the other's care. Then spoke of one more document. S.H.F. "Son, here is registration that all future creators must follow. It will ensure conformity, equilibrium, and justice for all similar labors in the future. I AM will set and enforce all mandates that all life forms must adhere. If there is any deviation the spark of life will not be allowed to enter. Son, make your first attempt simple, not to complex. Of course, they will contain your spark, which give them a chance to become a heavenly spirit, unlike your cretins of "Evolution." Those self-proclaimed corruptors will never see my light."

"Of course not Father. I will do my best in this endeavor; I will not disappoint you." Father, "Being disappointed in you Son is not possible. Before you Son is the Spirit image I have chosen for others to perceive Me. My Spirit image can change in an instant if I desire, but with what the future has before us., I AM what I AM. This is how I project my glory Son, I suggest you do the same.

For your creation and all that follows each must meet these required mandates. If they fall short of only one the spark of life will not be allowed to enter. Here they are:

1. Must be made of flesh and structure, not spirit.
2. Must be made to need nutrients and expend waste.
3. Must be given genetic codes directing it to survive, reproduce, compete, and have a yearning to prosper.
4. Must be given a nature, emotions, senses, and a creative intellect of differing capabilities.
5. Must be given a limited life span.

6. Must only exist in a three-dimensional blog of space, time, and matter.
7. Must be given a "free will" and knowledge that it may be used.
8. Must be given an inner sense of right and wrong, good and evil.
9. Must be given a "soul" and not an "orb."
10. Must be given an understanding of an "higher power."

With enthusiastic zeal Love took to his mission. Taking his Father's advice Love started slowly, with only one planet and two beings. He chose Earth for his home planet. He left "Evolution" to continue on other planets, which were producing higher intelligent species with each passing spiral, but on Earth He ended Evolution with a series of natural catastrophes. Most life forms were destroyed except for a few needed organisms that were allowed to survive, and the Earthly "Creatins" from Evolution; they interest Son Love; and He placed fossil records of Earth's pre-history accordingly. Then He constructed a "Garden of Eden" for his male and female to live. The beautiful ecosystem was a composite of luscious fruit trees, flowers with the most enticing aromas, and the gentle beasts were their friends. Where the dominant male was the husband and provider, one that, through his words and actions, gently lifts his helper, companion, lover, onto a cherished pedestal, as she becomes a willing submissive wife to her man.

In paradise they lived together in a perfect relationship, daily worshipping and praising their Lord. After breathing the spark of life into his creation GOD-LOVE explained to them that they were created to have a harmonious relationship with Him. They were made for His amusement, to obey and worship Him, that they could trust in Him and to depend on Him for all their needs. He then visited twice daily, once in the morning and once in the evening. The arrangement overjoyed Love and the children. Love's two gentle pieces of craftsmanship laughed, loved, obeyed, worshipped and talked face to face with their Creator. Total bliss is the best description of the honeymoon in paradise. Love soon realized how right the S.H.F. was.... the creator-creation dynamics is much more rewarding/exciting than the slow-moving game of evolution. Love, "Father, being a creator-parent is the most gratifying emotion one can experience. It makes me feel sincerely important, needed. That my existence has meaning and purpose." S.H.F. "Oh, you always had that Son; But now, for you, it's both as a Father and Son." As their light and warmth gently flowed back and forth from one to the other, the Father and oldest Son talked of life and what the future may hold.

John didn't know what he was feeling. Mankind has been introduced into existence. Is that how it really all started? John had to know more and kept reading.

When watching HIS son's Sophia could see the gleam in the Master's spirit eye. It would stir strong emotions in Her KLUZ. She wanted what the Creator had. She wanted to care passionately about a creation, HER creation, and have that child willingly return that passion. No longer did the back-and-forth banter with the Master satisfy that innate need. Actually, recently, He has made her feel inferior and unimportant. Like He did not want Her nearby. It hurt. But now her attention was on these new feelings inside Her core. They were very strange. She did not know how to process them. Later in time these new feeling would be called envy and jealousy, and to covet, all sins. She was no longer content and needed a change. Deep inside she knew just what the problem was. She wanted Her own creations! She felt that desire to be normal and correct. That she should be allowed to make Her personal designs. "That's a great idea!", she thought to herself. "The Master will have two families, doubling HIS fun. HE will provide for HIS and I will take care of mine. The son's will be cousins! It will be one big happy family." Her KLUZ was exuberant with the prospect! The anticipation of going to see the Father to ask for permission was exhilarating! With glee she quickly went to the Father. However, as she approached the glorious city she felt uneasy. Why? She knelt in front of the Golden Throne and lovingly requested a mother's desire. The Supreme Authority did not respond as hoped. "Sophia", He causally started out, "You sorely disappoint Me. You are selfish and greedy beyond compare! After all I have given to you, far more than any other creature, it is still not enough, your KLUZ wants more. The answer is an emphatic NO! Plus, you shall be made to remember your arrogance. As punishment I AM is removing your radiance. From now on your light will only be white, just like all the Angels. It will still be much bigger and brighter but no longer will you be adorned with beautiful decorations. Sophia, "No! No! Do not treat your loving companion this way! What I ask is not much. I ask for the both of us to enjoy all the creations. If you Son's can make life then why can't your one and only loving mate? IT will.." "Quit crying and complaining!", The S.H.F. loudly interrupted! "Your request is disrespectful, and I vehemently deny it! Also, for your persistent questioning and disobedience I am banishing you from the inner court for one period." The Holy One looked over at HIS country club courthouse buddies and they were all nodding their heads and giving the thumbs up. "The court approves, now be gone!" The Father looked over to Michael, the mightiest ARC Angel, and he took a step towards Sophia. Smugly she says, "You don't have to send your henchman. I know when I am not appreciated nor wanted. I'll go to a place where I am recognized for the special power that I am! "Well good luck with that!" jokingly said the S.H.F. laughing heartily, as were the elders! Bellowing so loudly as to echo throughout the entire domain! It was the first time something disagreeable occurred in the kingdom. Hurt, embarrassed, but mostly angry, Sophia went to Her own space, still talking to herself. "He says I'm arrogant, He's the arrogant one! If He did not want Me to create, why did He give me the ability to do so? (?) It is such an overpowering temptation! She stopped, relaxed, composed herself and started to concentrate. Wham! It came to her in a flash of light and a bolt of energy! She was frantic with excitement and YYYYYAAAAAAAAWWWWWWHHHHHHOOOOO!!!!!! She screeched her first howl! The ear-splitting sound shocking herself! "I know what I can do. I'll travel to the far edges of the wasteland, where the light is almost nil, I'll be almost hidden, there I will make my OWN son's! I will teach them; they will grow strong. Then, at the right time, soon I hope, I will present them to the (creep) for inspection. Their adorableness will melt HIS cold cold KLUZ. I will ask for, and HIS nature of mercy will not deny my request, to be accepted back into the fold, me and my son's. I will plead my case to the Elders, and they will judge in my favor. It is a good plan, it cannot fail." So, thinking that the creator/knower...of all things was ignorant of her plan, Sophia went off to the abyss to start her plan.

Meanwhile, Young Gods Love and Joy were talking. "Your Earth and garden are marvelous places!" said Joy. "There are so many things to do and watch." "Thank you, and I have a super relationship with my two creations.". said Love. Joy, "Yes, I noticed that. It looked like a lot of fun." Love, "Oh, It's much more than just fun. Maintaining their security and happiness is very rewarding, it fills my ORB with gladness. In our special relationship I experience their emotions when they do, but 10 times more intense! It's similar to how the Father feels about us, except this time I'm the parent." Joy, "Yes. What's that all about?" Love, "It's fantastic! It really makes you calculate your values and prioritize what is important. I will make tremendous sacrifices to ensure the stability of My Children." Joy, "WOW!" I have never seen you this passionate about anything." Love, "This is the most important task a GOD can do; create, care, and sustain. Only the Father knows but this may be my last effort at creating; so I'm going to give Adam and Eve every chance to achieve peace." Joy, "I like the cool names." "Thanks. Do you understand what I'm talking about?" Joy, "Enough that it has peaked my courage to go talk to Father about my test. I now have a great desire within my ORB to also create." Love, "Yes, you should, it will be our legacy." Joy, "I'm going to the Father immediately, with a glad heart.

Joy approached the golden throne, where the Father spent most of HIS time, but not all. For a moment Joy tried to convince his Creator that He was now both wise and responsible enough to succeed at creating; knowing failure at this task was not tolerable. S.H.F. "# 2 Son, you have only half the growth as when Love started His test." Joy finished with this, "Father, I have learned from Love, He is an effective teacher; and I am from you. I am from your Glory, I cannot fail, it is impossible." GOD, "YOU are passionate...full of eagerness! And persuasive." The Master hesitated. Joy was anxious, in a positive way. This was the most serious conversation, and the most bold, he had ever been with the Supreme Authority. S.H.F. "You can relax Son. Thus far you have done well and have verily pleased me. I think you can achieve what's in your ORB. You not only have my permission, but also my blessing."

It became a deeply ingrained knowledgeable "fact" that "blessings" ARE a special kind of gift of prosperity, or a dreadfull curse to be lived out. Love and Joy attained blessings. Joy, "Thank you Father. For Your permission but mostly for Your blessing, I know it is from Your Light." A warm glow radiated between the Father's KLUZ and the son's ORB. S.H.F. "Go now son, enjoy your test."

JOY choose a much larger planet than love's Earth and supplied it with even more vitality than Love's vision. Both had the same types of structure; atmosphere, geology, and biology. What Joy's planet had that Love's did not was the vast diversity of foliage. Trillions and trillions of square miles of flowers. Millions of varieties, all shapes, sizes, colors, and smells, each rich with Its own kind of nectar and pollen; with a unique formula, full of power and energy. Flowers in this story are important. This vast multitude of flora, that would possibly overwhelm an Earthly botanist, is the life source for Joy's intelligent creation. Then Joy began to create His own baby. Picture in your mind His dream. Compared to us it is hugh! Mack Truck hugh! 20 feet tall, 12 feet wide, with an 8-foot girth. It has the same basic physical systems of Adam; circulatory, respiratory, digestive, nervous, etc. It also has some interesting additions. Anchored on its back are two 10-foot wings capable of flying this 1000 lb. "Bee" 100 mph for 10 hours. For communications the Bee vibrates sound waves from two antennae that jut out adjacent from each other on the upper forehead. The message can be directed to one individual or spread-out wide angle for a group. The BEE can whisper or shout, it is a very effective method for "talking." In the future this ability will be diversified and expanded. Sitting a few inches above on the forehead and positioned in between the antennae, juts out a 4 foot long, razor sharp, triple edged, steel strong; yet flexible when needed to be; hollow tube used to suck nutrient juices from flowers. Different flowers produce different nutrients and other potent energies; it is a necessity to have the ability to cipher from each; this controlled tube can. This tool will also have other vital uses in the future. Like us this Bee has two arms and legs but prefers to "flutter." The real quality of each appendage is the velcro like substance that covers a four-inch diameter ball at the end of each limb. Here is how the Bee grabs, holds and maneuvers objects. One additional organ is called the "EMF." Short for Electromagnetic Force. This organ transmits an EMF that radiates from the velcro like balls at the end of the arm and/or legs onto any object that has the slightest measure of metallic properties. It is a fantastic skill. The BEE can lift objects twice its weight or be finesse enough to handle delicate microchips. Again, another resourceful talent for the future. Probably its most intriguing feature is its single eye, located 1 foot atop dead center; a circle 1 foot in diameter. The mechanics is the same as a human, rods, cones, optic fiber, etc. The real uniqueness is the swirling mucus within the eye. It is as thick as honey and can appear as a single color or as a mixture. The mucus liquid does not interfere with vision but does have a very telling feature. A certain color or mixture of colors reveals the emotions the BEE is experiencing. Thus, BEEs cannot lie about their feelings, or lie period. Here is an explanation for each color in the visible light spectrum. Red - Anger, fight, war. Orange – intensity, agitation, determination, work of either positive or negative outcomes. Yellow - worry, concern, problems. Green - the most common observed color, everything is o.k. normal, acceptable, satisfied, working, purpose, meaning; most of the time BEEs are experiencing at least one of these green emotions. Blue - happy, play, social, also a very common color. Indigo - love, commitment, duty, fulfillment. Violet - Only a few BEEs in BEE history have displayed the violet eye. A highly cherished and valued color. It stands for the "zenith" of true altruism. The highest form of sacrifice, but also words like humanitarian, patriotic, leader, and trusted, describe a BEE displaying a violet eye. For a BEE that had the right stuff to show a violet eye is derived from a lifetime of commitment and duty, and/or is sparked by a short period or even just a few spectacular acts of true heroism. It raises the BEE to the highest level of recognition and near worship. That is a brief description of the BEE's anatomy and physiology. According to the mandates Joy was authorized to place along the DNA genetic codes to make the BEE full of knowledge. On the Earthly scale BEE I.Q. would average 130. Also, a code for a strong work ethic was placed along the DNA strand, which greatly pleased the Father, who HATES laziness. HE is full of vitality; HE wants his creations to be vibrant. Another important gene was for an expertise in social engagement; other genes necessary to mention is the one for high moralistic standards, one for the capacity and even a strong innate urge to protect the weak; and last and most important, the knowledge of its maker. Satisfied, Joy said a prayer of thanks to the Father and blew the spark of life into all His creation. Unlike Love, who started with two beings, Joy populated His planet with millions all at once. His choice his desire. He sat back and watched His imagination spring into action. Momentarily He was overcome with emotion and shed some tears. He never calculated how immensely gratifying "creator-hood" could be. Thus, an alien race joins our story.

CHAPTER

THE "BET"

Back in the wasteland Sophia called the son's to Her for an announcement. She had forced them to grow quickly into young adults. Too quickly, without the instruction, teaching, discipline; just all the tools necessary to help a child properly learn how to grow into a responsible deity. Most of all they were not given the time or attention from a caring creator. Not until Sophia could use them to her own Crown did she fully engage them. They were brash, spoiled... plain nasty! She did not want to wait any longer to implement Her plan and decided to go to the Father by herself, leaving the brats at home. She called them to her, and it was easy to understand how their behavior would bring meaning and definition to their names. The oldest was named "Kao's", the middle child, Deceiver", the youngest was named "Anarchy "; if he was a junior high school student he would be classified with ADD. They were a handful, even for a Higher Authority. "Pay attention to this. "She would say, but they seldom listened. They had rotten schemes of their own making. She watched as they seemed completely unaware of her presence, they only lived in the exact second of their mind's environment, or it seemed so to her at the time. She told Kaos, "I am going to the throne, watch your brothers. Make sure you are in control, not like the last time or the time before that. If I come back to

33

trouble you will feel my wrath!" But they knew better. She hated to even scold them and often called her bluff. She left anyway and made her way to the inner circle. In her darkened mind she had devised a scheme to trick the Oh Holy One. Again, as she neared the Golden Throne with the Almighty sitting upright and strong, she felt more than uneasy. She was scared! But as her magnificent white light sparkled the court and all the Angels bowed down in awesome respect her confidence grew. The Master was unaffected. S.H.F. "Sophia, do you have a truth you wish to reveal?" Sophia, "I have no secrets. I have nothing to hide.", she defiantly said. "Oh, Great One, you already know why I am here, what do I need to say?" S.H.F. "Yes, I do. I do not desire and thus disapprove of your projections." Sophia had a prolonged strategy. Sophia, "That does not surprise me. But what are you afraid of? "NOTHING!" said the Master in a booming voice, blowing back the front row of Angels. "Did you not learn your lesson the last time. Again, your ungrateful attitude will garner harsh punishment." "GO ahead ", Sophia butted in! My sons are adorable. I love them unconditionally, something you are incapable of. You and your standards of conduct AH! AH! AH! "The Elders were stunned, shocked and murmured to each other. How anyone dare speak to the Holy Creator like that! She blustered onward, "That's hypocrisy coming from someone who brags about being a loving merciful God." The great "I AM "leaned forward in His chair, trying to appear unaffected by Sophia's words, but even the new Angels could sense the anger, and the Elders knew His KLUZ was infuriated. God slowly shook His head and said, "That's too much insolence! Your glory will be reduced to just above my Angels and your appearance will be that of a tar pitched snake/lizard. In a flash of light she was transformed and hideous to the sight. In frightened horror some Angels turned away. Oddly, some, apparently thinking Sophia had been treated unfairly, moved closer to comfort her. S.H.F. "Also, your name is changed to Mother Demon Spirit Llillth. MDSL MDSL, calmly, with no indication of fear, remorse, or panic, with reason said, "Why do you do cause grief for the one that not long ago you showered with gifts and affection. Is it My son's perfection that profanes you? Or has the virtues of loyalty and commitment escaped your KLUZ? S.H.F. "Silence! Your bickering will cost you more! Your son's will cease to exist. I will cause their life force to vanish." Sophia was no longer intimidated. Her plan will work. She became more confident, aggressive and applied more of her treacherous psychology. MDSL, "It's no mystery to me why you want to get rid of my boys. Do it quickly before your fans find out your son's have imperfections and mine... don't. Sure, vanquish them so nobody finds out who the better creator is; Me or You. We, You and I, know the truth; but don't let Your buddies find out; but now(?)... now, I think there will always be doubt. But that's o.k. with you... Master, that's why we have Free Will, and the knowledge that if we differ from you it is o.k.; because you want diversity. All life forms are supposed to have the freedom of expression without the fear of retaliation. I am just saying My boys could do some things better than Your boys. I'd bet a great deal on it." S.H.F. "LLillth, I know all outcomes. The best you could do for them is to buy some time before destruction is thrust upon them." Sophia, "Well on your Honor let's make it interesting. Only you can change the future. The "I AM "was getting impatient, "Get to the point!" MDSL, "Here is my point, Let's decide who is the better creator by having a fair and skilled contest between our sons'. It will bring you the thing you most enjoy watching, amusement by competition."

That's right! The Father likes CONTESTS! And He likes winners; as defined by those that work through difficulties toward a stated and timed goal, and with the faithful attitude of a good outcome; and if poorly is the result, then HE even more desires HIs creation to maintain their Faith. This will garner them Peace. It is even sweeter to HIM when a successful soul acknowledges HIM with praise, worship and works. HE blesses prosperity on those who commit, trust, and acknowledge Him. His Glory shines through HIS followers when they support each other, with a gleeful manner, in all endeavors. Actually, to the Father, sport's game winners and losers are trivial to HIM, however, HE is deeply invested in how all the participants react to the outcome. What is their nature? HE is thrilled when there are helpers and winners striving together, in this phase of existence. Doesn't it make sense that a supernatural Creator that WILLED himself into existence that within HIS KLUZ is a spirit of competition?"

For a moment the S.H.F. thought. Finally, an answer, LLillthe looked HIM straight in the eye, GOD....in the eye! "O.K. LLillith. But It must be done to my specifications." "Isn't everything? said the gambler." "You have no choice but to agree. You started this. If you reject MY proposal your son's will be vanquished. But, because I have absolute confidence in MY glorious KLUZ and thus MY son's abilities, we will have a contest of supreme value. LLillith, I have the courage to put MY son's future at risk, do you have what it takes?"

MDSL, "It sounds very exciting. Are you sure you want to do this? Will your sons accept the challenge.? "Do THEY have what it takes?" At this the Master sprang off HIS Throne! "You insult ME, question MY son's fortitude, and now try to squirm your way out of destruction! The competition is ON! "Within Her Demon KLUZ MDSL smiled! She had outwitted the Supreme Authority. She had manipulated the King into thinking HE engineered the contest, when all along it was Her handiwork; just what she wanted!

"What is the competition sweetie?" she coefully asked. The Father, disgusted by her tone yet inspired by HIS forth coming announcement. "Oh, here it is honey! Your oldest son Kaos will compete against my second oldest, Joy. All others, including you and I, will be spectators with limited methods to help. Your mind will be informed of the details. Within a stated and limited time period both sons are to create a "champion "species. Kaos must start HIS process on a planet of your making. Locate it at 180-degree angle from Joy's planet, three light years away from, and on the other side of Earth, so to be hidden from Joy's planet. "Why make a planet? Why Joy's pl." Silence! You always did interrupt LLiLLth. Just listen and let Me finish. We are almost completed."

The love and close appreciation the S.H.F. and MDSL once had for each other had plummeted from passionate love to sincere care, to indifference, to indignation, to disgust, and now, they just plain hate each other. The couple that at one time had the most wonderful relationship now want to destroy each other.

MDSL, "But Joy has an advantage!" "NO, NO, actually it's a disadvantage. But anyway, these conditions are fair and just; MY KLUZ cannot do it any other way. So, deal with it! Or reject it and watch your sons be painfully vaporized!" MDSL, "How can anyone stay around you for even a small amount of time. Compared to most I was a marathoner!" Upset, the Father continues, "Before the next rotation of your planet's galaxy Kaos must devise a creature that goes through three developmental stages resulting in a "champion." This champion leader and his armies must acquire the capability of space travel, locate, conquer, and enslave Love's inhabitants on planet Earth. Then, after enjoying the spoils of war for an accepted amount of time, report the news back to ME; if all requirements have been met Kaos will be declared the winner. During the same time period Joy must also construct a "champion "that goes through three stages. Simply, Joy wins if His champion stops Kaos's champion from completing his mission in the required time limit. Whichever son wins proves who is the better creator, Me or you. MDSL, "Is that it? Is that the contest, the bet? That's too easy! I am sure My son can better the competition. You might as well give me the trophy right now!" S.H.F. "There are no trophies Demon. The prize and consequences are much more substantial. Remember, I AM is the Supreme Authority, when I AM plays a game it must mean something. And here it is: The losing son and his family will become servants to the winner for all of eternity."

The stakes could not be any higher! Servitude forever! This BET is no joke. The inner circle, Angels and even the composed Elders did not know how to respond. There were some gasps, and "OH my, Oh my." Most just murmured amongst themselves. The dire consequences had stunned everybody. Except MDSL. S.H.F. "What do say now BEAST? Do you want to end it now, quickly? Save your boys from a humiliating defeat. Why draw it out and make your dogs suffer. For you I will cease them painlessly, quickly. Agree with Me to finish their spark now; or do you have what it takes? "The Father was having fun provoking MDSL, but she wasn't hampered at all. "So, you are saying... that this future IS NOT predetermined...and by the righteous justice of your KLUZ, you will not, cannot alter the ending or insert any contractual fine print?" S.H.F. "MDSL, you know MY KLUZ does allow any folly. Do you agree to the conditions? "Before HE could finish the sentence MDSL stuck out a hand, they formally shook, making the "BET" official. Nothing will alter its course.

The actions taken by Kaos and Joy in order to win the BET will determine the fate of three much different worlds and creations. Three species that have no knowledge of the BET, had no opportunity to accept or decline participation, and have no present understanding of the powers involved, or the consequences of defeat.

To most everyone's surprise as MDSL was leaving about one third of the Angels started to leave with the Mother Demon. For whatever reason their loyalty and service were now devoted to Her. As they left the court the Master clapped HIS hands and the glowing little Angels were immediately transformed into gargoyle demon spirits; miniature LLiLLiths. They were grotesque, smelly, and bent on doing MDSL's evil bidding. Flying behind their new Master they chanted in a baboon throaty growl, OORRREEEEOO....OREEO....OORRREEEEOO....OREEO.... OORRREEEEOO! They rejoiced that their new allegiance brought retribution from the HOLY ONE.

So, the first BET in history had been made. It pitted good versus evil with the fate of Earth in the balance, humans unaware of their future involvement. The quarreling and debate over who is the better creator will last until the battle of Armageddon. Who has the more perfected sons? Who is the better creator? Whose nature will rule the Universe?

John stopped reading, picked up a schoolbook and launched it across the room! "How can this be?" A crushing weight seemed to be on his shoulders, he slumped down into his chair. "Is this non-sense talking right to me?" "What is the meaning?" John took a hot-cold-hot-cold shower to free his mind. "The best thing I can do is to pray, listen, serve; be myself, wait for the meeting and try to be calm." So, as the day of the meeting approached and the tension mounting, John stuck the best he could to routine. Compared to the nervousness he felt preparing for the coming occasion the rigors of military cadet training was like a vacation. Occasionally family members would call and mostly console each other; they were all in the same boat, waiting. A week before the showdown they stayed at Mat's house to again discuss potential problems and their responsibilities. And then the morning of the historic meeting arrived. It was held in a mid-size auditorium, large enough for the 756 attendees. As mentally instructed Roy and Fuller arrived two hours early for "BEE orientation." Unlike the others they got over the shock of UKBA's enormity and quickly re-focused their efforts on the task at hand. They were all business as they knew the conflicting ideologies could erupt into more than just a heated debate. Through his mental insertions UKBA arranged for assigned seating, Western and Eastern diplomats separated by the center aisle, a symbolic gesture. Front row first seat was Artis, and to his left was a descending order of war hawks; The West was much the same. Roy and Fuller seats 1 and 2, front row. If they wanted to, Roy and Artis could reach out and hold hands, if they were lovers and not haters. A strong sense of suspicion was teasing anxieties. No turmoil had yet erupted, credit the professionalism and preparation of Mat and UKBA. Due to misleading information, wording of false documents and just plain lying the representatives thought this was a mandatory meeting sanctioned by the

World Security Council. John and Luke were out front on stage trying to look pleasant and congenial. Some mumblings and an occasional cough broke the noise of shuffling feet trying to get to their seat, but without incident everybody made it down. So, before an incident erupted Mat took to the podium to start his introductory speech.

Matthew, "Gentlemen, thank you for attending this historic meeting. Never has so many people of influence, of differing opinions, been brought together in such an enclosure." John leaned over and whispered to his father, "We should blow them all up while we got the chance." Barely, a visible smile darted across Luke's lips. Matthew, "This will be a fruitful gathering." Mat said with exuberance. "I'm introducing a person you have never heard of, but he knows each one of you very well. He knows the temperance of world politics. He has the ability to end world hunger, poverty, sickness; he can supply our energy needs, he offers comfort." There was much whispering and not very well-hidden motions of disbelief. Artis, in his natural arrogant and defiant tone, shouts out "enough of these foolish niceties. I am a busy man, get to the point NOW!" But even the West was shaking their heads in approval and saying things like, "Hurry up...what is it Mat...C'mon man!" It started to sound like an unruly jr. high convocation that has a boring speaker promoting safe sex. Mat, "O.K. Here is the truth. It is time to open your imagination to a place that has no boundaries. I met this person and he brought to my knowledge a new reality, a reality that is being thrust upon us with force and without permission." Was Matthew starting to ramble? "The posessorr of this knowledge is the representative of a friendly alien planet. I give you by title: Ultimate King BEE Angelo!"

An exciting buzz permeated the crowd. The curtain opened, and out fluttered a giant black and yellow striped, giant bumble BEE! His sheer size enough to stymie anybody. Fluttering to the podium he towered over Mat. His antennae started to vibrate and in perfect standard English, "Thank you Mat for the kind and informative introduction. And thank you to all the guests for your timely participation in this exchange of critical information. I am here to offer help, through the guidance and support I can provide; however, I am dependent upon your cooperation to solve the forthcoming problem."

Everyone was stunned! Speechless for moments. They shunned back from the monstrosity. They could feel a soft flow of air from UKBA's fluttering wings, as he "moonwalked" on stage, trying not to boldly alarm anybody. Artis was the first to re-gain his composure. Everyone else was scared to silence, but Artis is a child of the Dark, with confidence he spoke up, "Listen you inferior bug, events are in motion that you cannot control. A Goddess, the Supreme Authority, oversees my destiny and all in this room, and all around the world." Even the Eastern dignitaries looked strangely at Artis. Artis turned around to face his following, "This is technological mumbo jumbo. A hoax, a failed trick to try to lower our defenses. It will not work!" He twirled around to face his sworn enemies, "Oh, you of immoral fiber, insult us with such transparent deception. Fools that you are." Roy and Fuller sprang into action at the same time. "Hey, don't call us liars. We didn't have anything to do with this." Artis ignored them and continued, "Also, and this is for you bug. I have personal knowledge of who is in charge, and I worship her. The light can be of no service in this contest, so you are already defeated."

UKBA gently floated to be two feet away from and dead center to Artis's face. UKBA, "I know who you are Artis and what you are about." UKBA's shadow magnified his Hugh frame. The Eastern block was close to a panic, and the West was saturated with curiosity. Artis has a gold belt, it is metallic. UKBA used his EMG force to lift Artis off the floor up into the air. His mid-section was thrust upward while his arms and legs flayed about, trying to escape. In front of the whole crowd UKBA glided Artis up to the 100-foot ceiling. He then circled him around the large auditorium. Faster and faster with each lap did Artis soar! What a wild scene down below among the usually stoic diplomats! Some were hiding under their seats, some ran to the exits but found the doors shut and locked, others climbed back and forth over the seats trying to get their fellow on-lookers opinion. Most pointed and shouted unintelligible sayings. The West wasn't much better. There were all kinds of gasps, stares, and stirring around among their partners. But nobody crossed the aisle. After about 15 seconds of flight and a half-dozen laps of Artis being slid across the tiled ceiling, with him squeezing out muffled chirps for help; UKBA plucked him down in his original seat. Artis had passed out, the carnival show was over! The ordeal was hard to believe. Angelo was moving back to the podium when Dali, an instigator for peace from the Eastern delegation, a very respected cleric, "Pardon me your ..Ultimate... but this is very confusing. The words and actions of today are very disturbing. I cannot find any cohesion or understanding. Am I dreaming?" He paused for a second. "I do not think this will work, I am leaving, good luck in your travels." "Wait." Pleaded UKBA. "You are a true manifestation of your beliefs...it will all be good. Please enter in with me." Dali, "No. I will not stay. If you are who you say you are, then you alone will be able to cure our troubled and divided world. Good day sir." With those words he, and the rest of the Eastern bloc, left. And with few words, the West followed them out. The meeting was over and was a colossal failure. The organizers stood there together, staring at a passed out Artis. Then they saw an eye twitch, a finger move, and then Artis was awake. Immediately, in his standard smart-alec tone, "What are you doing, plotting my death? It's something you'll never witness" He looked Mat right in the eye, "Before you die old man, you'll see me rule the whole world, and what's left of your family." He let out cheerleader scream, making MDSL, who's looking in from above, also laugh out loud, like a maniac. John started to go sock him but was held back by a disciplined Luke. Luke, "Not now son, a little later." Artis, "Yes, not now son", said Artis, laughing even louder. "I am leaving now, by my own free will and volition." He turned and walked out the door. Those left in the room knew they had just encountered a tool of the devil. Not much was said by the good guys. UKBA, "We know where we stand. There is much to be done. The best you can do is stay prepared for any kind of worldly conflict." Fuller, "Well, I'm all over that." Roy, "Yes, Fuller and I will work closely, making sure our boys are ready to go to war." UKBA, "Good I will stay in contact. Mat, John, try to relax. John, good luck in all your school activities. School and work are the best distraction you guys can have right now. Again, stay alert, I will contact you all at the appropriate time." UKBA went to stealth and was gone. Mat, "Let's not get discouraged, and I just echo what our friend said. Let's go home and do what was doing before all this started and wait on UKBA. I love you boys; take care and I'll see you later."

John didn't say much on the long trip home, he WAS discouraged. Are Evil aliens going to destroy us? He felt like he was living in a "Twilight Zone" episode, and his brain is all locked up, like the first time he tried to solve a Rubik's cube. He took his elders advice and got into being a soldier; and once again began reading the far-out scroll. One thing Artis said did have him very curious, who is the Goddess?

CHAPTER 3

"THE TOTALITY OF SIN"

MDSL returned to the wasteland. When her sons saw Her ghastly figure, they screamed out in horrified delight. Kao's, "Mother, what happened to your light?" MDSL, "The bastard tricked and cheated me. He's a good Lier. A thief of others happiness. He thinks of only himself. Look how he has changed my appearance. Well,... now... I like it this way now. It magnifies the fear I wish to project. But the JERK hates our family and plots to vanquish our spark!" Deceiver, "I hate the Father! I want to squeeze the life juices out of him." Anarchy, "I can think of a dozen ways to bring him to his knees. I want him to crawl and beg for mercy." Kao's, "For your honor Mother we will crush him. Revenge will be ours to taste." MDSL, "Yes my sweet darlings. I have arranged a contest that will earn us much, very much. A way.." But just that quick the kids had turned their attention to their own devilish schemes. They rarely paid attention to MOM. "Listen now", she softly said, but again they choose not to hear her. "My children, "she calmly whispered, "if you listen, obey, and succeed, feel the pleasure I will give you. "With pursed lips she blew them a kiss and ohh so much more! Instantly their innards were caressed with carnal pleasure of orgasmic proportions! "Oh Mother do it some more "begged Kaos. "Whenever I want to my darling, and that's when your actions are up to My standards. Little ones, correctly do what I command, and much more will be for the asking. "Deceiver," Nothing can be better than this!" Anarchy pleads, "Please don't stop don't stop!" "Oh, but I am, "says MDSL, "your obedience will get you rewards but disregard My orders and garner THIS! "Instantly, their sighs and groans of sensual pleasure turned into screams of pain. Biblical kind of pain like being impaled onto a spike or soaked in gas and lit on fire. Words cannot describe the amount of pain. The kids were a constant blare of agony. "Listen to Me and be rewarded or ignore Me and suffer. Which will it be?" "We will listen! "They echoed. Kaos, "Mother, I sense a change in your demeanor. I now see a witch with an unyielding desire to stampede! I feel the vibrations of your greed and ruthlessness." MDSL had changed. She was done just being a companion and complement. Now, the desire to rule Her own domain is burning inside. Kaos, "I see you seeking out Authority and sucker punching anybody that gets in your way." Her slither of darkness had exploded into a cest pool of evil and sin. Her goodness blotted out by the darkness. She is the Queen of Terror. Her KIUZ was intent on eradicating the good light in the Father's kingdom. She would teach Kaos enough wickedness and coach him how to defeat Joy.

After feeling the difference between pleasure and pain the three kids were willing to do anything Mother said. She explained the complexities of the "BET", emphasizing the rewards and consequences. Driven to a frenzy by the opportunity to murder the Father and desperate with evil aspirations the three howled out like a pack of wolves. Kaos, "Mother, I will serve you gallantly. I will prove to be the better supreme commander and you the master creator; revealing him to be the hypocritical weakling that he truly is. One that does not live by the sayings he lectures upon his stupid droppings. I eagerly await the day as victor I can piss on his sissy son's head. It will almost be as good as the feelings I get from you!"

Kaos was a triple threat. He was determined, ruthless, and just plain mean; He sweated evil from his pores. MDSL, "You are the chosen one.

You will be king. You will make me proud. Come to Earth with me, sit on a mountain top and I will show you how to grieve our nemesis. It will formally start the fight and we will get in the first hammer blow!"

Together they made their way to Love's garden. Kaos was now intent on listening and learning. "Watch me son, "said the originator of sin, "this is how you use trickery." Mother Demon Spirit LLillith has the capability of changing Her appearance to humans. At first introduction to the innocent couple, she was a voluptuous female. Adam and Eve was shy but with cunning deception She put the two virgins at ease. Soon they were laughing and playing games. Then they sat close. MDSL reached for an apple, but Eve stopped her; "Our Lord says we will die if we even touch the forbidden fruit." MDSL, "You will surely not die." The Devil plucked the apple from the tree and handed it to Eve. Her and Adam each took a bite. Spiritually, they died. The Demon made some apple wine. They drank. Whispering and giggles happened. They drank some more. The laughter was more frequent and hardier. There was some touching and more whispering. They drank some more and became sloppy drunk. The brief touching turned into rubbing, massaging, MDSL looked like she was having fun, so did Adam and Eve. Caution and inhibitions were no longer a barrier to experimentation. The massaging turned into hugging and kissing. Then the three became physically intimate, as intimate as a threesome could get; already naked the three engaged in a drunken sex fest! MDSL taught them every natural and unnatural sex act. There was moaning and gentle groans of sexual pleasure; the sex became very intense. MDSL had successfully sown corruption. She would change from female to male and then back again. Looking from above Kaos became excited and gratified himself. This went on until... unbeknown to the children (not MDSL) God-Creator Love had entered the garden. As usual He was looking forward to the evening commune. Hearing the groans He thought His children was somehow in danger. Rushing up on the threesome Love was so shocked that He fell to His knees, hands covering His face, tears

46

flooding His cheeks; "What is this? ", is all He could get out. For the first time Adam and Eve was aware of their nakedness; in embarrassment and shame they quickly covered up with fig leaves.

To avoid confrontation MDSL quickly flew to Kaos. Wild yells erupting from Her sickened core. "See how easy that was son." Kaos, "So we can fool with Love's creations? ""More than that son. In the "BETS's" fine print the Creep allowed Me to slide in a provision saying we can torment Earthly creations until the completion of the contest, and at the end of the age there is a possibility that we can own and control their very souls. Also, as a MAJOR bonus inside the pukes and the planet Earth Herself I planted the seeds of sin. No one can stop its growth. The Creator promised not to interfere until a winner is declared. They looked down to see sobbing and hurting. "Oh what excerleration I get from their tears!" As they were flying off she heard Love say something about punishment.

Kaos, "Mother what is SIN? "MDSL, "Son I have released vast armies of demon spirits and evil forces. Together they will pervert the Earth and permeate the heart, mind, and flesh of humans. Even the offspring of these two losers will be affected: each generation more sinister than the last. Because of their weakness and stupidity, we will be allowed to torment them for all time." Kaos, "What about their soul Mother, can we snatch it and keep it forever, that's what I care about?" MDSL, "Listen, pay attention! At the end of the age those souls that have believed and accepted the Son into their heart We cannot touch; but for the ones that have not a relationship with the Father, the humans HE does not know, then We will roam the Earth like a roaring lion ready to snatch up unprotected souls. They have no escape, and our glory will grow and grow...Unstoppable! Kaos, "I can't wait to hurt His favorite creation!" MDSL, "We will use the sinners to cause havoc throughout Earth history and then torment them for the rest of eternity! ""YYYYEEEEEOOOOO!, "yelled out Kaos, "That sounds like fun. I hope no one believes. I sure like being a Devil! "MDSL, "I've got physical and psychological means to turn them away from their protector.

47

It will be easy. You saw how miserably weak and stupid they are. Ha! Ha! We will be kept busy by the number of pests to torture." Kaos, "What are your plans Mother, how do we turn them?" "We will convince them of two lies. One, that GOD does not exist and two, He lives but does not care about them, so why should they care about HIM? By causing personal calamities and hardships and spreading intentional conflict we will open the soul for invasion. Pride and the love for worldly things will be our allies. We will greatly celebrate watching the Father and HIS mutants mourn." Kaos, "Mother, you are the superb bitch! When do We start? "MDSL, "I already have! The Sin I placed in Earth has caused Mother Nature to alter the atmospheric and geological dynamics of the Earth. No longer is there just a gentle mist, warmth combined with cool breezes; Her new sinful nature will generate hurricanes, tornadoes, floods, droughts, tsunamis, earthquakes and volcanic eruptions, and other disruptions to create devastation and havoc. "Kaos, "And the worse the humans act the worse the disasters! "MDSL, "No son. Human behavior has no bearing on nature's actions. Disturbances happen because of the many different interworking's of energies and circumstances. But that's just the beginning. My octopus of SIN has many tentacles. NO longer can the lamb lie with the lion; Sin has introduced predator and prey, kill or be killed, fight and flight will dominate human living. It was not like that in the garden! And that is the short answer to the question, "What is sin? SIN is anything that hurts or corrupts humans; shorter, simpler answer: SIN is anything that wasn't in the garden. "Kaos, "Yeah... Yes, Mother that's great. Let's go, I can't wait to do My dirty work." MDSL stopped and coarsely rebuked him. "I will not let you be a failure! With the "BET" there is too much at risk. Heed My instruction, learn My methods." With a tight fist She squeezed his essence. Kaos, "Mother, Mother. "He could hardly get out the words. MDSL, "I will not permit a half-ass effort. This SIN will weaken and fracture the human spirit. It will pit brother against father and nation against nation. As they weaken spiritually, they will be easier to conquer. It will completely ruin his garden and infest his pets for all time. I will give the scum a plethora of addictions to fight; gambling, food, best of all drugs, all the afflicted will be morally judged and outcast; society will blame their lack of will power or the overpowering sway of hurting emotions for their downfall, when it is really the controlling persuasiveness of hidden SIN. Add in parasitic organisms, viruses, bacteria, and genetic mutations that will damage many with disease and complications. It wasn't that way in paradise! The dumbfounded worms always asking, "Why me. Why me? "At the vision of human sorrow and confusion the two howl together in laughter. WWWWWEEEEEYYUUUOOO. "The more pain We cause the pets the more pain We cause the Father. Better yet is when demons enter the weaker human pscyches. Negative emotions like greed and anger will lead to simple acts of indifference, prejudice, racism, blame, persecutions, and the strong religious differences will cause individual and state warfare. Yes, MY SIN will ruin life's, destroy the family unit, crumble civilizations, and eventually your brother Anarchy's roaming hordes of killers will bring final destruction to mankind." Kaos, "That's a lot of help, but I've got a lot of work to do; it all starts with Me. "MDSL, "One more tool to mention. It is the most effective. It is "Temptation. "Demon spirits will enter the mind and fester. Within time, just a moment for some, maybe years for others, but at some point all humans will act upon their personal temptation and forever remain under its spell. Its presence will have the most radical effect on mankind. There will be no rest for the Human Spirit. Temptation is like gravity, always probing 24/7, looking for weaknesses, for an opportunity to pounce. It is the beginning of all wrongdoing, the beginning of death. There is no escape from its seductive lure."

Kaos, "WOW! No one is conniving as you Mother! With every ounce of My orb I will battle Joy. I will defeat him. Oh Mother, all this devious news has gotten Me excited. Do you think I can be pleasured like before?" MDSL, "Of course darling. I understand your parts. In unison We will celebrate the death of Earth and humanity. So together they went off to exercise their own perversion.

2nd Son Joy had just left the Father's domain. He was still trying to digest the enormous responsibility and burden thrust upon Him with the "BET." He went to seek consul from His older brother who was in the firmament above Earth. Joy, "Wow!. Your punishment for them is severe. Was this degree necessary? "Love, plainly, "Yes. They had paradise with one rule, and they broke it. Yes, they were led astray by a cunning beast, but their weak moral fiber and innocence was like sweet candy to the Mother of Lies. Now, because of her, they are forever sinners; some are trying to do what's right; but look what my beautiful garden has spiraled downward to." Joy looked down upon the perverse and corrupt behavior of human offspring. "Yes, Joy said sadly. "What are you going to do with this mess?" Love, "I'm not sure. It's gone on since MDSL's intrusion; now all mankind has a sin nature, and I cannot change that. For some reason the Father gave her Authority on My planet until the "BETS" over. Her darkness has affected all My good design. The first-born Earthly son choose to be a murderer and was banished to their wasteland; but now look! "Joy could see creatin's and the descendants of creation fornicating and raising families without heavenly guidance. Joy, "I am sorry. I know you wanted and deserved better. It's a disgusting mixture of life juices." Love, "Look, the daughters of Seth, who I will never call by name, dancing around the campfires, spending the whole night producing offspring. All is sin. Sin is not allowed in Heaven. I must do something, I must think of a plan to overcome the wickedness of the whore's influence; so my children, all of them, can spend eternity with Me in the mansions I have prepared for them." Joy, "Well, it does not matter if I do not win the "BET." Love, "You will be the victor. You are from the Father thus superior in all ways." Joy, "I am confident you will find a solution to your heavenly problem. Time is a factor, I must go. I am on my way to prepare My babies for war. I feel unpleasant; but it has to be done and done successfully." Love, "Good luck. I go to our Supreme Authority to seek help. Good luck." The ever-eternal brothers went their separate ways.

CHAPTER 4

KAOS'S AND JOY'S FIRST STAGE

Kaos arrived at His newly formed planet to start the warring process. He was confident His strategy would earn victory. At the core was the belief that if his champion would have to compete with fierce rivals for food, water and shelter in his early development, it would strengthen Him for the ultimate battle. To improve His prodigy his race would go through the required stages, each time a mutation will occur, and one hybrid breeding ploy will make His creation the ruthless monster needed for domination. He called His protagonist the "Maulk." It is a large, red reptilian/ homo-Saipan type of creature. It has intelligence and is genetically engineered to have an unsatiable desire for power and authority. To test His creation Kaos constructed three diverse and formidable competitors. There is the flying 1000 lb. acid spewing dragon. It is 18 feet long, has 6-inch talons, and a four-foot spiked tail. Maulks are its favorite meal. Dragons are not very smart but have keen hunting skills and reproduce often. If it wasn't for another predator their numbers would over-run the planet. The next competitor is nicknamed the caveman, because he looks like the Cro-Magnon man of Earth's pre-history. To survive he masterfully uses two skills. One, he is an expert at camouflage. Like a chameleon he can change his shades of red to blend in with any background. It is shades of red because Kaos's whole planet is some shade of red. It is his favorite color; he is red. Moving with instinctual stealth even a large group of cavemen can travel quietly. The other skill is their very effective use of two sets of vocal cords. They can "throw "sounds, sending hunters in the wrong direction. They can mimic predator attack noises scattering smaller prey. Most importantly they learned the vocabulary of dragon grunts and snorts. Because he is weak but of good meat the caveman is constantly hunted by the dragon and this last species, which is by far the most dangerous. Physically he is weak and puny. He only stands four feet tall; the top half looks like R2D2, and the bottom like sponge bob square pants. Except in the middle is a 1-foot diameter circular buzz saw with razor like shark teeth; just right for slicing and dicing paralyzed prey. The "Stumps "genius is the mind controlling force that his brain wields. Get within 20 feet of a "stump "and he will insert action controlling thoughts into the victim's mind. Then, without hope, the prey is at the mercy of the stump, except the stump has no mercy. Usually, he'll paralyze a small number of captors and then enjoy a good raw meal. Many stumps together can cause a great number of deaths with their voracious appetite. Because their massive brain power needs so many calories the stump is constantly on the prowl to feed. Only natural reasons and the occasional lucky attack by dragons will end a stumps life. So, secured in cockiness, Kaos blew the spark of life into his creatures and a second alien species enters the race to 2060!. Soon, all hell will break loose.

When God-Son Joy reached His planet, He sat far above in the firmament. He looked down at the beautiful place thinking it was perfect. There were cities, hives, queens, farms, and families. His creation was busy and content. He knew they had a sense of purpose and meaning. They felt a worthy existence. He did not want to change a thing. But he knew he had to. The risks of the "BET "meant He couldn't keep his children in safety. His loved ones would experience much pain, bloodshed, and death. The coming rampage couldn't be avoided. Joy thought His creation had a solid foundation but like Kaos added some genetic mutations. One would allow the BEE to make, when called upon, a smooth transition from friendly socialite to one being accustomed to battle and the acceptance of death. Joy also added genes to strengthen its spirituality, righteousness and moral obligation. Joy felt the natural work ethic of the BEE would be a great advantage in the thousands of centuries long preparation needed to ensure victory. GOD, family, duty, and victory would be the corner stones of the BEE's "pyramid of consciences." Now, the genetic engineering would have to be tested. The warrior's response to the finality of battle and death is his only true measure. Joy choose a devasting killer for the first challenge to his loved ones. If they did not fight well they could be exterminated! That would force Joy to start all over putting him probably too far behind Kaos's development to win the "BET." Already it had become a do or die situation. Joy waited several generations for the mutations to be firmly established and then He released the monster. It came from deep within the planet, exiting from large polar caves located north and south of the eighth line.

It started like this: "Sir, there have been some hysterical reports from the national park. Something about creatures eating people. I ignored the first couple reports but now there's more and Sir, these guys seem real and are scared out of their wits. They warn me and fly out the door. We have to look into it." District Supervisor Alder told his park manager, "I'll get a hold of the police and go investigate." Similar conversations occurred at both poles. Police would travel in but not come out. It only took a couple of days for the governing authorities to realize something very odd and dangerous was happening. As the beast was fanning out into broader eating areas officials at the highest levels were meeting. Reagent Conners directed the meeting in section 12. "Gentleman, good day and God bless. May we gain wisdom and guidance from our creator. I personally want to thank Mister Gooding and the two Dixon's for moving this up the line so fast. Friends, this monster must be confronted and beaten. It threatens us with total elimination. I cannot impress enough upon you the extreme importance of this meeting. We face a devastating foe. Already he has eaten thousands of acres of flowers and hundreds of ...our... friends. It's 25 feet long, it's powerful front and hind legs have a sticky substance on them that it uses to grab and hold... it's...meal. It's front jaw juts out and is loaded with giant incisors. Presently they are feeding in the north and south flatlands, scientist think they ran out of food under world and came up to eat. When the food is gone they move on to new pastures, but soon our residential neighborhoods will be in their path. They are still coming out of the polar caves; they are hungry, and we are a favorite meal. Friends, this is the stark truth. If we do not find a way to stop this beast, (nervously T.C. went on,) nothing will be left of the BEE race! "Everyone in the room slumped over, a burnt-orange color in all the eyes. Nobody said anything, no thoughts, no answers. Just then a clerk came into the room handing Regent C. a paper. His eye changed to a glowing green and shouted out, "Cheer up men! This is from our fearless leader Ultimate Y. He has a plan for victory!" Cheers of yahooo and whoppii went around the room! "All right, all right. It's right here in my hand, let me read it to you. It says: "God bless and good day. Fellow citizens, without warning or justification a creature without a soul or God has invaded our land. He does not think, feel, or worship. Without guilt he secures his life by taking the life of innocents, he devours all before him, his only purpose for existence is to kill and eat.," C. hesitated for a split second and then raised the octave a few levels, "GOOD PEOPLE DO NOT FEAR! "For starting today, we stand together arm in arm as brothers, as one family, we will protect our loved ones and maintain our future! "In excitement the room full of BEEs rose up flying to the ceiling and circled the room. Regent C. had to pound on the podium to regain control. The message continues, "To do so we must become righteous warriors. We have moral permission and an ethical obligation to protect our families and way of life. The pest will not last! (More cheers!) We will send him back into the depths of hell from where he came!... (LOUD CHEERS!) ...I am confident that each one of us is prepared to make the great sacrifice to secure our common goal. It is of the most worthy cause. Now listen to your leaders. They have been sent the details of the plan, (C excitedly jolted a notebook in the air.) Commit all your energies to your duty. We will succeed! Always remember, God loves each and every one of you. Take care, and God Bless." WOW!!! The speech was as powerful as T.N.T. dyy---noo---mite! The demeanor of the room completely changed. Depression to determination, defeatism to enthusiasm! The men had total confidence in their leaders and a clear understanding of their responsibility. All was fully committed to the mission, eager to do battle. It will be their first time, other than the relative safety of heated athletic games. Ultimate King Bee Yust was an inspirational speech giver! C." Listen men. Go to your voting poll, it is being transformed into a military installation, (?). There you will be assigned to a specific unit and start training." Conners said one more thing, "Men, we will succeed or go to heaven trying. Either way I will see you later. I love you guys." Cheering like their team just hit the game winning home run they gallantly flew out the door, excited with anticipation. So, with much fanfare 2 billion BEEs around the globe reported for the first military induction. UKBY and his four advisors were responsible for the plan and should be credited for its smooth flow of effectiveness. UKBY appointed the top government official in each region as generals with training and decision-making responsibilities. They, in turn, appointed subordinate officers of each ranking on down the line. Everybody wanted to serve. Athletes would become the "marines "of the army; team captains and sport stars morphed into the navy seals, rangers and delta teams of the planet. The global passion united everyone in the noble and justified effort. It was a time of enormous patriotic pride! The grim reality of death just below the surface. The BEEs knew there wasn't much time so "specialization "would be key to victory. The first technique learned and put into practice was called the "Quickie. "It was to be used against the front line of the approaching menace. A four-man team would charge the mantis, up, down, left, and right of him. The overhead BEE would buzz the head. Through scouting we know that anything near its head is immediately attacked. When the beast rears up he will expose a soft underbelly, perfect for gouging. It was all theory. The BEEs have never purposely taken the life of another organism. However, Joy is confident in His genetic insertions. They would allow a BEE to kill without hesitation. The fateful time arrived. Ultimate Y. ordered an assault at the tip of the most advancing hoard.

Will Joy's planning succeed? The entire BEE world was awaiting news of the outcome; so was the Father; remember, this timeline has no set future; the life forces are determining their own destiny. It was an intensely nervous time for creations and creators.

A relatively small number of crack troops were sent to the target objective. The BEEs fought bravely! Joy's implantations did not fail, but the technique did fail! A few thousand of the enemy was killed but the whole company was nearly slaughtered, only a few dozen soldiers escaped. And still the violent creatures were coming out of the caves. Stalemates would not let the BEE race survive. Joy was worried and now the beast's food source on the flatlands was eaten up. The beast moved towards large populations. In order to buy time and to slow down the (PRAYING MANTISS), nature's "insect eater, "UKBY ordered more frontal attacks, knowing full well the disastrous outcome. He had no other choice but to send brave men into battle to do their duty, die. The generals would have to direct the course of action of the soldiers and citizens in his own region. It would be up to them to protect the people that voted them into office, the citizens they knew best, the kids they grew up with. It became very personal and emotional. The BEEs fought valiantly but took heavy losses. Divisions, companies and then small squads of soldiers would fight, retreat, regroup, and then fight some more. When entire regiments got wiped out untrained reserves and local citizens would continue the fight. Too many retreats, too many deaths. Something better had to be done.

That something better was being formulated in the lab rooms at "B.I.T. "Central. Scientist from around the world had been recruited to analyze and study captured dead mantis. They wrote reports about the anatomy, and from scouting reports made predictions of its social order and military strategies. They were trying to answer the three basic questions, what dictates their movements, what are their weaknesses, and of course, how can they be killed? To the relief of everyone they found the answers!

Never make fun of geeks, instead, encourage them. They are the ones that make the discoveries and make inventions. They keep our life safe and more enjoyable. The nerd findings enabled the war council to devise this four-part strategy. Quadrant Leader Fridley explained the plan to a consortium of generals. "Good day and God bless gentlemen. You will receive written details of your orders but I'm here now to explain the strategy and answer any questions. Are there any questions now......goood; here we go. One is called "Fire and Flood. "You know the planet has deep valleys covered with thick vegetation, and the valleys in between are lined by elevated hills surrounded by numerous lakes and rivers. The plan here is to dam up the water, draw the mantis into the valleys, and then light fires behind the masses. The fires will prevent escape and give the special forces time to burst the dams, drowning the mantis. Part two is called "Leap Frog. "The plan here is to quickly dig hundreds of thousands of miles of ditches along our vast plains, 10 feet deep by 10 feet across. The fill dirt is to be piled up running parallel to the ditch from whence it came. So, for the mantis to get to the next food source it has to jump in and out of the ditch and over the dirt. Now we have many eyewitness reports saying the mantis is such a good jumper that it will try to fly over the ditch and dirt in one effort, leaving its soft underbelly unprotected during flight. When the beast jumps two BEEs hiding in the ditch will fly from behind the dirt thrusting its head sword into its target, "Shish-ka-bobbing" and killing the foe. O.K., I'm reading from official war council orders. "He said as if somebody had snickered at the strategy. "Part three is called "Ariel

Attack. "Now most of our mountain ranges run parallel until they come together forming a giant flat mesa. In this plan the mantis is funneled into the corridors in between the mountain range. To get to the lush vegetation on top of the mesa the mantis will work very hard climbing up the side of the mountains. Now even those athletic legs will take some time climbing up the steep slopes, and during that slow crawl teams of our boys are going to bombard them with skull crushing boulders! "The General got a little fired up and fluttered back and forth for a second. All the Generals were eager to prepare their men for action. He continued, "Studies suggest that just like a well-disciplined marching band following the drum major the mantis will just follow the crowd, follow whatever is front of it. Apparently, they are not very smart, just hungry. The ariel plan is great, with the mantis bunched up we can't miss!" With more of a dead pan tone instead of his upbeat one he continued. "Men, because of the size and configuration of BEE planet (HE emphasized BEE) most of our forces will be deployed on the flat plains, facing our enemy head to head. Our biggest, bravest,....our best soldiers will be assigned this critical mission. Unfortunately, there are some scenarios where tricks do not apply. Thankfully our scientist has developed methods that reduce this type of confrontation, but they cannot be totally avoided. The hope is that our overwhelming numbers will ensure victory. Gentlemen, it is probably these battles that will determine the fate of our civilization." He and others were somber for a sec. "Are there any questions? "General Jones of the 6th Army did have a question. "Sir, that all sounds very good, but wonder if the mantis goes where our defenses are not fortified? It's a big planet. "A smile appeared on Fridley's face, "Good question farmer D. It's a valid concern. Here are professors Grider, Elder and Key. Key was the brainiest brainiac but was also captain and star player of the local sports team. He was respected in both fields. "Thank you General. Well, we stumbled across some information and then it all became very clear and simple. Through autopsies and very good medical intuition we discovered they find food just like we do, by color and scent." He held up two small vials, one red one green. "See these boys. This is the answer. The monsters will doggedly work through anything to get to the green liquid, but under no conditions will move near the red liquid. This combination of color and scent will create an evolutionary urge within them that they cannot resist. BEE's, we have the ability to direct the monster wherever we want to!" There were handshakes, smiles and congratulations to Mr. K. and his nerdy accomplices. So now a race was on. One side building dams, digging ditches, loading sorties and in training for hand-to-hand combat; the other side mulching and munching their way to an unknown showdown. One good fact is that there are no more beast exiting the caves. But soon the eaters would be within ear shot of public lands. So, with not much preparation or training Ultimate King BEE Yust made the call to initiate plan "Savior. "However, He gave all uniform soldiers 24 hours to spend with family and friends, he wanted to reinforce what they were fighting for. It was not needed to inspire the soldiers but was a nice and appreciated gesture. On the morning of the first assault Ultimate King BEE Yust. gave this speech. "Fellow citizens and honored protectors. We know the task before us. The risks are obvious. However, remember this; you are not alone. Before you were born, this day was destined for all of us. The glory of the Lord shall shine through you. We are his favorite chosen children. Do not grieve or be sorrowful, no, be of otherwise, of contentment and peace. The Father is in control, with faith He will bring us through this difficult time. Followers, God did not create us to succumb to an evil, soulless race. The day will be ours; the war will be ours! (the echo of cheers bounced around the planet) For our Fathers and sons, our love is in your heart. I know you will perform your duty with valor. I will see you when you return. God bless." With that 2 billion BEEs went into action. Hours before the special ops teams had sprayed designated areas with either the red or green liquids. It worked magnificently! Right on cue like Broadway actors the mantiss walked onto the stage! They moved to the vegetation near the dammed-up water, went in between the mountain ranges, and started leaping in and out of ditches. On the flat plains the BEEs were in hiding behind the mounds of dirt. The approaching herd was in a frenzy about finding new food pastures. The General at each battle site waited for the right moment to attack. Then all hell broke loose! Fires lit, dams burst, boulders dropped, and the gouging of soft underbellies! It was stupendous. The geeks and generals were ecstatic! Day after day, hour after hour positive reports streamed in from the battle fields. All like this one from Colonel Mock from 4th brigade, "God bless and good day sir. Casualties are few. The mantiss is not changing his tactics, he is very predictable. They have no leadership, no brains, they cannot comprehend our traps. Total victory is only time away. Congratulations to the geeks and war council." The strategy in areas 1,2,3 was doing great. However, the hand-to-hand combat on the flat plains was turning. The vast overwhelming number advantage for the mantiss was causing messages like this to be sent, from Colonel Terrel, "God bless and good day sir. Sir, our planned methods are no longer working. Sir, there are simply too many of them. They are packed so tightly together and are stacked one on top of another so close that light can barely pass through. Also, they seem to be in a frenzied crazed, killer state of mine. Just voracious! "The hopelessness in his voice was very loud. "Sir, there are a lot of good men dying out here. What are my options? What are my orders? "The commander would give the order to the Colonel, who would relay them to the Captain, who would have to tell them to the Sargent, who he and the grunt soldier would perform their duty. They were always the same orders; fight and retreat... regroup....fight and retreat.....hold them off as long as you can.....help is on the way! The grunt always has the same two thoughts, "Yeah, sure they are, and what they goanna do when they get here."

Everybody knew a different strategy or "trick "was needed on the plains. Then, a bad thing happened, and it got worse. The scientist theorized that the stench of their dead brothers was keeping the mantiss away from staging areas 1,2,3. So now, hundreds of millions joined the battle on the plains; that's where the food was. The BEE forces were completely overwhelmed. They could not retreat fast enough. The eaters started to move into the suburbs and cities. Military cohesion and disciplined crumbled. It was the beginning of the end. Like locust of the old American West, the mantiss would swarm into an area and eat all the food in their path, including all the BEEs they could catch. In the cities screams of pain and agony echoed through the near empty buildings. Panic and hysteria gripped the public. The army could no longer even put-up token resistance. Pockets of defensible areas became "forts of sanctuary."

Joy was nervous.

Then, one day a solitary figure appeared over a pack of mantiss. The salivating pack was heading for a defenseless infirmery. The nurses and doctors had been killed battling hungry mantiss away from the hospital; but now inside kids, elderly and wounded soldiers were left unprotected. The ruthless killers were only a couple hundred yards away when this solitary BEE, that was carrying a 5000 lb. vat filled with a mysterious liquid, flew just in front of the lead killer and started pouring the liquid onto the mantis's heads! On contact the liquid would burst into flames, sending the hated foe scurrying around in pain, until after a few moments they burned to a crisp; never again to do harm. Alas though, more mantiss were on the way but then also a smaller Bee with a smaller vat flew overhead pouring his liquid out with the same result. Again, just in time the older BEE had gone back to a nearby warehouse to get more purple elixir and made another direct hit, burning up dozens of predators. And then here again comes the younger BEE; several times the pair did this until there were no more mantiss in sight. The two fluttered for a moment, resting, thinking all was safe when out of nowhere two hungry eaters charged the hospital doorway. In an instant, without regard for their personal safety, the two civilians swooped in and went mano-a-mano with the killer beast. With precise maneuvering that would impress a jedi pilot they eluded the sticky grasps of the creature and with each pass the two

BEEs used their head swords to slice and dice the enemy to little pieces. Their expert swordsmanship would have made Luke Sky Walker applaud. The older BEE during this courageous deed displayed a fiery red eye of war. After the exhausting fight the smaller BEE collapsed and had to go back to the warehouse; but the older one transferred the couple of dozen patients to a safe (?) fort a few hundred miles away. It was an arduous feat requiring stamina and forceful will power. His eye was now a fretful but determined indigo. At bringing the last patient through the steel gate he was hugged and thanked from the tearful patients. Soldiers that were told of the story by the patients said it was a miracle, that he must be a saint. Then something happened that would change BEE future. This heroic BEE suddenly displayed the all prestigious "Violet "eye. All the people surrounded him, wanting to touch him, giving praise and worship. The embarrassed BEE just politely flew back to the warehouse. Word of mouth quickly spread the miracle about the violet eye story. An underground newspaper deep inside capital city printed the account of the heroism and super-imposed a "red "and "violet "eye on two pictures of the hero. The smaller BEE was also shown flying to the infirmary with a vat of the mysterious liquid. The feat was an inspiration and a moral boost to a shaken species. The story of valor and the magical potion quickly made its way to the supreme commander's headquarters. Commander Davis sent a special ops team to secure the two BEEs and bring them to him. They were found in their warehouse, brewing up more of the mixture. The team informed the pair who they were, and all swiftly made their way back to headquarters where this conversation took place. General D. "First let me congratulate you and say job well done. Your actions have lifted the spirits of everyone, the aroma of hope once again lingers in the air. What is your name son and where are your markings? (BEEs do not have uniforms but have arm bands showing name, rank, and serial number). "My name is Angelo Sir. I have been working day and night in my personal laboratory with permission and under the command of Colonel Key. I am a captain in the chemical warfare department. "Gen. D. "And apparently have found a new and effective weapon. As I understand, it is some kind of transportable fire? "Well sort of Sir. I call it napalm. "Why didn't you report it to Colonel K? ""Well it is very new, I didn't get the correct proportions right until just a few minutes before I used it at the hospital. It was the 38th combination I had tried, and it was this batches' first test! God willing it worked! "Gen. D. "It is very impressive and makes for a good story and pictures." Angelo, "Sir, my kids and I have been secluded in the warehouse working on the formula; what picture and story? "The General smiled as he looked at the dutiful soldier. "Here", he said, "take a minute to read this and look at your two pictures. "As Angelo was reading his eye suddenly changed from an observant yellow to a happy bright tealish blue. "What made you so joyful? Asked the General. "The brave smaller BEE they speak so highly of, he is my son. "General D, "Yes, a proud and satisfied father. Very good. Now, can your napalm be mass produced; can it be made to use in the war effort? Angelo, "Yes it can. I have already calculated the proper ratios for mass producing large quantities; I also have the methods to do so and the means to safely transport the materials to any distant location. The best news is that the ingredients are found in our beautiful flowers! We'll need all varieties from around the globe. "General D. "Excellent work good BEE. This is a game changer and just in time! We will use it against the entire swarm. Son, this could mean the difference between victory or defeat, survival or extinction. We must hurry, time is the critical variable." The BEEs in the room had a look of determination. Immediately a conference with the war council and learned individuals from surrounding schools, universities and all pertinent military personnel met to discuss utilization of the new potion. Final decisions were made, and Commander Hopkins assigned Angelo the responsibility of executing the plan.

So now there is another race on, and to avoid complete destruction the BEEs must win this race! Every BEE not involved in combat, young and old, was given a chore. From gathering shrubs and flowers needed for their potion, to working the assembly lines, to packing and distribution; Angelo and his son were the chefs; responsible for maintaining quality control of the mixture and supervised the entire operation. Thousands and thousands of giant vats brewed the energized pollen and nectar, the primary ingredients. The most advanced monsters had forced the population within the 2nd line both north and south of the equator. For the remaining BEEs, only a few million now, conditions were deplorable. Food, water, and medical supplies were scarce. Moral was at an all-time low. The military front liners were fighting bravely but the enemy had a large numerical advantage. They were bi-polar in a way. Vicious. Ruthless. Yet. Mechanical. Robotic. In their quest for food they just kept coming. No fear, no pain, no remorse... no emotion at all. They only kept eating, all the foliage and any BEE within reach. In two areas they broke through defensive fortifications and surrounded thousands of civilians. Finally, just in time, hopefully, enough of the potion had been brewed to make a difference. The most hazardous zones were bombarded first, and with great success! Through the whole massive swarm, across the rows, and up and down the columns; the fiery liquid burned the bast&^% into oblivion. The Bee bombers using the newly invented "flame thrower canon, "was quickly turning the tide. In a few hard-working months the victorious end was in sight. Angelo's napalm had saved the BEE race. He and his boy were world heroes! The pictures of Angelo's red and violet eyes were posted in all govt. buildings, churches and schools. The pictures epitomized the tremendous sacrifices and glorified the common people's bravery. Everybody knew who Angelo was and reverenced his violet eye.

Special forces hunted down and eliminated the last wondering herds of the mantiss. SQUASHED! At last, UKBY could make this announcement, "Good people of BEE planet... the war is over!" The leader knew to wait a couple of moments to allow for an instantaneous eruption of celebration. Then continued, "Honorable BEEs, understand this, our effort, our spirit, our belief and trust in our higher power was greater than the evil within these devils. Now, friends and neighbors, it is time to rebuild and generate. These will be our best days, days of glory, days for memories. The history books will forever speak of our sacrifices. Tonight, go home to your families and give thanks to GOD for delivering us from destruction. He is worthy of praise and worship. Celebrate with the Lord; next week, we work!" And celebrate they did! Every regional capital held parades, gave speeches, and entertainers performed. It was loud, even boisterous, and ...peaceful. But in a week they were back to rebuilding civilization. For a BEE it was natural to do so.

God-Son Joy sat back, basking in the glow of praise and worship his children offered him. He has great children, he feels. It brought a warm sense to his Orb. His plan so far was working. The attributes he implanted via DNA allowed his children to pass the first critical test. That's how quality Gods do it! He thought to himself. But he had a concern. Something UKBY said. The mantiss challenger did not think or worship. Joy pondered... "Did this strictly instinctual creature really been enough of a challenge to prepare my champion for whatever kind of stink Kaos was conjuring up. "Joy did not know the answer. It made him feel uneasy. Only time and the battle itself could put light on so many darkness's.

The two cousins had dramatically different methods to achieve their goal. Joy planned for social teamwork, moral obligation, and a desire to protect the innocent to get the job done. Kaos was depending on ruthlessness and a strong desire to rule others as the major incentives. Kaos was going to raise up three successive leaders; each one would be nastier than the previous. Their ideas and unsatiable desire for glory will shape Maulk Destiny and the direction of the galactic future. Kaos had made life on the Red planet very difficult. Large predators, poisonous reptiles, and flesh-eating plants made it stressful enough to make a battle tested Spartan shrivel up and cry. It was a major struggle just to stay alive. Contrary to BEE planet where the bad guy came from within the planet, Kaos's protagonist entered under-ground caverns to avoid the harsh and deadly environment. However, because of the Maulk's instinctual controlling desire to rule the others on top, they developed ways to secure safe settlement on the surface. For a long time they were like Earthen ants. Hunting parties for food would scurry around, hiding from predators; but it was very dangerous. Many Maulks died. It was a sad existence for centuries. Yet, as with every determined people improvement happened, progress was made. Like ants the Maulks became expert engineers. They developed concrete, molded lead, and other strong building materials. The Egyptians and Romans would have been envious of their magnificent architecture. Better weaponry and techniques made hunting parties more successful; yet still very murderous; but life had become easier. A feudal type of oligarchy arose. Kings, overlords, dukes, knights, serfs, and state workers composed the class strata, all underground. The military was the economic engine that sustained cities and villages. Eventually, after many regional conflicts, conquest, trade, negotiation, and compromise this shadowy world was divided into three empires, and then just two. Within each Maulk was still the innate need to rule the top, but at this time the domination of the entire Red inner world was the goal. And now "Bing", first global tyrant, loosely controlled the world but not with much cohesion; on the horizon was a new type of leader. Strong, intelligent, charismatic; yes, all leaders have those traits, but his was deeper. He had moved up the military ranks by leading masterful strikes against noted predators, and by challenging and defeating his superiors in mortal combat. That is how promotions are earned in the military on Red planet. If a majority of the rank-and-file soldiers vote yes when a lower ranked officer challenges his commander, then the two fight to the death. The winner gets command, as the loser cannot because he is dead. This new Maulk has many kills and successful challenges. But mostly it was his oratorical abilities, and what he was saying, that had soldiers and civilians alike excited. His sermon was one that had not been heard in a long time, yet people yearned to hear. He would say, "Follow me to the surface! Our God meant for us to rule the top, not to stay in the inferior bottom. I will lead us. Our generals have failed! I will not fail. In your heart you know I am the truth. "Throughout the empire he sang his independent message. He never kept his desire to rule a secret. He feared no one. His boldness, lacking in others, is what inspired people to follow him. One day this new warrior, named "Kahn ", called his superior out for control of the globe. The two Maulks knew each other well. Kahn is Commander Bing's war horse. Kahn's many successful surface raids had garner Bing many lands, slaves, and power. In the process Kahn had become a war legend, gaining hero status and prestige. Bing, "My young friend I knew this day would come. But why so soon? Is it because your greed is only surpassed by mine? Why impatient? You have much more time before your bones are as tired as mine, be still! Let me rule my portion and then it will be your turn. Out of respect no one else has challenged me. My service qualifies my time. You are in the wrong." "No! "Kahn emphatically shouts. "You have become weary of combat. Leading our people to the top is no longer apart of you. Corrupting yourself with the luxuries that your generals have won for you in battle is not the way of a noble king. It sickens me and those who deal in reality. "Bing, "We have different beliefs. I do not think our race is ready to live in the light." Kahn shouts back, "I will not let you insult my soldiers. Those that are trained in my methods have battled the mighty dragon and lived to talk about it! "Bing. "Yes, I know you won a few fights against average numbers. But you have yet to feel the full wrath of the dragon or the conniving traps of the stump. Others before you have tied to overtake the norm. They failed... you will to. I will maintain my rule; safety is better than slaughter. Now, go back to your cave and sleep. "Kahn, "I once admired you, but no more. You are a poor excuse for a Maulk dictator. With the universal support and approval of the First Army and the security council I officially challenge you for control of Pagan. Meet me in two days, noon, at the old coliseum."

The supreme death blow for total control! On that day, in the historic arena, in front of 150,000 immortals, Kahn walked into the octagon first. Half the crowd went berserk! Fights in the stands broke out; there were several stabbings; all to be expected at a Maulk heavy weight championship fight. Then, to everyone's surprise, Bing walked in with his sword of rule sheathed, ready for presentation. Bing, "Your words hurt but was true. My fighting days are over. Like the great kings before me I submit my blood to my God, (all Maulks have their own personal God, plus many more), The land and Army is yours to rule. It has been settled with my generals. They are eager to serve you; lead them well. Honor me with a good slice. "Bing knelt down. Taking the ruling sword Kahn lifted it high and swiftly bringing it down, slicing through the flabby neck. Kahn lifted the still squirming head. Squirts of red juices and a stream of blood poured out of Bing. Kahn dropped it to the mat, lifting his hands he called for silence. Kahn, "I am now the one and only ruler of Pagan. For the first time ever, the whole planet will be led by one vision. It is MY wisdom that will allow us to do things that no other Maulk has been able to accomplish. This moment is the beginning of a great movement. Generals, meet me in the war room in 70......You will learn my philosophy, training methods; we will plan for victory. Tonight, I go to my wife's and concubines for entertainment, all Maulks should do the same, it is my first order". Maulks, from their very beginning, believe that sexual conquest boost mental clarity, relieves stress, and most of all, increases the aggresive/dominant complexities of the Maulk psyche. Kahn walked off as if he was a god, perhaps he is.

Above in the firmament Kaos was pleased with the path. His champion won through fear alone, he didn't even have to proof his superiority. Now, thought, Kaos as he salivated all over himself, stage 2 will strengthen my Maulk even more. Joy does not stand a chance.

John finally looked away and thought, "This could be just any other sci-fi book I've read. But I know this one is different, because it came from a magical disappearing prophet, the respected Decipheress was kidnapped, and plus, I KNOW AN ALIEN! Only the weirdness of John's personal life is comparable to the fantastic story from the scroll. He wonders what's next in both.

UKBA had contacted grandpa Mat but no one else; and Mat said he was told to be silent on the issue. Something like that everybody knows not to pressure grandpa for information. He'll kick your ass! But Mat said he could relay this message from UKBA, "Things are progressing nicely." John and the rest of the family had to be patience with that. It felt strange to John going about his day in a normal routine at the base; with him knowing of the alien forces ready to take action and none of his peers aware of the dire circumstance mankind faces. Often, John must ask himself, "Is this really happening right now?" This reality was difficult to comprehend. But it was easy to read; so, during the day and other work hours he would be super-soldier, and during the night he would read the scroll. The story continued.

Love no longer felt glorious when he looked down upon his creation. Watching his once innocent children be turned into God-less fornicating sinners caused his "ORB" to cry out in pain. The good ones need help, he thought, and then corrected himself. No, they all need help. I truly love them all. It is MDSL's fault for their sin, not theirs; they were designed to be gentle; but now evil has taken control. I will find a way to redeem All my children." As Love watched Earth's inhabitants he was saddened at their lack of progress. Each successive generation faced multiple risks that could lead to their total extinction; starvation, injury, disease, killed by predators, killed by cretins. Worse, either they did not have the ability or simply did not want to make the effort to improve their conditions. Even after a long time, (much longer than even the "Evolutionary "game mutants), the created humans nor the cretins on Earth had not yet started to make and use tools (other than the spear and basic wood club,) they didn't understand fire; didn't know how to dig wells, plant seeds, or even domesticate animals. They were helpless. Hunt and gather, hunt and gather. Fight and fornicate, fight and fornicate, that's all they did. Love was already formulating a plan of redemption and wanted to implement it as soon as possible; but for it to be successful his children would have to be much more civilized. To solve that Earth problem God-Love was going to call upon the services of the most advanced cretin society from a distant planet. It is a spiral rotation older than Earth's garden and has reached an altruistic level of appreciation. They search the cosmos looking for truth and knowledge, their two equal Gods. Like all players in the evolution game, they began as a one celled organism floating in an ocean. But quickly went through the evolutionary stages; including global conflicts, intergalactic conquests, colonization of thousands of planets, and now their technology is so superior to the few other cretin species that are also travelling in space, that they seldom have to use their weapons. This race now promotes peace and the abolishment of any and all forms of slavery, (rampant among cretin societies on every inhabited planet) The only time they interfere in another species timeline is when that species is helpless in avoiding extinction. Then, when they do help it is incognito. They are the perfect candidate to help Love. God-Love is not the Father, but he still has lesser god like powers. With those powers he explained inside the collective mind of the, (helpers,) as they will be called, their mission. How, during their travels, they will come upon a weak species inhabiting a blue green planet, that needs personal hands-teaching/leading/manipulating. How they are to take the appearance of "demi-gods "able to perform minor miracles. They are to choose the leaders of various cultures and to impart wisdom and knowledge to them. God- Love ordered them to teach and model the best ways to govern and how to be governed. That the helpers were to teach the basic talents needed to sustain a civilization. Gradually, on Earth, order and stability became the norm. Eventually, Kings, pharaohs, empires and kingdoms came and went. The helpers had completed their mission. The Earthlings now had enough general knowledge of themselves and the world around them that their free-will inspired soul can make decisions concerning their eternal life. After the helpers had established this solid foundation for the Earth to flourish, they left, leaving its stewardship to the natives.

"UH!" Thought John. That History UFO channel was right all along; aliens did come down and jump-start civilization! I knew it all along, John joked to himself. The scroll seems to be confirming events in history. "How much is me and my family involved?" John settled in to read for a hours. It was 4th of July weekend so he was off from school and had a whole day with nothing to do but read. He got some snacks, drinks, limited his phone reception to Mat and Luke, (Mark if he could), And drifted away into the scroll, anticipating special feelings.

It was an exciting time on BEE planet. The Mantiss is eliminated! HAPPY! HAPPY! HAPPY! Families were together, food and water were plentiful, important work needed to be done. Perfect! That's all a BEE wanted! They were rebuilding and everything was better.

The BEEs are a democratic society, and it was time for an election. Most of the leaders had been killed in the war. Local positions needed to be filled, and a worldwide vote was needed to elect the Ultimate; the world leader. On BEE planet they take voting and elections very seriously. They understand the difference a quality leader can make, compared to a poor leader. As the 13-week process went along it became obvious to analyst and anybody with common sense that the Ultimate position was really just between only two of the four candidates. The incumbent, Ultimate King BEE Yust and the war hero, Angelo.

The Angelo family was at their farm discussing the vote. Young son #2, "I'll be glad when this is over, and you are the Ultimate. Angelo Sr. (#0) "I feel good for the people because any one of the four quadrant winners would be an excellent leader. I believe they are sincere in putting the needs of the people first, instead of any personal gain. We'll be O.K. no matter who wins. "Oldest son #1, "Yes, but you would be the best ruler, dad. You qualified with more achievements than anybody else, even the Ultimate! World Housing Authority, Capital City Planner, Bonds Supervisor, and of course your work in the chemical warfare department, you won the fight!" # 2 jumps in, "That's right. But we know the two Real reasons why dad will win the election: the two pictures! "The pictures showing his heroism and valor had a monumental effect on the spirit of the people. Hope can do wonders for the soul! The napalm and newfound optimism turned the tide of the war. Also, no one since the great "Nuses "had shown the highly valued and extremely rare "violet eye." It is worthy of value. "You are truly a great man father." "Whoa, whoa...interrupts senior, "I am just a man trying to help his people, that's all. Let's not get carried away. At some point in time everybody is asked to step up to help his fellow man, that's part of life. "#1, "Yes, father, but you are the most devoted to doing it consistently. The whole world knows it. "Sr. "Well, I'm sure everybody remembers Ultimate Y's. inspirational speeches. They were well timed and loaded with information we needed to hear. He was a good war time leader. "# 1, "Well the war is over and now you are the best man for the job! "Sr. "O.K. you guys go play. You're trying to give me the big head. "The kids eyes turned a bright blue as they flew off to play dive bomber games. Angelo, also showing bright blue, proudly looked on. Later, his kids were proven right, Angelo had won in a major landslide. UKBA was now in office.

God Joy now had his chosen leader in position. Just as scripture states in many religions how "Powers and Authorities" arrange circumstances on Earth, God Joy decided who was going to champion his people, not fate.

Progress on BEE planet continued. Every sector that could be measured was off the charts. There was a boom in modern infrastructure, sports and entertainment venues were thriving; arts and sciences were advancing the culture. Much of the credit for the rapid improvements was given to Angelo's new policies and leadership style. He got the most out of everybody and every situation. After this particular workday he was fluttering on his veranda watching his sons and friends play a game of "tag. "He thought, "Young boys, so much energy, flying so dangerously fast and close to each other!" Gradually, suspect, an eerie quietness fazed itself in until there was no noise at all! None from the distant city, or from the nearby woods, or from anywhere else. Angelo thought it was just him, but the boys stopped playing and tried to adjust their antenna. This was very peculiar, and then a stranger thing happened. In the surreal quiet thousands of small bright crystal balls started to circle the planet! They moved randomly, magically. Slow at first then faster and faster. Un- believable that there were no collisions. Angelo looked at his boys, "I do not think we are in any danger. Let's just enjoy the show." The whole world, just like the Angelo's, was totally mesmerized. The strangeness wasn't over! After about ten minutes the crystals faded away and about 50 moon size objects rolled around the planet. The giant objects looked so close it felt like you could reach out and touch them. Peaceful. Peaceful. That's the effect of the crystals and moons. And there's a next.... the BEEs eerie feeling had changed to calm; during this calm moment the entire sky turned into a rich violet color; the most trusting and reassuring color to a faithful BEE. To the serene BEEs the violet sky was awesome! All the tag players were circled around UKBA and had bright, teal-colored eyes. Every BEE citizen around the world was comforted by the aura. God-son Joy was about to give his first talk to all his creations, and now he had them at ease. When he spoke a small wave like ripple, a gentle disturbance, flowed through the violet sky.

God-Joy said, "My little children, do not be afraid. I am your Creator and God. Consider me a caring Father. This is the father talking to his children." His voice was firm, yet soft and smooth; relaxing. "I have been with you from the beginning and will to continue to be close at hand. My loved ones, listen intently, "He paused...." listen intently, I am pleased with your praise and worship. Your altruism is of value. Because you have lived properly, I have chosen your race for a great quest! You are to do my bidding. With your faith I am going to prepare you to travel a far distance.

You are going to a distant planet to meet other friendly subjects. The purpose is to give me glory; and to spread my message of love, joy, and peace. You are commanded to teach these accepting creatures the proper way to exist. With meaning, model for them an altruistic lifestyle. You must not fail this mission! It will not be easy, no, it will be hard. There will be difficulties and obstacles. Also, disappointments and sorrow. Listen with seriousness: "DO NOT RELENT! "Joy repeats it with a booming voice, startling some BEEs, "DO NOT RELENT!" Joy had to convince his creations the importance of the mission. In his caring Father voice he says, "Be of steadfast accord. Heed my words. Beware! ... Beware! An evil one desires to strike you and the others. You must prepare and be ready to confront the evil leader and his followers. The innocent ones you seek are frail. They need your protection. They are special to me, just like you, and must be saved. Your duty is to find and protect my other loved ones from the evil that wishes to destroy them. You and your son's son's and so forth must not let this happen. It is an honor and privilege to serve your God. I know I can depend upon you, that is why you have been chosen. The Holy One that watches over you sends his blessings. Go now, immediately start your mission. I offer you, my blessing." Then the surroundings came back to normal. WOW!...Again...WOW! How can I describe the soaring emotions the BEE planet children must have been experiencing!? How can I explain the emotional outpouring that must have occurred when your Holy Father, Creator, talks personally to you and all the other BEEs around the world at the same time! And in such a magnificent manner! Not only truly documenting his existence but giving the BEE race a very meaningful assignment. A mission to spread his glory; and to save other loved ones. A mission that includes danger! Again, the whole world was unified in a worthy cause. Just like in the old Mantiss war when everybody was together. One mind, one spirit, one goal.

After a few minutes of boisterous family excitement, the Angelo's went to the Ultimate office. UKBA first met with his four Quadrant advisors, and then with the entire cabinet: and then with all of the district representatives in the house of jurisdiction. The mood was of stupendous optimism and positive enthusiasm; how could it be any other way? After the initial jubilation and exclamations of joy, scholarly work produced fruitful results. Various committees were given the work of defining goals and objectives; and methods to achieve them. A plethora of social and scientific revolutions exploded. Every facet of society produced futuristic improvements. Cultural, intellectual, and technological advancements transformed the world. Conveniences, luxuries, and even excesses permeated every family. A top priority, and one that made leaps and bounds, was in the newly formed aerospace industry. Numerous scientific inventions and discoveries was quickly making space travel plausible. In just one BEE rotation computers, satellites, lasers, holographs, new durable composite materials, and a powerful type of rocket fuel came to be. The BEE's had set a goal of space travel and after much generational persistence and dedicated work Angelo # 3, who had won the 10th election after Angelo Sr. and #'s 1 & 2 retired, could give this speech.

UKBA, "Today my friends God is looking down on us with a bright blue eye! We have crawled, took baby steps, and now as an adult we are ready to fly. This ship and its brave crew will rocket off to our nearest planetary neighbor. We are not sure what awaits them, but it does not matter. It is there; we shall go to it. We will obey our creator and satisfy our own curiosities. We will glorify the Master by spreading his message. Gentlemen, good luck and God speed." The whole BEE world rejoiced as the rocket blasted off. Everyone had helped in some fashion with the space project. The first adventure out of BEE planet atmosphere had begun. More importantly to God-Joy, it appeared to him that he was ahead in the race.

CHAPTER 5

KAOS'S 2ND STAGE

The ragged Maulk Army returned to their homes as Kahn and his generals started to work on new war plans. His first and second attempts at establishing a large permanent base on the surface did not go well. Although Kahn was credited with great service. Scouts were sent out looking for new opportunities of conquest.

After a few moons it became the "season of birth." The Bi-annual time when all impregnated females would give birth. Kahn's first wife, he has four because polyonymy is the norm, gifted him a healthy baby boy. Kahn vowed to himself and his personal god that he would stay in power until he could pass the "Ring of Rule" to his oldest son. Out in the farmland, past the suburbs, a hundred miles from capital city, a son was born to a civil servant. Dad Zeke was going to name him Klautu; but only seconds after he was born his father almost killed him. It is allowed by Maulk law and tradition that a father could kill his son immediately upon birth if any physical defects are observed. Klautu had an abnormally very large head! But it was his first child. Out of compassion and a want of a boy Zeke decided to give this baby a chance at greatness; so, despite the abnormality he let him live. In his early school years "Klautu "was nicknamed "big head! "Because of the constant bullying and street fights, where he was always outnumbered, big head---- I mean Klautu----Klautu... became a loner, an outcast. He insulated himself and concentrated on his studies. He became an intellectual. Then, during his adolescent years his frame caught up with his Frankenstein's big head. He became massive! He was bigger, stronger, quicker and smarter than all his peers. Although his thick-skinned skull was still large this physical growth spurt gave him great confidence. He developed a personality and even became witty! Older kids and even adults wanted to be around him. Nobody ever made fun of him anymore; he was just too big! He was the smartest on the academic teams, fiercest in the military field exercises, and star player on all the sports teams. His father was sure glad he didn't kill him!

Like all male Maulks Klautu had a strong desire to fight and conquer. All young boys try to gain recognition and status among the group they belong to by doing daring things. In Maulk society it was an economic boost to have slaves. Klautu's father had three, well below the average and not very financially stable. One-night Klautu' and his best friend "Kai "decided to help both their families by going to the surface to capture some slaves. This pre-planned escapade was dangerous and risky. Just what they wanted! Before they went to the top they had a ceremonial toast of "plume." "This is to us, the greatest assassins ever!" "To our glorious capture, it will go down in the journals." They grunted for satisfaction and exited the tunnels leading to the light. And then it seemed suddenly there they were ...on top ... alone. They had been on top during the relative safety of military escorted school projects, but never alone. They took the first few steps, snorted, looked each other in the eye and then got into ninja mode. Their training and Maulk D.N.A. directed their movements. For miles they travel as though invisible, not even the flightless gu gu bird spotted them. Better yet, they had stayed hidden from the stump. If detected by them they would become a meal. Suddenly, Kai stopped and touched his friend on the elbow, nodding to the south as he did so. There they were, a dark mass moving in extreme quiet through the dense jungle,

15 ft. and stop for 5 sec. move 15 ft. and stop for 5. They ARE quiet! But Klautu and Kai could see them. They looked at each other, their gleaming canines dripping saliva. Nothing like capturing slaves together to bond an already close friendship. They silently took out their crossbows and prepared to shoot. Then, without reason, the mass erupted into a violent ball of U.F.C. bloody fighting. The cave people were choking, gouging; hitting and clawing; doing all kinds of crazy things trying to kill each other! They were yelling, screaming and making some noises the boys had never heard. Then, at the same time, the two teens realized the cause of the strange behavior. STUMPS! Stumps had taken control of the cave people's mind, forcing them to kill each other. Already, in only a matter of seconds, the stumps were starting to slice up and swallow the dead bodies on the periphery. Now all this was new to the boys, but all the instructors said that if this scenario ever occurred the best thing to do was to RUN FAST! One must get out of their sphere of influence before they grab your mind. But the two youngsters were scared, they never been confronted with their own death before, for a few seconds they were frozen with fear. Maulks are not prone to fear, but the presence of stumps would frighten even the most hard-core warrior. Then Kai jumped up and started to run, getting a head start on his buddy. But Klaus's longer strides quickly caught up. He looked over at Kai and noticed that he didn't look good. Veins were popping out on his forehead, he was profusely sweating, eyes glazed over, and he was shaking and running all at the same time! Then Kai pounced onto Klautu and started to choke him, really choke him! Kai was trying to kill his best friend! Klautu stumbled, falling to the ground. "Kai what are you doing," thought Klautu, as he couldn't get the words out. He couldn't breathe and started to lose conciseness. Klautu looked into his friends' eyes and didn't see the guy he grew up with. The stumps had full control. Kai was as good as dead. In dire trouble himself he still had a moment of sadness about Kai. Then he had to save himself. Klautu, being bigger and stronger was able to jump up and throw Kai off him. But like a ball shot

out of a canon he charged again, kicking and punching wildly. Klautu sadly concluded there was no hope for his friend and applied a sleeper hold. A few red salty tears flowed as Kai was gasping for his last breath. To save his own life he had to kill his best friend. The stumps didn't make him do it, he did it. Klautu was looking down at Kai, grieving, when he heard some rustling behind him. To his horror three stumps walked up on him. They were well within their range of influence. Klautu didn't even run, he knew it was too late. He stood there, waiting to be transformed. But nothing happened! After a few seconds the stumps teeth started chattering like an old-school typewriter. Klautu took a couple of steps toward them and still nothing happened. They seemed nervous. He walked closer. Then, suddenly the stumps turned and ran! Their little two-foot legs were no match for Klautu's athletic prowess. He quickly caught them and was able to hold all three midgets in one arm as he began stabbing and stabbing with such ferocity that in a short minute the stumps laid on the jungle floor in a gooey mess. Breathing heavy Klautu stopped and sat on a log to catch his breath and think about what just happened. "I'm the first Maulk to survive a stump attack. Certainly, the first to kill one. But how; why me? "Slumped over he felt emotionally exhausted. He leaned over to get up and hit his head on a low hanging branch, it didn't hurt, and he shrugged it off. He picked up Kai, he was going home to, and the gooey stump mess. As he was walking back it came to him. "It's my big head! That's the only difference between me and Kai, or any other Maulk. My big head is too thick to take control of." He is right. Destiny made the bones and flesh around Klautu's head to thick for the stump brain waves to penetrate. He is immune to their power.

After walking all night with Kai on his back he arrived at his friend's den. He explained what happened but to his dismay Kai's parents blamed him for his death. They said he should have never talked Kai into taking the stupid trip. It cut him to the bone. His hatred for the stumps intensified. He vowed to himself and his god that he would eliminate the stump race from the planet. He entered his house and boldly proclaimed to Zeke, "I have killed stumps. I am a stump killer!" Zeke waved his hand and said, "Son, slow down and make sense. What do you mean? "After explaining the episode, they decided to take the dead stumps to the regional commander.

Klautu's story was met with much skepticism, but nobody could deny the smelly stump bodies laid out on the floor. They waited two hours in a conference room when finally, a group of clip board toting white coat doctors came in asking a hundred questions. The stumps were taken away for examination. They left and then two hours later a heavily armed squad of soldiers escorted the pair to the Czar's office. The Czar's office! Wow! thought the two farmers. "The great Kahn wants to see us!" They entered the plush office and was introduced to the Czar. "So, you are the boy that didn't succumb to mind control and then stabbed these stumps to death." "Yes Sir," meekly said Klautu. "Your big for your age. "Zeke, "If I may Sir,?" "Go, ahead, said the Czar with a stern eye. "Thank you, your excellency, I almost killed my son at birth because of his big head; but I decided to give him a chance at greatness; I believe he is going to achieve it." "Hey!" shouted the Czar, I don't want to hear your family stories; how did you kill these stumps? "Zeke ignored the angry Czar and continued to tell his story. "I believe a prophecy has been fulfilled. My son is the "chosen one" Zeke says proudly. "Our prophet, Hopkins, says one will spring from the soil, we are farmers, and will rule the ones from the stars, whatever that means. "Czar, "Well good. The chosen one has shown himself," said the Czar with thick sarcasm. "Son, you smashed the stumps so bad that our scientist couldn't make much of it. That's O.K. I know the pain that revenge causes. That's all for now. We will call at our discretion, be ready. You may go now. "Zeke stood up and said, "but your excellency, my son is valuable. He may help you go to the top." Czar, "Go now." "But..." started Zeke, but Klautu cut him off, "That's all right father. We are not needed or wanted. Your greatness, we will be at your service when you desire. We will go now. Let's go now father, "firmly said Klautu. Czar Kahn, "Yes, it is best if you leave now." As soon as the two farmers left the room Kahn said this to his errand boy, "Go to our spiritual leaders and tell them to find everything they can about Hopkins and his prophecies. For now, the matter is closed. "Kahn's next two campaigns to the top also ended in disaster. There was always a fatal flaw in the strategy, or a tactical error made during combat that would result in the dragons feasting on thousands of Maulks. After the two calamities the Maulks once again lost hope about living in the light.

During the next birthing season the great Kahn was gifted with two baby girls. He shipped them off to one of the thousands of "institutions for formal education." All females were entered for schooling. This is where they are taught how to best serve Maulk society, according to their talents. Females learned how to teach school, work in the mines and factories, plow the fields, raised the kids, cook the meals, and how to attend to her master/ husband. All males were given up to 5 females for wife's or concubines. Commitment to reproduction was a necessity because of the large number of casualties in the hunting parties. So, polygamy is how it is supposed to be, it was never any other way. Actually, life on the Red planet is not that bad, for them that was used to living that way. See, because of the ruination effect of sin MDSL never introduced sin onto the Red planet. Of course not! The Mother Demon isn't going to ruin her son's creations! Therefore, in order to become a stronger race, capable of subduing the surface, and more, the Maulks created a society devoted to promoting the welfare of all its inhabitants. There was no food or shelter issues, govt. supplied. There were professional types and blue color workers. The Maulks were educated, and goal driven. The only thing we'd consider bad is the fact that these are evil cored living beings. The act of killing and death saturates their urges. They wish to impose their will upon every other breathing organism. No act of cruelty is beyond their scope. But sadly, they do not even realize the bastards that they are. There is no sin, just genetically engineered creatures to be violent, racist, intolerant rulers who have no qualms about enslaving, torturing, and killing anybody different than them. All thanks to Kaos.

In a way it's like my very loyal pet dog (princess) that I cared for very much. She would never hurt anybody in the family or any nice manner stranger. Yet, years ago, when my mother was still alive; her, me and my bother would feed the squirrels in the backyard. In the morning and after dinner we would do this. It was a big backyard, big enough for princess to go out and do her business without stink' in up the place. With Princess inside Mom would sit on the back porch and throw peanuts out in the yard under a large shade tree. About a dozen squirrels would frolic around, chasing each other, running up and down the tree and all along the branches and fence top, it was a free circus show! My mom loved it. She laughed at all the folly. It is a favorite memory. One day when we all got home from eating a restaurant breakfast, we noticed princess prancing around like she was in that famous dog contest; and she had that stupid dog grin on her face, so we knew something was up! She had a sparkle in her eye and led me outside towards the bottom of the squirrel tree. There, lying on the ground was an innocent little squirrel. It was dead. Princess must have killed it when she was let out in the morning to pee. The squirrels usually hear her but she can be quick…this one didn't make it. It had little eyelashes, and squirrel nails. It had a frighten expression on its face. It broke our hearts thinking our loving pet could kill such an innocent playful creature. It seemed as if princess was giving it to us as a trophy or gift. I think princess thought she had done something good. She is part border collie and German shepherd, a real hunter. She was acting on instinct. It was her nature. Couldn't help herself. She didn't even know it made us sad. We couldn't get mad at her. It is the same way for the Maulks. The EVIL GOD KAOS MADE THEM INTO THE EVIL THAT THEY ARE.

At the Zeke household they were also expecting. With much anticipation they waited for the delivery. It was a boy, a boy with a normal size head. Proving, in Klautu's mind, that he Was the chosen one, that his big head wasn't a fluke. Before the "season" he had devised a plan and now it was time to carry it out. He got his crossbow and knife and headed for the surface. His father met him at the door. "I can't let you go son," said Zeke. Klautu, "I must find out for sure; you know I do." His father knew he was right but still impulsively blurted out, "Well then, I'm coming to!" "Father," said a disappointed Klautu. "I had to kill Kai to stay alive, I won't kill you, do you want to kill me? "Zeke could only look down, "No son. Be safe. I'll be here when you get home." Klautu, "Don't worry dad, I'm sure it wasn't a fluke. Years ago, you were right, I was born for greatness, to help our people. I'll be back before daybreak, with more dead stumps." Zeke sat in his favorite chair to wait for his 1st born. His wives sat nearby. They waited...waited.... waited, it was taking too long! The women shed tears and tried to comfort each other. Then the back door opened and a bloodied Klautu walked in. His mother's gasped and rushed to him. "I'm all right. This is stump blood, not mine. There are 5 dead ones in the barn. This time I cut them clean, the doctors can get what they want." Zeke, "There is no time to rest. Clean up and we'll head to capitol city. "Klautu, "I agree, there is no time to rest. Destiny is waiting for me." They went to capital city. Kahn to Klautu, "Congratulations, young man. My, your even bigger. "Klautu had grown a foot since their last meeting. "Yes sir, but it is the thick skin and skull that defies the stumps mind control. "Defy, yes, I like that word. It describes your abilities very well. Since our last talk I had some research done. That's why they call me Czar Kahn. Because I get things done, remember that boy," said Kahn with a cold stare, then continued. "There is no "chosen one. "We are all of equal beginnings. Some, like me," he says and slams his fist hard onto the table, "rise to elevated heights that others only dream about." Zeke and son shot a quick glance, they have read the scripture together, they know what it says. Kahn, "There have been some reports about some other babies born with "freakish" size heads." Kahn had emphasized the "freakish" as an insult.

He waited for an emotional response but didn't get one. "You may be the first but there may be others. So, I have a very important mission for you." Excitedly Zeke asks, "A mission to serve the people, I hope." Kahn shoots back, "You serve me, not the people." Anxiously, Klautu asks, "Well, what is the mission, I'm ready to lead?" "Lead? Said the Czar, as his and Klautu's eyes lock." Settle down cub scouts. I assign missions every day, you're not special. Be calm. "The two relaxed, a little bit disappointed and dismissed. Kahn "I want you to take a squad of men and circle the planet, going up and down and all around," Kahn smiled at his rhyme. "Keep records and document any" fat head babies! "he said fat head smugly. "When you have travelled the required distance report to me, (if your still alive, he thought to himself.) Zeke, "It is a very honorable mission. Let's go son." Kahn, "I know I can depend upon you. Here are your traveling papers and security clearance. It the imprint of my ruling ring's signet," he said as he held up his golden ring of rulership. It was magnificent. "One day this will be my son's, "winking at Klautu," He will be king. "After a couple days of preparation for the Marco Polo type journey they departed.

How many others are there like Klautu? They had only travelled a short 30 miles when the group came across a caravan of about 1000 people. A centurion, the apparent leader, spoke up, "Do not go near our old village, you'll get eaten. "Is that why all these people are on the road?" asked Klautu. "I am Bork. Retired Colonel and leader of this clan. We had to leave our homes. At night the stumps come in and eat their fill. They are too smart for our traps." Zeke, "But you are so close to capital city. Why didn't you send for help?" For two years our requests have fallen on deaf ears. They live in luxury; they do not care what happens outside their world. All the surrounding villages suffer the same fate. We feel helpless." With disgust Klautu shakes his head and shrugs his shoulders. This made his hatred for the Czar and what he stands for burn hotter. Klautu "I am going to your village to solve the problem. I am called a "Defyer. Stumps cannot harm me." Bork, "You are not making sense. In the village you will be eaten, come with us, you are welcome. "Zeke, "Listen to my son, he speaks the truth." Klautu, "It is my head, "Klautu turned to go and got the last word in, "I simply have to prove my invincibility." As Klautu walked alone towards the village Bork could only sadly look on. Father Zeke spoke, "Rest tonight, tomorrow be amazed!" At daybreak Bork came out of his tent to see Klautu waiting for him! "Your alive!" he exclaimed. How did you escape the stump? "Klautu, "I didn't. I sought them out. Gather your people and follow me to a clearing in the woods" "Is it safe?" "Of course it is. I am here to save our people from danger." The clan walked behind Klautu and when they came to the clearing there lying on the ground motionless was 20 dead stumps, 20! Some females gasped in horror and stepped back in fright. Others, overcoming their doubt, picked up sticks and started beating the dead stumps. I will go back tonight and get the rest. "He did and the next morning lay 25 more dead stumps! Again, the next day he went but retuned empty handed. Klautu, "It is safe to go back now. There will be no more danger. They have mind control and are smart but within their spirit they are cowards. They will stay away from whence they have been killed. "Bork, "You are brave and surely must be the chosen one that is written about. We ae indebted to you for giving our village and way of life back to us." As they formed a large semi-circle around Klautu he stood up on a cart and gave an impromptu speech. "My friends, do not give up hope. Our race is destined by the gods for us to rule the surface and beyond. (?) Pagan (their supreme God) himself has selected me to lead an army of defyers to eliminate the stump and dragon. It can be done! Not one will remain, I promise. They will cease to exist. Be patient, I will return. The prophets have written it."

The template was set. The same thing happened in other villages, towns and small cities. Klautu would kill all the marauding stumps and then give his "follow me, I'm the chosen one to lead our race to the top speech." Most often to packed crowds cheering enthusiastically. The people soon became adorned with Klautu, pledging their allegiance to him. He was always successful. Being the only one able to kill stumps gathers popularity real fast. As they left this first village Zeke had some news for his son. "Son, in their clan was a newborn baby that had a big head. Klautu, "Are you sure? "Zeke, "Well there's no mistaking a big head son. I've done some quick math. That was a clan of 1000. According to the last census our race.......uuumm...uuummm; Zeke was squirming around with excitement as he whispered the total. "What did you say?" Asked Klautu. "1 million! That's 1 million! Son, theoretically, there could be 1 million defyers...now that's an army! My son, everything we believed in is coming true! "The conversation of a defyer army with Klautu as its commander quickened the pace to their next adventure.

News of Klautu's victories over the stumps spread quickly, always preceding the next stop. Crowds and official welcoming groups would meet them on the road and escort them to city hall. Mothers would invite him in for meals, fathers would listen intently to his stories of conquest. Daughters wanted his offspring. His star was raising rapidly.

Kahn's spies took notice. Kahn's # 1 agent explained the situation to the Czar. "Your excellency, His achievements and fame cannot be overlooked. The masses are loyal to HIM! He has great support. Already, after just a short duration, 25,000 men walk with him. At that rate he'll have 100,000 warriors when he returns. Sir, I suggest hang him now for treason; before he gets too powerful. "Kahn, "I dare you insult me!" he says to the spy as he slaps his face with a hand whip. "You underestimate me slug. Guards, take this man out and hang him for treason. I'll send the paperwork later. "He was hung in the public square; but few cared, people were hung in the square every day. Kahn turned to spy # 2, "Go back and instead of monthly reports I now want them weekly. Do not fail me. "Kahn wanted to pass on the ruling ring to his son so he could be the "puppet master "behind the scenes. So, before Klautu's popular return, through intimidation, blackmail, and pay offs, Kahn persuaded the war council and military generals to anoint his son Czar. His coronation without going through the proper challenger process was corruptness of the highest magnitude. When the first duke that complained was hanged it ended anybody else's idea to contest the crowning. # 2 Czar Kahn now wore the ruling signet. Young and brash. Eviler and dastardly than his predecessors. He ruled even more harshly than his father but had limited experience on top and soon became content with just giving orders and making promises. He received reports telling of Klautu's dominance of the stump and of his tremendous army of supporters; many who were warriors. He disregarded them as exaggerations. He even ignored the eyewitness accounts saying Klautu was only about a weeks' time from capital city. He acted as if his arrogance would make his rival go away. Until one early morning he was awoken by the sounds of clashing symbols, blowing horns, and beating drums! He made his way to the window and was shocked to see large crowds of people in the street. He told security to get his war vest and sword. General Tork met the young Czar in the street and went on to champions' square. When Kahn # 2 reached the fight zone Klautu was already there. No words were spoken between them. Everybody knew what must take place.

Soldiers supporting the different fighters called out to their own God, asking to give courage to their champion. EEEYucj HFstttyyy.. fufhn..dnmfurnf... Many kinds of screams produced an iconic noise. The electricity was unimaginable This was for total control of the Red planet and a fight to the death! Both fighters lifted up his arms as a show of force, except Kahn # 2 shouldn't have. Klautu is probably the biggest and strongest Maulk on the planet! Klautu started jogging towards Kahn, gaining momentum as he went. When he was about 20 feet from the Czar the ruler suddenly crouched down and propelled himself right into Klautu's knees.

"How does it feel to be hit you punk? Stumps don't do that do they? I'm not a little something running scared! Said the Czar, laughing heartily. "You do not know combat as I know combat," he says and beats his chest."

Long before you were known I went on many "kill hunts "with my father. Klautu, "It no longer matters. My people will not follow you. You have no respect. I am the better, we all know it." They circled and again Klautu speedily moved to Kahn, with balance this time. Arm's length away Klautu throws a left jab and makes a wild kick at Kahn's thigh. Kahn calmly blocks each one and his fans cheer loudly causing some fist -a-cuffs in the stands. Zeke isn't worried, he knows his son well. The two fighters were in close quarters now and Kahn threw a powerful right cross. Reacting lightening quick Klautu reached out and grabbed Kahn's smaller fist, he pulled hard jerking Kahn forward and then Klautu twirled him around, kicking his feet out from under him all at the same time. Then, as Kahn is falling Klautu pounced on him like a crazed killer. The two became intertwined rolling around on the ground. The worst possible scenario for a much smaller Kahn, it was like a toy boxer going against a pit bull! Klautu ended up on top and leaped frogged himself forward so his knees were pinning down Kahns arms. Kahn struggled mightily but with Klautu's size combined with having a very advantageous position,.... well, it didn't look good for Kahn. Klautu started to rain down massive blows to Kahn's face and head. Kahn frantically waved his arms and kicked his feet, but Klautu was just too strong! The energy in Kahn's wavering arms started to diminish. There was less and less energy. Kahn would try to speak but would get smashed in the mouth! He is helpless and his backers know it. After a few more moments and a dozen crushing hammer blows Kahn's arms became frail, he was barely able to keep them struggling. Shortly, Kahn's legs fell prone to the ground and his arms fell lifeless. His chest heaved a couple more times and then there was stillness. The fight didn't last two minutes! Klautu took off the signet ring and fitted it on. As he thrust it in the air all the soldiers knelt in solidarity. It was easy for a race that honors killers for all of Pagan to pledge their allegiance to Klautu. Klautu, of course was ready with a speech. "Listen my glorious warriors. We will be thirsty for stump and dragon blood! Destiny has chosen this champion and you gladiators to fulfill prophecy. Our enemies will be vanquished. Meet at the new moon to plan our domination. Until then, go to your dutiful women. A bright future awaits us. Go now. I am eager to celebrate the new beginning by experiencing all my carnal pleasures."

Kaos and MDSL was discussing their progress. MDSL, "Your champion hasn't done a thing! It is a violation and forfeit of contest if I help you. But let me give you some encouragement. OOOOUUUUUU that hurts! Kaos was in pain and begging his mother to stop the torture. "Mother, it is early, have some confidence in me. Things are good." "Good? "Growled MDSL. Find a way to spur your man to do better. You cannot fail dumbass! "MDSL left and Kaos contemplated. "It is early. I like my methods, MDSL doesn't know how to do everything perfect. I'm good at this and I'll show her." His personal pep talk was motivating and reassured himself that his plan IS the best.

Over a long period of time, from Angelo # 3 to Angelo # 7, the BEE's had finally found life. It brought some initial fanfare, but it was not intelligent life, and the notoriety wore thin. Still, the BEEs had learned a lot. They had left research and development teams on dozens of worlds. And even through generations without luck the people were still undaunted. Still very much determined to find the ones that need their protection; always watching their back for the evil one.

On the Red planet Klautu was holding his first war council meeting. "Maulks, sit down and prepare your mind for something different. "He could sense the uneasiness in the room. Klautu, "Someone speak up for the group. What are your thoughts? "Cleric, an elder from the older campaigns, and regional warlord spoke up, "We are not satisfied with this system. We want more autonomy over our lands. Plus, you are so young. Leading a world of Alpha Maulk males is more difficult than killing defenseless stumps! We are not sure you can handle the stresses. Can you really control a vast army? "Klautu, "Is that what you think, Cleric? "Before the old man could answer Klautu ran and jumped on the conference table, sliding himself all the way to the other end, Cleric's end, and just before he reached him Klautu pulled out something a kin to a Jim Bowie knife and jammed it into Cleric's heart. "Now "said Klautu, as he wiped the blood from his knife, "is there anybody else thinking I'm not strong enough?" Of course, there wasn't a word. Father Zeke laughed out loud and said, "Do not be doubters. My son IS special. Look, listen, and learn. Soon you will be believers." Zeke then distributed pen and pad to everybody, this was new. Klautu, "I just wasn't out there killing stumps and counting babies. Father and I recorded valuable information about the stump and cave man. We will eliminate them first and then concentrate on the beast. We have developed tactics that utilize the "defyers" talents. They are being taught right now to thousands of young defyrers in military academies we established during our travels. Believe me, this is a well thought out plan. Read and understand my book, "How to win a War." It will lead our race to the top. So don't die old-timers. Stick around to enjoy the spoils of victory." The generals and the army liked what they heard and became very confident. As they prepared for attack there was finally a time of peace and prosperity. Training and weapons production dominated time. The war machine was the fabric that wove society together. People were dedicated to the cause.

On a need-to-know basis, long before Klautu took control of the planet there was a sect that believed the "chosen one" was not to be born of chance; but was to be directed by other Maulks, to become the best that each generation could offer. So, for multiple generations, fathers and sons and sons of sons; these fanatical idiots used genetic breeding, hybrids, hormone therapy, and chemical enhancers to manufacture the supreme Maulk. Each hot season the male and female with the highest quality genes and desired character traits were mated. Each time producing a bigger, stronger, smarter, more determined offspring. And then one birthing season a hybrid was born that was far above all that had come before. The genetic effect had quadrupled the desired traits. Mostly, he was EVILLER than any maniac could hope for. It was obvious to the genetic engineers and those with knowledge that this male was to be displayed to the world. Their tweaking and experimenting had led to this product; destined to be king champion! Forever ruler! The leaders of the sect decided to implement the next phase of the master plan. The timing was just right. He was one the first to enroll in Klautu's military academies. Immediately he dominated every facet of military training school. His peers, professors, and fellow combatants were all extremely impressed by "PEU. "PEU and his handerlers had a hidden secret: his "creators" engineered an "emperor", not a slave. PEU had one genetic goal, "I will murder Klautu and assume my rightful place." Although he was young and had no challenges or victories yet, every fiber in his being told him he was to rule Pagan. "Patience is key," PEU said to himself, "when the time is right, he will be mine...he will be mine."

In time two million well trained "defyers" were ready for action. Klautu spoke about how the Gods had paved a "golden road of victory" for them. They headed for a mountain range clustered with a system of large, connected caverns. Tens of thousands of stumps lived there. Klautu and his army didn't need much of a plan. Without mind control the physically weak never had a chance. The massacre played out a thousand times all around the planet. Next, they concentrated on the cave people and got the same results. I know that just two sentences to describe the near annihilation of two species doesn't seem fair, (a few cave men and stumps were spared); but there is a lot of foundational history to establish about the two alien races and how their progression becomes relevant in human history. Klautu was working hard to make sure that everything he predicted was coming true. He was good to his word! Then phase 2 was put into operation, the destruction of the dragon. Except there was an unforeseen consequence of killing most of the stumps. They had been limiting the dragon population and now there was an explosion of the Maulk eating monster! Perimeter defenses had to be updated and improved; and travelling restrictions for times and locations were vey limiting. Also, and maybe worse, was that with no slaves to work the trivial, menial, but definitely necessary jobs, society was starting to crumble! Male Maulks were made to be warriors! They refused to do things like trash pickup, repetitive factory work, any type of agricultural field work, and any work of domestic value. The females did more than expected, but they just had too many other family, educational and social duties to make up the difference. Losing 99% of the domesticate work force was devastating for the economy and the general welfare of the public deteriorated. Civilization went backwards. Now, only the ones rich with land, power and a few working slaves, could afford food and shelter. For the first time there was a set of hungry and homeless Maulk. Class warfare and riots were a daily occurrence. Only by Klautu's Charism and his speeches detailing the "new plan" for greatness prevented the world empire from imploding.

One day Zeke had this conversation with his son. "Son, I have some news for you that needs to be heard. Klautu, "Father, I am aware of the problems and have perfected a plan to solve them." "No. That is not it. There is talk of rebellion; to replace you. There IS a worthy challenger lurking for you." "Bullshit, "exclaimed Klautu, ""I'm bigger and badder than anybody out there and I can still fight!" Zeke, "I know you can, son. But you spend a lot of time in your office planning campaigns. You do not see the everyday soldier like I do. Son, it may be hard to believe but this young stud is bigger than even you! It is said that the "underground crazies" were smart enough to somehow make him, but that's hard to believe." Maulks now choose not to live underground, the few that do are labeled "crazy." Zeke continued, "He's a hybrid of some kind. His name is "PEU "but that's all I know. "Klautu, "We'll get the full run down right now. Sargent, send in that talkative rep from down the hall, you know the one I mean. "Yes sir. "Apparently everybody knew the talker. Zeke, "A rep? Are you positive? "Klautu, "Oh, this one will know the whole story and be spot on! "She came in and Klautu got right to the point, "Ms. tell me all you know about PEU." Her eyes lit up like a junior high school girl. "Oh, he's so special!" "What do you mean?" growled Klautu. "People are excited to see him because he is sooooo big! "Sighing as she glanced away in a daydream. "After he gives his speech in each town, he always chooses a female to mate with. To stay behind and raise the kids, start an office and handle the business affairs, and be there when he needs a wife. I hope he chooses me when he gets here, "again sighing. "How do you know so much?" "Well I'm a member of his concubine club! I get a newsletter and received free tickets to his lecture in Kork, just down the road!" Klautu, "Well don't plan on seeing him this week." "Why Not? "Klautu turned to one of several security guards, "Take this traitor out and hang her in the square." She screamed and struggled as they drug her out the door. Her pleas for mercy and forgiveness just satisfying Klautu all the more. Klaus's security secretary brought in the requested dossier on PEU. She was instructed to start reading. "Yes Sir, it is quite lengthy; recently promoted to Colonel, approved by both you and general Tork, "Klautu had to but in, "I just O.K. what Tork puts forth; from now on I'll read every fine print." "He has risen faster in the ranks than anybody, even you Sir, he has 17 successful challenges and is undefeated in the war room H.O.E. games. He just beat the supposedly unbeatable "Spolk the Excellent." "He is presently on vote for security council membership. "She turned over her packet to continue. Klautu, "That's good. Your dismissed. Klautu, "Messenger, tell PEU to be in my office early morning."

The next morning four-armed security personnel led PEU into Klautu's office. Klautu was surprised by PEU's stature but did not show it. He stayed in his chair, he didn't want PEU to see that it would be the first time that he had to look up to anybody. Klautu, "Sit be comfortable. "PEU, "No. I prefer to stand. "An awkward beginning. PEU knows his size can be intimidating. Klautu stood up. These were the two biggest, nastiness sons of bitches on the planet! A showdown is inevitable. For a few silent moments they glared back and forth, sizing each other up.

Klautu, "I usually do not grant treacherous dogs an interview; no, I snap my fingers and they are hanged. "PEU, "You sent for me, and yes, I am unique. In your heart even you desire to serve me." Klautu could feel his blood boil! Klautu, "My desire is to squash your heart in my fist! "The guards and others in the room could feel the tension skyrocket. Klautu, "I am the first defyer, the one that got the job done. "PEU, "You failed, but more importantly, you mis - interpreted the sacred writings. You are not the CHOSEN one. And now your decisions and policies have left us for dragon fodder. My handlers read the books and correctly followed the directions. With Gods approval Maulks created the perfect Maulk. I am the preferred stock of the Gods. I have been patient. Now is the time! "Shouting this as he rushed the guards standing between him and Klautu. "Seize him and send him to the gallows! "Yelled Klautu. There was a frantic scuffle, four to one, four and a half if you count Father Zeke. But in a flash, before anybody could get killed, General Tork and two members of the war council stepped in, shouting the fighters down, separating them and demanding that they give tradition and the army justice by having a public challenge. The Alpha males stepped apart and shook their head indicating yes. Zoar, Chief member of the War Council, "You two shall battle for dominion of Red planet. The historic colisium. 2 days noon. "The historic coliseum! A generation ago was the last time a challenge fight for supreme commander was conducted here. Klautu had won that one in a brutal display of force. No one since had crossed him. Before the main event there was preliminary bouts involving slaves, lions, baby dragons, gladiators, and some blood spilling. The rampage gave the place the proper aroma needed for the monumental championship fight. Watching from above the buzz and excitement had Kaos all worked up. His final stage champion was ready to start his reign.

The referee made the introductions. By sight PEU was much bigger, the fight already seemed over. His fans were going nuts. As soon as the announcer finished the last syllable PEU rushed towards Klautu and

Klautu rushed PEU. Two bulls charging. They moved so fast that the announcer couldn't move fast enough and was crushed in between the two giants! Squaaaaasssshhhh! Referee body fluids squirted all over the octagon, soaking the front row spectators! They cheered wildly at the gruesome scene. In a split second PEU spun around and got Klautu in a death lock. Klautu swung his arms around, barely landing some minor head blows. PEU responded by throwing him down and riding Klautu like a small pony, grinding his nose into the coarse flooring. The first blood to flow. Calmly, and with Klautu not able to put up much resistance, PEU repositioned his arms and hands to fully apply the universal sleeper hold. The fight was going to be over in 10 seconds! Kaos loved it! But as PEU looked at his almost sullen soldiers he loosened his grip. And then he put on a show of pain; it was all about control, power. And he knew that his warriors expected him to enjoy putting Klautu through pain. So evil! He went about torturing Klautu and suffice to say the episode ended with PEU ripping out of socket each limb and throwing it to the frenzied war pigs in the four corners. Then he took the head, put it dead center of the octagon and SHIT on it! The gladiators had never seen such a bold show of arrogance! This exhibit of raw power and brutality is just what Maulk society needed. This was surely the Maulk to avenge all their losses and disappointments. The warrior blood was boiling. PEU's savages would do anything he demanded. They would find out later that he rules with an iron fist. Above, Kaos was salivating. "Oh, Mother, Mother. Did you see that" "he smugly asks? "This is the champion that will crush all before him. Now, confidently I can go to the next step ...space travel and domination. We are ahead of schedule and the puke. Mother, come with me to My environment, you will enjoy it! "Whatever that means.

CHAPTER 6

FIRST INTELLIGENT CONTACT

PEU had a completely different idea concerning the Maulk relationship with the dragon, stump, and cavemen than any other previous Maulk Czar. Instead of eradicating them he intended to use behavioral modifications and positive incentives to domesticate the stump. By feeding the stumps large appetite with plenty of calories and keeping his mind active on constructive duties the synergy was like Maulk/Master= Stump/Pet. However, it was thetalents of the slaveman/caveman that was instrumental in procuring the trust and cooperation of the dragon. They acted as translators as the one time deadly rivals negotiated and compromised and in soon order appreciated the advantages of working together. However, the critical factor of why the Maulk's became the rulers of the other three species is the fact that they could feed them. In short time the native inhabitants became lazy and yearned to be fed. Also, soon they became compliant and even eager to serve the Maulk. The Maulks were smart enough to give intellectual freedom to the stump. And did it help society! Almost immediately the stumps analyzed the military/industrial complex, making sweeping changes increasing production and effectiveness. The same could be said in all the arts and sciences. Civilization was on the move again! PEU, as he states it, received visions from his superior God telling him to travel to and conquer the "lights in the sky. "The Maulks did not know what that meant, but the stumps knew! Space travel is possible! And with PEU's permission worked on it diligently. A few generations of Maulks came and went but ordained by God Kaos, PEU did not age: further solidifying him as the true chosen one.

The stumps constantly strived to reach the stated goal of space travel; until the day PEU gave this speech, "My fighting gladiators. Today, this vessel flies off to find our first enemy to conquer. The statements I made to your forefathers have been proven! Never doubt the great PEU! I will not grow old until we have planted the Maulk flag on every planet in the galaxy, (cheers break out all over the world.) This ship is the eyes and ears for the military. We have a fleet prepared for battle, we only need a destination and victim. Now.... PEU was unexpectantly interrupted by a thunderous sonic boom! Then, an unidentified flying object appeared. A ship of different style went streaking through the sky. Its color was not red, which really freaked everybody out. Suddenly this fast-moving craft just stopped; didn't slow down to stop, no, it was going super-fast and then just stopped! Maulk airships do not have that capability. Excited civilians were recording the incident. Then, faster than anything in the Maulk air force, it jetted to PEU's podium, hovered 1000 feet above a few moments, and then much faster than before it soared up, up, and out of sight in 2 seconds. Causing an even louder sonic boom. The crowd of killers were confused and acted like it. PEU started giving orders. "Security... maintain control and set up a perimeter, no one leaves. Control tower, postpone liftoff until we have some answers. My people do not be alarmed. Through visions my God told me we are to conquer alien races, that ship will be our first space kill! "Some spattering of applause and cheers sprinkled through the crowd, but mostly everybody wanted to know what just happened. "Give all recording devices to security and soon you will be contacted for questioning. My staff is to meet in the war room immediately to discuss this event." After only a few hours of analysis the stumps had it correctly figured out. A caveman translator explained to PEU and he explained it to his staff. PEU, "Most fierce warriors, intelligence is convinced we have indeed been visited by an alien race and they are most assuredly monitoring us right now. Of course, their technology is far superior to ours presently but that will change. That's a dictate! We do not know their purpose for coming here and we certainly do not fear them. The great PEU will no longer allow this event to hamper or further delay our endeavor for planetary conquest. It reaffirms my strong position of first line of sight. We will not be surprised again. Also, more funds from the general treasury will be diverted for research and development. I want the best armor and weapons! We want to be able to take a punch and then deliver a knockout blow! Committee leaders will go over assignments and details. I will see you at liftoff."

PEU was right. Undetected, the alien ship had released four spy satellites. They would secretly orbit the Red planet recording for audio and visual effects. The BEE crew was able to record PEU's speech and it was the first message to be sent home. It will take three years to get there.

When it did finally arrive back in BEE Space Defense Offices Commander Z. briefly looked at the material and then took it to UKBA # 7. Entering the office Z. couldn't hide his enthusiasm. UKBA, "Why is your eye such a bright blue.? What has gotten you so happy?" Z, "A scout ship has located a level 5 intelligence Sir, a level 5!" Z. exclaimed. Angelo couldn't believe it! They both gleefully fluttered up to the ceiling and around the room. UKBA, "A level 5? Are you sure? "Z. "Scans have verified it. They are right here in my hand, and more streaming in every hour. Captain Mock of the scout ship did a great job of secretly deploying our beacons in strategic locations, like right above their central government building. A planetary decision maker resides there. But sir, I only briefly looked at the report. Before we make any announcements, I suggest only you and I first view the tapes." UKBA, "I agree. Let's go watch privately." UKBA called in speech and language experts and had electronic converters transform Maulk grumblings into BEE talk. Then, much to their dismay, the two friends watched hours of public hangings, gladiator style fighting's, easy to believe for real war games, and just the Dailey shedding of blood without any remorse or consequence. It was clear to them that this was not the little innocent ones they are searching for. More than likely this was the evil one they must confront. An emergency meeting of the full jurisdiction was convened, and UKBA took to the podium, "May God bless this congregation. My fellow achievers, long ago our creator told the ancients of this event that has occurred. "With a dark orange eye and a monotone vibration, he continued. "We have found the evil race." There were some gasps and flapping of wings and then UKBA had more information. "My friends I am sorry to disappoint you. The recorded material is clear evidence that this is the ones we must do battle with. Before you are transcripts of pertinent conversations between these vicious killers; also, here is an edited version of a speech the ruler of their world gave just before their first spaceship lift off. It sums up the attitudes and goals of the aliens. "From PEU's speech, "Myself and the stumps have correctly concluded that the alien ship is from a weak race on a small planet three years from here, a short distance. My bloodied warriors, we have found our first victim! "Shouts PEU as the army sways back and forth yelling war chants. "The first of many to feel our pain. My fierce killers, in our lifetime we will revel in the spoils of galactic domination! Nothing can stop us. We will double our efforts to quickly go to war. Soon my zombies we will swim in the blood of the tortured. "When the snipit ended UKBA said, "Men of honor, we are now facing the enemy our God and a host of Angelo Ultimate's have warned us about. They are a species bent on the destruction of us and the other special ones. Although we are a people of peace, we must fervently prepare for war. On every front our best must be put forth or risk complete and total elimination. Men, now is the time to come together."

For many years the Maulks and BEEs built more scout ships and a bigger battle fleet. On both sides every technological advancement was applied for military use. But the BEEs had a big advantage having the spy beacons. With the surveillance they knew of the Maulks progress, and a few times was able to copy their improvements.

Enough time had passed that two more elections on BEE planet was held. The citizens, being of sound logic, still had upmost confidence in the Angelo's. UKBA # 9 was now in office. Things progressed at the same rate for a while until Commander LTZ. buzzed into UKBA's office with the brightest blue eye. UKBA # 9, sensing something big, asked for the dream, "Is it the news we've all been waiting for?". LTZ, "Yes Sir, I believe so. There is some evidence of violence but appears to be necessary for survival. The leaders have problems of greed, power, and corruption; and the masses are easily led astray. I am pretty sure they are not an evil being, but I am not convinced they possess a soul. They might be another formation from the seas, like on some of our colonized worlds." UKBA, "It sounds like you have a thorough study of the findings." "Yes. During a history seminar I read where the last sighting of level 5 life was at first mis-interpreted, I didn't want that to happen on our watch, so I took a good preview of the report." UKBA, "Good job. What do you suggest?" Commander LTZ. "Well, sorry sir, but I can't decide if they are cretins from the sea or God's creation. I do not think anybody presently has enough information to make a reasonable decision. I propose we send a dozen beacons to gather more information." UKBA, "For how long?" LTZ "We must decide before the Maulks make a decisive move. We don't want to be caught with our wings down." So, after only weeks of brain storming, negotiating, and compromise, a plan of action and method of implementation was mandated by BEE jurisdiction. The BEEs put the plan into motion and sat back waiting for information to flow back to them. Other drama was unfolding in a different location.

Love entered the Father's inner circle and approached the golden throne. He was hoping to secure a blessing for a unique solution he formulated to solve the sin problem on Earth. Love, "Father, you are aware of the separation that exist between me and my children, because of the corrupt sin tampering of the whore. They are now and forever innate sinners not allowed in the kingdom because of their corruptness. It is not what I had planned but I cannot overpower the bitches doing. "The Most High Authority, "That's right. You can't by my discretion. I have knowledge that is too rich for you. It is not wise of me to revel all truth to you at such an early age. Trust Me. All things work to the best for those who commit themselves to Me. One day you will understand, but that day is not today. Love, "I accept that fact Father, and will always gladly submit my forbearance to your decisions. But I have a creative idea that may satisfy your absolute demand for righteousness and justice concerning how I may redeem my children and earn them a place in paradise; to live in the mansions I have prepared for them. It is a novel idea that of course needs your approval, and hopefully blessing. "S.H.F. "Good! "The Father bellows out, surprising his oldest son. "Father, I've been gone a little while, ...you seem very... robust. "S.H.F. "Yes. I AM is robust. I was not going to fix your little problem. It is not good for a father to manipulate every detail of a son's path; it stunts their growth. It's good that you took the responsibility to do the work yourself. Besides, you are of the best stock. Use your God given attributes. Now get to the point with the short version of your idea."

Love did not think that the ruination of his loved ones a "little detail "but moved on anyway. "Here is my plan of "salvation," as I call it. In chronological order, I will first cause men of Earthly repute to prophesies about a savior that will come to release mankind from the bondage of sin. They are to record my revelations and events on paper for future generations. Father, here is the unique solution that I hope is enough of a propiation of sin for my children to be forgiven and sanctified. I am willing to go to Earth to be born a flesh baby of a virgin, live a sinless life, I will

101

perform miracles; also doing signs and wonders, giving people a reason to believe in me. For a short time, I shall preach the glory of the Father and Heavenly Kingdom. Next, I will be harshly persecuted and unjustly crucified by the demon work of hell; at this time Father I wish to spend three days in hell preaching the gospel, securing the keys and releasing those in bondage from spiritual death: and then humbly ask that you raise me from the grave. I will give my apostles final instructions on how to inform all of mankind how to escape from the clutches of MDSL. They will take the word to the four corners of the Earth, preaching to all races and nations, writing my commands and teachings in books and letters and such; all that needs to be known for the meek to receive the gift of my ""Salvation." Then, through Earth history, those free-will beings that believe what the prophets said about me; that I am the son of God, and choose to acknowledge me with their mouth, and then invite me into their hearts to live, then with your permission Father I would like to bring those believing souls to your magnificent paradise to live for eternity. What are your thoughts, Father?"

S.H.F. "I think it is worthy of glory...glory for you and I. But before I give my final yes I must make sure you are willing to walk the Earth as flesh; to face all the temptations that MDSL will surely confront you with, remember, remaining sinless is mandatory, (I certainly will!) shoots in Love, S.H.F. continued, "you will experience rejection, humiliation, great physical pain, loneliness, deceit, disbelief, and many other unpleasantries. If you can say yes to passing this test, then I only have a couple more stipulations that you must agree to before I give My blessing." Love, "For My children I will suffer any amount of pain that is necessary. What are the stipulations?

"S.H.F. "The behavior of your Earthly creations sickens me! MDSL has won too many victories over the undisciplined weaklings. Thus, life on Earth will start all over. Pick one family and the needed animal husbandry and devise a method for them to survive a devasting flood; that at the end of it they will re-populate the Earth with righteous sons and daughters. Also, for the purpose of the "bet "I will alter one gene of the first-born male child in each successive generation. Coating it with an undetectable substance that greatly encourages him to confront evil of the fiercest kind; the first-born male of each generation will inherit this valuable gene. The power in this valuable gene can only be harnessed by MDSL and I AM. It is of a precious nature that only MDSL and I AM knows of its treasures. MDSL will kill to snatch that tool from the Earthling, to use it for her own trappings Because this gene and the seed that caries it is so valuable, (also for many other reasons the Master has not yet spoken of) it's security must be maintained. To survive the many treacherous situations this male linage will be caught in, because of its "courage "gene, my Wisdom has assigned a beautiful quartet of "Guardian Angels "to protect the special one from death. (Marie, Donna, Liela, and Betty were kept very busy!) S.H.F. "Also, make it known to your masses that it was I, I AM, that sent you to do this work and that you receive all things from me. And I beforehand, before the day comes, let it be known it is I, I AM, that has pre-destined who shall enter my heavenly kingdom. Of course, if they enter into your plan of salvation that means that I have pre-destined them for heaven. Now, consider what I have put forth." God waited. ""What do you say." Love, "I accept the commitment. There is no hesitation in my spirit. I will be the sacrificial lamb to ensure the peace of my children." The Father said yes and blessed his oldest son's idea. It gave the Son his most rewarding and fulfilling emotion yet to date. Love was thrilled that his creations have a chance at redemption! He has the Father's approval, cooperation, and best of all his blessing. And the story jumps forward.

CHAPTER 7

SCOUT SHIP FAILS

This is a message from a BEE spy ship positioned over Red planet capital city, "Sir, this xl7 reporting #1 emgff is sputtering, switching over to # 2. Emgff stands for electromagnetic gravitational free force. After a few seconds the captain reports again, "Sir, # 2 emgff is not working either. Re-trying #1. It is not turning over; I repeat she is not turning over. "The experienced captain tuned to the engineer, "we got to have one reactor working or else our stealth will be comprised. "I know, "retorts the engineer, I helped build this ship!" From above in the cosmos the Hemi-Spheric Commander asks, "Is the problem fixed yet. This has never, I repeat never, happened in the history of BEE fleet. Two faulty reactors at the same time! "Engineer can you explain this? "irately asks the commander. "Sir, I started this job when you were just a pupa, my experience tells me this entire unit has blown a socket, I've never seen it before. As you know we will not be able to maintain stealth or altitude." "Check that, prepare to be towed." The Captain, "Sir we have entered their atmosphere, we are visible and are rapidly descending." Commander, "take evasive maneuvers and remember your oath! ""Don't worry about this crew upholding it's oath, I may still have time to fix it "said the captain, "as he looked under the control panel. The commander almost hysterically yelled out, "you don't have time, hit the switch, hit the switch! "In the background the Commander could hear the crew shout, "watch out for those trees pull up, pull up!" The Captain started to hit the button to vaporize the vehicle and crew, but heard the hum of a reactor starting, he hesitated, and then it was too late. The ship clipped some trees, too many trees. On his visual the Commander could see the tiny BEE spy ship dive into the forest, slide out of it a mile away, and then slam into the side of a rocky embankment. The button wasn't hit, an oath was broken. No vaporization occurred. The ship lay there exposed with all its advanced technology. The Commander had the option of pulverizing the wreck, but almost instantly, like a swarm of flies on a pile of dung, a Maulk military unit team burst upon the crash site with great speed. The Commander gave the only remaining order for this situation, "Captain, you and your men get in the escape pod and eject. I repeat, eject the escape pod!" There was no response confirming the commander's worst fears. Either the crew was badly injured or dead and would soon be captured by this evil predator. He quickly sent a preliminary report to BEE headquarters.

With anxious caution the Maulk investigation team approached the wreckage. It looked like the ship they had seen years earlier. With instrumentation the stumps started to analyze the prize. The Colonel in charge was in constant contact with PEU. PEU, "I'll have your ass if you screw this up! "He always ruled with fear. Kaos liked his ways. "What do the stumps say?" "They say it is composed of an unknown substance; and add that the decoded panel markings indicate that this is a spy ship; loaded with surveillance equipment. ""Your Excellency, there is a gaping hole in its side and the stumps are asking permission to enter. ""Of course! "Barks back PEU. "I'll be there soon, do not screw anything up or you get screwed up! Until then communicate to me all matters. "Yes sir. I am now entering the ship through the one hole, other than that the ship is intact. The interior has a different layout than ours.....OOHH....... OOOhhhh Sir, a great discovery!" "What! What! "An excited PEU asks. "Sir, there are four dead alien creatures around what must be a control island, and best, there's one moaning and groaning, he sounds just like us when we are in pain! ""Fantastic! We have a prisoner to torture and extract information. Make sure you keep him alive." Captain, "Sir, I have no knowledge of their living processes. How can that be expected of me? "PEU's only comment, "If he dies, you die." Captain, "Another concern Sir, the stumps are frantically moving around the spaceship in a frenzied pace that I have never seen from them before." PEU, "Well leave them alone, they will learn much. This is an historical day for us. Now listen you punk. Take the intact ship and all the dead bodies; keeping the one alive, to underground bunker # 17; I will send you an evacuation team and meet you at 17. Let the stumps study everything. Their analysis will answer all our questions."

PEU was at 17 when the evacuation team arrived. "Here is what I want done. In this corner set up a medical team for a thorough examination and autopsy of the creatures. How can we kill them? Is what I want to know. Over here put an engineering/physics team. Tear apart the machinery and find out how we can copy it. Then, Captain organize some specialized units to understand their guidance, weaponry, how do they accomplish "invisibility", understand the total electronic configuration. Captain Tad, you are in charge. Do it right and there will be rewards, moots and mollies, (?); that is the only option soldier." PEU had to go put down a small rebellion. Maulks are violent, it doesn't take much to stir them into a massacring mob. But as he had told Captain Tad he would return in two weeks and right on schedule He stalked into hanger 17. Lucky for Tad he was up and busy! "Hello, Sir. How was your trip?" PEU, "That rebellion, I killed it, and to eliminate any further uprisings I buried a thousand prisoners up to their neck, poured honey on their heads, and let loose about million red ants on them all. Even I was amazed at the outright crazy sounds when a 1000 nakeds are slowly eaten by red ants; WWWHHHHEEEWWWWWW!! It drives me to smash heads! "Shouts PEU jumping onto a tabletop. He jumped back down and stared at Tad, "whaddda got for me puke?" "Oh we got plenty Sir, "kind of cocky. PEU liked it but didn't show it, "We'll let's see it." Captain Tad, "Mechanics did a great job. We figured out their jammers, sophisticated guidance systems, laser canon capabilities, stronger composites needed for deep and extended space travel and finally, more powerful thrusters. There are no boundaries to our domination. We found out how it all works! Your Overlord, this is like a thousand year leap, HHHOOOOWWWWWWLLLLLLLLLLs... In true demon fashion PEU howls out louder than any Maulk had ever heard! Captain Tad, "The medical team also discovered much. They are of robust physics. Muscular, with a large and well utilized brain capacity, Internally we are similar; basically, they die from what we die from, blunt force trauma, HA HA HA HA!!!! They got a good laugh on Pagan gift day. Each Maulk had a quick line of how they were going to dispose of their first alien. Tad, "In a fair fight we win every time, he said all goose bumbely, excited. All the Czar's advisors again started laughing at Tad. "Fair fight! "jykels PEU. "Rookie, we take stacked numbers and overwhelming firepower when we go into a fight, dumbass. We are Maulks!" Tad did not respond but kept reporting. "Your Greatness, I have saved the best for last." "Good move, young man. "(His accomplishments promoted him from punk to young man.) "We were able to keep the prisoner alive and was able to interrogate him. Interrogation is too harsh of a word. We just asked him questions and without applying any kind of force he would tell us everything he knows about the subject." PEU, "Say your words straight. "Tad, "Intelligence thinks this species is incapable of lying! Whatever the reason they just ramble on when answering a question." PEU, "Sounds like spy school 101 to me. "Tad, "No; electronics and even better is the stumps say it is the truth. Can't argue with that." PEU, "No. No, you can't. If they can fool our stumps, then we are already defeated. We will trust our God that we are doing the right thing. What did you find out? ""A lot before he died. Well, Sir allow myself to brag, (on the Red planet bragging is an accepted and condoned practice,) when we was sure we had all the facts available I beat the shit out of him! Hitt'en and kill'en something from a different world felt strange, strange and addicting; I want to kill more of these disgusting pieces of shit! "PEU, "I think you do have some Maulk moxy! said an approving PEU. "You will be with me on the first historic landing on another world. What did the prisoner say? "Tad, "Two major points Sir. One, presently, at this very moment, there are 24 spy beacons circling the planet and 2 more stationary satellites directly over capital city. They can record audio though semi-permeable materials, like ours; and have been taking still pictures and recording movements in major govt. centers. "PEU interrupted, "There listening right now?" Tad, "Yes Sir. According to the prisoner this race has known about us for a very long time and consider us an enemy." Peu leaned closer, intrigued by what was being said. "There is more important information. They have prepared an armada capable of coming here with the purpose of destroying our people, total." PEU, "WE..", Captain Tad courageously butted in, "That's not all Sir, perhaps a desired trophy awaits. "PEU, "For the last time, use straight words." "There (ONE) God ordered them to protect innocent siblings on a distant planet from attack by us; they mean to do so by destroying us." PEU, "All they have is one God. Any species that can be supported by only one God is not powerful enough to battle us!" Tad, "There God attaches some importance to the weakling." "Yes, for some reason they are important, "said PEU with a gleam in his eye. "Captain, you are now a Maulk, (a great compliment!) Take two weeks off, grap a portion of females and mollies and go to shore. One more time, they can hear us right now." "Right Now! Thank you for the generosity, Sir." PEU saluted and turned to his sr. advisor. "Go prepare the "Red "bunker. The Red bunker is a heavily fortified, state of the art Secret Bunker formulated from the cave dwellings during the ancient days. It is soundproof with no visual clues. "Implement the plan of scourge. "Said PEU. Members of all war team were quietly and without notice hurried to the top-secret bunker. PEU was confident that not even the sophisticated spy devices the aliens had could penetrate his security system. He was right. The BEEs did not know of the meeting. Whatever those topflight officials discussed and planned during that time remains a secret; even from me.

CHAPTER 8

THE FLOOD AND ADOPTION

As a concerned creator and prime "BET" maker the S.H.F. called Son Joy to the throne to clarify some facts. S.H.F. "Joy. ""I am here Father. "S.H.F. "Understand this, your champion is the most integral part of the contest. Listen and heed my "Advice." Joy, "Of course Father." "Go to your planets leader and impress upon him these points. Reassure him that Love's creations are the chosen ones to be protected. However, at this point in time the rules state "no earthly contact," so instead, for now, each BEE family is to "Adopt" an Earth family. Find a method to induce a strong emotional bond between family members. Emphasize that one day BEEs will be asked to sacrifice their life to safe the Earthlings. It is God's will. During this time I will arrange that the Angelo family will "adopt" a specific Earth family that the I AM highly values. It is imperative that you spur your children to the highest levels of altruistic quality. Go now, do your best, be wise." Joy, "I will do my best. I will not disappoint you."

That conversation started the second Earth Age. At Joy's request the Father sent his most effective messenger to inform UKBA. At midnight the Angel entered UKBA's room and awoke him. "My friend Angelo do not be alarmed. I am here in peace, even more, be of good cheer. I am Gabriel, a Guardian Angel and messenger from the most High Authority.

I am here with vital information." Angelo, remembering the strange tale of BEE God speaking through the sky, opened his mind to the possibility that what was happening was real. Gabe, "Angelo, what is asked of you and your people can not be denied. Your action defines the separation of peace and prosperity from death and enslavement. Time will answer all your questions, but you must start the action immediately. Know these truths; the Red planet harbors the evil destroyers; the second alien race on the blue planet is the innocent children that requires your help. And thirdly, Gabriel briefly explained the adoption process, saying it will become clear shortly.

For the next few days UKBA # 9 organized his thoughts and then called a meeting of judication. With Gabriel's internal inspiration and with meaningful clarity # 9 explained the situation to his officials and the general public. It was a lot of information to digest.

But from the onset the adoption of the Eathlings took precedence over fear of the red one. It was the Bees caring ways that guided their energies. An Adoption committee decided the procedures for choosing and the order of selection.

On Earth, Love had become so disheartened by his creations that he regretted their existence; but his devotion to the Father's ideals kept him from destroying the whole human race; instead, keeping in the forefront the Father's wishes, he decided to start all over with just one family. With flood waters reaching the tops of mountains he ended corrupted human life and then entitled all Earthly treasures to one righteous family. For the rest of human endurance this is the family, and its descendants, that God desires a personal relationship with, they are sanctified. Yet, very soon after disembarking, the youngest of the clan committed a humiliating sin, so God's Earthly representative, the boy's father, laid a curse on him lasting for all time. This curse carries a high debt of consequences and mankind is still paying the bill.

Now, the Heavenly Father is in control, of all timelines and matters happen at his discretion; in His wisdom he made it so that when the

Humans were stepping off the Ark, after the devastating flood, the Bees had the technology to view it. Years earlier, soon after the Angel Gabriel's message to UKBA, the BEEs sent highly technical satellites to Earth. The humans were oblivious to their actions, they did not know they were being spied on. Also, for their pleasure, the BEEs came up with an ingenious way to secretly watch humans interact. At the time of their birth, no matter their location, each baby will inhale an invisible mist which contains something like a GPS chip, except much more sophisticated with many more uses. The mist enters and harmlessly mingles with the human brain. It is undetectable to human technology. This is just a brief and very oversimplified description of this advanced culture's capabilities. It is how they hope to safely and emotionally be an unknown part of their adopted families' Dailey life. This chip has the capability to emit a four-dimensional audio and video landscape back to BEE planet for "owner's "eyes only show, or, if the adoptive parents choose to, have a public viewing. Again, this technology is a star's age beyond us. The owners can have a public or private viewing, show different angles, and can even replay the scene! So, the BEE can see what the human sees, or the preverbal "fly on the wall" scenario can be clicked. This will be streamed 24/7. The planet is wildly anticipating its first use; but for now, there are only 8 humans! The committee decided that UKBA should have first choice to adopt; and go down the ladder of accountability for each remaining pick. But as we know the human population soon skyrockets.

And now the time is here. On Earth the water had receded enough to walk on dry land. The Ark's giant doors swung open and out stepped the family. Very unimpressive! To a relative strong and energetic species, the Bee thought the humans were very meek! No wonder they need help. Immediately, the hearts of this passionate race burst into tears. A grand yearning to attend to the humans every need and want percolated throughout the BEE spirit. Both God and Joy sensed the devotion. Joy's planning and organic designs were proving correct. They were pleased.

From the eternal urgings that the Holy Father placed within him, UKBA # 9 picked the son that had the "special gene "attached to his DNA. The gene that makes him courageous enough to fight bastardly evil. Also, significantly, this gene is passed on to each first-born male child, for all generations, never to be interrupted by human means. The gene is of high value!!!

Very soon the Bee world was mesmerized by human activities. They laughed and cried with the first family. It was a major social event on BEE planet with each human birth. It meant someone received the honorable mission of bonding with that family. It meant the actual male BEE that adopts his Earth family has obligated, always happily, to all his future sons, and their sons and so on, the responsibility of bonding, perhaps caring, and perhaps dying, for their human family. Through the decades and centuries more and more BEEs completely involved themselves in the human psyche. They rejoiced, they grieved; human imperfections could be heart wrenching. Pain and suffering are horrendous. They are trying to understand guilt and shame, not experienced often on BEE planet. But probably even stronger than what the Earth parents offered, was the unconditional love the BEEs always maintained for their loved ones. Joy's plan was working magnificently!

For much time worker BEEs were in the factories, shipyards, and manufacturing plants preparing the fleet for invasion of the Red planet. Families and society in general were happy and content, living through their normal routines. UKBA performed his Ultimate duties of supervising policies, administrating orders, delegating different responsibilities, and authorizing work projects. He constantly monitored the progress of the fleet and events on the Red planet. Since the failed scout ship report the information he received was bland, boring. UKBA was suspicious. What happened to the frenzied pace? His advisors thought it trivial, he let it go.

In this short amount of time Angelo's boys grew tremendously. Physically, mentally, and emotionally they had matured in great strides.

Anglo thought it was time for them to meet their Earth brothers. That morning he brought #'s 11 & 12 to his office. # 11, the oldest, "It's about time you allow us to see OUR brothers. All of our friends have viewed their Earth family for a long time; we know their families and not even our own." #12, "Yes, we have to listen to their stories and have none to tell." UKBA, "Well parents do not raise their kids the same way, on the same schedule. I do it how I think is best. Just like DAD. I believe you are better for it. You need time to figure out who you are; what are you going to do with yourselves? Your judgement and ability to discern right from wrong needed rooting. Your values needed cemented in the right way, which should be molded by ME and other good role models. Not by the whims and fluseys of a very morally weak human race. We were sent to help them because they DO NOT live the right way. They are to learn our style; we were not meant to copy theirs." The observant # 11 quickly throws back, "Well; it's too late for that. Everybody acts like a human! It's pretty hot!" "NO! No, it is not! "Said UKBA in his deep authoritative voice. "And not everybody acts that way, only a small percentage of the youngsters; the 1 % you need to avoid! Most BEEs watch out of care and entertainment, not to emulate. "# 11, "Sure Dad, sure." Just then two people of distinction came through the door. Two old friends, Space Exploration Director Stein and Invasion Commander Admiral Bo. UKBA, "Hey boys. Come on in and get comfortable. We're getting ready to view our Earth family for the first time together.

BO "The first one? Wow, your late! "UKBA had to look away from his laughing boys. Stein. "Yes, me and my boys signed up for the deluxe package. It's excellent! On the public frequency we have touristed many ancient archeological sites. It is very interesting and educational. Imagine. We can witness from a very far distance, the loved ones that we have all adopted, and will protect from the evil one with our last breath." UKBA, "Yes. I have had, "the talk, "with the boys. They are aware of the circumstances." # 12, "Father, can we do that, visit old sites?" UKBA,

"Well I programed the box to zoom in on our family member. Many years ago, I watched the first humans, his ancestors, start Earth civilization all over again. I was the first to choose and now this is the 10th oldest son from that original group. Here we go! "Angelo turned on the converter only to hear this, "We are sorry. Due to heavy use, we cannot complete your request at this time. We apologize for any inconvenience. Please try again later. ""Are you kidding me! "Says a frustrated UKBA. BO. "Wow. That tells you how many people are watching. Stein, "Yes, I heard of a small plant taking a time break to watch some "royal wedding." UKBA, "Well a work stoppage is going way too far. People must maintain their decorum. I'm going to call the cable guy. Surely the Ultimate can get a little extra care." After a few moments of talking UKBA said it would be fixed in ten minutes. "How about that for some pull! "Bo, "I hope so, oh so great circled one, (Angelo had a weight problem.) Stein, "Right, glorious one bright as the sun!." Only good old friends can make fun of the world leader!

11, "Father while we are waiting tell some stories of our Earth family." UKBA, "Yes, good idea. It's something you should know. Being the Ultimate I had the privilege of choosing the first son of the first family. Japeth was the oldest of Noah's three sons. We will be watching one of his descendants today. His linage was blessed by Noah, the patriarch. Accc..." Just then the box crackled on. Before them was a strange scene indeed. # 11, "My gosh they are grotesque! They don't have any wings! "# 12, "Sound comes from that...hole(?) in their...(head?) Look, they ONLY walk, they can't fly! These guys ae backward! "UKBA, "Life forms may be different, it doesn't mean they should be made fun of or treated unfairly. "Father UKBA, always teaching. "Stein, you are the Earth specialist, what are we looking at? Stein, "Obviously they are in a large stadium, 25,000 I'd say. And studies about human behavior suggest this crowd is drunk! "UKBA, "Drunk? What is drunk?" Stein, "Humans consume, drink liquids, to stay at a mandatory saturation level, a pretty high number, but some kinds of liquids alter their mood, attitude, and behavior. This "alcohol "elicits

a wide range of emotions from any who drinks it. Anything from wild laughter to physical violence can be the result. Looks here though as if everybody is having a good time." BO. "That's what it looks like to me, I think it has something to do with those people crowded together under that podium thing! Look, the converter has marked that big male out front as your adoptee. He sure is big, biggest by far." UKBA, "Well good for him! "Then something happened that got everybody in the stadium excited. "What's that? asks UKBA, worried. Whatever those large hairy beasts were, they were charging right towards UKBA's son! "Stein. What's happening?" asked UKBA with a slightly high-pitched tone. Stein, "I don't know but it doesn't look friendly!" Just a few feet before the animal reached the son the one in the lead was mysteriously swept aside and jammed into the beast following him. They grappled, raising up on their hind legs; when they did the son bolted and grabbed the hind paw of a beast. Quickly he stood and swung the lion around like a discus thrower would and slammed the beast's head into the other's head. They smacked together with a mighty thud, leaving both lying dead on the dirt. UKBA, "Whew, he's all right. It's O.K. boys." When it became clear that their brother was in danger they had moved closer to dad. It was the first violence they had ever seen. Still speechless they watched more. The Earth son walked over to a (ruler's box?) A person adorned in a beautiful white robe trimmed in dark purple, rose and spoke. The converter box automatically translated the speak into BEE language." "You have done well but seem not to appreciate your gift. You have your freedom. I overturn your guilty verdict and release you from a lifetime of bondage. With pleasure you can watch the show as a free man." The son spoke up, "Give me a chance to also win their freedom." He was referring to a group of about 20 men, women, and children, probably families. They were huddled together in the middle of a large, circled opening surrounded by 20,000 screaming drunks! The son, "They have done nothing to deserve death." Ruler, "You Christian brothers make me sick! O.K. I'll give you a chance, but you'll give us a show before it is all over. Hopefully, and more than likely, you all will be slaughtered! My fan base will love that! The great Herc meets his demise in my stadium, named after me! I'll enjoy watching you get ripped to pieces, for I have what will end your folklore stories of glory. "He turned to the guards. "Bring out the cyclopes! ""What's a cyclopes? "Asked a nervous UKBA. Stein, "I don't know. In all my studies of Earth I never read about a cyclopes. Hey, your son's name is Herc!" Bo "Know anything about it?" UKBA, "Just that I like it!" BO. "For some reason the guy doing all the talking doesn't like your boy, boss. "(boss, term of respect)"

Loud roars was coming from behind a very large gate at the back of the stadium, slowly it swung open... and then whammmm! You could see a hugh disfigured foot kick the doors open! Out walked the biggest, ugliest freak anybody had ever seen. Gasps of shock and disbelief rumbled through the stadium. The army had learned from a sorcerer how to use specific odors and aromas to direct the cyclopses behavior. With those tools and trained elephants to help control the monster it lumbered into the arena. Its size was stunning, frightening to some. A 16-foot tree trunk! Massive arms and legs, reddish long hair, big nose, pointy Vulcan ears and one eye right in the middle of its forehead. A real looker! He was spitting blood and food morsels out from a previous meal and when he belched; the awful smell caused some spectators to vomit and others to rush away. Four brave soldiers unlocked the chains attaching him to the elephants on his feet, animals and men quickly scurried away, luckily not becoming a meal. The monster took a step and then suddenly, moving faster than one would expect, he was able to get to the seating section and pluck some spectators from the bleachers. He immediately chomped one in half, gulping him down headfirst. With a glossy eye he glared at the spectators stampeding to the exits. Then he bit the other guy's head off, gulped it down. # 12, "I've never heard people in that much pain before. # 11, I've never seen fear like that. Our brother doesn't stand a chance! "UKBA, "Let's see what happens. Our clan, both here and there, is of special stock." The cyclopse glanced over and noticed the regrouped Christians. They were defenseless, out in the open. Some kind of distorted grin came across his face and he moved toward his next meal. Instinctively Herc ran to their protection. He placed himself between the monster and the group. Bending he picked up and flung a fist full of dirt into his enemies face; and then thought, "What the heck am I going to do? He's bigger than the two headed serpent I destroyed at the big sea. "That's right, it's me you want ya ugly dog. "The cyclopse did not understand the words but didn't like the tone. With a groaty roar he jogged towards Herc, the Earth shook with each pounding of his foot. Unable to think of anything smart Herc just jumped up and grabbed his lower leg. The monster tried to fling him off and then tried to shake him off, but Herc had a stable grip. Herc then ducked to the backside but the monster reached around and grabbed him! With both hands the cyclopse squeezed! Herc struggled but the life was trickling out of him. He kicked and squirmed but of no use, the giant was too strong. Suddenly, the monster started to sneeze! Knee jerking, stadium crumbling strong sneezes. His grip loosened and Herc jumped free! As the monster tried to compose himself Herc looked over at the scared Christians. Then he glanced up at the laughing Emperor. Even if he could escape, he wouldn't. He is the only hope the others have. He turned back to face his foe. The cyclopse was pissed off, hungry, and it was past dinner time. He slowly waltzed Herc's way. With each step he would swing the 6-foot-long chain that had connected him to the elephant. It could easily slice Herc into little morsels of finger food. But each time the chain was close he would dodge it; but also, the chain appeared to move a few inches by itself, always in his favor. After a half dozen times it just seemed magical! Funny to a rip-roaring drunk crowd. The monster stopped. Raising his hands and looking around in confusion he roared out in anger. The emperor was mad. He and the mob wanted bloodshed. Standing up the Emperor strutted over and said something to his soldiers and then a blue mist was squirted into the monster's face. In a second his face contorted, muscles bulged out, he was meaner than before, and headed right for Herc. The monster continued to swing the chain. With each step he would swing the chain around in a circular fashion. Again, if it hit Herc it would slice him like a peach. He retreated, the monster sped up; but being the big goon that he is, the cyclops lost his balance, lost control of the chain and it wrapped around both feet. In a clumsy fashion he stumbled and fell. Herc moved as if he had a plan, but he was making it up as he went. He ran a few steps and got a different chain that was thrown to the side. He was going to put it to use. The monster wasn't paying attention to him because he was bent over tying to untangle his feet. Herc quickly snuck up behind him, threw the chain around his neck and clamped his legs around the monster's waist. He had a firm hold. Herc, thought to be the strongest man on Earth, tightened the noose. The monster's face got redder and redder. His arms were flailing around trying to hit the culprit. He even got on the ground and rolled back and forth. A small dust storm sprang from it. How could Herc survive that? But he did! It is hard to describe that minor miracle. Working so hard cost the monster his breath. His eye started to bulge, and his breathing was shallow; the end came fast......dead, just that fast. Herc got off the cyclops to a standing ovation! Herc-Herc-Herc! The fables of his extraordinary accomplishments must be true; but this was the greatest! The mob was throwing flowers and other tokens of appreciation, again chanting his name. He leisurely walked to the front of the ruler's box, the Emperor lifted his hand and all was quiet. "You have done well; the Gods have smiled upon you." Herc had to speak up, "I worship the one and true GOD. There is none before him." Emperor, "Do not test me. I am not in the ring; I win every time. What I say happens. Be good and go in silence. You have earned freedom for you and your friends. Now be gone, I never want to hear of you again. "Herc left the stadium and UKBA turned off the converter. # 11, "Father, our brother is a courageous hero. I want to get to know him better." # 12, "Yes Father, I think even you would approve him a good role model. He was willing to risk his life to save others. If he was a BEE it's possible he would have a violet eye." UKBA, "Do not let your emotions rule your logic." BO. "He is full of altruism, but I have to speak up. My own Earth son was confronted with some religious zealot trying to behead him and the group of travelers he was with. Well to make a good story short he freed himself, beat up the hoodlums, and led some strangers to safety. Everything as a father I would have taught him to do. I felt pride. I want my children, adopted or not, to live in peace. Friend, why are we still on BEE planet? Our mission is out there. "As he points up to space. Stein, "Well, I can't be silent now. My Earth son also beat back robbers trying to steal goods off a well-travelled road. One of his children was killed. He cried, I cried. What are we doing? They are fighting evil on Earth right now. Are we going to wait and let the Red one sneak in and destroy our loved ones? We were given a mission from God; I believe we are ready to act. "UKBA, "I think there is much good on Earth. We, as a race will no longer sit on the sidelines as spectators. We will join the fray. I will address jurisdiction very soon, very soon." The three friends slept well that night, satisfied with their decision to head for Earth.

Another being that slept well that night was Herc; because he was alive TO sleep well! The S. H. F.'s Guardian Angels had again saved the "linage" of the chosen, special gene. The family whose first born pre-chosen male will challenge the most evil demon. Many times throughout Earth's short history has the Guardian Angels (Steve, Deb, and David this time,) kept the linage intact.

John closed his eyes. He had just consumed a lot of information. He got up from his desk and chose to walk around his room; moving his feet always freed up his mind to think clearly. He asked himself the obvious question, "Am I related to Herc? Is that why the secretive, prophetic scroll was meant for me only? That I am to learn the destiny of two worlds and my fate among them?" John didn't want to think anymore. He decided to get some fresh summer air and walk to the library. He had a research paper due and would Enjoy looking up some other worldly information.

He went to the 3rd floor resource center and as he walked by a reading table a magazine cover caught his eye. "Newton predicts 2060!" He walked to the proper book aisle, and thought, "2060…I'll be alive then. What is happening? John is naturally curious, but that title should get everyone's attention. John, "Really?" John knew he had to go back and read the article.

It began like this: Isaac Newton, everybody knows about the apple. His parents wanted him to be a minister, like his father. Instead, he grew up to be what most historians agree was the most influential scientist of his century. His work on Optics, Mathematical Equations, and his three Laws of Motion earned him a chapter in every general science schoolbook. His two most famous publications: Mathematical Principles of Natural Philosophy, and On the Motion of Bodies in Orbit, made him the most celebrated of celebrities in London's Royal Society. Men like Edmund Halley and Robert Boyle came to him for advice. His contributions to God and country were so substantial that he was knighted and became "Sir Isaac Newton." He was a respected man of integrity and principle. He was not known as a storyteller, to exaggerate, or to create falsehoods. Most people do not know that he was a devout Christian and spent more time analyzing the bible than solving universal mysteries. He was often heard to say, "I believe the bible to be written by God inspired men and read it daily." He became obsessed with Revelation and the date of Armageddon. When would the final battle between good and evil be fought? The quest to find the answer became an unquenchable thirst.

Recently, in Oxford England, many of Newton's personal papers that had been secretly hidden per his request, has been released to the public. In them, Newton, a man of truth searching for the truth, confesses that God himself had bestowed a talent upon him. No one before him or since has received this gift. God gave Newton the ability to decode secret verses in the bible. The decoded verses gave Newton the answer to his quest. The message was clear. The final battle between the sons of light against the demons of darkness will be in the year 2060!

John quickly counted the years in his head. The article continued: That is the year of reckoning. It is when all mysteries will be resolved, and judgements rendered. All biblical truths and prophecies will be fulfilled.

That's all John needed to read. He immediately went back to his room. He was going to keep reading until he got to the year 2060! John wandered how close the scroll was; it continued:

CHAPTER 9

GALACTIC WAR

UKBA, Bo, Stein, Jurisdiction, and the BEE people agreed that they must destroy the beast first, and then travel to Earth to revel Gods glory. A launch date was set. Many families did their best "last thing" before lift-off. UKBA decided to show his sons their Earthly family. Most BEE Fathers have "parental rules" regarding T.V. viewing time. Angelo must be present when his sons watch; so because of UKBA's busy schedule this is the very first time for the kids. Angelo remembered how excited he was at his first viewing. Actually, the first viewing is like the "birds and bees" talk that Earthly father share with their sons. Because of his constant involvement with the development and the preparations of the new fleet UKBA was unaware of the situation on Earth. All he knew was that his Adoptive son was named Peter.

The boys came into the den and for an hour he explained the enormity of the cosmic plan and their place in it. Making sure that # 12 understands that he is to adopt the next male born Christlink. "You and your Earth brother will be co-patriots. Many adventures will you stretch in your golden years." # 12, "Together father, he is there, I am here." "I believe that will change by the time of your full maturity." This is Peter, your adopted brother, follow the star."

Wow! # 12 had shivers. His heart was fluttering.! He felt a lump in his throat. He couldn't explain to himself the rapid vibrations and overpowering emotions. He only now has seen his brother for the first time, seconds ago! But running through his head was words like sacrifice, devotion, protection; or phrases like, finish the work, do the job, complete the mission; or a sentence like, he will never be alone, I will always be nearby. Then they watched Peter as he walked and talked. It was early February, Southeast Asia, Vietnam. Peter was involved in an incident that for a brief while saddened the Angels in high places. He was a 25 old Army Ranger Captain, on a swift boat leading a secret mission behind enemy lines. HE is to deliver ammo and medical supplies to team 6 who was rescuing captured jet fighter pilots.

As Pete's boat moved close to the bank the boys were mesmerized. They had never been so captivated in their life. Of course, the box converter converted all speak into understandable talk. "Lorio, Hurd… hide the boat under the trees in the deep cove. Brian, Charlie, come go with me, Lorio, if we're not back in two hours head home, no questions, no guilt, just follow orders." Pete jogged ahead of his two best friends, "Follow me boys. We're either going to find team 6, the prisoners, or gooks, no matter what it's going to be fun!" The Angelo boys had difficulty comprehending Pete's sarcasm.

Brian, Charlie, and Pete had gone to school together, military boot camp and then signed up for the Rangers together, they knew each other well. They have won highschool state championships together and that teamwork carried over to their military combat. They complemented each other very well. But the Angelo's didn't know that. They could only see their loved one move down a barely visible path until a loud noise dove them to the jungle floor. Pete, "Brian, climb that tree and see what's going on." Brian, like all three, was an outdoors man from the Montana woods, he was up and down in 10 minutes. "They got our guys strung up and whipping one right now, he's not going to last long." Peter was thinking of a plan when Charlie spoke up, "Well there's no way I'm leaving until we get those men out." "Same here." Chimed in Brian. "This is the reason we joined the Rangers, to do the tough jobs like this." Pete, "I know all that guys but we just can't rush right in; I'm formulating a plan in my head. Do some more recognizance and I will meet you back here in an hour; I'm going back to the boat to get more firepower...we're going to need it." The jungle is dense and the load heavy, but Pete made the 4-mile trip in under an hour. "Good hustle Pete, I know that wasn't easy." "Take it easy. You know any Ranger could have done it. What did you guys find out?" Charlie, "The one guys dead, whipped to death." Pete's jaw stiffened with determination. The three viewed crude maps in the dirt then came to a consensus on a plan of action. With watches synchronized and confident his buddies were in position Pete slid through a loose opening in the bamboo fence. Hiding behind a jeep Pete raised his M-1, the rescue was to start with his first shot, and POP! One shot one kill. On cue Brian ran through an opening and like Jim Brown in the "Dirty Dozen." He ran in between the barracks and dining room throwing hand-grenades into each window. BO..Bo..BO..Boooooom! 2 buildings, 4 windows, 8 explosions! Vietcong came out running on fire, haphazardly shooting their rifles. At the exact same time, (because their good), Charlie lifted his 50-caliber machine gun and blasted away at their machine gun nest in the bamboo tower. Crashing down it turned into cow feed. While Brian and Charlie had the enemy pinned down in a crossfire Pete ran to the prisoner's barracks. He cautiously moved inside, "I'm of the United States Govt. here to rescue you." The five frightened and confused prisoners cowered and stumbled around until Pete corralled them together and offered some reassuring words, "Don't worry. Your safe now. The Rangers are here. Follow me." The sickly group stuck close to Pete, sneaking around pallets of machinery and military equipment, making their way to Brian and Charlie, who had relocated together behind a troop truck. They were in a fierce firefight. Pete came up from behind to avoid enemy fire. "Hold them until we get to the boat, then circle around to the boat, ditch the gooks and I'll pick you up under the burned-out bridge. Good luck boys" Pete always threw in his "Good luck boys" every mission. "Don't worry buddy, there's only about 30 of'em. Piece of cake," said Brian. Pete knew Brian wasn't being funny or sarcastic, he just honestly thought it would be a piece of cake." He played along with a straight face, "Right, I'll see you back at the bridge." Pete and his group made their way to a hole in the fence on the other side of a shack. Just before he exited, he took a last look at his buddies, there they were, fighting together side by side against Las Vegas odds. It almost looked like they were having fun, almost. "Get moving!" Pete said in an angry tone. Least he still heard gunfire, that meant his friends were still alive. "Head down that path." "You call that a path." After 20 minutes the shooting stopped, Pete didn't like that. "Hurry up, 30 more good minutes and we'll be at the boat. Later, from the rear Pete heard footsteps a short distance away. He whispered, "Get 10 feet to the right and stay down, they're coming." Two figures ran by, Pete recognized his friends, but they were too quick to get a word out. He was just glad they were alive. "Pick it up, let's go." They were 5 minutes from the boat. Pete heard loud rustling from the rear, no doubt who this is. "Stay down, stay hid." The squad of soldiers sprinted by, in a couple of minutes they heard gunfire.

14, the youngest, Father, this is too intense. Do I have to witness the death of my brother the first time I view him?" UKBA remembered his first encounter with his Earthly son, his was no different. The "Christlinks" just seem to gravitate to trouble. UKBA, "Buck up son, you're an Angelo."

Pete burst through the brush to see Charlie in a hand-to-hand struggle with two V's. They were to close for Pete to take a shot, so he unsheathed his custom-made hunting knife and charged the scuffle! He quickly approached from the back and immediately slit one of their throats, then gutted the other one from the back side. He turned to see Brian's arms flailing about breaking the water's surface then disappearing. Pete, an Eagle Scout graduate. Took quick aim and buried the blade deep into the assailant's spine, he was reaching for it as he sunk into the water, Brian exploded out gasping for air, saying "Thanks" with a thumbs up and smile. The skirmish was over.

13, "My brother is brave, I will be just like him." # 14, "Not as brave as I will be. I will be fearless, trying to save the innocents, just like our brothers." UKBA, "Boys, I do not think his troubles are over, let us continue to watch."

The senior officer spoke up, "Have you been informed of the circumstance?" Pete, "We were to deliver supplies to team 6, we couldn't find them but found you. What's next, Sir." "We are not jet pilots, AS important as they are we have much more critical information and was being prepared for Hanoi." Another officer spoke, "Two men have already been tortured to death, because they didn't give up any facts. They Will come get us. A company of regulars were on their way. But they'll never get this," as he tapped the side of his temple with a bloodied index finger. Charlie, "We don't stand a chance going through the jungle." Brian, "Or floating down the small channels. There's only one hope." Pete, "We gotta run the "Gauntlet." Prisoner," What's the gauntlet?" Captain Pete, "There's two miles of enemy controlled river before we get to the Marine held bridge at DaNang, beyond the curve." That's the problem, the gooks will throw everything they have to get your valuable information. "OK, that's what we'll do," said Pete as he exhaled a small windstorm. Pete took the controls. "Let's get lucky Sir." Said one of his crew. "There's no plan "B?" "No." "Get down and hang on." With all in the correct position they headed down the muddy delta to "Thong Point." After a few twists and turns highlighted by sporadic gun fire, the Point was in sight. From there it would be two miles of an organized and concerted effort by a determined foe to blow them to smithereens. Pete and the others didn't worry about capture, they would not allow that, but to die was a real possibility. Pete slowly pulled close to the corner as a dragster pulls up to the start line. Just before he punched the accelerator Pete said a quick breath prayer, "Father, save this

sinner from destruction so I can serve you better, I can't serve if I am dead."
Elegant. "Get ready boys, I'll be flying like Richard Petty! Pete turned the
corner and floored it! Within seconds the on-slaught hit him like the smell
of a dead skunk in the middle of the road! The ping, ping, ping of small
arms fire hitting the side of the boat and explosions sent waves over the
top, soaking all the passengers. The speedster boat, pushed hard by her
Captain, went faster and faster. Soldiers were shooting over the top, but it
was lucky if they hit anything; speed was their best friend. 100 yards went
by, 200, a half-mile and amazedly a mile. A glimmer of hope, was safety
possible? Then a canon blast hit directly in front of them raising the front
end high into air and then slammed it down into the murky delta with
extreme force. "We should be dead, or at least swimming." Said one escape
to another. "Yeah, this sure is a sturdy boat." They bounced a few times
then again gained momentum. The Marine held bridge was in plain sight.
"Go baby go, we got a chance." Charlie, an old track teammate. "Sprint
the finish Pete, sprint the finish!" Closer you get to the bridge the heavier
the fortifications are, and more powerful weaponry does the Viet Cong
employ. Heavy machine gun rounds started ripping holes in the sheath
of the craft. Several massive explosions shook the entire skeletal frame
and vibrated human ribs off the bone. Pete, in expert handling, settled
the boat and then went full speed ahead. With hungry eyes the disparate
crew looked toward the bridge. They were so close. About 800 Yards away
the Marines stated shooting over their heads, trying to give cover. Pete,
"C'mon c'mon." As he was pushing up against the control panel, hoping
the extra push would get them to safety faster. "Hold on,", screamed Pete,
"A few more yards and were good." He was right, a few more yards, but a
beady eyed gook took dead aim and fired a high velocity bazooka round
at the boat. It was heading dead smack center, finishing them. A perfect
shot. Wouldn't you know it! The last shot that had a chance to destroy
them was a perfect shot!

But it didn't go that way. A few feet from the boat Guardian Angel Sue placed herself in front of the shell and it exploded with devastation in Sue's mid-section. After many centuries of work and many rescues, especially this horrific event, the constant trauma caused her Spirit cohesiveness to lose its integrity. Even Angels have a limit to the number of catastrophic disturbances one can withstand. Her essence began to slip away. The atoms, sub-atomic particles and other tangibles of Gods physical creation started to drift apart. They will be gobbled up by other materials to be used for some other purpose. Nothing ever vanishes. The Angels in Heaven looked upon the scene with extreme sadness. They began to cry, weeping heavily. Sue sang in the choir and cared for helpless animals. She was a compassionate greeter for new arrivals. The sobbing was deep and real.

Then, in his wisdom and undying love, The Supreme Holy Father scooped her up, mended her, and said, "As it is written in John 15:13 "Greater love has no one than this, to lay down one's life for a friend." Sue is a great example of servant, mother, and child of mine; she has done well, I AM well pleased. She will be rewarded by returning to her previous chores. The ones I know she loves and enjoys."

The bombs stopped, they were out of range, passing under the bridge. The mission was over; another success for a heroic Christlink.

Pete and his team are good, but again as through the ages, it was the love, loyalty, and duty of the Angels that prolonged the gene and the special properties it can harness.

Pete retuned home just in time to witness the birth of his first-born male child, (new possessor of the gene.) He and his wife Rachel named him Matthew. Back on BEE planet the Adoption Board told # 13 he qualified to adopt one boy. The timing was remarkable. # !3 watched Rachel give birth. Matthew was cuddled lovenly in her arms; Rachel and Pete admired their adorable son. # 13 turned to his Father and asked, "Father, explain my feelings to me. I am trillions of miles from this baby, we have no common blood, neither he nor his parents have any knowledge of me; yet I feel a strong sense of devotion to this child. Inside of me is a wealth of protective care. What is this?" "Yes, it is mystical, I have the same emotions. Maybe it is because many generations ago we as a race was instructed to do so by God. Now, as a society it is just automatic that we Have these feelings; to have an innate desire to become their helpers. # 13, "I yearn for the day when we can shake hands, that's how they greet people on Earth." UKBA, "Son, as you know events are coming together leading to some kind of cataclysmic ordeal. I feel that long ago God set an unchangeable timeline for events to occur that must be done before a deadline. I sense it is fast approaching. I fear, yet also oddly hope, that you and Matthew will be involved in some great battle…a showdown between good and evil. Prepare yourself son, and your son's son. I will do what I can to help." # 13, "Father, do not worry. I will gird myself and answer the call. There is bountiful strength in my soul. Nothing will stop me from defending God's command." What a father, what a son! UKBA, "Together, let's watch Matthew grow into a man." So, they did.

They watched his first birthday party, 6th grade graduation, singing Christmas carols at nursing homes, his first kiss, his first and last drink of alcohol. They wish they could have been best man when he married his high school sweetheart, Sarah. Matthew was a uniquely talented induvial. Athletic. Intelligent. Humorous. He applied and was accepted at Annapolis Naval Academy. He excelled in the classroom and was being groomed for top gun. Well-liked and social he was known on base and in the public. In 1985 He and Sarah had a baby boy, they named him Mark, # 13 also adopted him. # 13 Had to look up the names when a doting father-in law described Mat as having the courage of a Joe Namath, charm of a Cary Grant, and the wit of Johnny Carson. Mat's military resume 'quickly became legendary. He flew the most dangerous covert missions and had many secret accomplishments. He was the first to fly the stealth fighter. Plainly said, he was a hero. He recommended changes in composite materials and craft design. His ideas were approved by high command,

and he was transferred to the new Base "51." He was the test pilot for a new plane, setting unpublished records for flight duration, air speed, and altitude, the triple crown. His boldness earning everyone's respect.

Son Mark followed in Dad's footsteps. Matthew, through his actions, taught his son discipline, humility, importance of commitment, and to live by Godly morals. At age 50 Matthew was named Director of NASA's Mar's program. The same year Mark was highly decorated for successfully rescuing diplomats and civilians from renegade terriosts. No one yet knows how he accomplished the minor miracle. But it was the birth of Mark's first son that made the family prouder. Mark named his first son, Luke. And life went on.

In jubilation and much fanfare, the BEE space fleet left for the Red planet. Optimistic anxiety (?) best describes UKBA and Commander Bo's feelings. The Gods anticipation of the first battle elicited different reactions. MDSL and Kaos raised their level of evil throughout the Fathers Earthly kingdom. Joy, Love, and the Creator watched with care.

After a few years of travel the BEE armada was close to its destination prompting a high-ranking officer to walk into PEU's office with a sealed envelope. After being acknowledged he looked PEU in the eye and winked, and said, "The mail is a day early your Overlord." Then he again looks the boss in the eye and winked three consecutive times. No mistaking that. Peu walked to a safe and removed a different sealed envelope. He read the first line to the officer. "Is that distant thunder I hear? "The officer read from his paper. "Yes." PEU, "Go and shelter my house. I will feed the children. "They looked at each other, nodded once, winked once, and then both quickly left the room. Within the next two hours all those on a "need to know basis "was told what they needed to know. They all went through a similar code exchange and then acting normally, not to draw any attention from the spy beacons, made their way go a previously assigned post. The BEEs were unaware of the Maulk's preparation.

On the "Queen Mary," flag ship of the fleet, Captain Fitz spoke to Commander BO "Sir this is fantastic. They do not have surveillance pods out, so we are moving free." BO, "Yes, we have not detected any pods. Strange, they have had that technology for a hundred years. I do not trust them. Order all ships to maximize range and scope of electronics. "Captain Fitz, "Sir, will the increase in power possibly alert their sensors? "BO, "I want to know what's out there, I order it. "Back in the underground red bunker PEU and his generals could see the BEE armada approaching. Through the captured spy ship and the stump brain wizardly the Maulks were able to invent satellites and space technology superior to the BEEs. The BEEs were clueless to the fact. Biff, the Overlords top general, "It has worked! You are a genius! "PEU, "Yes I am. "shouts PEU, and then with a fist pump to his own chest with each stated syllable he rants, "I...am a gre...AAAATE lea----derrR! None of you puny weaklings forget that! Now let's watch our lasers zap their front line. Ha Ha Ha."

Years ago, after the stumps acquired the knowledge from the crashed spy ship, PEU, his generals, mostly the well-fed stumps, during the meeting in the Red bunker, had devised a plan of deception and misinformation and have been spoon feeding it to the hungry BEEs like a new born babe. Because of this deception the BEEs think the red menace was intellectually behind, inept, and not prepared for war. In reality, the exact opposite is true. As the BEE scout ships and light cruisers got close to springing the trap PEU and his generals let out their own personal war yell: ohohohu, hhhhhheuuuioioi, aaahahaaaahha. hk,mhkhmhkkhmhkm, and a half dozen others. At the moment of impact, when 100's of the most advanced BEE vessels got vaporized, all Maulk soldiers forced out, from their deep innards, an odorous belch, another war yell, and spit out some kind of gooey mess onto the floor! "Quick, get me a Slout! "Demands PEU. A slout is a rat like rodent. Peu takes a live three foot live one by the tail and chomps its head off! As rat guts and juices run down his face PEU moans out in ecstasy, "After causing that devastation I needed some satisfaction."

The entire BEE fleet felt the enormous disturbance. BO "What happened to our scout ships marking lights? "Captain Pomy reported from the front destroyer that the advance line of cruisers and runners have disappeared. Enormous explosions blew them away. BO immediately ordered all ships to hold position. Until Fitz said, "The engineers and graphics have analyzed all the data and have concluded in front of us is a massive spider web like structure fitted with high explosives. "BO, "If our sensors did not detect them, it means that our intelligence reports are faulty. They are more developed than first thought. Tell the captains in sections 12 - 34, to focus their weapons on one distinct and common spot and see if we can poke a hole big enough to safely pass through." Relatively soon, F.Z. happily reported. "Sir, able to report a small slit has been forced open. We can solve the problem." "Good, well done. Expand it enough to complete the job. "It took several days to expand the opening big enough for a moon ship to pass through but finally the destroyers finished the job. With caution the fleet silently floated by the snare. Commander BO, "We anticipated early casualties. We will not be deterred from our stated goal. On with the mission!"

Back in the Red room PEU threw his arms up in jubilation. "You fools are so predictable! My killers, prepare phase two. "When the complete BEE force had passed through the hole PEU gave the orders, "My assassins, this is the moment you have trained for, it could not have unfolded in any better way. Go for the two big ones on the far right. They are the most isolated and vulnerable. Complete your mission and be glorified. Your reward will be virgins in Pagan's beauty. Now, go do your job!" Their job was to die! They were committed to it. If they could take out a troop ship then all the better. F.Z. quickly fluttered up to BO." What is it F.Z.? Why so nervous? (Deep yellow eye) F.Z. "Sir, radar detected several small craft moving at a high rate of speed toward our left flank. #'s 49 & 50 are the farthest away from our attack group. "B. "Yes, but their battleship escort should be enough to handle that small number.

133

Still, send two reserves to their location. Take all steps to remain alive."
The firing had just started when the reserves arrived, 7th cavalry style. It
seemed like over kill; the BEEs had a three to one advantage in attack
ships. The BEEs were wrong again. Colonel Rasp to Commander BO,
"Sir, our weapons only do minimal damage to their outer shells. We have
not penetrated their defenses and their firepower can demolish our ships!
With five to six hits our men our destroyed. We already have lost 23 good
spirited fighters. Our technology is overmatched. We must face the facts.
"B. "Rasp, I'm giving you permission to make in battle decisions but try
this first. Go to defensive formation "stack house "and focus many canons
on only a few targets. Tak'em out one at a time, individually. Proceed." It
was a good strategy. In multiple levels surrounding the most crucial moon
ships the destroyers and the blitzkrieg could coordinate their firepower
with many laser canons shooting at one intruder. PEU, "This is so perfect!
"He knew the dedication of his pilots. "Captain BGh. Line up in two
columns, zero in one area until you can blast trough their defenses and
get to the prize." The fanatical warriors did just that. Two at a time they
would streak into a barrage of canon fire; shooting their own guns at the
shield protecting the giant troop ship until they were blown to pieces then
the next two in line would take their shots. Both the Maulk's armor and
weapons were better than the BEE's. It was part of PEU's master plan
not to reveal advancements in Maulk wisdom and knowledge; now, Peu
was reaping the benefits of his correct foresight. In quick action the two
alien species fired on one another until all the BEE gunners were dead but
there were still two kamikaze Maulk pilots alive. They barreled down,
aiming the point of their attack ship at the battered troop ship. Taking a
dozen hits themselves the pilots steered the cruising bomb into the gut of
the ship. BOOM! Except a hundred 0's between the B and the M can't
describe the enormity of the explosion. For ages it was the largest recorded
disturbance in the cosmos. It's concussion waves toppling over the closer
boats and shaking the whole fleet. PEU, "Tremendous, not only did they

complete the mission they also killed and killed. Now that's how Maulk's do it!" These honorable warriors make me proud to be a Maulk. "PEU's exuberance was matched by B.'s sadness. Extreme, intense emotions at the opposite ends of the spectrum. PEU, "All right, get the envelopes, on my mark turn the mic's on; and be real, or be real dead!"

Bo. "Gentlemen, take a minute for prayer. Give condolence to those close to you. F.," Sir, finally, some good news. We have intercepted transmissions from their leader, PEU." "Now, at this time?, "thought a perplexed B. "Put it on speaker." PEU was in mid-sentence and sounded like he was pissed off! "Say what?" Biff, "I regret to report that our entire air force is destroyed. The last two were able to destroy the cargo ship, the priority." PEU, "Priority? Our attackers are vital. You stupid idiot. Subdue this man and throw him out the waste bay. He doesn't belong with us. How are we to defend our homeland without aerial coverage? We are now open to invasion. Send in the stumps and then leave us. I must devise a quick plan of resurrection.

"Commanders, but more as friends, B. and F.Z. looked at each other. They have been duped twice by the enemy. Bo. "They could be lying. "F.Z. "Yes, that's what the reports have said; as inaccurate as they have been. Lying! That's got to be hard to do." Bo. "They seem pretty good at it, no remorse, no guilt." F.Z. "What to do sir?" B. "We have a mission. Regardless of truth or lies we must force the action. I order to execute plan "swarm", may God help us." The remaining BEE armada maneuvered into swarm formation and prepared for invasion embarkment. Unbeknown to them the Maulks had staged their planet with acceptable landing zones for space aircraft but had erected camouflaged landing hazards, defensive fortifications, and tactics for overwhelming the intruders as soon as they set foot on the red planet; another well thought out trap. The Maulks were able to use the ages old tunnels of the "underground days" to hide their war machine. The BEEs were again oblivious to their predicament. PEU, "Look how it is working by my design. God Pagan is proud of me. My rewards will be astonishing! Today, after generations of planning and work, the blood of victory will drip from our teeth and drench our chest." Hesitantly, Bo. gave the order, "Moonships touch down, escorts secure the perimeter. "The deluge of BEE disaster started immediately. When the transporters touched down, just in the perfect spot for the Maulks, millions of hydraulic lifts loaded down with technically advanced weaponry sprang into action, unleashing ultra-sonic laser canon fire with devastating effectiveness. This new ray, secret from the BEEs, melted the protective shielding of the moonships. Then, millions of Maulk "units", a unit is a Maulk and stump riding on the back of a dragon, rushed out of caves and underground bunkers spewing acid and heat rays from a handheld device. Surprised BEEs were mowed down instantly. As soon as they exited the ship a stream of super-heated rays would penetrate the BEE torso, dissolving him in great pain. But it wasn't all one sided. The counterattack suffered many causalities on the Maulks. The scene is of brilliant red, green, blue, and yellow streams of light, ear deafening explosions, and the sight of giant Bees battling fire-spewing dragons. Luckily for the BEEs the latest design of the "gallion" was the most sophisticated and dangerous weapon in the battle. Its production was unknown to the enemy. It started to neutralize the larger Maulk force. PEU, "O.K. the machines have done what was asked of them. Now it is time for hand-to-hand combat. We will get close enough to them to render their big guns useless. I am surging to go out myself and again feel the rush of killing with my own bare hands, that's the best! Release the reserves to the North, we will hit them at the weakest point." A billion Maulk units headed for Bo's flank, his weak spot. Bo. to Captain Hunt "My good friend Hunt, "Take your troops and head N,N,W, I'm going N,N,E. Meet me at their worship mount and together we will make a plan from there." Hunt, "Yes sir. we still have some limited air cover, if we time it right." Bo, "Get your dozen best, a small crew, locate and take out PEU. At all costs you must get the job done." Above and around Maulk capital city was a shimmering kalidiscope of war sights and sounds. It overwhelmed the senses. The actual hand to hand fighting took place about 50 feet above the paved streets of the capital. Maulks flying on their dragons, stumps hanging on, blazing acid fire snorting from the dragon's nostrils, laser rays, light sabers, and decorated BEE head swords being used as deadly weapons. The BEEs were quicker and more agile than the dragon and after shooting his handgun the BEE would dive into the Maulk unit, gouging it with his all-powerful head sword, sending a gored up Maulk to the dirt; likewise, many BEEs were sent flaming through the sky and thudding to Earth in flames. The ground below was a mixture of limbs, tails, and various alien body parts, a foot deep in a bloodied guts from both the Maulk and the BEE. Wounded soldiers moaning and groaning, crawling to the enemy, still fighting to the death. This went on for three days, the ebb and flow of contested battle wearing on all participants. The outnumbered BEEs had retreated and circled the wagons on worship mount. The Maulks were inching their way through the ranks, sacrificing everything they had to finish the doomed prey. An ending was near.

Above, F.Z. reminded Commander Bo. of UKBA's final order. "Sir, you and the Queen Mary are too valuable to lose. It was the Ultimate's final order that you both return fully intact. The fight is over, there is nothing you or this vessel can do to change that. The time to leave is now. "Bo. "But my boys, there gone. "Bo. wavered for just 2 seconds. Bo. "It is not over, only delayed. One day we will avenge our brother's death and full fill God's mission at the same time. I will lead our forces. Yes, we are a determined people and have a righteous God. This set back is nothing, it will only make us stronger. "Bo. was inspirational, but it was much too early to forget about defeat. Bo. barely whispered, "let's leave." His eye had a strange, unusual color, a weird mixture of colors and emotions; who knew what B. was thinking? As the respected Queen Mary lifted into the upper atmosphere those soldiers that could see her momentarily stopped and saluted the pair of icons. Commander B. almost broke down and then the radio crackled.

From his war room PEU sent this message, "That's right you cowardly leader; run from the battle just when your men need you the most! I didn't expect anything different from such a weak leader and race. I will allow you to scamper home because I want you to explain this humiliating defeat to your superiors. Remember this! Never interfere with the Maulks again! And forget about Earth. That treasure is mine! Stay away. Yes, I know about it, there is much you do not know of me, but I know all about you. Be warned and beware! Now, from your master and conqueror, you have my permission to "skedaddle." This message altered Commander's B.'s already fractured nature. Within himself he vowed to bring honor and victory to his family and planet, no matter what!

On the far edge of the battlefield, behind a mountain range and out of sight to everyone was a small BEE spy ship. It was the only BEE craft to survive. When the Queen Mary left it stayed behind. 2nd in charge, "What are you doing? Are you crazy? We must leave with the mothership. Captain, "NO, we are going to stay here and send reports back to headquarters. We're O.K., nobody knows of our presence. Isn't that what spies are trained to do? "# 2, "Soldiers are trained to stay alive." Captain, "All of our beacons are destroyed. We are the only ones that can obtain information and secretly send it home. We can be a big help to the mission. We are in desperate times. Turn on the recorders. Concentrate on that building near the plaza, that's where the transmission to Commander B. came from. "# 2, "Well, I guess we might as well die doing something worthwhile." Captain, "It'll be O.K. "So the little spy ship hid out and sent important messages back to BEE planet. In time they will become very valuable.

The battle had ended in a glorious victory for PEU. He was the tool and extension of Kaos and thus MDSL herself. They were thrilled that there're champion had executed the plan so expertly. Kaos, "Mother, you are worthy of all praise. Soon, the cosmos will bow down to you." MDSL, "YOU have done well thus far. We knew that punk Joy was no match for your worthiness." Kaos, "Mother, a critical first step is completed, yes I have done well. Can I get a reward?" "Of course my darling. Here, I hope you enjoy this as much as I do." Upon the gratification Kaos turned himself into a big black wolf, big as a world, and howled at the kilotons eruptions, a show in a place Earth has never heard of. "What about us? "Asks Anarchy, as Deceiver stood watching, his hand moving back and forth. "Your pleasure will come when you do something good for me." "Well Mother then give us something to do." begged Anarchy. "Shut up and be patient." Angrily, MDSL rose up her spirit, but the boys sped off before she reacted any further. MDSL, "O.K. my bastard. Here is the next part of the plan. I am going to change your appearance into a hideous grotesque snake/reptilian type creature." Kaos, "All right! Will it scare some to death?" "Absolutely. You're the worst they could expect. I am sending you to the red planet. Through intimidation and a display of power you will become their leader. I want you to personally lead the invasion to conquer the peasants on Earth." Kaos, "But Mother isn't that against the rules?" MDSL exploded into a large mass engulfing a nearby solar system! In a rage she flung some boiling energy at Kaos. "Think son THINK! We are DEMONS! We make our own rules. We don't pay attention to others; we destroy them! "On fire and his spirit dripping it's essence away Kaos begged his Mother. "Stop, I know, I know now what to do, I won't make one more mistake! "Having your essence on fire must really hurt. MDSL, "You are ready. Hurry, go do a good job. I want to win the bet as fast as I can. Like a sexual rush I wish to dishonor him by squirting my juices all over his chin.! HA HA. I hate him for all those ages he consumed me. Now go, you look just right for the role."

As Kaos was entering the upper atmosphere of the Red planet PEU was in the middle of Overlord plaza, giving a speech to thousands of his "invincible "soldiers. Of course, he was bragging and taking all the credit for the massacre. No one was stupid enough to disagree with the biggest, nastiness, son of bitch in the universe! With a booming voice and a foot on a BEE prisoners neck he exclaims, "Because of my ferocious attitude, leadership skills, and appetite for killing, ...he hesitated as a large black cloud was slowly dropping from above. Its color was black and not red, which elicited a fearful anxiety from the mass of Maulks. A lone figure started to descend from the cloud, heading directly for the plaza. As it drew closer it got bigger and bigger. Some Maulks started pointing and murmuring; others got in a fighting stance. "Do not worry. Whatever it is your fearless king can kill it if he chooses to." The crowd relaxed. They knew nothing could withstand the fury of PEU. As the figure came into focus it looked different. The creature had a pit bull type jaw, and its mouth was filled with pointy yellow teeth, they blazed in the red sunlight. He had two emerald, green eyes, glowing! Two small horns strutted out from his forehead; his muscular physique was covered with reptilian like fish scales. Four-inch thorns transverse down the middle of his spine and whatever the creature is, it was jerking a two-foot crocodile tail back and forth on his way down. His reptilian scales was as black as Texas crude oil. Very intimidating to a Maulk! He held a 25-foot trident in his right hand and lightning bolts dazzled from his left hand, a slight acidic mist wafted from his pig nostrils. He continued down until the crowd moved away forming a Hugh circle around PEU. From a short distance the Maulks could smell the creature's nasty breath, body. This was the closest to shock that a group of Maulks had ever been. They became frozen, just staring at the unique being. Until Kaos got close enough and slammed his spear into the ground! The whole valley rumbled as though it was a quake. At the same time, he (Kaos) caused everyone to have a choking sensation. Not only the Maluks at the plaza but all over the world Maulks were clutching their throats, trying to force air down to their lungs. Kaos's first caustic words, "Kneel down and pay homage to me." They all did, allowing 1000 BEE prisoner to fly off, trying to escape. Kaos raised his free hand and zapped them all at the same time with streams of high voltage electricity! They were turned to BEE goo, splattering those below. Then he turned and shouted profanities and cursing at those who knelt. "That's how you treat defeated enemies! The softness of this race sickens me! Especially you!" as he kicks the bent over PEU in the back of the head, sending him flying into the crowd. "From now on you are my Bitch! To deliver my every whim." Kaos looked at the kneeling worshippers, most still struggling to get breath. "My name is Lucifer. I am the one truth." He took a dramatic pause...." There is none before me. I have come down from my gold throne to lead the Earth invasion. It is a treasure that I desire, it Shall be mine! Right now every female Maulk has been impregnated with my jism, they will give birth to a devil, like me. Killers at my calling, to do my will. I and my war dogs will conquer Earth. Do not feel slighted or unworthy, with a good performance you too shall enjoy the spoils of victory. I will explain the strategy to my Bitch and she will assign your roles and duties. Do not disobey...or...disappoint." Kaos pointed his trident at a distant mountain and without warning it exploded; really blowing it's top! He says, "I can do that or do this." This time he swept his trident from left to right, mummifying all the Maulks caught in its focus. "It is not wise to question my Authority. "Just then the captain of the BEE spy ship, in a panicked knee jerk reaction, bolted out of a cave streaking to outer space. Lucifer pointed His trident at it and a glowing black light of pure energy shot towards it: yet in another display of invisible force, just before the ray reached the ship it flattened out, dissipated, and harmlessly disappeared. It never made contact with the ship. Lucifer again slammed his spear to the ground. Nothing happened! Nothing even came out the tip! Then a booming voice from the heavens firmly spoke to Lucifer. "This one may live. Let it pass safely." Everyone heard the authoritative voice. And then softly so only Kaos could hear, "Now, Kaos, YOU kneel down.!" Kaos started to say, "This is forbidden by the...,(it looked to the Maulk army that Kaos was fighting an invisible force; that was pushing him down to the tiled plaza floor; that's exactly what was happening. Kaos ..." ny the game contract, I automatically win!" S.H.F. "It is open for interpretation. (Do even GODS scribble the line between right and wrong?) "For now the contest resumes, with all items still in place. Unless you want an all-out war between you and I ... or do we let the kids settle this? "MDSL, from above, "Honor your words! she said from a distance. They stared for a moment then both Authorities removed their essence from the location and Kaos continued. Lucifer stood up and fiercely shouted, "Only by my protection are you not destroyed! It is I who saved you. Come Bitch Peu. Come get the details of my plan." Lucifer ascended towards the black cloud. With an invisible force he towed PEU 100 feet behind him, upside down. The whole incident was very bizarre to the simple minded Maulks. Stumps did all the thinking.

The boss (PEU) that they thought could never be challenged was just man-handled by some "black" creature. To the Maulks now it seems that the black creature is the most powerful thing there is, until! A different magical unseen force started controlling him, forcing him to kneel! So... PEU is getting invasion plans, every female Maulk is having Lucifer's baby, and a BEE spy ship is heading home with invaluable information. The showdown of 2060 is fast approaching!

CHAPTER 10

HUMAN AFFAIRS

UKBA, # 10 called in his son, # 11, he had a special announcement for him. # 11 had quickly surpassed all expectations regarding all fields of endeavor, athletics, military training, intellectual capabilities. He was wise past his years. Politicians respected him, military elite sought his consul, and the voting public admired and trusted him. He led from the front, by example. When he came into the office # 10 got right to the point. "Son, because my energy and stamina has diminished, and of the critical issues confronting our people, I have decided to turn in my resignation. This job needs a young man driven by optimism. My boy, I have been notified by all the proper authorities that a vote will be put forth to the Advisory Board and the Jurisdiction to qualify you for the position of "Ultimate." Once approved the public will have a "yes" or "no" vote to grant you "Ultimate BEE," without the normal election process. Also, you have been given a 100 % credit to begin an early transition to the office. Of course, you have to accept; the procedure allows a two-day thinking period." UKBA # 10 did not notice a calculated change in his son's eye color. "Are you neither happy or surprised? "# 11, "Father, if I had been surprised it would mean I wasn't prepared for the job. I am prepared. Long ago it was easy to see this coming. It is my duty to be ready for any contingency. I have been reading the pulse of the public; reviewing policies and procedures, and our numbered list of priorities." # 10 just smiled, his son would be a much better Ultimate then he ever was. His eye was a dazzling blue, a very proud father. # 10, "Can you tell me what you have in mind?" "Camelot!" Said # 11 as he straightens his spine, lifts his wings high, posing like the statue of the original Angelo. The one that sits in front of the newest space observatory. # 10, "Camelot, Isn't that an Earth term? "Yes. And like the knights of the round table my friends and I will vanquish the evil that threatens galactic security. We have a strategy to eliminate those that sow discourse. Father, is there any secret memorandums that I need to know about?" "No son. You are up to date. For all intents and purposes, you are now the acting UKB. # 10, "You know the Queen Mary is the sole survivor of the invasion fleet. "UKBA, "I know. God is asking more from our faith, and we will gladly offer it. I believe it is a test, the weak of heart will quit. But for those that continue to do the work, but more importantly trust in the Lord to supply our needs, and then give the credit and glory to the Heavenly Father, then we will be the victors. The quest for the innocents is the goal. It is the answer to all things. Our mission is very important. It cannot be made trivial, for the Earthly man's sake we cannot fail. "# 10, "Yes, I agree with your wisdom son. One of their Earth religion books sums it up very nicely, I liked it so much I trust it to memory. It is called EPHESIANS, chapter 6, verses 12 and 13. "For we do not wrestle against flesh and blood, but against principalities, against powers, against rulers of darkness in this age, against spiritual hosts of wickedness in heavenly places. Therefore, take up the whole armor of God, that you may withstand the evil in the day, and having done all, to stand." # 11, "Yes, that's exactly it! In the end, I will stand! Father, your wisdom makes me feel small and humble, yet very important all at the same time. # 10, "Yes, I am humbled to. It is evident that God is in charge but wants his devoted children to dedicate themselves to any cause He sets forth. Despite the horrible defeat I think our warriors will return with enthusiasm." #11 paused. # 10, "What is it son" "I also have good news. I have been approved for adoption, Two boys. #'s 12 and 13." # 10, "Oh son, Oh son. You have completed me. I have come full circle. Thank you for being a thoughtful son." # 10 took a deep breath and fluttered close to # 11, practically whispering he says, "Son, very important. Soon. Tell them of our "special" relationship with the Christlinks, our Earthly family. Remember, ours is of a higher calling. Harp on them about the Angelo oath and fight to uphold the Christlinks; adopt and stand the oath. Son, I know you will be a great Ultimate and Father. Teach your sons well. Things are moving very fast; at the chosen time it will be your sons that will be asked to do much. Be prepared." The two Angelo's embraced and then # 11 officially went to work. Once UKBA # 11 took over the administrative duties and started leading the world his optimism re-energized the populace. The depth of Commander B.'s humiliating defeat only sparked more dedication and commitment to the mission.

PEU made a "launch "date speech to bolster his somewhat diminished stature after his Lucifer encounter at the plaza. However, unbeknown to him and his security team, The BEEs were utilizing their new "re-wired "spy beacon and heard Peu's plan. Thus, UKBA, his staff, and the knowledgeable BEE world, knew they had to immediately get to Earth. It was UKBA speech time.

"My fellow citizens, may our God in his full grace and mercy grant us peace of mind and good health. People, tune in intently and understand my words. From the very beginning the most high God has foretold of this day. Once, long ago, he told the ancients of an important and dangerous quest. They accepted his calling and so have we. He then equipped our race with the talents and desire to accomplish a worthy goal. Our forefathers found the innocent little ones that we are to protect and save, thus confirming and extending the covenant. Together, we have matched the monumental effort of previous generations. And now, the critical message is this, our spy intercepts reveal that the red menace is soon to depart for Earth. But be of good cheer. We are ready to overcome the challenge. In God's destined plan He has chosen us, this generation, to confront and defeat the red eyed menace. It is our time to give God His glory. With altruism we will protect and save our adopted loved ones. I know we our willing to make the greatest sacrifice. After our victory, and with humility, we will model the proper way to live. We will spread the Holy Creator's message of Love, Joy, and Peace. It will fulfill our obligation and complete the quest. Truly, IT IS a GLOURIOUS time! When I finish Commander B. will give you the necessary detailed information. Now, I have a personal note I must share. The matter I am about to speak about is already decided and is not open for debate. As an adoptive parent and BEE planet ambassador, myself and son # 15 are leaving immediately for Earth." There was a rustling and most of the general public was slightly shocked. "Generals Norris and Gnat and two destroyer escorts will accompany me. The route has been scouted and is perfectly safe from Maulk detection. I will do my best to represent you and the entire planet; first to my Earthly family, and then to world leaders. Hopefully, they accept what is happening is for real. I have always appreciated your efforts and attitudes, thank you now for the warm vibes! All my days you have filled my soul with gladness. Take care and I will see you on Earth, we will have a picnic!" UKBA tried a little humor to soften the blow of departure. "Here is Commander B. Thank you. "Within an hour the Angelo's were gone.

During the long trip there was a diverse range of topics, # 15 was super inquisitive.

"Father, is our Army ready to fight the red snake again, last time he beat us bad? "UKBA, "We learned some valuable lessons the hard way, through experience. Commander B. has never been the same. He feels responsible for the loss, it's personal with him. It won't happen again. "# 15, "How can you be so sure? "UKBA, "Well son I'll answer you this way. I've been reading some Earth literature and I like this proverb so much I've committed it to memory. It's # 3 and goes like this: Trust in the Lord with all your heart, lean not on your own understanding. In all your ways acknowledge Him, and He will direct your path. I do not believe our loving God would give us this mission, prepare us, and then send us across space, just to fail. I trust Him. He may test our faith and fortitude, but He will give us every opportunity to win." # 15, "He has demanded many sacrifices from us, and we have never scorned Him. "UKBA, "That's all true, great things do not come easily. We have chosen what is hard to do, it isn't the BEE nature to take the easy way out." Often, they would watch events on Earth. # 15, "Father, they are so backward! Did we ever live so crudely? "UKBA, "Remember, our civilization is much older and thus more advanced than Earthlings; but in the beginning we were the same type of hapless creature. It takes time for a species to mature past their primitive greedy desires, it has for them anyway." The excitement grew as the sighting of Earth grew bright in the window. They were right on schedule. It was preplanned that they arrive at an annual 4th of July picnic that many Christlinks were sure to attend. This year was no different, about 50 extended family members showed up to fellowship and watch the famous fireworks display.

15, "Have you got your speech ready? "UKBA, "Yes, I have practiced it many times. "They both giggled like school children. They marveled at the festivities below and was surprised at the many similarities between the species "family picnic." Celebrations, games, socializing... it all looked familiar and fun!

CHAPTER 11

THE FIRST MEETING

John greeted his dad and they walked to the staff car; it would be an hour drive to the fireworks. John, "I'll be glad to get around the family again, laugh a little bit." Luke, "Yeah, I always feel refreshed when I'm with family. Hey, Grandpa wanted you to bring him some reading material, something about a scroll." John, "I'll run back up the stairs and get it." John unlocked the door and looked at a near empty desk. A folder, pen, paper, but where is the scroll that was in the middle of the desk. "I wasn't gone 2 minutes!" Naturally he traced his last steps. NO; there's a place for everything and everything is in its place, my lock box should be right here. John went back to the car and told his dad of the theft. "That Fast! Are you and pops keeping something from me son?" "No dad, I wouldn't do that." Luke. "Well, what was in it, what did it say?" John, Um. Um. Wait a minute…Its right on the tip of my tongue. Scroll…2060..BEE..I don't know, I can't think." I was just looking forward to the fireworks and seeing grandpa; I'm done doing serious things for a while. Winning Nationals was enough drama and hoopla for ten lifetimes." Luke, "Sounds suspicious." John, "No, I've been reading it, but I honestly can't think of its content." Luke could see the uncomfortable look on his son's face.." Luke, "Well, for the next two days let it go, we all need a good vacation. NO issues, only laughter." "All right!" exclaimed John. So, dad and son had a joyful trip. They arrived and started to mingle with missed family members.

Uncles Roy, Fuller and nephew Luke was politely talking and eventually, like always, it turned to politics and the military. What's next Luke, you've done everything, what's next? "Asked his uncles. "Gentlemen, gentlemen, please, this is so big I can't even tell you about it," said Luke, in a joking, lightly bragging attitude. "I can't believe that! "Said N.A.T.O. Military Chief of Staff Roy. "We probably already know of it. "Chimed in War Department Chief of Staff Fuller. "Right, were the two most powerful men on the planet, think we don't know what's in front of you? "Luke was only playing around but now he was concerned, "what's going on? "Roy, "Some big things are coming together Luke, a new world order. It's finally and definitively put the bad guys on one side and the good guys on the other: for easy distinction. Then you know it won't take long for a showdown." Fuller, "That's right. Our job is to be confident that the good guys are informed and prepared." Roy, "Keep guarded Luke. Your skills will surely be at the tip of the spear." Luke, "That's what my next mission is all about...hey, it's safe to tell you guys right? said Luke with a smirk. Just then probably the most respected diplomat in the world walked up, Grandfather Matthew. "Boys no shop talk today. We are here to celebrate our forefather's bravery, including all the Christlinks that served in the armed forces. We are to commend and give our appreciation. The fireworks start in 15 minutes so come over here and we'll all sit together. I don't know how many more of these events I got left in me, so I want to spend them with my favorite people. ""Hey, hey, hey said the boys. Don't talk like that. You know you're going to outlive all of us!" As they laughed and grabbed the prime chairs the family always reserves from the city. Front row seats for the best show on Earth. "Luke, "said Mat, "go get little John. We are the unique three, (?), so we need to sit close together." Just then John, Luke's son and the youngest male Christlink, (first born and possessor of the special gene), pulled up a chair by his great grandfather, giving him a big hug as he squished in side by side. Right before the start Patriarch Matthew said a brief prayer for those close enough to hear, "Father in Heaven, please accept praise and worship from this lowly sinner. Your grace and mercy are immeasurable. Thank you for all the blessings you have bestowed upon this family. We ask for your guidance and wisdom this and every day. Lead us away from evil and his temptation. May we give our best in serving your Majesty. Amen. "Amen, Amen, Amen everybody echoed. Precisely at 9 o'clock the first sparkles erupted.

"WOW! This is great!" said 10-year-old John. "WOW! This is great! "Said Angelo # 15. His first live Earth fireworks. "This is so much better than seeing it from a module!" Patriotic symphony music could be heard between fire work explosions. The smell of sulfur and gunpowder was in the air and there was rousing applause after each song. It was a spectacular show! Slowly, moving in from the West and behind the enormous display was a giant thunderstorm. In 5, 10, 15, minutes the storm had quickly moved closer and gotten even bigger. Young Angelo had never seen one before. # 15, "What a pleasing God they must have! Look at the awesome show he is bringing them… much more incredible than their own artwork. UKBA, "Yes, He is very kind." The fireworks displays were closer, loud, and really neat; but the ear-splitting thunderclaps and overwhelming expanse of the dark clouds and lightning bolts put into perspective the fury of Mother Nature. Matthew leaned over to John and said, "Kind of lets you know who's in charge, doesn't it?" "Oh, I know who is in charge. God told me last week, "said John in a matter-of-fact manner. Smiling, Mat asked, "Well, what did He say?" He said, "John, I AM is your friend. I control all things. I have a future plan, and you are a part of it. I will tell you more later." Matthew sat speechless for a moment. He didn't think such an innocent child, his blue-eyed blond hair great grandson, could make up something like that up, could he? Mat, "Well when He tells you more tell me, O. K.? "O.K. grandpa. "Mat turned to his other side and said to Luke, "pretty good show uh? "Luke, "Yeah, I don't mind these kinds of explosions, not like the ones over the canal. That was the worst ever. It was more dangerous than Iran. But I didn't lose one guy! "He said proudly. "Not because of any heroics I did, I just have a super crew! We'd die for each other but fornately haven' t had to. "He stopped short as not to say "yet." Mat, "Yeah, I know the feeling. Every Christlink, from the very beginning I'm sure, has always put themselves in harm's way to vanquish the bad. But I must admit you have done more than most. Let's see, you've destroyed WMD's in the Philippines, fought and sunk a rouge Russian destroyer before it could use its nuclear weapons." Luke, "Yeah, I don't know how we averted WW3 on that one." "Then of course the mission over North Korea was the Mt Rushmore of danger." Luke, "Grandpa, only a handful of top officials have knowledge of that. How'd you find out? "Mat, "Well I know, but I can't tell you, "said Mat laughing, "You ain't got the clearance youngster!" He said with a big smile. Luke was a fantastic pilot but nowhere close to the behind the scenes planner and manipulator that ol'e grandpa was. Mat, "I'd say your Guardian Angels have been working overtime." (Mat had no idea how accurate that statement is!) Luke, "Yes, I have a full prayer life." Mat's intuition was correct. Luke's Angelic protector had been Carol, a most special spirit, now she has a watchful eye on John, Luke's first born male child. Mat, "What was the boys badgering you about? "Luke," Oh, they think they know something, but they really don't, "leaning closer Luke whispered, "I'll tell you grandpa, it's really super. Tuesday the black ties are flying me out to 57! says Luke, very excited. "What's 57?" Asked Mat dryly. "It's the new and actually secret aerospace camp, all military. It's the 51 of the 50's. So hidden the president and other top brass don't know about it." .... Luke hesitated, "Pops, do you know about it?"

The cymbals clashed on the final crescendo as the fireworks ended to a standing ovation. The Christlink's started to clean up their area. Mat started to walk to the nearby woods. "Where's Mat going? "Asked one of the cousin's wives. Sarah, Mat's wife, answers, "Oh, it's a ritual with him.

Every year he goes down to his favorite bench and throws a penny into the pond. He says it brings safety and good fortune to the whole family." Toni, "Being so military I didn't think Grandpa was superstitious." Sarah, "Well. He's really not. But as often as our men are put in dangerous predicaments, I wish he'd throw a whole role of quarters in there! "The women laughed out loud...deep down knowing the possibility of a new "predicament "was just an order away.

1000 feet above the pond the Angelo's were fluttering with excitement. UKBA's eye color was a swirling mixture of anticipation, wonder and tingling excitement! He turned to his first assistant, "Is everything ready? Nervousness coming from his antenna. "Yes, your Ultimate. The milk and cookies are the correct temperatures." "Good, good. That's important." 2nd in command relays to UKBA, "Sir, evacuation protocols are in place. Mr. Mat will arrive at the extraction point at the expected time; except Sir there is a variable. Young John is running down the path trying to catch up to his great grandfather. What shall be done? "UKBA hesitated as thoughts formulated, then # 15 had an idea, "Father bring young John on board to! We will meet and become friends. I will talk to him while you and Grandfather Mat discuss the issues." UKBA does not hesitate this time, "A stupendous idea! General, make it so!" As Mat reached the pond John ran up beside him. "Grandpa, I have my penny... plus, I have to tell you...." but before he could finish there was a gentle tug on his metal belt buckle. Before either Christlink could say anything, they were softly being pulled upwards into the night sky. John shouts out, "What's happening Grandpa? ""I don't know, but we'll be all right, I'm sure of it." He wasn't sure of it, but don't let anybody try to harm John, that's how Mat felt, down to the bare bone! Higher and higher they went. Below them they could see their family and the rest of the park. They didn't know it at the time they were in stealth mode, invisible. In a just a short time, seconds, they were guided through a large door, entering a disc shaped object. They were placed upright in a furnished room. Both felt a "release. "They glanced at each other, looking for abnormalities. The room had a sofa, four lounge chairs, two t.v. dinner trays, a very large screen and strange markings on the walls. Then, a sliding door opened and in walked two giant Bumble BEEs! The humans were speechless! Mat and John stepped back. John hugged Mat's waist, but soon let go, although he still held his hand. Then it got even more weird! Without a mouth to move somehow a voice came from one of the BEEs! "Matthew and John do not be afraid, no harm will come to you." With unbelievable expressions Mat and John could only look at the giant BEE, and then to each other. "Yes, I know your names. Please try not to be alarmed, you are not in danger. My name is Angelo. I am the representative of a friendly alien planet." Without warning John reached up and pinched Mat real hard in the soft belly. "Ouch," yelled out Mat, looking over to John. Who just shrugged his shoulders with a "Well, I had to see! "Look. UKBA continued, "I expect this first meeting will overwhelm your senses for a while, but eventually we will be able to communicate." Angelo turned to a third BEE that was in the doorway. They did not talk but the antenna (?) on top of their head (?) vibrated and then the BEE left the room, but quickly returned with what looked like a food tray of cookies! UKBA "Here, please sit down and relax," (the lounge chairs were replicas of Mat's favorites on the patio,) "Enjoy this cold milk and cookies. Oatmeal and raisin Mat, your favorite." Mat thought to himself, "They are my favorites, but how did he know that." He sat there trying to observe and take in all the details he could, for the report. A smaller BEE came into the room and said, "John, do you want to come over here with me to play, while the old guys talk? "Without a thought John jumped off the couch and moved towards a "gaming "area. Matthew shot out of his chair, "Wait! "He lurched out for John but he was already past his reach. UKBA, "It is all right Matthew. I seen John when he was born and watched him grow. I have looked upon him nearly every day of his life. I have witnessed his failures and achievements, I also cried when his dog Princess had to be put down." Angelo # 15 turned from the play area to add, "Sir, John is my adopted brother who I am very fond of, I am willing to protect him." The two kids started to play again, this time "thumb wars." Matthew was touched by the statement. He was surprised to get a warm trusting feeling. He sensed the youngster was honest and sincere. He felt safe enough to start asking questions." Your round thing in the center, it changed colors, what's that all about? "This round thing is my eye, to see things, the mechanics works much like yours; except the swirling colors inside is an indication of the emotion I am presently experiencing. My mood changed from the teal of intelligent behavior to the bright blue of a proud father. The smaller BEE is the oldest of my two sons." For a few moments the two parents watched the boys play with laughter. UKBA, "He is a good son." Mat, "Yes, that is my first impression." Mat sat back down. "Now, let me get this straight. Me and John just flew 1000 feet in the air, and we are sitting in an alien spaceship, enjoying some very good cookies and milk. Plus, I am talking to a big bumble BEE that says he is the leader of a friendly alien planet." UKBA, "Very good synopsis Matthew! Except I prefer the word representative rather than leader." Mat just sat there. UKBA, "Mat, little John already pinched you to make sure you're not dreaming, what more scientific proof do you want?" The two Angelo's turned to each other, they both had a little shiver as their antenna jostled, and their eyes went shocking green." Hey, said Mat, a sparkle in His eye, "you guys are laughing! Laughing at me! Ha Ha" As Mat belted out a hearty laugh. UkBA, "That's right Mat. It was a spontaneous joke that neither my son nor me knew was coming, the spontaneity made it extremely funny to us aliens!" "Yaa, I guess it was "said Mat, with a wide grin. "Wow! A giant alien with milk, cookies, and a sense of humor! What's next? "The mood had turned jovial. They were interrupted by even louder laughter from the boys. The adults turned to see Angelo tickling little John. He wasn't being hurt; he was having fun. "Be careful son, "called out UKBA, "they are of weaker frame than us. "# 15, "We will play another game." "Matthew put down his cookie and in his political voice says, "We are weaker, and technologically inferior. Sir, what is the purpose of this encounter?" The meeting started much better than could have been hoped for, now it was time for business, thought UKBA. UKBA, "Matthew, I am glad your shock and awe is over. Because there is critical information I must share with you. First, let me give you a simple background. Trust me my friend. Our God, whose name when translated to English is JOY, has given our people, our species, an important quest that we cannot fail. It is an integral piece to the cosmic puzzle. At a later time, we will discuss those complexities. For an age we have observed your planet. With few exceptions your populace has been unaware of this. This is the crucial comprehension Matthew, each family, we have families just like you do, each family unit has "adopted "an Earth family. Over a period of ages and many, many generations our society has developed strong emotional bonds with their Earth siblings, sons and daughters." "Children and siblings?" asked Mat. "What about you, do you have children and siblings?" UKBA, "In the beginning, to be the very first and original, by Godly decree, my forefather and thus each first born adopted male, including me, had the privilege of choosing the first of the new age; it was your ancient father. The Chrstlinks and the Angelo's are destined too always be together. I myself has watched your clan invade and spread throughout Asia, cross the Atlantic, help to found America, fight in every war; I am emotionally invested in you and your children Matthew. Many times it drained me. Yours is a daring breed. And now, my son has adopted your grandson John as a caring brother. Already he has a strong agape type of love for John. He will never forsake him," said UKBA, almost defiantly. Matthew began to say something, but UKBA sternly cut him off, "Matthew, there is much more, there is more to what my son said earlier. To be a protector to us means willing to lay down one's life to preserve what he believes in, we believe in our God and in our mission. Right now, Mat there is 2 billion BEEs coming here in 100 million vessels. They are travelling here to save their adopted Earthly family from destruction. That's how strongly we feel for our families. We

have gratefully accepted the duty. It is an honor and privilege to do so."
Mat stood back up and said somewhat sternly, "Wait, wait, wait, I don't
know what's really going on; there may be a war, but if so it'll end, they'll
be a winner and a loser, and the sun will come up and life will continue.
Us Earthlings will deal with it; we don't need any alien help." UKBA,
"Matthew, here is the critical message you must hear. Now open your mind
to the truth. You may want to sit back down." Mat sheepishly looked up
at the intimidating figure and slid into his chair. "There is also another
alien race on their way to Earth. They are full of hate and evil. They are
determined to conquer, dominate, and enslave humanity for all time. This
species was created by an evil God that he himself is leading the invasion.
His name is Lucifer." Matthew sprang up, coughed, nearly choked, and
said, "Whoa, Whoa," says Mat as he stands and spins around with his
hands up like a helicopter, "That's too much... that's too much like bible
prophecy. It can't be real, it's a fancy trick. "Just then John went to the
person he loves most, "It's O.K. grandpa. God talked to me again, but I
didn't have time to tell you because we started to fly in the air. You told
me to tell you when God talked to me again." Mat, "Well hurry son, what
did he say? "God said, "John, let your new friend help you. You will have
fun. I will be with him. He and those like him can be trusted. Grandpa,
Angelo is my new friend, I am having fun, and I know we can trust them."
Geez, thought Mat, John is only 10 years old! Within his mind Mat was
having a philosophical debate. It only lasted a moment. He looked down
at his own flesh and blood and knew John was sincere. Mat, "I believe my
grandson, and thus also believe the incredible fact that I am in an alien
space craft and this is not a hoax." Just then a much larger BEE(!) came
into the room with antenna vibrating wildly! Angelo, "Sorry, a unexpecting
event will cause the ending of our talk. "What is it" "UKBA turned to
Matthew and wavered for a second. Although Mat had just met UKBA it
seemed that this answer made him uncomfortable; his eye was orange, "An
advance scout ship from the evil planet is approaching." "Well, how close

is it? "Asked a very concerned Mat. UKBA, "We didn't expect an enemy ship here for another Earth year. They must have moved up their invasion date." "Invasion date! "Almost screamed John. "Our technology will allow us to stay hidden. It is still superior to theirs. We will safely return you. For now, it is best NOT to report this to the authorities. ""That's improper, but due to the unusual circumstances I agree with you. "Said Mat. UKBA "Here is a recording of everything that has transcribed since you left the picnic. At the appropriate time we will contact you." Mat, "How will you do that?" "Mat, we are an advanced civilization....it will get done. Now step to the door and you two will safely be lowered back to the pond, no one is there now. Take care. View the tape. Gird yourself for trouble. Before the next full moon, you will hear from me. For safety you must go now." The two Christlinks stepped to the door and John waved goodbye to # 15. "Blood brothers for life my friend!" # 15, "Threw thick and thin, you can count on me! "They sounded so earnest and devoted, thought Mat. John, "I know I just met him grandpa, but I feel drawn to him. I think together we are going to achieve something miraculous." "Amazing, "thought Mat, I am sure these two will have many bold adventures together. I hope the All-Mighty will guide them."

It was a soft landing, and immediately they heard Sarah say, "we've been looking for you. Let's go now so we can beat the rain, at least make it to the car to stay dry, you know traffic's not going anywhere. "Mat and John didn't even have time to re-adjust to normalcy. John, "What can I do grandfather?" "Nothing that I can think of son. Do not tell your father. I know that seems wrong, but UKBA is right. Keep this as close to the vest as possible. That means you and I are the only ones to know of this. Do you understand John? "Said Mat in a caring voice. John, "Yes I do. When do I get to see the tape? ""As soon as you can make it to my home. It was midnight when Mat and his wife got home, way past their bedtime, but Mat was too charged up to sleep, he had to see the tape. "Honey you go on to bed, I'm going to the den where it's quiet, watch some late night t.v.

I'll see you in the morning. "Sarah questioned how he still had energy and Mat joking said it was the overflow from all the excitement of the picnic and fireworks, then he quickly scampered to the den. Mat had to see from a third person perspective exactly what was said and happened during this unimaginable evening. He is hoping the tape will provide an accurate depiction of the events. Mat watched the film. Nobody could have made this up or go to such great lengths for some pathetic, impractical joke. No. He was convinced of what UKBA preached was real. There was going to be a showdown between destroyers and protectors, with humans caught in the middle. Like UKBA said, Mat sensed that this confrontation was just part of a bigger mystery, a slice of a designed plan that must be followed through to the end. Later, and far away in New Orleans Luke and his old school-good friend-side kick Dave was getting in a cab heading for the French Quarter. "Do you think it is a good idea to meet your crew in a bar, in the quarter? "Asked Dave. "Shouldn't it be in a conference room or a big meeting office?" "Hey, I know these guys well, "retorted Luke. I scouted them when they were still wet behind the ears. I recruited them, trained them, and gone through vicious dog fights and bombing raids with them. Let the record speak for itself!" For some reason Luke was getting fired up! "Can't deny that, most decorated team in Naval history. ""Any history!, "Luke shoves in. He considered this a work/pleasure trip and decided to have a few drinks with his subordinates. Luke, "Watch me though, you know I don't drink very often, I can't handle much. ""Why now? ""No reason." Dave, "Hey, no one in this crew has suffered serious injury, let's keep it that way boss man, ""Boss man" was an inside joke from their pre-teen years. "Sure thing. "Said Luke. Knowing that the six were special, the envy of every squadron commander.

Together, this six won their high school 5 A state championship in both football and basketball. They went to the same military academy, joined flight school as a fighting unit, was spotted by Commander Christlink and the rest is history. Every Air force facility around the world has studied their techniques and successes. Because of their familiarity they didn't need to meet in a formal setting; no this was the "singing 6!" Luke showed up at midnight on Bourbon Steet, French quarter, at the House of Blues. It was Tuesday, amateur night at the mic and the 6 was about to kick some ass! Word got out that the boys were in town and would be performing, there wasn't an empty seat in the place, they were that good! When Luke and Dave walked in they were chauffeured to a reserved table, how nice of the boys thought Luke. There they were! On stage jammin, in front of a wild, jam-packed audience, shaken' their booty! They were known for laughing, loving, singing, and killin'; killin' cover songs and enemy pilots that is.

Tip, the lone white guy, was on the mic rapping out old school melodies of the Four Tops and Temptations, the crew was busted out dance moves in perfect rhythm. There was T.A., the powerful tightend that made all the stone crushing blocks for the team's vaulted power sweep, and also caught the game winning pass in the title game. There's L.S. The front man on the feared 1-3-1 half court trap that spearheaded the groups basketball championships. Even very good opposing point guards wilted like a dried-up wheat under his tenacious pressure, plus, he hit the crucial last second free throws to beat N.E. in a hotly contested final game of the season. A lot of celebration on that one! Again, Tip. The smooth vocalist womanizer. He was a two-time State middle linebacker AND wrestling champion 195 class! It was just plain stupid to mess with him! Then, there's "Smoke, "because he was too fast to blink fast. Lightening quick yet built like a brick house. He'd hit the hole and cover 5 yards before a linebacker could take a step, then run over him for another couple yards. Also, his blazing speed got him 44 points in a big basketball game, it was a record. Then," G. T." The do anything to get it done player, in any sport! During the course of games he seems to be the "big play specialist, "not so much the last second hero stuff, no, when the opposing team would get it going, sucka all the momentum out the stadium, or gym, G. T. would make the big play, or a string of them, bringing the team back from defeat or hitting the clutch jumper or gaining the first down, whatever it took to drain the optimism from the enemy. Then, there was their leader, two sport captain, "Mr. W. "as his team-mates called him. The glue no-nonsense man that always said, "O.K. guys, we Are going to do everything we need to do right now to win the game. "And that was just in practice! Now they all lived in a Florida community, Godfathers to each other's sons, except Tip, being single he travelled when off duty, but he always kept in close contact.

After a standing ovation they waltzed to Luke's table. W., the leader, was first there. "Whew, whew, look at those bars, COLONEL Luke! "Luke, "Yaa, you studs earned me another promotion. I sure appreciate it. I'll tell ya though, after 10 years you guys can still kick it." L.S., the jokester, "Shoot, Colonel we'll be 90 years old in wheelchairs and still be whoo'em." Luke, "I believe it, you guys look sharp." They told old war stories, trying to keep it light. Until Smoke, the ultimate competitor, spoke first, "What's the word Colonel? "Chairs squeaked across the floor as the boys scooted closer. "The word? ""The wo..." The fellows looked at each other, trying to hide their snickers. The legend was drunk! "OK. All right. I'll be OK. I never drink but I thought this announcement justified it.....it didn't! Whoop! The boys never seen their stone-cold commander drunk. He WAS human! "Sir, should this be postponed" A pretty looped Luke stutters out, "The occasion, the "word" Luke emphasizes word, doing the air quotation sign, """ "is BAM..BAM..BAM." Oh Boy! This was too much; the crew nearly fell out their chairs with gut busters! They finally caught their breath and asked again. "Sir, can you tell us why we were asked to meet with you, you said it was important and needed to be immediate, that's why we met so soon and here at this whacky place." Luke straightened up like a standup comedian's dummy. He was hilarious! "For 6 months I've been at a secret location... SSSHHHHH.(The boys tried to hold in but couldn't help snickering,) Testing a new fighter. It's a game changer! Not just a single progression of technological advancement..NNNOOOOO! Somehow, we got a big leap past the competition. (Ha. HA. HA.) No one can touch it, can't touch us. "Luke's first concern was always the safety of his men. Although he volunteered them for suicidal type missions, he was always on the point, he always did the most difficult job. "I'm not that drunk, it's just that advanced. Now, fellows this technology is beyond my comprehension and explanation ability but here's a few easy highlights. Guaranteed we'll see them before they see us, all within our own console. We shoot a magnetized sound wave, insulated in a carbon vacuum tube. It glows as it wriggles toward the mig, and then hits it and just rips the metal apart. I see it on a slow-motion film, it looks awesome." Said Luke, stumbling as he shot his arms out, pointing like he was shooting a laser. "Get more baby", it's rubberized Styrofoam collects and then repulses rockets like that ole playground saying, "whatever you say bounces off me and sticks to you ..I think it goes ... "Luke sat down, the boys helped him sit down. "One more, the best, it's got an anti-matter reactor, first of its kind, we never run out of gas or ammo, take that jack! "That was it, the most classic drunk show there will ever be! The 6 couldn't hold back the tears from gut splitting laughing. TIP, "So you've seen this machine before sir? We've all heard the miracle stories before just to have the information turn out to be faulty. It's disappointing." "Seen IT? "belches Luke, raising his voice and as he carefully gets out of the chair. For the last six months I've been flying it ever which way you can, "says Luke, straightening his shirt and tie; and they shot...shot and HIT me!" "Hit you? With a missile? A couple ask at the same time. "Yep. Dead center, and it's pushed slightly back and then boom, the rocket explodes but most of the concussion waves are forced away from you. Look, they didn't tell how it works, but I proved it does work. We can't be stopped. We have superior technology." And were the next Guinea pigs?" "Bingo, we leave next Friday. I cannot tell you where we are going, it's a secret. Do your all-pre-flight home preparations. You'll be gone for at least 3 months. All right, that's it for me, the Dave will contact you tomorrow, get the details. See ya later. "Just like that the legend was gone. The singing six talked about the possibilities. With eagerness in their hearts they went home to their families and had difficulty sleeping; except Tip, he got his little black book out and made some phone calls.

Above in the realm Love was smiling and telling Joy how successful his little maneuver was working. Joy, "So you used the cretin species that was of service earlier.? ""Yes. They are at the zenith of evolutionary development. They have far surpassed my expectations for maturity." Joy, "But they do not believe or acknowledge you; they have never praised you, why did you recognize them?" "They are not composed of evil. They worship truth and knowledge. Presently they are their Gods. It could be worse, plus it worked. They were able to deliver to a particular race on Earth the components necessary to raise their level of technological sophistication. They correctly, through my persuasiveness, digested the information and now can be of assistance to your BEEs when they arrive.

"All the High Authorities were manipulating their pawns for the upcoming showdown. In her realm MDSL was explaining her next ploy to Kao's. "I am going to Earth to speak with "Artis." He is a pawn that through flesh manipulations I have risen his status to a position of power and influence on the world stage; and now it's time to show him who is in Authority and make him willing to serve us. Watch and learn my biggest devil." Artis is presently the Ambassador to the United Nations for the newly formed A.E.A.R.; Alliance of Eastern and Asian Republics. Right now, the only members are the old Russian states, China, North Korea, and Iran. But Artis is flying to United Nations to give a "recruiting "speech, to sign up more puppets. However, during this flight an event will happen that will change the course of history. Artis was sitting comfortably in the Russian State's private jet when suddenly it took a severe nosedive! Because of the sharp incline of the plane, it was hard for Artis to regain his balance and to stand up. As he pulled himself over the upright seat the Atlantic looked mighty big in the window. Taking long strides and a big step over a passed-out stewardess he made his way to the pilot's cabin. To his dismay the captain and co-pilot was unconscious. He pulled one out of his seat and grabbed the con. He has no flying ability and made things worse. Looking out the front window all he could see was the massive ocean. Hope was disappearing more with every puffy cloud he glided through. Artis was staring death right in the eye and wasn't much of a man about it. "Why? Why me? I've paid homage." (Artis did pray to something, and he always asked for more power) "I will do more, do not take my life, (just what MDSL wanted to hear!) Artis didn't get an answer. The Atlantic was nearly on him, so he surrendered to death. At the very end he counted the seconds to his smashing. 3...2...1... .... HIs eyes were closed but nothing! His mind said, "I should be dead. This is strange, strange indeed. "He opened his eyes to find himself sitting on a puffy white cloud, overlooking the deadly ocean. "What is this, was my prayer answered, "Artis questioned. Unlikely, although Artis did pray he played the part of a pharisee, making dramatic public prayer, quoting verse and law but in his heart, he really didn't believe in a higher power. Then a grotesque horrifying vision waft in front of him. MDSL! Her fright inducing figure caused Artis to scream, AAHHH AAAHH! And then, with less fight and theoretics he screamed again. AahH, aahh." Are you through? "Asked a calm MDSL. Surprisely, especially after the little girl scene, Artis was at ease and asked a questioned, "Who are you and what's going on" "Two questions! MDSL, with Authority, said, "Listen carefully. I am the most supreme high God. I rule all. Nothing happens without my permission. I am directing you Artis to do my bidding on Earth. It is because of me that you have riches and power; now with your arranged position you have duties for me to perform. I will give you directions and your results must be positive." The naturally greedy Artis asked, "What is in it for me? "MDSL, "Look yonder, all that you see is yours, if you reach my goals. "Artis looked "Yonder" and seen mansions on mountain tops, a fleet of boats loaded with gold and silver. Best yet, to Artis, was to his left as far as he could see was beautiful women of all shapes, sizes, and colors." Or continued MDSL, "You can deny me, or fail, and suffer this." Immediately in front of Attis was a giant King Cobra snake! The T. Rex size reptile slowly swayed back and forth glaring him in the eye. Attis was frozen solid with fear. It struck in an instant! Swallowing and gulping Artis whole, gobbling him down it's throat. MDSL could see his bulge slowly being constricted down the snake's long intestine. His muffled pleas for help garbled by the muck of digestive fluids. MDSL laughed at the delightful scene. Artis could feel his innards pressing against the outside of his stomach walls, absolute agony! He was at critical mass, ready to burst! MDSL waited two more seconds............... and with a thought returned Artis to his puffy cloud. "Well what will it ..? "Before she finished Artis said, "I will be your most committed servant, forever executing your commands. "MDSL, "The expected answer, the only answer Artis. Now, continue and complete your United Nations objective. I will command you later with more functions. "With a tone of Authority, and a hint of fondness MDSL finishes, "You are mine now, be proud and strong." The next instant the plane was landing, everyone else was oblivious to the event. Artis signed 56 nations to a pact agreeing to attend a general assembly meeting intent on promoting Eastern Independence and subverting Western Idolatry. Eventually 54 of the 56 joined the new coalition. The A.E.A.R. Alliance of Eastern and Asian Republics was now the largest and most powerful military/industrial/trade complex in the world. The member nations agreed and signed a manifesto stating their common beliefs. Ban all Western influence from entering the new Alliance; including, but not limited to, all forms of fashion, music, literary publications, arts, Hollywood style entertainment venues and the biggee, the internet was blocked; all trading deals, treaties, all types of agreements with "Westerners", were to be re-negotiated. Self-reliance on member nations was a general theme. It is expected the severe penalty of enforced decapitation will be an effective deterrent to those seeking out Christianity. And, secretly, not given permission to be in this book, was the approval and strong encouragement from the elite leaders for terrorist organizations to be fully funded and given means to perform acts of defiance and instigation. Anything to dismantle the Western confidence in their ideology was the terrorist goal.

The East and West was different. Lifestyle, values, human rights; there is so much difference it is foolish to start enumerating them. Within their Eastern boarders there was a staggering division among the classes. The Government and military were completely pure, according to their parameters. Their linage free of any DNA pollutants from other races. Those on the fringes, all those" sub-human" types was used as forced labor. The mentally, physically, and emotionally "weak" individuals that would drain societies resources; instead of aiding them, they were eliminated. Coldly and without remorse their culture now accepts that tradition as normal, as correct, and believes the West is wrong for criticizing the practice. Jews, gypseys, gender questions, and the discontent was put into forced labor camps, for life. The justification was that they received free room and board, medical, (got to keep the work healthy,) but here is the kicker. There is no uprising or protest in the East, not even from the persecuted labor! They are satisfied being menial 3rd class citizens with no hope or desire to improve. They do not yearn for challenges, or opportunities, they choose not to be noticed.

The future looked bright for the A.E.A.R. The united military was very powerful. The citizenry was content and committed to political goals, war mongering had started. There would be no hesitation to go to war. One political cartoon depicted three Scottish Highlanders with pig faces, dressed in kilts and playing bagpipes, marching over, rather, trampling over little Asian looking babies! It was graphic, showing the babies crying and spitting out crimson red blood. The caption read, "If you don't stop the imperialistic pigs, who will?" The record for volunteer military enrollments got shattered for three months in a row. Artis had been the director of the first assembly and now was awarded the most powerful and prestigious position of authority in the Alliance. He was voted "Premier" of the A.E.A.R. That would make a Politian happy, and

it made him happy, but what overjoyed him was that MDSL was pleased."
"Are any rewards attached to this promotion, "sheepishly asked Artis?
"Why yes." Responded a smiling MDSL, she just liked pursing her lips.

The success and rapid economic expansion of the new coalition sent the Western world into a turmoil. The lack of trade, closed boarders, and the ceasing of cultural exchanges was shattering its economy. Western leaders were confused and it was taking too long to make the proper adjustments. Capitalism and democracy move like a snail. Also, something that made the generals nervous, the balance of power had shifted. A.E.A.R. was now titan. The stability and solid foundation that N.A.T.O. once provided was now crumbling apart. Apathy, the lack of will to spend the necessary funds, and a dissolution of trust among original members, (finger pointing) allowed the organization to disassemble itself. A "for rent "sign might as well been at N.A.T.O. headquarters. Something had to be done to equalize the threat from the East.

About a decade ago Roy and Fuller seen this coming like an off-speed knuckle ball. To help prevent the collapse of Western civilization, (that's how serious it was,) the two uncles founded a new organization to replace the old structure. Over a period of years, they conducted numerous private meetings with a few national leaders; contingency plans were approved and implemented; and thus the E.A.A.C. was created. It was a union of free trade nations that agreed to partner their militaries for the purpose of discouraging the East from intrusion. Confidence among the member nations soared! Again, there was a balance of power; the fear of attack, retaliation, and mutual destruction ushered in a period of tolerability. We're tolerate the sickness of the other, just don't try to infect me! England, America, Australia, and Canada are the E.A.A.C.; along with a few "friends with benefits nations." Divisions were strong, both sides thinking they were the good guys. Israel pledged assistance but did not join because of its geographical location and delicate international relationships. Mostly, nations were on one side or the other, except Mexico and Columbia.

Nobody trusted their government nor was smart enough to manipulate the drug lords. Drug kings are the kings, in their corrupt world. MDSL drugs still infiltrated the world, she sure knows how to ruin a soul.

After six short weeks of training the "Luke's "were ordered along with the 9th fleet to the Mediterranean Sea, just off the coast of Israel's new settlements. And it looked like the wrath was coming! An A.E.A.R. army, supplanted by Iran and Iraqi forces, was charging towards Israel's newly constructed water plant, her first of many. They are the only country in the world that can economically, and profitably for them, produce and trade large amounts of fresh water. They have the technology but will not share it with anyone! Since the worldwide decades drought, resulting in famine and millions of starvations made Israel's abundant water a valuable bargaining chip. Civilization had already drilled the water table to historically low levels. The East was upset with Israel because they charged the East twice what the West paid for the same amount of water. So, they decided to get it for free. A confident Artis contacted the E.A.A.C. This is his announcement to the E.A.A.C. "I will get right to the matter. I do not want WWIII. But I mean to end Israel's arrogance!" said Artis in a huff. "I will prove they are not the chosen ones. "Then quickly, "No. No. NO! I am the one chosen to be King!" he said with a flare. The East generals looking at him curiously as he danced around the floor. Artis, "Let's do this by biblical tradition and historical precedents. You send your best squadron, and we will also send our best jet fighters. Do you wish to lose a few, or many? Answer me in two minutes, I will wait on the line." "Wow, talk about arrogance! "said Fuller. Boy, I bet he's a joy to be around." Roy, "Premier Artis, we accept your challenge. Keep this deal between us, no one else needs to know. My pilots are on the way, seven birds, that's all I need." Artis, "Your beautiful. I will send 10…no..I will send 50, what do say to that you weakling. Ha Ha. Sorry, that's the deal" "Sure. "Said a cold stone Roy. "Call you later, "Roy, "That's the weirdest national leader I have ever had to deal with. ""Yeah, he's a strange one. But I'm sure we gotta'em!" The two uncles did an old school high five and headed back to the conference room. So, the first major skirmish between the world's two new superpowers was about to begin.

This was Commander Kloak's orders to the Luke 6 in the flight room before takeoff. "You'll go against 50 super migs. 50! He said with disgust. You'll be outnumbered but from what I've heard that doesn't matter. I hope everything I've heard about this machine is true, because a great deal is riding on the outcome. "Luke and his team barely look up. The training had convinced them of the invincibility of the A1 Falcon. They were patiently waiting to show the world. Kloak, "You know they will have a surprise somehow, Truthfully, I voted "NO, "to sending just one squad; I lost the vote to Admiral Houston, his vote vetoed everything. I guess he knows something about you that I don't. ...Well, so good luck! Now go do your duty." Once they took off and was in formation Luke gave the final instructions and received a "Green "for go signal from the whole crew. This was it, according to time, distance, and speed calculations the enemy should be coming within their visual range; miles and minutes before the migs will be aware of them This dog fight, conforming to video gaming etiquette, and today's, "I got to have drama in my life every second of my life, society," would be broadcast over satellite stations. Artis, who manufactured the tense relations with the West and devised these attack plans, was confident of victory, glory, and rewards. Roy and Fuller needed a win for the obvious military and economic reasons, but also for a boost in the morale and confidence in their leaders and the newly formed E.A.A.C. From a staggering distance, (to everyone except the shooters,) the Luke 6 fired the first shots. Seven super migs were ripped apart from their rivets! Luke, "Great men, just great! This Falcon is the real thing, I think it's gonna perform past all specifications. Our training is true, stay in ranks and let's go do some devastation!" Seconds later and out of distance from the enemies land, sea or air radar systems, they dropped seven more migs with the "magnetized sound wave "(?); they did a "gooseneck ", the now famous move that Luke first used to get out of a life and death struggle in the DMZ zone separating the Koreas. He taught the move to the team and they now used it to bring down seven more camel jockeys. Luke shouts out, "OK, that's 21, 29 more to go, piece of cake! Luke said with boyish enthusiasm.

MDSL was furious at the success of the A1 Falcon. MDSL, "The human has been given help from the outside! I will demand a proper explanation or a forfeit from the %&*&$$!! BUM. Turning to Kaos, she screamed, "Act as if nothing happened, continue on with my plan; I will return shortly. MDSL went to argue her point with the judge, jury and hangman. The result will come later.

Back in the battle Luke had some news, bad news. Commander Kloak from the "Christlink," the super carrier named in recognition for the many achievements and contributions Matthew has made; Kloak notified Luke that 100 more migs were on the way, and worse; a regiment of A.E.A.R. regulars were being transported in personnel carriers toward Israel's defensive barricade. "Boys, 100 more to go. And you're on your own. I'm going to stall a charge until reinforcements arrive. Wilson, take over, use the "circled wagons" strategy. I'll be back. "Wilson, "Sir, we never tested this machine under such conditions. Will she hold up against so many enemy fighters?" Luke, "I'm sure. So sure, I'm reserving seats for your next show!" Nobody said another word but sure had a big smile on their face. As they redirected the Falcon for a new dog fight the migs also received instructions for a new tactic. They employed it with little success. But, in a different defensive formation and technique the Luke's didn't get as many kills as they did before. Some migs broke from the fracas and was able to score hits at the water plant facilities below." Boys, we gotta do a better job! Go red loner and stop the lower attack. I'm busy with the North ground assault. "Luke had 1000 men and machine bearing down on the main hydro plant. He laid down suppressive fire and dropped a dozen thermo explosive bombs. Completely disorganized, the enemy troops were forced to retreat and regroup, allowing Luke to re-join his team. "Red loner" resulted in massive losses for the bad guys. But the new technique by the migs were also scoring many hits on Luke's planes. Each Falcon was taking numerous blasts to their wings and fuselage. The "rubberized Styrofoam" and the new compound called "xelomite, "performed terrifically. They did seem invincible; but how many direct hits can the new jet fighter withstand? The migs were swarming around the 6 like moths to the light. The traffic was so heavy that a couple collisions occurred.

Artis was furious! "If nothing else gets done...destroy at least one enemy jet. By God, it damn well better get done! "Artis did not need to relay his feelings, his fiercely determined shooters burned with the same thought. Luke, "Men, you have done a fantastic job. No one can question your bravery or the magnificence of the A1. But now it's getting down to the nitty gritty. We will draw a line in the sky and not permit any breakthroughs. Let's go get it on! "Luke's enthusiasm could be felt through the sea of air. It became total chaos! Migs and the super-fast A1 jets weaving and banking so close to each other made the ground radar look like a whacked-out video game. Slowly, with precision shooting and expert maneuverability of the complex Falcon, the good guys got the upper hand. Mr. W. "Sir, this has been a privilege. This day, under your superb command, will be written on the walls of Annapolis, and forever etched in our memory. It is a miraculous victory." Luke was about to respond when, "Sir, this is T. A. I'm in a little bit of trouble way out West of the dessert." A single MiG had run away and when T. A. tried to catch him two dozen focused killers zeroed in on T.A. Two different groups taking turns riddling his armor with metal ripping gun fire. "Sir, I lose one group and another dozen is right on me. My Xelomite is white hot, I've never seen anything glow like that. What can I do Sir", said Luke's friend, with a hint of desperation in his voice? "Dodgem buddy, I'm on my way. You other guys stay here and clean up, I'll be back. "Luke pushed the reactor harder than he ever did in the test runs, but a pilot that he trained and helped raise into a solid man was in danger. As Luke banked toward T.A. he could see his predicament. Artis had ordered an all-out effort to destroy at least one Falcon and now T.A. was the logical victim. Luke could see a furious effort by T.A. to evade the dog determined migs but nothing was working. They were on him like 2-dollar perfume on a main street hooker. It happened just before Luke was in range to help. BBBBBBBLLLLAAAAAMMMM! A reddish-orange ball of flames engulfed Luke's entire range of vision. It was all he could see. His hands fell from the controls, his legs became numb. His mind went blank. Momentarily he refused to comprehend the death of his friend. All the responsibility, tension, and stress of too many dangerous missions in to short of a time caught up with Luke. Temporarily his mind went bezerk.

After their one achievement the losing migs started to head home. Thinking that the other Luke's would also be willing to call it a draw. Five were, not Luke. He was crazy for revenge. Cruising at top speed he chased the fleeing migs. W, "Don't do it Sir. It has been a tremendous victory. It is a win, do not tarnish T.A.'s memory with an act of vengeance, he wouldn't. Sir, you have always modeled the correct behavior in a sparkling career, just keep moving on, follow me back to the "Christlink." W. wisely mentioned the name's sake carrier of Luke's grandfather, surly that would jerk Luke back into normalcy. But it was if he was made of the effective "xelomite, "W.'s well-reasoned logic bounced off Luke with no impact. In a real scary Jack Nicholson voice Luke said, "That's right I'm angry, real angry. I'm gonna do what I'm gonna do. This is for T.A. Good vs. Evil. Now you go your way and I'm going my way." W. Tried to connect with his mentor but it was no use. From its maximum range the Falcon weaponry blew apart several migs. The A.E.A.R. pilots did the worst thing possible, they tried to outrun the super jet. They didn't know about the new technological wonders and wizardry of the Falcon. With ease Luke would simply look at the screen and push a few buttons. Colors of a reddish -greenish stream would Criss cross the sky in a corkscrew fashion searching for, and Always catching its target, blowing it to little pieces. Credit the engineers and scientist. Luke hit more buttons and before the clock struck twice all the migs were gone! He then turned and headed for the ground troops. They had over run the Israelis, but the Luke's crew had already beaten them back to the original boarders. It didn't matter. Refusing to follow Admiral Kloak's orders and the pleadings of his men Luke bore down on the near defenseless soldiers. He zoomed in very low....gliding from left to right, positioning himself directly over the top and dead center of the 100 remaining soldiers, then soared straight up into the atmosphere as he did he released 1000 gallons of a new highly volatile liquid. 10 times more flammable than the old napalm. This new type was a sticky fiery fluid that immersed itself into the tissues and fibers of whatever it lands on. The molten fluid produced a terribly painful death. Luke couldn't look down at the agonizing picture below. He wished he hadn't done it. He landed on the Christlink and was escorted to his room. MPs was stationed outside his door. In his room Luke cried a little, prayed... and slept peacefully.

CHAPTER 12

THE POWER OF ARTIS

A month prior to a highly controversial and much anticipated speech that Artis was giving at the U.N. a secret meeting was held in Washington D.C. Only the members themselves knew that this highest level of security even exists. They are President Fletcher, C.I.A. and N.S.A. Directors Cotton and Flynn, the Christlinks - Roy and Fuller, and representatives from England, Canada, and Australia. U.S. President Fletcher, "What's the latest info gentlemen, is it time to move?" "Cotton, "Sir, since the arrival of the AEAR and Artis the number of domestic and foreign terriosts captured or killed has doubled; also, there is a 28% increase in the number of monitored cells." Flynn, "There also has been an increase in military production throughout the AEAR. There're in the planning stages of something dangerously big. Intelligence is warning us of multiple catastrophic attacks during or immediately following Arti's speech." "President Fletcher, "We can't allow that to happen. Use all resources needed to prevent the carnage. What do you say Mr. Roy, "We must take visible action of deterrence; move our navies into defensive locations, and all electronic weaponry brought online. "Flynn, "Attacking on the 4th is Artis's style of arrogance, it's a sure bet; "with a almost a moan he added, "the mall of America is on the target list, among many other sites that would have a probable death count in the thousands."

At 9:00 P.M. Moscow time, on the 4th of July, Artis Addressed theU.N.. His name was called, and he strutted to the fancy podium. At first, he just stood there, arms extended, hands resting on his side. He didn't say anything and looked uncomfortable. Then he slowly gazed at the seated inventory, some was already owned by him, the others will either be seduced or raped. His body language and facial expression turned from a look of uncomfortableness to a message of disgust and discontent. "This will be short and to the point. I will state the concrete policies of the AEAR. Since the ruthless Templar knights led the blood thirsty crusaders into a content and peaceful Islamic Jerusalem the arrogant West has tried to pedal and force it's immoral and corrupt culture on an unwanting East, "His voice gained more grit with each sentence. "Down our throats you have shoved your meaningless and extravagant lifestyle. For centuries the capitalistic empires had the economic and military might to act so gaudy; but they could never sway the upright character nor decay the moral fiber of a humble people. (Fuller and Roy hypocritically yawned at that statement.) You have been wrong about us FROM THE VERY BEGINNING; just as you are now; you mister, (Artis looked right at Mat,) are terribly misconstrued about our true wants and desires. You will soon find out the truth, because now everything changes. Starting now the glorious East will no longer acknowledge the existence of the deplorable West. They will be as a vapor, as a mist that vanishes in the night air. In every facet the world is now divided into two halves." Artis stood a little taller and spoke in a "Commander and Chief "voice. A large screen in view of everyone showed a world globe with an easily seen black line dividing it into two halves. On the East side was neatly drawn letters, A.E.A.R. the other side had a poorly scribbled, E.A.A.C. Intentions were obvious. Artis, "The world is now split for good. Do not seek us, we, as a sovereign republic demand that we be left alone to carry on what is good and correct. "Then his tone changed gears and his statements were accompanied with waving arms, foot stomping and chest pumping; Hitler was a putz compared to this wild man. Artis, "No longer will we share our wealth with you! You cannot enter land, air, or advance into our water boundaries; if you do it will be a provocation to war; Cyber and intellectual properties are monitored and are forbidden to the West. We will use our own resources, I suggest you do the same, again, do not disturb us. Justifiable death will come to all violators. "Roy and Fuller just sat there gritting their teeth; as if in high school you accidently heard the opposing coaches' speech to fire up HIS team, that would be enough to make you want to duke it out, mano - a - mano style; but due to years of other disciplined necessities the two sat there in silence. Patiently knowing that they will strike back at their discretion, surprising Artis. The insane man continued, "That's it! Western crying, deal making, negotiations, compromises...NO. NO.No.. NO! This behavior will no longer be tolerated, you have been forewarned, now be heedful and beware. The last thing I have to say is.... It's about time and GOOD riddance! "As Artis was swiftly leaving the building the Eastern half of the world gave him a rousing ovation. Leaping to their feet the standing jubilation and hand clapping lasted several minutes after his departure. The Western half just sat there quietly, leaving when part of the crowd moved the party out of the aisle and into the forum. Artis hurriedly ran to his armored car and sped to the airport where he immediately got on the massive state fortress plane and flew towards home. He was moving fast because Flynn and Cotton was right, as soon as Artis crossed into protected airspace all hell broke loose throughout the EAAC nations. The scope of the terriost activity is too wide and numerous to list, suffice to say that every member nation of the EAAC suffered casualties. Bridges, warehouses, manufacturing plants, and other "smaller" targets were attacked, with considerable number of fatalities. Most of the more sophisticated plots, the ones that took more time, money and planning were thwarted. Like the yacht that was loaded to the brim with high plastic explosives getting within a mile of the Hoover damn before being confronted with gunfire until finally the boat exploded in an retina burning glow. Another was the Mall of America as predicted. Several United States law enforcement agencies combined tactical units to stop the attack. A paid informant spilled his guts so when a half dozen escalades with ten well-armed martyrs each, dragged raced their way through stop lights and inter-sections, screeching their tires through the parking lot. But when they slammed on their brakes in front of the main entrance their plan had to changed. Instead of bum rushing the front door and blasting away everybody in their sight, they were faced with hundreds of well-placed camouflaged specialists. Snipers picked off the first out of the vehicles and regular sharp shooters finished the good work. Within a minute either all the bad guys were shot dead or had turned the gun on themselves, cowards. But besides the tens of thousands of murders from cruel acts around the world there was one devastating victory the bad guys will point to and brag about. In very late June the owner and top executive of a prominent lawyer firm, that lived across Lake Pontchatain, an hour North of New Orleans, was kidnapped but held hostage in his own home until the late evening of July fourth. That's when four unidentified men shot the family members, filled their two personal/corporate mid-size planes with thousands of gallons of high-octane fuel, and took off to celebrate. They had scouted the location and rehearsed this scheme many times for more than two years; from a distance they knew the family well. Poor Kitty will never make it to graduation. GPS set the speed and path to coordinate their destination at a certain location precisely at midnight, what partyers they are! To avoid radar detection, they flew only a couple hundred feet over the 26 mile long lake; when their target came into view their eyes glittered as much as the decorated city. Inside the New Orleans superdome was a festive atmosphere of shared hope and jubilation. A wave of good vibrations filtered through the audience. They were oblivious to the fact they were singing their last verse and dancing their last step with their favorite star. Side by side, wingtips almost touching did the racing jets slam into the domed structure, exploding into a massive fire ball. The terriost had logged many simulator hours practicing being expert pilots and crash artists, preparing for this specific site. The AEAR kept the hidden cell well-funded. The superdome structure crumbled from the force of two speeding jets smashing into the dome's top side. Thousands of revelers were killed and tens of thousands more badly injured.

Across the country hundreds of smaller targets were hit. Normalcy was disrupted, lives lost, and confidence shaken. A success for the bad guys. It was the final straw for President Fletcher and the EAAC. Cotton and Flynn contacted the international network and a special segment of the "Houston "plan was put in motion. Special agent code named JC was notified to execute his one assignment.

Gustave was preparing Artis's wardrobe for tonight's special July 5th speech, only to be broadcast within AEAR limitations. It is a new holiday for the Republic. To commemorate the separation of the two philosophies Artis formally proclamated July 5th the most acclaimed of all A.E.A.R. holidays. Artis, "Yes, I have made this Republic into what it is, it's stature is of my doing, without me none of this happens, "as he swirls around looking at a painting of the new Premier's mansion and capitol building that he personally oversaw as project manager. "Do you think I deserve this acclamation Gustave? "The new holiday is named, "Praise Artis Day!" He didn't wait for an answer. "Tonight, my Gustave I am going to introduce my Goddess Queen. The one from which all predictability flows. She, the ultimate power, has chosen me, Artis! "He hesitated for a split second soaking in all his dreams, "To lead the Earth, I will have total power and control. Soon, as her word has said, at her direction all mankind will bow down to me and all riches will be mine and all females will be mine! "As he seriously did drewell a little spittle. "You will be right behind me Gustave, just like these last years. You have seen the work I have put in, now the rewards are there for the taking."

After a small meal and short nap Gustave made final preparations for his Premier. Outside the national palace thousands of devoted citizens waited for their idol. Artis put on his red velvet dinner jacket and stepped out onto the magnificent balcony. The crowd was in a crazy frenzied pitch that would make any rock star envious. In his charismatic foot stomping and arm waving method he stirred up the fanatical crowd until they knocked down the barricade, rumbled over and around security personnel, risking arrest and injury, and charged to the balcony area, just to get closer of their precious leader. A dozen feet behind Artis, stood Gustave. He was in the master bedroom that led to the "speech balcony "; the room where Gustave did most of his work, he knew the room very well, did servant Gustave.

For 15 years Gustave had been religiously carrying an extra cell phone around in his pocket, he never used it or even acknowledged it. For over a decade it was never noticed. Long ago he quit trying to figure out why he HAD to carry this phone on his person at all times; like it was a death curse NOT to have it. Only once, twelve years ago he did not put it in his pants and his sub-conscious made his skin breakout in rashes, itchy rashes. He quickly understood the correlation and now the cell phone is handled in habit, without thinking it has become a part of his leg. But now, for the first time, it is vigorously vibrating. As in a dream he answered it, "Is this JC? "Said a melancholy voice from somewhere. "Yes, this is JC. What can I do for you? "As if reading from a pre-addressed script the voice said, "The dew is on the ground and the bird is singing. Do you understand?" Without hesitation, as if he knew this stranger with the strange voice "I must take out the garbage. "It was the response the Houston plan initiator wanted to hear. It meant that the two decades of training, behavior modifications, and brain washing, might have been fruitful; that this agent/robot might have been worth all the time, effort, and money. Gustave put down the phone casually, as not to draw attention, went a few feet to his personal section of the Premier suite. To nobody's knowledge years earlier Gustave had installed a fake electric meter panel behind the clothes rack. Removing the front cover of the panel revealed a small compartment, just big enough for a 38 special. Gustave slid the pistol underneath a silk robe that Artis liked to wear; he was instructed to have it ready at the end of the speech. So, guards and security agents did not even glance his way when just seconds before the final sentence of Artis's electrifying speech, Gustave walked out onto the balcony and appeared to start to hand his boss the robe, but instead he ...BAM! Right in front of the ocean of spectators the .38 caliber bullet cut through his thick-skinned skull and parted his brain like the red sea! It was in plain view of his lovers and the millions watching on T.V. The Houston plan was a success; and then Gustave quickly turned the gun on himself and unwittily pulled the trigger, total success. Aides wrapped Arti's falling apart head the best they could and rushed him to the capitol hospital. In the ambulance the doctors hooked him up to heart and lung machines and transferred him to a well-furnished private room located in the basement of the palace; only selected nurses, doctors and military Chiefs of Staff knew the facts of his securement.

13

CHAPTER

ARTIS RETURNS

In the year 2053 events were quickly occurring, nearly simultaneously, that brought the showdown of 2060 closer to fruition. MDSL and Kao's was ready to launch their next stage of domination, which included a revived Artis. In an invisible miniaturized state MDSL flew through the hospital to Artis's room. With telepathic powers she summoned the main medical unit to the room. Just before they entered the room MDSL used her Middle Ages wizardry to heal Artis's wounds. He was better than before. Yes, The Holy Father, In His mysterious wisdom, bestowed MDSL with great power and Authority. Those normal humans in the room were completely baffled. How did Artis survive that devastating gunshot to the head? and who was he talking to? Artis awkwardly climbed down from the bed grumbling, "What am I doing here?" "You got shot you imbecile! "With a mixture of surprise and anger Artis shouted, "Well why didn't you stop it? "Instantly Artis realized his mistake and dropped to his knees, with hands cuffed he slowly reached up to His God. But it was too late. Artis couldn't speak but the agonizing grimace spoke volumes. He somehow tilted his head a single degree to be able to look at the nurses. It is a cliche to say but they were frightened stiff, but it's true, they were too scared to move. Wouldn't you also be if you just witnessed a patient that once needed machinery to live get out of his bed completely healed, and then in just a few seconds later he was on his knees as you watch, almost feel, his fingernails melt and then his boney fingers and then his melted hands were dripping down to the floor like thick syrup rolling off a stack of pancakes. His fluid began to puddle on the floor. Men and women fainted or stepped back to the farthest wall. Then, just as fast, he was made whole again. "Don't ever question me again!" she snapped. Artis," No, I will not. I am your servant, what is required of me? "MDSL, "My glorious son is bringing his army of beasts and demons. We will crush all resistance on Earth and in the Heavens. You are to execute the simplest of plans here on Earth. You are to destroy those that refuse to worship me and enslave those that swear obedience to me. You will be informed of the details. A good performance is necessary; there will either be rewards or consequences. Now get to it." MDSL disappeared and the medical unit was shaking his hands, congratulating him on the miraculous recovery. Artis's told them, and the public in the next day's headline story, "my massive tissue loss was regenerated by my tremendous self-determination and amazing will power, couple that with the desire to finish the job before us, and thus added together those facts inspired my spirit to do the impossible." For days every Western news outlet ran the miraculous story of Artis's "Regeneration." The West absolute understood and respected his motives and intentions; but now some fear was creeping into the Western psyche, it didn't feel right. In the East Artis could no wrong, he was invincible, the public's conscious awareness had turned him into a Demi-God.

Kaos was feeling invincible. His plan was coming together magnificently. He believes that his three-stage champion is a much better product than Joy's dud. It was proven in the first intergalactic war. His Maulk's dominated! Now, with everything in order, all the pieces in place, he was going to maneuver the final victory. The one that proves the Dark should rule the Light. He urged the Artis psyche to move accordingly and he did, and not in secret.

This is an excerpt from the next Artis rant. "Now, at this moment I order my generals to attack. The plan and its goals are burned inside their hearts, they will not fail! "As he nearly sprinted up and down the same balcony where he was almost asasinated "Join me and my armies in the annihilation of God's worst enemy...the idoltors... of the adulteress West, they will be put to shame and then put to the flame." For minutes thousands of cult slaves chanted Artis...Artis...Artis.! "Do your part, get your share.""

W.W.III started in the year 2054. John was a 19-year-old Academy graduate. Top National honors for marksmanship, he and Michael had dominated. The two were waiting orders from General Mitchell. Tonight, though he and his sniper buddies were going out on the town before being shipped to the war. Being the best he and Michael were sure to be an intricate fiber in the woven plan of success. Many graduates had similar schemes that night and ended up at the "Toot Your Horn" Blues bar. John's crew were not socialites and didn't venture off the base often, let alone consume large quantities of alcohol, but they had a designated driver so tonight was going to be the exception. At the bar John was right in the thick of pickup lines, the worst exaggerated stories of some kind of personal conquest... or blown-up headlines about a sports play; or just about anything to garner bragging rights. Except nobody in the room was talking about Artis or war; that can wait a little while. John and company was moving to the pool table but was roadblocked by a rush to the stage, "Hey, what's the deal? John asked a stumbling toy soldier, thinking he must be a regular. "This awesome girl started singing here a couple years ago, she's awesome! "he said again, making the hour glass shape with his hands, grinning with wide eyes as he raked his way to the front. Suddenly, there was a small explosion on the stage! Man did the fly boys like that! Arms up, navy hats waving around, whooping and hollering. John forced his way next to his informant. "Isn't she something, "he shouted, luckily John was able to read his lips, the joint was too noisy to hear anything else except what was right in front of you. And then BAM! She came running out from behind the curtain to a thunderous applause. She WAS awesome! Now, John had a big grin and wide eyes. The long-legged hot babe was dressed in black stretch leotards, a dainty white lace bra (filled just perfect!) sailors cap, seductive cosmetics; her beautiful smile was the clincher. Her powerful rock-roll voice had the crowd bouncing off the walls. Her charisma and energy had John's heart speeding like a formula 1 race car. After prancing and dancing she was moving from the far end of the stage to his end; John was caught up in the excitement and shoved his way to the best spot up front. John had to get a closer look at this girl. As she gyrated closer, he felt excited. This was new to John; he usually only gets emotionally invested with his family ... or war games. But he felt like he is supposed to get to know this person. Suddenly she was right there in front of him! She was belting out the tune, stepping in dynamic rhythm, and then, looked down and pointed right at John! Dead center forehead with her gleaming eyes piercing John's soul! With a sparkle she screams Janis Joblin style, "Whadda gonna do boy, run home to momma or take a wild ride with me. "Man, that girl is incredible! I've got to meet her. He started to inch his war to the back dressing rooms, but the dense crowds and zealous college security beef made it useless to try. When she finished the song two roadies immediately ran out two cement blocks on a table... she was running right behind them.... all at a quick pace they put the blocks on the table...and then out from behind the curtain came a flying chain saw! Like a pro ball player, she gripped it out of the air and all in one swoop muscled the saw through the two blocks! All that was surging through John was," Man, that girl is dynamite." Without missing a beat, she hop-skips to the other end of the stage where two massive goons had grappled some lucky guy from the front, put a mask on him and threw him in a king's chair. "Why not me? "Thought John. Still skipping she moved to the winner; some roadie from the back threw her a 12 foot (?) leather whip. From a close 8 feet she snapped the bull whip at the stranger and blood spurted from his chest! It couldn't (?) have been real but it sure looked real. Sci-fi magicians are un-believable. Still kicking the beat and making her way back to John, she again looks dead at John, making him think this message was for him, "The choice is clear, the time is near, if you don't bend over and take it in the rear! "And just like that the music stopped and she ran off the stage, show over. He saw her turn the corner and sneak a peak in his direction. John had to lecture himself." Really meat head. You got NO chance with that 10."

"The lights dimmed and flashed a couple times then the DJ. started to spin the discs, it was time to leave. On the way to the parking garage John bumped into the soldier from inside, for some reason he felt hopeful... but for what? "Hey, again. Tell me what you know about the singer, ...please. "Corporal, "Not much, nobody does. One rumor says she's under-cover; another says she's some wizard from Langley. She never mingles, keeps everything a secret." When John closed his eyes that night, she was his last thought.

Once again, the "Luke" 6 was aboard the Christlink. They just rounded the horn of Africa heading for the Suex canal, a vital target. General Norris of the First Naval Task Force was giving final briefings before takeoff. "Gentlemen, our allies are in control of the Pacific Theater, there is a stale-mate in the Central America's, The Euro-Asia conflict is just heating up, and we have been given the toughest task: control, protect, and maintain transportation lines for the water; the # 2 priority is the oil refineries. The drought and clean water shortage are going to make objectives in this war different than any other. The site on the Mediterranean shore is massive. It was built with EAAC money. Norrris, "It won't be easy, but we do have the best jet fighter in the world." "Oh, that's right, we do have the best jet and...and the best pilots," Said Luke as he poked Wilson with an elbow. W, "OH, Sir, it's only us, the most decorated pilots in history, but we do have a good plane," as he jostled back with the colonel." "I know you boys are good, but let's not get cocky. "Norris fixed his strengthening gaze on the

"6. ""Be safe and giv'em hell. "Pastor Simpkins patted Luke on the back as they passed each other. On his knees did the humble man offer praise, worship, and asked for favor from the Holy Protector, the hard floor gave no mercy to the Pastor's rickety knee joint. In a blur the friends were in the blue sky looking for trouble. "Business as always boys. Lock in two targets, after that you are free to single out kills. Fire at will. "The onslaught began. The A1 Falcon was the superior weapon. Surely, as whoever used the first club, then gunpowder, and then technology; whichever side had discovered or invented the better tool to kill with usually won the fight, or battle, or world war; this time the good guys had made the technological leap of the century! How did they do it?

The Luke 6 was unstoppable! In a very short amount of time the 6 had eliminated the entire air fleet of the AEAR. From the meetings and preparations held on the Christlink the crew knew next to implement phase two. "OK boys, put it in the next gear. Zero in and destroy your phase two designated ground targets. When your through with that pick out targets of opportunity. Do as much damage as you can." The 6 had cleared the path for a massive land invasion of the Middle East entering from the point of the Mediterranean. All around the world the EAAC was winning.

CHAPTER 14

2ND GALACTIC WAR

Just outside the detection range of Earth's satellite system another battle was about to begin. Again, because of the superior brain power of the stump, the Red Armada was able to swiftly run to the Milky Way, undetected by the innocently foolish BEEs. Their nightmare was about to start. Kaos/Lucifer was sitting in his commander's chair giving orders. "Damn it!" I said triple check your calculations. We do not want to engulf Earth, its star, or any surrounding planets, just the scum."

Long ago, since their capture and enslavement by the Maulks, the stumps have been studying different mechanisms and mysteries of their surroundings, including space physics. They discovered some useable, and controllable properties of the famous "Dark Matter." A simple comparison of the complexities of this new energy available to the Maulks is that of saran wrap. The kind you would pull over food so you could put it in the frig for cool storage. Imagine four moon size generating ships, that house a machine, device, that produces this "saran wrap." Its unbreakable, molecular bound fabric is composed of dark matter. On command 24 dozen tug like boats will pull this fabric away from a rolling type of large cylinder positioned on the generating ships, as it rolls off the cylinder the tugs gently "guide" this sheet of dark matter in the desired direction. The field will expand and travel at a very precise and predictable rate. Any c+ 9th grade Algebra student could determine its size and speed at varying distances and thus its location. At the appropriate time the generating machines are shut down and the intended target will be enveloped and basically "digested "by the dark matter. When the job is done the Maulks have the engineering capability to "pull the plug "and drain the wrap of its energy, until it completely dissipates into simple atoms floating away to somewhere else. It is a formidable weapon. However, it is extremely dangerous, difficult to manufacture, and the Maulks have a limited supply of it. PEU, "Your excellency, the calculations are correct, there is zero chance of collateral damage, and the optimum number of ships are just now come into range and is in our line of the roll out. "Lucifer, "Great. Shoot the first layer, show these bitches whose boss. "When completed diagonal the generators so as to sweep both sides of the planet, we should have enough core material to do that." PEU, "Very good Master. The first volley is away."

"Scout ship YIO629 on the outer most surveillance ring reporting a large disturbance of unknown origin and energy source. "Queen Mary control, "What do you mean unknown energy source?" "It's moving our way sir, slowly, but it is coming and what I mean is that I have never seen this energy signature before. I do not know what it is or how it makes locomotion." "Is it a danger to us?" "It is... The dialogue stopped. For this very type of reason Commander BO had positioned his Queen Mary on the far side of Earth, impossible to detect. 2nd in command Fitz from the Western flank. "Sir, something again must be wrong with radar, communications, again our blue dots representing the advance force have disappeared, gone. What do you say Sir?" "Again? "Thought the somber leader. "They outsmarted us and destroyed our fleet the last time with dark sorcery, how can we let it happen again" Bo was a frustrated furious! BO, "Keep sending transmissions, check for electronic malfunctions, and update me with the smallest of details." Just then 3rd in command Gnat reported in with the same message, his advance force on the other side of the planet was eliminated. Again, BO was out of blue dots. This is just how the last devastating defeat started. If it happened again the Earth families will be lost to the evil force; and BEE planet, their home, will be left defenseless. The stakes are at its zenith; nothing of more importance is before the Bee warriors, they all realize the scope. BO, "Fitz and Gnat, has there been an intrusion of Earth's atmosphere by this new force? "They both said no. BO, "It seems they do not wish to harm the Earth or humans. Take your armies and report to your assigned Earth Atmospheric location. Stand by for further instructions. Radar tech, "Sir, there is no indication of Maulk interference. "BO, "Oh their out there somewhere, within striking range. We didn't lose 40 % of our fleet by accident. I hope we have enough to win this fight. Surely our God is going to help us.

The Maulks drew first blood in the second intergalactic war, and it was some serious bleeding. The alien battle would now be fought in Earth's upper atmosphere, viewable by humans. But the Earthlings were fighting their own battles. So, it was a four-way slug fest, West vs. Easts below, Maulks vs. BEEs above; it would soon be an Alien / Earth tag team match. Fortunately for the West, their experience, cooperation among member nations, and freedom for trusted regional generals to make real time battlefield decisions and corrections was overpowering the monopolistic, egomaniacal controlling method of strategy and leadership style conducted by Artis. Around the world AEAR armies were taking a beating. Artis was confused as a 6th grader trying to put together a broke down truck transmission. "What's going on? I give you fools plans for victory, and you come back with news of defeat. What kind of losers are you, the dead kind?" Krog, leader of the northern Armies, "Supreme Emperor, in the course of battle circumstances change, adjustments must be made quickly. Field Marshall's cannot wait hours or even minutes for your instructions." And then with bold caution, "My good leader, when the enemy does not wait for your participation it puts us at a great disadvantage. The few generals that have made their personal decisions public were executed for treason. It is not a good way to win a war." Artis looked at him and then said, "Sir, you are courageous and bold to speak your disagreeing mind. "He turned to his security detail and pointed, "take this courageous and bold traitor to the gallows. "The other generals stood there waiting for orders.

"You will not lose this war from me. I will be ruler of the world! Now get out of here while I strategize another "FOOL" proof plan. Get out! "Get out shouted Artis, slamming his foot on the carpeted floor. He walked behind them ushering everyone out of the room. The instant he coded the lock he knelt prone to the floor. "Oh, great creator why have you forsaken me? I have done all that you have asked. Why isn't victory given to me? "Artis's prayer was answered. MDSL," Oh my dog Artis. I gave you to many human frailties. They make you so insecure, what a pity, I will pity you. HA! HA! HA! MDSL loves to make herself laugh at other's expense. Don't worry. My glorious son, who has attained status above the Angels, is on his way to rescue the helpless. Again, don't worry you fool, it is a scheme of mine." Artis, "I apologize, It should already be imbedded in me that you control the universe; I am a willing pawn. "MDSL, "Go about doing my business, I will return shortly."

Matthew, now 94, was slowing down quite a bit. He was at home with John, 19, watching the war on T.V. John was still waiting for a call to arms. He was eager for deployment. Everybody was now sure that he had the "right stuff "of a Christlink. They were in the same room where they had told their relatives of the Angelo's. Since the war started the two had ben glued to the T.V. John couldn't understand why his squad, the best in the nation, hadn't been called up. He is unaware that Angelo, again through sub-cortex mental insertion and false documentation, arranged for John to remain home with his great-grandfather. Angelo would need John's services later on.

Since Lukes first confrontation in the Middle East, aerial dogfights have been broadcast worldwide. Mat and John had nervously cheered for their blood kin and the A1 Falcon. But no need to worry. Nothing can compare to the fabulous jet. It is unbeatable. That's the way of Americans. They have a strong desire to be number one in everything, I repeat... everything! And they are willing to make great personal sacrifices and work extremely hard to be the best. Also, Americans will root and support winners, usually decorating them with hardware and accolades; whether it be to immortalize the Super Bowl Champs, or the National Spelling Bee champ or the backyard softball champs; or watching their countries best jet fighter and its pilots bring down the enemy.

This afternoon Luke was again heading for the Middle East. Back home Mat and John couldn't get close enough to the 5'x 9' screen. Suddenly the house started shaking apart from the foundation and then the roof lifted and was gently placed in the spacious south 40! Floating down from the invisible spacecraft was the Angelo's. "I am sorry my friend, we are too big for the door. "Mat. "Well, what about my house, what am I going to live in? "UKBA, "No need to think about that, the D.C. metropolitan area is targeted for destruction." Mat, "What do you mean. We are winning the war. Luke and the A1 has been amazing." UKBA, "I know all there is to know about the A1, but my good friend, the real war is nearly upon us. The evil one himself has arrived. "Mat stopped what he was doing, and a blank stare rushed across his face. Just then they heard the announcer on the T.V. loudly exclaim, "Oh my God look at the size of that Red ship! It's impossible for a monstrosity like that to be able to fly! Look! Dozens, maybe hundreds of smaller ships, the size of an RV are coming from inside. No! NO! Several just zoomed by firing at ....and just vaporized two Falcons, I do not see them anymore. That's never happened before, this could be bad for us. People, start praying fervently." A sound like a microphone being dropped was the next noise over the waves. Mat and John sadly looked at each other and then moved even closer to the screen.

They were looking for the markings on Luke's jet, but the action was too fast to tell who's who. Mat could see the fear in John's eyes.

"Son, your father is the best pilot there has ever been, he will be fine." Mat patted John on the shoulder but he was also trying to cheer himself up. He was fearful for his grandson's safety. Angelo, "My friend I can empathize with your concern, but it is much too dangerous here, we must leave immediately, meaning right now!" UKBA started to lift Mat but he waved his arms and UKBA released him. The three started to move towards UKBA's ship and as John was turning off the tube he exclaimed, "There's dad! That's his number and six of those red beans are after him. "In an excited pitch Mat yells out, "Move your ass son, lose those sons of bitches." John looked up at his pops, who was standing firm behind the chair; John could see the passion in his great-grandfather's eyes, the fight. John had always heard about his pops being the warrior/ philosopher; and listened about his many famous military victories, as told to him by other family members, his great- pops never talked about killing with John. Once, when he was very young, he was up late at night to use the bathroom and his uncles were in the kitchen talking with pops. He was young and didn't understand what was being said, but when Mat raised his voice, just a little, his two brothers scooted back in their kitchen chairs and raised their hands as if to say, OK, we've had enough, whatever you want boss. "That's how it seemed to John back then. John studied his pops closer. Determination, the type of strength that you can depend upon, the type John strives for. John, "He will be OK pops. No Tic-Tac is going catch dad, he's too good." John tried to help a little.

In his cockpit Luke was doing everything he could do to stay alive. "Move Dad move, speed up. Use your stuff!" yelled John. After doing his patented backward corkscrew move Luke went ballistic, straight up to the sky's zenith. Luke was hit several times and the xeylonite did hit's job but how many times can you depend on that? "I'm in a dog fight with a demon, never imagined I'd be doing this when I was in grade school, "said

Luke over the air waves to no one in particular. With explosions all around him Luke turned the nose downward and headed for the dirt. Faster and faster he went; in his visor the Earth was getting bigger and bigger. Close to being smashed he jerked the stick a hard left; hoping to finally leave these guys in the dust or maybe their wings will crumble under the stress. 3 2 1 go! The acceleration threw Luke back into his seat, momentarily he bolted away from them. "Ha Ha! That's how it's done boys!" said a relieved Luke. But right on cue all 6 of 'em made a perfect synchronized 90 degree turn and was again right on Luke's tail; firing ballistics at him. Mat's heart sunk; John's eyes got misty. Then a miraculous thing happened; all 6 craft just tumbled away; far, far away. UKBA, "Good. Your God has saved Luke, he must be worthy. "John jumped up and down squeezing Mat. "Thank you, Lord, thank you. "As they started to move to the ship they heard a volcanic thundering boooooomm in the distance. The ground slightly shook, in the distance they could see a massive dust cloud of debris rushing towards them. They scrambled to the ship and made their way to the control room. The projection screen displayed a nightmarish scene rushing towards them. Mat and John wasn't sure they'd make it; UKBA didn't seem bothered, "Full speed ahead. "He calmly said. As they elevated out of the clouds they saw the ominous giant red Maulk space craft. UKBA, "Stealth mode please." The red ship was emitting a red mist like substance onto the surface of the Earth, scorching all materials on contact." I wasn't worried about the dust, but if that mist hit us we would have been vaporized into nothingness. "The group knew D. C. was destroyed but were still waiting on other reports of the war. No one knew if Luke was dead or alive. Angelo, "The A1 Falcon is a tremendous weapon for Earth warfare, but it is no match against a foe with a million-year head start." John, "Can you defeat them, Angelo? asked John. Angelo searched for some good words but could only come up with, "Probably not." "What do we do then, "asked Mat. UKBA, "For the next few hours the best thing this group can do is fervent prayer, asking that our merciful creator take this evil out from our presence." So they all started to pray

Luke also said a prayer thanking the savior for his good fortune. He was now in hypersonic speed in stealth mode and low to the ground trying to avoid detection. "Here we are," he said to himself, "We'll blend in like a brown tick dear in the Mississippi fall woods. His destination was the EAAC base located an hour's flight away. He hoped they had fared better than his fallen buddies.

The first thing he seen was plumes of grayish black smoke spiraling into the blue sky. Still from a considerable distance something looked odd about the base; a closer inspection revealed the charred remains of infrastructure and military equipment; burnt shadows on the ground was all that was visible of any humans. "These guys really took it hard; then a faint Beep...Beep...Beep.Beep..Beep. "Wow! Morse code, that's sneaky." Luke continued to listen, EAAC friendlies, and then the coordinates. "I know that location. It's an old war time bunker we built years ago. The red eyes must not know about it, "Luke mumbled. He lowered his Falcon for a soft landing, got out and started to walk where he was hoping there would be a camouflaged door on the mountain side. A rat-tat-rat-tat scattered the sand close enough to brush the side of Luke's leg. He stopped cold and listened to what would surely be forthcoming directions. "Identify yourself." Luke quickly ran down the required serial numbers. A few seconds later two sergeants appeared from behind a fake boulder and directed Luke to get back in his Falcon. A dozier towed him to an underground hanger where several other aircraft was stored. The two marines escorted him to a backroom door. Following the marines Luke had a good look at the expanse of the interior, completely invisible to any casual passersby on the outside, if there were any. They walked through a door into a futuristic looking mega-complex. "Man, those camel jockeys must have spent millions of their heroin profits on this place." An officer came up to him, "Hello, I'm Captain D.H. Come with me, there are some excited gentlemen eager to greet you." Luke couldn't guess who it might be. Entering a conference room doorway Roy and Fuller were there to meet him. Roy, "Luke, my boy. Bob and I had agreed earlier that if anyone could survive the alien on-slaught it would be you." Fuller, "We sure are glad to see that your safe. But don't get comfortable. We will need a briefing on their weapons and together we will formulate a plan." Luke, "Then the war isn't over? "Roy and Fuller looked at each other with that Christlink determined glare. Roy, "It is for now, but were not through." Fuller, "Yeah, we took a real hard punch, but it didn't knock US out. You'd be surprised how many are left and how fast we are regrouping. It might take a while to mount a serious comeback, but it will happen." He sounded confident. "How do you like our hidden facility? Its size is enormous and is supplied with food and armament. "Just then Captain D.H. came up to them, out of breath from a hurried pace. "Sir, I know this is going to sound crazy, but I must inform you that there ae two civilians and one large," to illustrate the size D.H. held his hand as high as he could and also jumped as high as he could, "A very large ...BEE sir," and then quickly added, "that's right Sir I said a very large BEE, that talked to me! Should I let them in?" The family laughed together and waved him in. As the two groups walked down the hallway to each other, from opposite far ends Angelo jr. and John ran to each other and high fived, Luke and UKBA embraced the best they could.

Joy and Love from above had great emotions springing from within their "Orbs." It is very rewarding when a plan that was formulated millenniums ago, and has to work the first time, comes together perfectly and just in time. The necessary bond between the BEEs and their adopted Earth families was unbreakable, stronger than Joy had ever dreamed of.

Mat was also sprinting down the hall, old man style; John did a quick high five with Jr. and then sprinted to dad, beating his grandfather to him. "Dad, "he started out joyfully, "I didn't think I'd see you again, we saw you in that predicament and thought you lost." Luke, "No, son, I don't lose!? His jokingly wide grin touched a nerve and Luke shed a few tears of emotion, the first in a long time; and then of course Mat and John teared up; and then in a few seconds rock solid military men Roy and Fuller was hugging all of them! It is the most emotionally stable, and of those in command or of those that much is required, that ARE the most emotional, they are the ones that offer their total effort to a commitment, the ones that offer a complete dedication of all their energies to a cause, without expecting any rewards besides the personal gratification they enjoy from the sense of accomplishment they get when a task is successfully completed. Sometimes a release is needed. That is what the Christlink clan is experiencing right now. Mat, "That was a tremendous miracle that our Lord thrust upon you," then Mat looked up and said, "Thank you Lord for saving my son from destruction. "The rest bowed their heads and nodded in agreement.

UKBA, "I must go now, my people have also suffered devastating losses. But we are planning a counterattack. I will notify you of the detailed strategies. If we coordinate our efforts, we will stand a better chance for victory. "Mat, "Yes, our races will fight together, just as your God directed." UKBA, "Thank you for trusting, even from the very beginning. Together is our only path for survival. Gentlemen, be of sound faith, once again there will be peace among the stars. God bless and good day." As UKBA glided towards the exit the magnitude and severity of the situation fell on the group like a ton of bricks. Probably the only thing that may prevent the extinction of the human race will be the perseverance and intestinal fortitude of this small group of inspirational men. The six went to the dining room to get a decent meal. To their pleasant surprise Reverend Radke and Pastors Donna and Simpkins from the Carrier Chistlink was already seated. Matthew, "OH, I feel much better now. Godly men and women allow the spirit to nourish the soul! Friends, your faith and encouragement are better than a juicy steak!" Pastor Simpkins, "It warms my heart knowing that everyone is saved, (Roy is not) Mr. Mat, you did an excellent job of raising a Godly family. Bless you. "Pastor Donna, "Amen to that. We all will see paradise with the Son, praise him always." Reverend Radke said a prayer of thanks for the food and then added, "This is from First Chronicles, "And say ye, Save us, O God of our salvation, and gather us together, and deliver us from the heathen, that we may give thanks to thy Holy name and glory in thy praise." I don't know how or why but that verse just popped into my head, I could see it." Pastor Simpkins, "Yes, sometimes that is how divine inspiration happens, and it fits the times." They ate together as warm friends, choosing not to think of the approaching turmoil. They went to their separate sleeping quarters, each hopeful for a good night's rest.

The next morning, they were jovial at first but the buzz of activity around the complex reminded them of the heavy load they must carry. In a caring and thoughtful tone Pastor Simpkins said the breakfast prayer, "Dear Lord, we worship and praise your majestic glory. We give thanks for all your blessings. We are reassured knowing that you are in control of all things. We have hope that the test before us strengthens our faith. We trust that it is through these such challenges that we may prove our love and show our dependance on your mercy. Thank you for grace, Amen. "That's pretty much how everyone thought. They filled their plates in silence. 5-star general Roy took a hefty scoop of hash browns and slammed them down on to his plate, splattering his neighbor's. "Sorry, I didn't mean for that to happen. The mood was turning depressing. Reverend Radke, "I know the last few days have been overwhelming, emotionally. I have consoled many confused and troubled young men. Pastor Simpkins, "Yes, Donna and I also have. They are troubled by a world full of pain and hate. The death and destruction of war itself can be nerve-racking, but then add in two warring alien races and it can throw the human psyche completely off balance. Roy, "Nothing personal but I hate to think I just lost 40 million men over some ethical test! "He bit each syllable short before blasting it out." Silence again. John spoke the obvious, "Well why

DOES God test people? "Rev Radke, "I think Donna has it right. Trials and tribulations reveal our true feelings for the Father. During crisis some people criticize and with draw from the Father; others yearn to be closer to him and learn how to depend upon his grace. Pastor Simpkins, "Yes that's true. Not only during the tough times does He test our commitment to Him, but he will also allow fortune or fame to come to a person to see if he gives God the glory or will he take the more common route of sinful pride and boastfully takes all the credit for his success." Donna, "That's right. We serve a jealous God that desires and deserves the glory." Matthew, "Let's be perfectly clear, to help mentor young John and for Roy's sake who I believe is still unsaved. "Roy, defensively, "Yeah, that's right, just haven't got around to it yet, I will on my own time. "His family members disregarded the comment and continued to listen to Mat. "John, anybody that sincerely accepts Jesus as their Lord and Savior into their heart and confesses it with his mouth then they are forever saved. For those that are saved...if they repent every day, serve the lord well, and faithfully pass the trials and tribulations of Earthly living, they will be rewarded with "Crowns" to be worn and displayed in paradise. They will receive positions of responsibility in heaven that to them will be meaningful, purposeful, and FUN!. Can't ask for more than that; by the way, that includes a loving personal face to face relationship with the Father, Son, and The Holy Spirit. "Mat sat back satisfied with his speech, the others looked content. But Luke had a question, "Pops what about those daily temptations to do something you know is wrong? What about those? "Mat, "Oh No! That's not God, he will never ever test anybody with sin. God uses personal challenges that are tough to overcome so we learn to depend upon him, he wants to be involved in your life and he wants us to succeed, but it is the devil's sin that will tempt the flesh with carnal pleasures." Mat fell silent and seemed to age about 5 years. Mat, "and UKBA is telling us we are up against a devil that originated from a distant planet, that seeks our demise." And then Mat became a fiery young man again. "Satan will not separate us from the Holy Creator.," he shouted, pointing an experience looking index finger toward the ceiling. "Let's go now and plan our victory." Mat jumped up the best he could and headed for the strategy room, he turned around to see everybody still sitting and eating. Mat's adrenalin rush caught them by surprise. With firmness Mat called over to them, "C'mon boys, let's go write history! "His excitement was contagious, a motivator; just like when John witnessed years ago when Roy and Fuller scooted their chairs back, they did it again. Fuller, "Your right Mat, let's go plan a rebellion!" Roy, "Mat, where do you get the energy?"

The others, being non-military, stayed and finished a good early meal. Walking close to his most special person John asked him, "Pops have you ever been tempted" Mat, "Sonny, I sin and repent every day! "John looked over at his do-no-wrong- great-grandfather and felt.... and felt older and more mature.

CHAPTER 15

EXISTENCE ON EARTH

Celebrations were being held in the Imperial Palace, Moscow. MDSL's highest creations were present. #1 Son Kaos, Artis, Peu, and newcomer Abad, commander of the devil brigade. MDSL, "My fornicators, you have done well. Victory is almost complete. Without thinking Artis interrupted, "But Master, their Army is destroyed, we have won!" MDSL, "Shut up and listen dumbass, the snake can be brought back. "Peu smugly laughed at Artis's rebuke. "When we have totally dominated, enslaved, and then enjoyed the spoils of war for a reasonable amount of time, only then will I brag of my victory to the defeated. He and his sons will be forced by the nature of their Kluz to honor the agreements in the fine print. His righteous KLUZ leaves him no other choice but to serve me for eternity. She let out a scream that would make Freddy Krueger shiver. "Now, before I go here are your new responsibilities." I know mine already, "said Artis, trying to be teacher's pet. MDSL, "Shut up bitch before I put you to flame." Peu laughed again and Artis shot him a cold glare. Peu stood up but glancing at the Goddess he quickly sat back down. In the future the bad blood between these two will have dire consequences for their evil cause. MDSL, "Artis, you and your soldiers are to maintain security at all the top-level priority sites. Implementation is at your discretion." It was

Peu's turn to play the fool. Peu, "Master, should a miniscule mutant like Artis be held accountable to make decisions? "Before Artis could retaliate MDSL shot a steam of burning acid from her eyes to Peu's eyes. Down to the floor in agony did he wallow. "Never question my Judgement. Pain, more pain... and then death is the punishment for such insanity. Tell your soldiers that, if need be, in the performance of their required duty, they are expected to die. Peu, your dragons will be the bounty hunters. The more humans or BEEs that you bring in as prisoners you will be paid a stipend of mocs and mollies, (Whores and drugs.) You must imprison them and assign them to work details. This Commander Abad, his devil brigade will roam the planet doing my bidding. You others do not question their actions. "Raising her demon voice she growls, "A resurgence is not tolerable! It would be the end of all of you, so for your own good make sure it doesn't happen. Now, me and my sons are going away for a short while to celebrate our victory. Perform your duties well; or else. "So, Artis, Peu, and Abad went to work on Earth, Kaos and MDSL went to enjoy themselves, Roy, Fuller and Mat was organizing a rebellion; The Maulks oversaw security, UKBA was planning a surprise attack.

For the Western losers on Earth it was a sorrowful time. Four words can sum it up for the beaten humans; hunger, disease, work, torture, add prostitution for the bigger females, and a few males. Worse, the humans have no hope; hope is a powerful motivator, it can help the spirit survive for a long, long time. That's a terrible void, having no hope, knowing that it is never going to get better, that things are never going to change for the better, in your favor. But the human slaves were unaware of the millions of Earthlings that had escaped persecution and was hiding out around the globe. Most didn't know that a revolution was being engineered and that great progress has been made. New developments were constantly improving the chances for success. UKBA's BEEs did most of the commendable work.

The Maulks were over-confident and didn't even organize search parties. On Earth under the direction of MDSL appointees, organization was not a priority; but corruption, power quarrels, fornification, underground drugs, in fighting and many other forms of personal gratifications is what consumed the invaders time. If MDSL knew how her subordinates were conducting themselves pain would be served up. Two new improvements made the rebellion a real possibility. The BEE space stealth system was miniaturized so it can be used to hide small objects like a one-man ship, or a jet plane, and maybe even small enough for individual use; and the second help was made in the communications department. The BEEs were able to manufacture a hidden transparent frequency that can "piggyback" on other seemingly unimportant transmissions. Because of this the BEEs and top Western brass can freely communicate with each other, with no worry of being caught. This was a great benefit and advantage; also as good, this new BEE technology could secretly steal all incoming and outgoing calls made by the enemy. Basically, the West and BEEs knew exactly what was being planned by the evil forces. However, the very best reason that the rebellion has a real chance of winning is the evil ones themselves. Not only did they forgo search parties but most security was either not instituted or was very laxed. Security was almost nil. But the spoils of war were in high gear! From the very beginning the Maulks have had a drug and sex problem. Now, just a short time after conquering the Earthlings, the Mexican and Colombian cartels are having success manipulating the addicted MAULKS. The glory after such an overwhelming victory had the Aliens thinking the Humans were too meek and was incapable of mustering even a futile attempt at resistance. So, whenever they could individuals or whole squads of Maluks found their way to the local drug house; where they would just quietly sniff, snort, and shoot their way into a stupor of euphoric sounds, colors, and tingling sensations, usually lasting for 24-36 hours. Only the expertise of generational drug lords could get the best of a fierce Alien killer like the Maulk. The drug lords became the street corner "Pimps "and "dealers "to the hundreds of thousands of Maulk security personnel. This greatly helped the serious and determined EAAC rebels. Peu and Abad was carousing and mainlining with different big Earth women every night, sometimes for days at a time. They knew of MDSL's consequences, but the ecstasy of the drug and the feel of the women always overpowered their better judgement. They were extreme addicts and whoemongers, their actions condoning the same behavior from their soldiers, real role models. However, it was hell for the Earth women, most if not all were patriotic spies, sneaking very useful information to their commanding officers. They should be considered heroes. It was an all-out effort by everybody. Artis was also basking in gluttonous luxuries. Ancient Roman Emperors would be envious of his extravagant parties, and he was always the center piece of attention. Drunkenness, debauchery, and nakedness let the wild imaginations of the evil bastards run amok. Artis, Peu, and Abad grossly ignored each other, communicating only about the most necessary of subjects. Security details were the least of their concern. The building of the new "Artis Coliseum" is a perfect example of their unwillingness to cooperate with each other.

Artis, "Peu, you filthy animal! Why haven't your slaves finished my stadium. What's taking so long? I have a new betting game I want to try out. Six humans are released into the stadium and then I let five hungry lions in there with them, then you bet on the human that you think will last the longest: actually there's numerous betting schemes. Luckily there are plenty of humans and lions to entertain me. I want to be entertained, now where is my stadium you peasant, get off that slut now and do your job! Peu, "You little punk-ass; you're lucky an accident hasn't happened to you ......yet! Artis, "Don't threaten me. MDSL needs me much more than she needs you. "Peu, "You dumb-ass, the Goddess doesn't need anyone. Now never bother me again with your trivial desires." Their fierce animosity trickled down to the subordinates, one army didn't like the other, including the devils. Like the breeds they are, they were selfish for their own desires. Control of the defeated humans was low on the to do list. The war was over with no chance of a rebellion; it was over, the humans are finished and will conform to Maulk will. Drugs, women, and self-satisfaction was all that was on their mind, thus, the planning and preparation for a rebellion progressed forward. If MDSL had been their things would have been different; but she was out with her sons enjoying the victory in their own mind-blowing style.

Captain D. H. led John to a "strategic Maneuvers" room where he would receive instruction about the spy network and the equipment needed in an upcoming operation he was to command. They entered the room, and someone immediately caught his attention. "Who's that over there, "he asked the captain. "Who? ""Oh, c'mon man," snickered John. "I'm sure everybody has asked about THAT girl. The one sitting behind the conference table." D.H. "Oh, that's Mary she's been here the whole time. She's really good at her job. Some kind of super genius, but one thing is for sure, she's got the three f's." "Three f's, what's that? "She's fine, fresh, and fierce." He said with a grin of lust on his face. For some reason it rubbed John the wrong way. "To me it looks like she deserves more respect than what you are giving her. "Cap. D. H. "Oh I definitely respect her skills, she really knows her stuff, but it's that body that grabs my attention." Again, with the same irritating look as he made the "hour glass" shape with his moving hands. John felt himself getting angry..." Hey, straighten up or I'll give you a fourth F. ""What are you saying?" John, "Disrespect her again and I'll box your F'N ears in, "said John with the classic John Wayne stare down. Captain D.H. says, "You know I'm the ranking officer, you could be in serious trouble." John, "It just doesn't seem right Sir, you saying those things about the nice lady." D.H. "You don't even know her... but she really is a nice person, I was just throwing some men's locker room talk around, nothing serious. You can't be that edgy around here, loosen up when you can." John didn't respond and after a couple moments of silence the captain changed the subject. "Anyway, her brother is a field agent, hopefully you'll get as good as he is. John, "Ya, well I come...just then the speaker came on telling everyone to move to a shelter. Captain, "C'mon, hurry but don't be in a rush. ""OK' said John, thinking "whatever he meant by that. "Just by chance Mary stepped in front of John as they moved into a semi-dark enclosed room. They were told to sit down with crossed legs and folded arms, like they did for nuclear attack preparedness back in elementary school. Some people behind John got "in a hurry" and bumped into him, causing John to clumsily fall into Mary. "Oh Oh I'm sorry." Said a nervous John, "I didn't mean to do that." Mary, "It's all right, things happened." John's forearm and the back of his hand had brushed lightly up against Mary's breast. Mary," Please just sit down and be quiet. "Because of their proximity John couldn't help to notice the clean fresh country smell of Mary's hair. The sensation from the enticement was branded into his memory. Their arms and shoulders were pressed together and John felt, "Man, how soft is this girl?" For the next two minutes of the scare John's heart was racing, and he pretty much held his breath the whole time, and it wasn't because a Maulk war bird was in the vicinity. Once it moved a safe distance away, they got the signal to go back to their work stations. John was surprised, and tickled, that Captain Dave led him to Mary's post. D.H. "John, this is Colonel Clark, she oversees this department, she will instruct you on how to have a successful mission. Nobody knows more about your mission than her." Colonel Clark, this is Lt. John Chistlink. He comes highly recommended by Chief of Staff's Fuller and Roy." John appeared nervous and stiff. Cap. Dave, "Just concentrate on the training, John, and you'll be alright. "Dave was chuckling about something. John, somewhat embarrassed, stammered a little bit, "Yes, yes Captain. I won't miss a thing. "Captain Dave, "Oh I'm sure you won't miss a single meeting," he said laughing. A stately Mary ended the jousting, "Thank you Mr. Dave. Your services are no longer required, have a good day Sir. "She politely dismissed Dave and he didn't mind at all, Mary's beautiful smile and soft voice, just short of sexy, left Dave walking away with a "good boy" look. Charm oozed out of every single pore of Mary's body. She tuned to John, flashing her pearly whites, and John's knees nearly buckled. "Get ahold of yourself knucklehead, she's just a girl, there's no reason I can't be master of my own domain." He came back to reality with a question from Mary, "Are you related to the aircraft carrier?" John, "Yes, same family. There's been some heroes before me. "Mary, "Well our side needs a hero right now Lieutenant, are you up for it? The country pleasant tone Mary used with Dave had changed to a determined, matter of fact, let's get the job done attitude. John was impressed. With his most serious deep voice he practically shouts, "Yes mam. I will be ready when called upon! Mary let slip out a grade schoolgirl giggle and smiled right in John's eye. His heart skipped a beat. Mary, "Look, this is going to be a one-on-one training seminar. You and your mission are very important to the rebellion. I designed this plan and its method of implementation. You are going to be the leader, the man in charge, so I thought it best to give you individual instruction; smaller groups of team leaders are being trained by my staff, but your mission is first, it must be completed successfully within a short time period.....it is difficult and dangerous and if my plan or you fail. "She stopped talking. Then added, with a slight hint of desperation, "Got it?" "Yes Mamn! "Mary, "Hey I'm only 29, I'm not a mamn yet." she said, again flashing that killer smile. They laughed together, it seemed like they had similar natures and personal demeanor, but it's much too early to tell. Mary, "Your young. Why did they choose you over more experienced soldiers?" John, "Well, I finished first in all my academic classes, won Nationals in the Master Sniper division. I set 6 world records, but I think it is my last name is why they picked me to do this job. My family heritage says I got what it takes to get the job done and I feel that I am up to the challenge, whatever it may be. "Mary just sat there, unmoved by John's statement. For a moment they sat in silence, just looking at each other. For the first time, beside his older family members, John felt a little intimidated by someone else's confidence. "Man, this girl has got it all together, you better be at your best around her, "John said to his frontal lobe. Finally, Mary spoke, "OK. I will trust the decision of my superiors, they are...smart." Good, thought John, Mary's on my side, I'll be OK. Mary, "Look, for the next three months we are going to be spending a lot of time together. In private I'll call you John and you can call me Mary; in public your still Lt. and I'm Colonel Clark. Deal? "Good deal "Mary smiled, and John's felt a surge of adrenalin. John had never met such a heavenly creature. He had to force himself to concentrate on the work. "So, I'll be in training for three months. When does the rebellion start, when does the real action start?" Mary," Think of it this way, when you and the other teams are ready, you and your team's action will start the rebellion. It's the first event we have scheduled to signal the beginning of the revolution. John, ... I and others have been in this room for weeks planning this surprise attack. Our elite staff and all the decision makers scrapped the other plans in favor of mine. My plan is the ONLY plan, I am going to give everything I have to make sure you are prepared for this critical mission." For the first time John gently took Mary's hand. He caringly held it saying, "It's OK Mary. This is the beginning of a great ending, together, let's make sure we do everything just right." For the first time they looked deeply into each other's eyes. Mary, "We will John, we will. "For a second they gazed into each other's soul. Mary, in a cheerful tone, "Well, all righty then. I feel better. I sense that you are a good man. Let's get to work."

So, with childlike enthusiasm they started. For the next 5 hours Mary explained the basics to John and laid the groundwork for further study and preparation. With the preliminary teaching completed they left for their separate sleeping quarters. Lying in his bed thoughts of Mary prevented John from sleeping, he couldn't get her out of his head. Everything about her appealed tom him. The smell of her hair, her beautiful smile, warm to the touch; he liked the way she walked, and talked, the way she taught him his lessons; even the serious things like her professionalism and dedication to the corps. In tonight's prayer he asked for the substance necessary to do his job, not wanting to disappoint Mary. Two months later and right on time per a pre-arranged meeting date and time, Angelo's cruiser pulled up to the camouflaged mountain side. The ship floated in, and everybody was whisked away to a conference room. All the pertinent officials were there waiting, (except two tardy individuals.) UKBA, "Good to see you, dear friends." Good to see you to. "UKBA, "When peace is here my friend, we will spend many hours in luxury together. "Mat, "or we could go fishing!" The group laughed and Mat added, "Peace better hurry and get here, I'm getting old! "The Angelo's laughed hard, The Christlinks... not so hard. Mat's family is aware of his old age and frailties. Young Angelo asked where John was. Roy, "Captain, "Go and get the Lt. and Colonel Clark too, you know their together. "Roy, "Is the next shipment ready? "UKBA, "Yes I have delivered 50 disruptors to your staff."

"And you are sure they will disable the steering mechanisms of the Maulk fighter jets, rendering them useless? "Yes, as long as they are properly transfixed onto the transponder located on its underbelly, then the ship will not respond to its guidance system and they will not be able to pilot the vessel manually." Fuller, "Can it be fixed? "UKBA, "Not by the time our combined efforts destroy their space fleet. "Luke, "So proper placement and installation is the trick then, right? "Luke's mind flashed to an innocent 8th grade picture of John that he keeps in his Falcon. "UKBA, "You have been training people for the mission, I'm sure. "Luke stood tall, as if called upon, and firmly stated, "The best we got!

"DH knew he could go right to Mary's room and the both of them would be there. He knocked on the door and heard a sweet, "Come on in, it's open. "Sirs, uh, Colonel, your presence is needed in the main conference room. The Chiefs are there as is the two BEEs. John, "Good, great! Mary you will finally get to meet the Angelo's. Junior is my best friend, imagine me saying that, saying an alien giant BEE is my best friend. Super people, well, you'll figure it out once you meet them. I've only known Angelo a short time, yet I consider him my best friend. Is that strange Mary?' Mary,

"No John, it isn't if you feel it in your heart. Always follow you heart John. "When Mary said that the two good friends were walking down the hall holding hands, Mary squeezed John's hand when she said, "Always follow your heart, John."

Coming through the door and seeing two giant BEEs for the first time Mary's eyes got really big and for a moment lost her breath. She took a step back when UKBA's antenna started to vibrate, and then took two more steps back when sound came from his direction! "Hello May, I am Mat's friend, UKBA. It's nice to finally meet you. I've heard so many compliments of you." Mary, being the type she is, quickly regained her composure. She shot a quick glance hitting John between the eyes. He just lifted his hands and shrugged his shoulders as if to say, "Well, I might have mentioned you a few times to grandpa." John, "uuuMmmm, Colonel Clark is my field instructor, that's all. "UKBA, "Oh? All right, but my sophisticated sense of the human psyche led me to believe there was much more to your relationship, from both of you. But I guess I can be wrong occasionally." said UKBA with a sarcastic color in his eye. Mat, "What! You be wrong about the human condition? Well, I do remember the one year you picked the wrong team to win the super bowl. "UKBA, "Well, pardon me but nobody saw that upset coming!" John, "Well upsets do happen you know, people and BEEs can be wrong occasionally." Mat, "OK, sonny, take it easy. You and your father get your feathers ruffled so easy." Luke and John, in the same exact manner, shook their head no. Roy, "Let's get down to business. You two, (pointing at John and Mary,) sit over here by me." When everyone was seated Roy nodded to Mary and asked, "Colonel, you're training the lead men, how is he doing? "Mary, "Lt. Christlink is doing just fine Sir. He is progressing on time and with comprehension of the material. "she said quite frankly. Roy, grinning, turned to Mat, "Look! She already gets her feathers ruffled; they make a great pair! "Oh boy! Everybody broke apart on Roy's joke; at the pair's expense everybody was able to get some comic relief, at least for a moment.

For this meeting could determine the fate of the world. Except Mary and John weren't laughing. It was if everybody knew something that they didn't. "OK. Let's get busy for real this time." Said Fuller, as he was catching his breath. Fuller, "Has the 50 disruptors been delivered to each base? "UKBA, "Yes. A leader at each base has been trained, just like here, and a squad of agents to perform their duty. This is my last stop; at the other bases I reviewed their individual attack plans and generally made a few revisions to improve it and to synchronize the movements of the total scheme. "Roy, "OK Mary, it's your baby. "Getting up Mary's eyes was sparkling; was it because she was excited to give her presentation, or did she just like the word "Baby."

For the next two hours she explained the details of her plan. She was professional, polite, clearly spoken, and with perfect clarity made the complex plan seem simple. John was very proud of his instructor. Matters such as logistics, the effective use of the new "stealth motor scooters ", communication uplinks, the disabling of the supposedly impenetrable ionized fence surrounding each enemy base, and the all-important correct placement of the disruptor on to the transponder located on the underbelly of the war bird; it was critical. Also critical was the timing between the teams located at each base, the ones holding the warbirds. UKBA was coordinating the movements and actions of the individual teams. The key was to transfix the transponders around the world at the same time; with them all disabled at the same time, a worldwide attack would be launched simultaneously. At the end of the meeting UKBA congratulated Mary on a fabulous plan and had no revisions. UKBA, "Thank you Mary, nice work. There's one obstacle that only time can resolve. We have intercepted info stating MDSL and her son is coming to inspect Artis and the others. His security is a joke. If the High Goddess is too displeased, she may stay on Earth. That would change everything. Hopefully they heap praise upon her and fill up her gluttonies need for attention, if satisfied with circumstances on Earth she may go back to her depths, when she leaves that will be our time to attack." Everybody was in agreement. UKBA, "It seems our work for now is done. We'll wait to see what they do, and react to it; stay hidden and safe, all protocols are in continuance. Mat, how about some milk and cookies, and I brought some sweet nectar for me. Let's go to the big screen and do some fake fishin! ""AAHH that sounds great to me. Kids don't bother us, unless of course you must. Let's go buddy. "No matter how many times you see it, it still looks odd to see a man and BEE going down a hallway, TALIKING!. Angelo Jr. turned to Roy and Fuller, "Want to go get some ice cream (Angelo the BEE liked ice cream!) Roy, "Sounds good to me, you two wanna go?" John, "Ice cream sounds good to me. Want to get some ice ceam Hoone... I mean Colonel. "That mistake busted everybody's gut! HA. HA. HA. John, "Guys that is not normally how I address the Colonel. "UKBA, from a distance, "Luke, I have sensitive hearing, and I don't think my senses about the human psyche was wrong ole sonny boy." Mat practically had to be held up by UKBA because he was laughing so hard. Mary was embarrassed but managed to say, "Well, it was nice to meet you, your Ultimate. I'll never forget this experience. I'll see ya'll later. Lt. Would you be kind enough to escort me back to my quarters." "Yes mamn...Colonel. I'll see everybody later. "The young couple turned away walking to her room. Mat and UKBA watched the two youngsters walk hand in hand; Mat felt lucky to be able to see pure innocence again and UKBA had the kindest of colors swirling around his eye.

John was standing in Mary's doorway when two privates playing around chasing each other bumped into John knocking him deep into Mary's chest... and then she wrapped her arms around him and wouldn't let go. John wasn't fighting her; he lowered his hands and for the first-time kissed Mary! Mary, "John, it took you so long to kiss me, I could hardly wait! "John, "Well I wanted to kiss you the very first time I saw you but was concerned about being a gentleman. "Mary, "Well, you are a gentleman, but you don't really know the first time you saw me. "John, "What do you mean? "Mary gripped a hairbrush to use as a microphone, jumped on the bed, started running and jumping somehow on it like a sprinting gymnast, then glazed with a laser like sharpness right in John's eye and belted out, "the time is near, the choice is clear, unless you bend over and take it in the rear. "Wow! That was you! Unbelievable! "John moved closer. He couldn't believe the "have it all together beautiful women standing in front of him wanted to kiss him! "Well, how much of a gentleman can you be?" She said just before she pulled him chin to chin. A millimeter before their lips touched, she whispered, "You ain't seen nothing yet, here's something you're never going to forget." John had a super adrenalin rush affecting every part of his body, and then he planted one on her! After a couple of seconds John pulled back a couple inches to look into Mary's beautiful eyes, they were sparkling! Then again they searched for each other's lips and kissed passionately, I said PASSIONATELY!. They stopped and gazed into each other's eyes again for a few seconds and then kissed again...... Mary stepped back, "You still a gentleman now flyboy? "John, "Well, I AM a full grown red-blooded American male" Mary, having a good time, threw a soft pillow at John, "That's what I thought! Well, that kiss is all you get jarhead. "John, with a smile as wide as the Grand Canyon, "I wasn't suggesting anything. ""RRRiiiigght. "Mary fires back. "If I nodded my head you'd be all over me! "She said giggling. John took a step closer, "Are you nodding Mary? asked a curiously hopeful John. Mary, "John, you've never even told me how you feel about us, or even what you think of me. "John, "Don't you know by my actions? ""A girl likes to hear the words... and with feeling "she quickly added. John "The truth is Mary, what I mean to say...." then the worst possible timing. There was a knock on the door and an announcement over the loudspeaker at the same time, "Attention Lt. Christlink you are to report to the strategy room at once and on the double. John, "Mary, I've got to go now. I don't want to rush this. I'll express my feelings to you after this emergency meeting, whatever could be so important. I'll be back." John softly kissed his love on the lips and left. Their fingertips were the last thing to touch as Captain Dave pulled his friend down the hallway. Entering the room John could tell the mood was terse, something was definitely wrong. "Is my grandfather alight? "Roy, "He's fine. It's a military matter. We have a problem that needs to be solved right now or it could jeopardize the whole rebellion. ""What is it and how can I help? "Luke, "Pay close attention son, it is an unusual situation. "Fuller, "John, a field agent has been captured. Just before his abduction he was able to tell us his location. He was mapping huts used for warbird storage. He must be rescued but not with a large force for fear of tipping our hand. The problem is that he has knowledge of our entire operation. And this million-year-old species has perfected methods of abstracting information from prisoners. You understand right? "John, "Yes, of course I will go alone and rescue him. I volunteer. Give me the needed details. "Fuller started with the worst part, "John, the agent you are rescuing is Mary's brother, Joseph. "John's mood became more somber, but also more determined. John, "Does Mary know? ""No. I don't think any good would come of informing her at this time." John, "What's the plan? ""We know the location of the drug house that he is being held. They know he is a spy, and they always torture to get the information. Luckily, we have agents that are delaying the interrogation. "Who's doing that? "Asked a quizzical John. "Pimps, prostitutes and patriots." John, "Boy, this is weird. "Roy, "Yeah, but the drug lords have really helped our cause. Without the Maulks strung out on drugs right now and fooling' around with our women they for sure would have cut the info out from Joe's tongue and the whole enterprise would have to shut down. "Fuller, "Most of the hard work is already done. All you have do is all the cloak and dagger stuff." Roy, "Yeah, just sneak in, shoot all the bad guys, grab Joe, and get away, ""Without being tailed, "added Fuller. A nervous smile appeared on everybody's face. John, "Yeah, simple cloak and dagger stuff." Fuller looked him square in the eye, "here's the real deal. Joe doesn't have to be rescued, but he can't be allowed to give up that information. Do you understand?

"John solemnly nodded yes. In his mind he thought there's no way he was killing Mary's brother. He was going to get him out safe or die trying. John, "OK. So, I travel 100 miles on this "invisible "scooter, get Joe, travel back with this new untested bike at its maximum weight and distance per tank, all undetected, is that right?" "that's right" was the echo. Roy, "You got it ace. "Fuller, "Except time is the essence, go as fast as you can, there and back." Luke didn't like his son being put in such a risky and very important chore. Luke, "Sirs, I am the best pilot in the force and the pilot with the most experience, it should me doing this mission. "John, "Give it a rest dad. I've learned about the Maulks and have trained for situations like this. I am the one better prepared to do this job, sorry Dad, "said John, trying to sound disappointed. "Don't worry, I can pull this off." He added. Luke had to say, "I'm very proud of you son, I'll see you when you get back." With that John took off on a dangerous first mission. On the way there he couldn't help to think that there must be a better way. He felt like a guinea pig trying out the new devices, the first time to be used in battle. But if his supervisors have faith in them, then so did he; anyway, he would have volunteered to rescue Mary's brother no matter what the circumstances. At midnight, with a full moon, John could see the dimly lit drug house. It must have been built especially for the large newcomers because it was long, tall, and just big! Perfect size for the predators. "OK. Now I just have to trust this "stealth bubble. "No quick movements and there not supposed to be able to see me." John slowly, silently, crawled over to the house and by standing on an outside table was able to peer through a busted out window. These monsters were like a rhinoceros stood up on its hind legs! Not Angelo big but was still a good 10-12 feet big and all muscle! John slid back down and regrouped. John remembered a saying an ole college team-mate used to say before doing something impossible, "Nothing to it but to do it! "So, John got to it. There was 4 of them either passed out or sleeping on the floor. and one was laying on a beat up ripped apart sofa. He could hear moans and yelps of pain coming from two probable bedrooms in the back. Piles of cocaine, heroin, and other drugs littered the room. "OK, I have been instructed that when I shoot my weapon it will disengage my bubble and can't be re-activated until I get back on my scooter. Uhm. Almost whispering to himself he thought, "My best chance is to shoot first and kill'em all before they have time to re-act. John then heard a moan from a darkened corner. He looked over to see two normal size feet extending from behind the sofa, the shadows blocked the top half, but it had to be Joe. This is it, then one more psyche up, "Go big guy go!" Running through the door he disengaged his bubble leaving him in plain sight. Immediately he started blasting his machine gun. ZZZZZiiiiiiipppp zip zip zip... He put several rounds into the Maulks passed out on the floor, even their blood smelled rotten. The only one that had a chance was the one sleeping on the sofa, but he didn't even make it to his gun. The whole episode took about 4 seconds. During that time Joe had stood up took a couple of steps and then tumbled into the light, falling on dead Maulk carcass. John could see a mangled and bloodied Joe. "Watch out. "Thumbers "coming out of back be.." John swung around and heard a Bam..Bam, and then his ear was stinging! He hit the floor, rolled over to his knees and took quick aim; in front of him standing in the bedroom doorway was a scratched up Maulk, panting heavily. Then a large black women came from behind him and tried her hardest to struggle with him, but he was too big and strong. He backhanded her, smashing in her face and sending her head so far sideways it nearly flew off her neck, but her gallant effort bought John enough time to shoot. ZZZZZIIIPPPP! He splattered the dude! Some screams and pounding came from the other bedroom. Quickly, but not in a hurry, John went to the door and peeked around the edge. Another horrifying scene. The largest Maulk in the house was using the butt of his rifle to pummel two more large black females. They were obviously dead, but he just kept banging away. John wanted to strangle the beast with his bare hands but knew he didn't stand a chance with such a monster. So, being the expert marksman he is, John first shot the weapon out of the monster's grip and then shot him several times below the knees, dropping him to the floor, unable to get up and walk. John felt ok, but not the euphoria he thought he would. The Maulk, a true warrior, was scratching and crawling his way to John. John knew that the girls had saved his life. He was in a hurry but out of guilt and shame he took a moment to say a quick "beath prayer. ""Father, please forgive me for my lack of compassion and my sin of judgement. Bless these ladies' soul, they suffered to help others." Then John released a barrage of gun fire into the rapist crawling on the floor, ripping him to small bloody pieces. He moved to Joe and heard him say, "Hurry up, the real soldiers ae on their way. "He nearly passed out, but John helped him to the scooter. They were in the dark and as they were taking their last steps to the jet bike they heard a commotion from the house. "Oh no!" said Joe in a scratched voice, "These guys got anger problems. "All of sudden somehow the devils were right on top of them. Gushes of wind zoomed past John and Joe as the ground was eaten up by gun blasts. The scooter exploded and all seemed lost. John was running in the dark shadows trying to find a good place to hide, dragging Joe behind him, grimacing in pain. John threw him behind a big boulder and opened gun fire at the closing devils. They shot back cracking the boulders protecting them. John, "Two more rounds and these blocks are gone. Got any suggestions? "Joe, "Yeah. Next time have a better plan... I want you to know that I didn't give up any information; and it hurt like hell! I didn't want to let anybody down so the lights still green for go. What's your name?" "John. "Joe, "My rescuer John. I have all the important information and they know I have it. I don't want to go through that pain again, I don't think I could take it twice. If I'm captured, I'd probably talk this time and then they kill me any way. "They had to slide to their left as the Maulks were out-flanking them. John, "You'd better finish your thought then we gotta do something spectacular." Joe, "If you get out of here tell my sister she is the most precious gift the good Lord put on this Earth." John's gut tightened. Joe, "and the hard item, don't let me get captured, you know what I mean, it is what I want, but it is for the good of the cause that I am not taken alive." That's as serious as it gets. John re-fortified himself and tried desperately to think of a way out of this deadly mess. Then the miracles of all miracles. UKBA's stealth spy ship materialized right in front of them! Green and blue laser lights melting and vaporizing every Devil in sight! The ramp lowered and out running, and fluttering, was UKBA, Luke, and brother Angelo. Luke's laser gun searing the black night air with pinpoint accuracy. Angelo hoisted the two agents up and put them in the safety of the ship. Luke ran back jumping through the door and they rocketed off. Father and son briefly hugged and nodded they were OK. Luke, "UKBA showed up around an hour ago and when we told him of the rescue plan he really blew an ear gasket. I've never seen him upset and I sure don't want to ever see him mad! Son, to accept a challenge like this took real man courage, I'm proud of you." John kind of blushed and politely asked, "You got anything to eat? "Dad smiled warmly. "No. We'll be home in ten minutes. Let's bandage your ear. "John felt that it was good to be back to normal. When they putted through the bay doors John was surprised to see about 200 people there to greet them. "What's going on? "Asked Joe. John, "I'm not positive but this might be for us. "Of course, it was. As the two new friends walked down the ramp, they received a hero's welcome. Everybody was cheering and clapping, Mary was right out front. Before John was on solid footing she was in his arms. Mary, "John your hurt!" "NO, no it's nothing." They hugged and kissed, elevating the crowd to a crescendo. Mary, "John, I never want you gone from me ever again. I want to marry you, raise a big family, grow old together and then die in each other's arms! The slower Joe had been out of ear shot and did not know of the two's relationship. Joe, "Hey, hey, baby sister, remember me? Field agent in constant danger, doting brother." Mary ran to him. "Joe, I didn't know it was you they were rescuing, nobody would tell me exactly what was going on like it was some big secret, but now I understand why." Joe, "Well I didn't think I was worth the effort but here I am." John strolled up. Mary, "John, you went on this suicide mission to save Joe? "John, "Well, it wasn't a suicide mission because I'm standing right here, and you know your brother, doesn't somebody always have to get him out of trouble." Mary and John giggled and held each other. Mary, "That just makes me love you that much more John." Joe, "Hey buddy watch it. What are you trying to do with my sister? "John, "I'm doing this. "Right in front of the 200 people John got down on one knee. Looking up at his love, "Mary, I love you with all my heart. More than anything under God's blue sky, my desire is to be your forever loving husband. Mary Clark, will you be my caring wife forever?" Mary, "Mister John Chistlink. I love you now and forever. Yes, I will marry you." Somehow the crowd applauded louder than before! Most women had tears in their eyes and the men looked jealous, their expressions saying, "why couldn't I meet a girl like that and sweep her off her feet with the kind of charm he has." Joseph was the first to congratulate them. "Well done life-saver! I hope we become good friend." "We already are." replied John. After much hand shaking and congratulations Mary and John went to her room to start planning the wedding.

As the party was breaking up the elite staff went to the strategy room. UKBA, with a burnt-orange eye, meaning trouble. UKBA, "Fortunately we intercepted an encrypted message before the Queen of Evil was upon us." What are you saying?" said Roy. "She and her son the devil will be at Earth in one week. She notified Artis to have pomp and circumstance ready for the visit and we basically head her word for word. Hopefully her visit will go smooth, and she will leave, in her presence we cannot start the rebellion. I know from Luke's brave interdiction that patrols will increase so we must have supreme diligence. No power surges or unwarranted travel or communications. Keep in-house noise to a minimum and security vigilant. I will contact you later at the appropriate time to discuss the launch date of the rebellion. I must leave you; I have crucial work to do. God Bless and good luck. "He was gone before the anything else could happen. A loudspeaker announcement about the arrival of MDSL was made and the necessary arrangements and precautions were handled throughout the complex: then quietness. The shared joy of engagement was replaced by a somber mood.

Back on Earth the three stooges were acting like stooges, but they aren't complete fools. They realize the good gig they got on Earth and knew that if the Holy Goddess wasn't pleased with their effort it could be taken away from them; or worse, they could be subjected to intense pain leading to a very slow death. They acknowledged the lucky notification, instead of a surprise visit and immediately started to cooperate with each other in order to put on a great "dog and pony show." To emphasize their dedication to improvement they ordered the execution of 100,000 known Maulk derelicts. Suddenly efficiency increased. Soldiers started looking and acting like wanna be killers again. When MDSL and Kaos arrived, the gala began. They had a concert like event tour of the larger bases around the world, where they were entertained by the torture and be-heading of millions of prisoners. The infallible Gods had nothing but praise and worship heaped upon them. It was quite impressive. MDSL, "My dastard, soak in the appreciation and glory. I am confident the time is now! "She screamed and howled at the same time. The Earthlings have been conquered, enslaved, and now we are enjoying the spoils of war. I, I say I" she was in a frenzy that you just don't confront, "OH, I feel the jams of my boiling pleasure centers scathing my insides! "MDSL was slobbering all over herself. I will shoot the Father with my pleasure! We must hurry and announce ourselves and of our stupendous victory to the puny weakling, very soon to be my eternal slave." Kaos, "I will notify our puppets of our intentions and have them stand by. "In a instant he was back, "Mother do I have to ask after such a victory? ""No, son, do not ask. "In plain view of surrounding demons and devils they do what those kinds do, and then they were off to see the great "I AM."

Escorted by the devils and demons MDSL was determined to make a grand entrance. The closer they got to the Father's domain the more she rambled on. "His KLUZ cannot allow him to escape this pre-war contract. It was stated that only one future free- will can be the result and outcome of the signed document. His sons will be our servants, his Angels will be our dogs, the Elders will be made to wallow in their own vomit for eternity, and I will sit upon the Golden Throne!" Kaos, "Mother, my blood also boils, I am salivating, and my limb is stiff. This is better than death and destruction! he exclaimed with enthusiasm. MDSL, "Of course my adorable son, this is the reward for death and destruction."

But many other important inter-related events were happening at the same time as MDSL was entering the Father's inner circle. To ensure the proper timing and correct cause and effect sequences several corresponding occurrences must be examined in quick succession. So, as the two Gods of Darkness was about to come face to face with their nemesis another couple was taking a shorter journey.

It had been a month since John proposed to Mary. It was the shortest engagement period Mary thought was permissible. Now they were walking down the aisle with all the dignitaries present. UKBA was even able to upload a link so Grandad Mark on Mars could see his lineage get hitched. The Angelo's were there for the wedding and to finalize the rebellion details. Not since Romeo and Juliet had two people been more suited for one another. After the "I do's "the couple found their way to a specially made "honeymoon suite." The generals and all pertinent staff met in the strategy room. EAAC Secretary of war 5-star general Mr. Roy opened the discussion. "Gentlemen and your Ultimate, welcome to this historic meeting. Today, our consensual agreements will alter the course of mankind. At this hour we choose freedom. We choose to make our own destiny. Let us harness the courage within us to make the hard decisions. We not only contend for the here and now but for our kids' kids and all future generations. We will strive together to make sure their path is wide, straight, and smooth. Consider not our fortunes but those that come after we have done some work. We are committed to look evil in the eye and brush it a side. "Roy sat down. In pursuit to prevent the destruction of the human race the men were galvanized. They got down to strategizing. After a week of constant struggle, debate, conformity, and finally consensus, the participants were exhausted. Fuller gave closing comment. "Men, it is settled. We have done well. This final plan will succeed. We shall pray to God to give us the resolve to force the desired finish. With the help from our willing protectors humanity will survive and once again enjoy the glorious bounty of this wonderful planet.

CHAPTER 16

DESTINY?

Long ago, before the existence of anything else, while the "I AM "was still marveling in his private personal glory, he began to desire more than just loneliness. He contemplated different ways to amuse himself. Many, many, many, experiences transpired. One of the most appealing was inter-reactional relationships. Thus, creation manifested. Sons, friends, worshippers, warriors, and a special "companion" provided social entertainment. For a while it satisfied Him. But the Great Authority, being a self-willed created super-natural all-knowing Deity; wanted more, something brand new. He decided to engage in a challenging contest, again, because one of His many spirits IS competition; although there is never any doubt of the pre-destined outcome, but on this one and only occasion, to create His most exciting match, the Great "I AM" permitted the most qualified counterpart, (Sophia at the time), to eliminate "predestination "as a stipulation. That's how the "bet "came to be. And now it was the time for the Founder of Wisdom to make a Masterful move. He instituted a time freeze/shift to all game participants, except Him of course. The cunning stratagem is unknown to EVERYBODY! HE is the only one that has knowledge of its implementation, not even HIS son's no of its use. During break HE called Son Love to HIS throne for a confessional conversation.

The Holy Father, "Son, I am proud of you. The courage and resolve you displayed on Earth to save your creations was inspirational! Your depths of patience and strength you exhibited to maintain your humbleness, and the magnitude of persecution you choose to endure to secure the "plan of salvation" greatly surpassed the expectations of the Elders; but you didn't surprise me. I am your Creator; I know who you are and why you were made; and it is to do a great thing; and that great thing is this: My number one son...the finish is here! The showdown between good and evil, that was forever meant to be, can now happen. Son, you must now decide to change from the sacrificial lamb to the warrior King that the instructed prophets on Earth wrote about. Son, I am dependent upon your courage to make the correct choice and to take affirmative action. Your goal is to defeat the Queen of Sheol. "And then a sentence from the First Original Creation that he should not have ever had to utter. "Son, if you are not victorious, if you are defeated, all the creatures of light will forever be slaves, to serve the Darkness of Evil for eternity."

Love, with no indication of calamity in his voice, "I will Joyously fulfill my destiny and complete my calling, bringing about Peace. "Without hesitation, without fanfare or parades of sendoff, Love headed down to Earth with eagerness, to judge the best course of action.

So, back on Earth for all creatures, without detection but with logic and reason, time jumped from March 24, 2059, to December 25, 2059. It was significant to GOD's realities of the competition for this to happen.

Believers in the Western world was starting to celebrate the birth of their savior while those from the East was trying to make the West miserable.

Within the base complex it was impossible and against the rules to try and get presents from the city into the bunker. Due to the close launch date of the rebellion no one was allowed outside the complex. It's understandable. It was John's and Mary's first Christmas as a married couple. After dinner in their small one room bunker apartment John handed Mary a box wrapped in brown kitchen paper, it had a homemade bow of aluminum foil. Mary, "John, I didn't expect this, we agreed not to exchange gifts. We can't afford it plus, there's nothing to give or get. "John, "I know. It's not much. I don't want anything. Go ahead and open it." Mary opened the box to find a tiny, cute, pink teddy bear! Mary, "John, I love teddy bears. I'll sleep with it every night your gone. How did you get it?" John, "That's top-secret Colonel. "John and his best friend laughed together. Mary reached under the bed and slid a present to her husband. John, "Oh you kidder! I really believed you didn't get me anything. "He opened it and inside was a shiny locket with a stunning picture of his wife. Her long hair, beautiful smile, sparkling green eyes... just her presence made her comparable to Venus the love goddess. John, "Mary this is the best gift I ever got, where I go it goes. "Mary, "I got another gift for you, well actually it's a gift you gave to me.. no.. no it's a gift we both received from God. "John, "I'm confused. "Mary, "John, Mary hesitated thinking John should have guessed from her excellent clue, "John, I'm pregnant!" She happily looked John in the eye, leaned over hugged and kissed him. John vigorously hugged back and let out a WWWHHHEEEWWWWW!!! "How long. ""1 month. "John, "You're going to be the best mother." Mary, "John you're going to be the best Dad." John, "This is just the beginning. We have so much life to live, Mary I want to live on the edge, make every second count, you and me together. "John was so excited he had to stand up and do a cheerleader dance! Mary, "John we are going to have many children, a big family, "she said, spreading her arms wide, "you will be the grand patriarch of a family rich in Christian values and traditions, we will serve the Lord and HE will bless us with health and happiness. "Mary, you make everything better, mostly me. Let's be able to look back and say we have no regrets.... that together we lived our lives to the fullest, and that will be our gift and legacy to our generations." Mary, "Oh John, that was beautiful. You ae a wonderful noble man, I am lucky that you love me. "John, "Well, I thank the good Lord every day that I'm able to be close to you. I'm the blessed one." They melted into the bed.

CHAPTER 17

IT STARTS

In some ways the last days before the rebellion went to fast, and in some ways to slow. Too fast because John wanted to spend as much time as he could with Mary before he went off to war; he desperately wanted to witness the birth of his son but now that looked very unlikely. Too slow because the mind can invent scenarios that probably Won't happen, but you think about them anyway. Some of his daydreams were nerve racking. Mostly, he just wanted his mission to be over so he could know if he failed or succeeded. Hero or goat, dead or alive. A lot was riding on his courage and abilities.

It was early evening Dec. 31, 2059. John was lying in bed waiting for the alarm to go off, it did at 12:01. He sat up and poked Mary on the shoulder, "You can get up now and quit pretending to be asleep." "Well, who can sleep the night before such a daring mission, and with you first at bat. John, you got to stay safe. This baby is going to pop out any day and it is going to need a father. "Mary was going a mile a minute. John, "Don't worry, I have to be here to tell my son his purpose and meaning in life, like pops did for me. By the way honey, happy new year." The married couple kissed; words were not necessary. As he was leaving John tuned back to Mary and said, "Don't worry honey, 2060 is going to be our best year ever! "John was to report at 1:00, he walked into the flight bay at 12:45, Lombardi time; somehow, as a little baby he thought he heard the oldest Christlink that he can remember, Pete, shout, "get their 15 minutes early, Lombardi time. "He made his way to the disembarkment stage and like everyone else, inspected his equipment. At 2: 00 General Fuller started the final prep. "Gentlemen, our plan is solid, you are well trained, we are in the right, God is leading us. He will not allow evil to end his creation. Everyone do your job and we will be all right. Do it right and on schedule. Let's not have any indecision. Because when John is done and the rest of us can move into action he will be hanging out on the roof like a stranded goose. (John didn't like the image.) Any questions? "There were none, so Pastor Simpkins gave a short moving prayer, all were thankful for that. Pastor, "Father, at this time of violence we ask for your protection. Bless each man with courage, and the knowledge of forgiveness. Amen. "John synchronized his time piece with the space digital, as did all the team leaders around the world, all 560 of them, each team composed of between 50 to 100 "Freedom Fighters," as they were calling themselves. His team left on the tick of the second hand. John was carrying on his "stealth "scooter a 100 lb. "De-ionizer ", meant to dis-arm the security field surrounding the Maulk base. To help ensure the surprise and secrecy of the world wide effort each team commander, (just like John), was to install and activate the engineering masterpiece precisely at 5:00, (his scheduled time). Timing was critical to the dismantling of the entire Maulk warbird fleet at the same time around the world. If one team fouled up the whole mission could be jeopardized; and then the lone BEE flag ship (The Queen Mary) combined with the inferior EAAC Space Force, would be no match for Maulk numbers and technology. As John's team flew to the Maulk base he was again talking to himself, reviewing his prescribed steps. "OK. I get there, in my invisible suit as before, crawl up the framing poles to the top of the "hut, "install the de-ionizer, dis-engaging the safety of my invisibility, turn on the silent machine, and watch to make sure the security field is down, call the troops in, while the whole time I'm on top of the world in plain view, then, when all 50 of the men that me and Mary trained have successfully placed the De-ionizing disruptors on the underbelly transponders, and have safely left the base, I am to re-activate the security field as though nothing happened. Then, when we attack, and their space fleet cannot function we will rain down destruction upon their heads. "John got psyched up thinking about his crucial part in the grand scheme. "If we buy them enough time even our jets can knock out a sitting duck!" John and his team secretly arrived at the base and John was glad to see there were no guards around. The West can sure tell the difference between when MDSL is here running a tight ship and when the three stooges are in control. Covert intelligence did say this was the best time to strike, because most of the Maulk security would either be asleep or strung out on drugs. Looked like they were right. He hid his scooter according to plan and went to the designated pole to climb, Mary's plan was very detailed. He put his suction cups on, checked his timer and on the second started to climb the pole. His first step quietly plunged through the thin rubber like invisible material and John seemed to materialize, there for anybody to see, if they were looking. "I sure hope nobody wakes up; can you grant me that Lord. "Asked John. Mary's training took over and John made the 400-foot climb to the top in the same exact amount of time that he had practiced it with Mary, he could almost smell her hair. With no incidents he completed the first step and radioed his men that they were safe to sneak in. Each unit scurried around the base to their assigned task like hungry mice carrying away a chunk of cheese. John's adrenalin was really kicking in, reminding him how fear and courage are always partnered together, like a couple dancing a tango, struggling to decide who is going to lead. John was lying down flat as he could to avoid detection. During the months of training his men lowered their duty completion time from 19 minutes to 8 minutes. Right now, John wishes it was about two minutes. As soon as they all get to their scooter and leave John can go to the next step and be closer to home. He counted to help his patience. "2...4...8. minutes, hurry up boys, but do it right. He felt how fast 10 minutes passes when he is with Mary but this 8 minutes has been like an agonizing hour. Then a vibrator on his belt meant bad news. It was General Roy, "John, "we have been spotted in sector 66, soon the Maulks at every base will be alerted. You are ordered to pull out immediately, your progress is to be muted. Again, pull out immediately. "John didn't have a chance to question, which is probably for the best. John notified his men; he was too busy to think about the negative percussions from the one and only rebellion plan that was beginning to be foiled. Deception and invisibility were out the window. John, through his training was able to slide down the 400-foot pole in a few seconds and then it happened. Bam. Bam. Bam. They were shooting at him! He slid backwards the last 10 feet, summer salted into his bike, spraining his ankle in the process. As he stood to get on his transportation a bomb exploded near him, the concussion waves knocked him to the ground and left him groggy; but his pain bought him back enough to just in time Zip. Zip. Zip. The National marksman shoots three times and gets three kills, more precise, three Maulk heads blown off. Pain always punctuated his aim. He was separated from his men and somehow lost his communicator. He crouched behind a waste dumpster and tried to invent some options. He didn't have any good ones. Then the Maulks pounced on him with relentless gunfire. He was in a fierce gun battle and knew he was being flanked but couldn't put up any resistance to the move. Bam.Bam.Bam. Zip. Zip. Zip. The shots went back and forth but John was vastly outnumbered and had a field disadvantage, he slumped down thinking that this might be his last duel. Then from the rear he heard a wonderful chorus of gunfire! His men had come back for him! They didn't have to, it wasn't ordered or expected, well it was kind of expected, deep down in John's heart he trusted he'd have help. That's what he would have done if the tables were turned, he would have come to some soldier's rescue. That's what Marines and Ranges, and all branches of the military and actually your American neighbor down the street would RUN to the rescue. Americans stick together. Now it was the Maulks that was outflanked. Behind him John could see his First Sargent in Command, Aloi. He loved the guy, in a military uniform. but out and about he was basically a hard ass. The sign in his yard didn't say "beware of dog," no, it said "Beware of the Bullitt up your ass." He was out front directing his men to the left and right, he loved playing war. Part of Mary's plan was for each soldier to carry a handheld powerful explosive, much deadlier than the old normal hand grenade, just for situations like this. At his friend's command 50 orange-reddish exploding clouds of destruction eliminated the company of Maulks. Aloi jumped on his scooter and swiftly picked John up and they sped back to their base. As soon as the two was off the scooter Aloi was on the war again. "Well, it's on now Sir, WE are going to give them hell, they just don't know it yet. "His positivity was encouraging, refreshing. "This war is ours to win and I want right in the middle of it. "To make his day John told him, "Hey dude, thanks for the Audie Murphy rescue, you and your men were awesome. Audie Murphy was Aloi's W.W.II hero, who became a Hollywood movie star. John got his ankle taped while he was debriefed. The sergeant was right, there was intense fighting all around the planet. It was do or die for humanity.

Far away in the upper heavens the time/freeze had been lifted. MDSL continued to enter the Fathers domain, unaware of the Master's ploy. There were companies of millions of devils and demons lurking behind their Queen, coarsely chanting dark chords of malevolence. It was the total opposite of the harmonizing tones that used to accompany her beautiful radiance. MDSL, with Kaos two steps behind and to the right, stopped at the foot of the throne, glaring up at the sitting figure. This time she did not offer praise but instead blustered, "I declare myself the VICTOR!, "she shouted directly into his face. You must relinquish your throne to me and bow down in disgrace. You will no longer have a name. Your son's must lick the bottom of my son's hoofs, your buddies, the Elders, will wallow in their own vomit for all eternity. This is only the beginning of your consequences for your foolish arrogance. S.H.F. "Oh, one of little wisdom. Again, you are wrong. A new battle has begun, there are competing armies on Earth. You can declare nothing, except what a fool YOU are!" She looked down to Earth to see war and shouted, "You cheater! You do not play fair! I won fair and square." She sounded like a spoiled third grader complaining because she didn't get a star on her paper. S.H.F. "I wouldn't cheat even if MY KLUZ permitted it. Anyway, I don't need to cheat to beat you loser. I'm not a cheater but I do completely read the rules, which you apparently don't do. There was a clause that allows a one and only use of a certain ploy, all legal, I guess you missed it, what a shame, "as HE turned to HIS buddies, hooking a thumb over HIS shoulder pointing to MDSL; they laughed together. Motivated by aggravation MDSL raised her hand to release some energy. The Master balked at her, "Do you really want to start something now? "MDSL hesitated then jerked around. "I'll go finish the job myself." In a frenzied state of anger she bolted for Earth. The Holy of Holies looked over at his cohorts and again started laughing, their look said it all, "She just won't learn! "Before she got very far the Great Authority took his thumb and index finger and slowly brought them together, like a teenage girl would do to her younger sister to keep her quiet, when they touched MDSL, Kaos, and all her munchkins experienced another time/ freeze; this time only affecting their darkness. The S.H.F. explained to Arch Angel Michael, "She would have failed but I don't want her to enter the fray yet, she can later. "So, it was. The Father controls all outcomes, glory to him.

Back on Earth General Roy updated the rebellion's progress to the Angelo's and John. "Our underground network was able to steal prison security codes and released about 50 million soldiers; they have found their way to our side have been equipped and are now fighting on the front lines. Also, the genius of the Bees was able to send a "magnetized pulsating surcharge of different electronic frequencies, (?) through the nuclear armament of the AEAR. That prong of our attack went smoothly, unlike the disruptor part." Fuller, "Yes, the good work has leveled the playing field pretty evenly for the humans, but it's the space war that counts. Just one of their warbirds could rule the world. The coordination of all allied forces will come from this office." UKBA, "Yes, very logical. I will take our only remaining scout ship and help the effort in Bagdad. "General K.S. is in control there. Roy, "Good idea. Take Captain Christlink with you, his foot isn't so bad that he can't be of some assistance. John, "Thank you Sir. "UKBA allowed John a few minutes for a quick goodbye to Mary. Being instrumental in the rebellion's original plan and her expertise and knowledge of war strategies Mary was an extremely important and busy women. Their goodbye was a quick tear, kiss, and "be safe, I'll see you later."

In the ship Angelo # 15 told John, "Right now our chance for victory is good. You Mary's plan is working." UKBA forcefully stepped in, "Young men, your optimism is immature. Learn to deal with facts. Hope is well intentioned but must be caried forth by accomplishments. They still have a formidable space force and the evil one has yet to come. Now you two put your brains together and come up with our next best option." UKBA was right. Nothing worthy enough to end the war had yet been achieved.

Someone else was waiting for the evil Gods to arrive. Artis was prone to the floor shouting, "Where are you? Why have you forsaken me? I have done all that you have required of me. It is Peu and Abad that is at fault. Come and give me my rewards. Punish them as they deserve to be, I am the one true heir to Earth's possessions. "His Generals would pause in disbelieve; pull him up and coax him back to the war table. He would participate for a minute and then end up prone to the floor again, pleading to those listening, "Can't you comprehend that there are powers and authorities greater than our war machines that will determine the end result of this contention. Then he would pray again.

The critical space battle was under the direction of Commander Bo. Because of his inferior technology he wisely decided to use a "hit-and-run- method of offense. He knew the fight for space superiority will be the deciding factor in the revolutionary war. At first the guerilla style sneak attacks worked. But after many BEE victories and Maulk losses the losers changed their tactics. Both sides had good reason for the last man standing to fight to the death; the BEEs to uphold their oath of protection, the Maulks just because they were ruthless killers. There were no retreats or surrenders from either side.

CHAPTER 18

EARTH LOSES

Despite fierce and brave fighting the human rebellion against the evil forces was going badly. E.A.A.C. land forces needed a boost from the BEEs, but all they have to offer now is UKBA's special scout ship and General BO's flagship, the Queen Mary. General Bo contacted UKBA, "Let me report Sir that our 12 battle cruisers destroyed 120 Alien warbirds. That's a remarkable kill ratio for being outgunned and having less armor. Only the courage of the crew and the abilities of the commanders made that possible." UKBA, "Yes, outstanding! Back home the gallant men will be honored. What is the outlook General? "With noble pride the General spoke up, "Sir, I have decided not to run to buy time to recharge the crystal grid. I'm just going to slug it out. The Queen will surprise them with her armor and firepower, this isn' t some ol'e tugboat ya know."

General Bo loved the Queen Mary. He designed it, supervised its construction and has been its only Captain. Bo, "I'll try to keep reporting but soon I may be too busy. Tune in to all frequencies to stay informed. "UKBA, "Yes, soon we also will be busy. God Bless and take care." BO, "Sir, be confident that someday, somewhere, we will spend peace together." That lifted UKBA's spirit, but his eye quickly transformed to a greenish/ purplish, with a mixture of grey? Nobody knew what UKBA was feeling,

I think he wanted it that way. Angelo's fast scout ship, with its relatively weak weaponry compared to the Maulks, but overwhelming firepower compared to the A.E.A.R. air force, was able to wrestle away Bagdad from the EAST. They left behind tanks, cannons, and to Luke's joy... aircraft. Without constant maintenance the A-1 was unable to fly. The mechanics at the complex did not know the intricate complexities of the futuristic aircraft, nor had the parts.

"OK boys, there not the Falcon but they'll match anything we'll fly against. Change the markings and suit up!" Luke was ordered to protect the H2O plants, the most important objective of the war. General Roy, "Luke, you know how the rising sea levels infiltrated the clean water aquifers with salt water, now these freshwater plants produce more potable water than all the rivers. Soldiers must hydrate. HUUH, damn climate change. If the aliens destroy each other this will be the most sought-after prize. That's why we're putting our best right here with us. "Fuller came into the room like it was a scripted play, "Luke, we need you at your best. The rest of the AEAR air force is coming our way." Luke, "Just turn me loose and point me in the right direction." Fuller, "Luke my boy they have 60 migs left, their best Russian, Chinees, and Iranian pilots are at the controls. Luke, "That's it, 10 to 1, piece of cake! "To a stranger Luke might be talking unrealistically or may seem overly optimistic or just plain cock-eyed stupid, but John knows his Dad is a true warrior...and champion. Luke had been in many successful dog fights, he felt at ease in battle, it was his natural realm.

Rat Tat TAT, SWOOSH. Luke made his first kill nose diving from 60,000 feet. Something not many good pilots can do, but Luke made it look easy. Then he zoomed down and curved even to the sea, jerked the stick back pointing the nose straight up and while withstanding a G-Force of 10 shot another Mig out of the sky, something else that wasn't easy, but Luke is not easy, he's hard, very hard in dog fights. Luke, "C'mon boys whdda doin... I got two already! Luke was special, the others were not. From the many-colored streams of laser fire, the exploding bombs, and plumes of smoke in the blue sky above to the soldiers below the dog fight looked like a moving jig-saw puzzle. The soldiers couldn't tell who was winning and who was losing. Luke knew. "Smitty watch your back! Smoke, get that guy off him! Bank Gant bank! I'll be there in 2 seconds. "Luke was doing the work of three good pilots, but the other team was pretty good too, and the numbers were against his team. One by one they disappeared. Smitty, Smoke, Gant, and Lassiter splashed into the Mediterranean Sea. Only Wilson and Luke were left of the Luke's and most of the other EAAC planes had been destroyed. There weren't any funny comments now, only a struggle to stay alive. Luke was using every good maneuver he had ever tried. All by himself he was evening up the numbers. Then, right in front of him before he could help, Wilson's jet exploded into a ball of garish colors. Luke goosenecked right behind the shooter and put three times the amount of ammo needed into the plane's cockpit, following him all the way down to the brink, still shooting as the mangled bits of metal plunged into the brine water. In a rage he jetted at full force to the sky's peak, and then tipped the nose, turned off the engine; he was now free-floating toward the Earth. He relaxed and felt a sense of freedom. He could see for miles and miles. He was amazed at the size of the H2O complex, and then just before the horizon the enormous oil complex. It blew his mind though how poorly its blueprints were. One well-placed direct hit at the right spot could start a chain reaction of devastation. "We gotta get these guys before one of them gets lucky, "said Luke to only himself. He was thinking that if he was losing that's what he would do, if we can't use it then nobody's using it. A couple of miles away Luke was surprised to see only three jets remained. Two Migs were bearing down sending rockets and cannon fire at the lone EAAC pilot. Luke put his Master Sniper skills to use, again one shot one kill. Down he went but so did his lone teammate. It was one on one for all the marbles. Luke remembered what General Roy said to him and oddly imagines of

John, Dad, and other notable Christlinks flashed before his eyes. Luke was lucky to quickly gain the upper hand. He bore down on the Mig... andnothinghappened.

In the frantic pace of combat Luke made a rookie mistake and did not check his dial indicating armaments. Luke had been spoiled by the unlimited supply of the Falcon but now he was out of ammo!. Then he made it worse by letting his concentration lapse for just a second and ... ooppps! His adversary, who also must be a really good pilot, did a fancy move to slide behind Luke. Luke immediately went into defensive mode and tried all his best moves to lose the Mig fighter. But this guy didn't fall for any of them, he was super! The first opponent to ever stick with Luke. Luke checked the screen and gritted his teeth; the pilot was good enough to get in perfect position for a perfect strike. Luke knew it was too late to dodge a heat seeker, but again nothing happened! The Iranian also must have been out of ammo, what a miracle! He had sure gained Luke's respect. Luke slowed down, he wanted to see the guy; the highflyers were good enough pilots to get close enough to get a good look at each other. To Luke he looked like a normal guy, he looked normal enough that he could drink a beer with him and play some Texas's hold'em; a shame thought Luke, how people in control, that never do the fighting, start all the wars, and usually over something that the average dude doesn't even know about or care about. Course this war was much different, aliens, Gods and eternity were involved. The two warriors waved to each other and went toward their homes. But Luke glanced at his radar screen and noticed the Mig swerve back again heading for the complex. "Oh no you don't, "yelled an excited Luke, "Not on my watch!" Luke turned around and put on the after burners. The Mig started to nosedive so Luke took an angle he hoped would get him to the Mig before the Iranian could kamikaze himself into the tankers below. Luke had always been good at calculating geometric measurements. It looked like he would make it in time to stop the chain reaction; so, he took a quick look at a smiling picture of an 8th grader John;

a lump formed in his throat. "Father, forgive my sins, I have tried to do right according to your word. Please take care of my loved ones. Thank you, Lord. "A few moments before contact Guardian Angel Sarah devised a brilliant plan of rescue. As she moved The Holy Father above gently rebuked her, in his wisdom and desire HE said this to Sarah, "Wait my child. It will serve me and the believers that he is permitted to perform this noble act. Therefore, let him be. "Thousands on the battlefield, millions watching on T.V., the Angelo's and John on the scout ship, watched Luke slam into the Mig; in time and a far enough distance away that the base suffered minimal damage. Another Christlink war hero! Luke put duty and honor first, before all else. He was an inspiration to the entire EAAC. Like Sargent York of WWI, Murphy of W.W.2, and now Colonel Luke of the great rebellion. UKBA tried to comfort his grandson, "You know John, most men don't care enough to choose something to be passionate about, and then even fewer have the opportunity or guts to live and die with glory, your dad chose both." "Thanks, "said John simply, I'm going to go to the bathroom for a minute. "He was left alone. John was sitting on the toilet and heard a commotion out front. He thew some water on his cheeks and ran to the action. On the giant 160 x 90 screen everyone could see General Bo's battle had begun. John was blown away by the graphics and visuals, it really was like you were in the middle of the battle; Of course, he wasn't, General Bo and his men were. Laser lights, massive old fashion nuclear explosions, something like a lava flow streaming from the warbirds, it was a cosmic horror show. The Queen Mary was the only ship they were aware of, after Bagdad UKBA's scout ship had successfully stayed hidden. The Maulk bastards threw everything they had at the Queen, they only have 30 warbirds, their entire space fleet, no reserves held back. They used several different methods of attack; but nothing penetrated the structural integrity of the Queen Mary. As the birds were coming to and fro the Queen was taking pot shots at them during each pass. Thus far, for a 24-hour battle, both sides shields were holding up. No visual damage to any vessel. UKBA, "My good friend how long can you take this kind of bombardment?" Bo, "We ae still 90 % strong. But I fear we will never have the opportunity to cool down our power crystal grid. If we don't then in time our shields will weaken. We have to hope that our weapons destroy them first." UKBA, "Hang in there. Our prayers are with you. "That's the best thing the scout ship could do, pray. 24 hours turned into 36, then 48, and then 72 hours into the battle came the first sign of damage. One of the warbirds burst into a red flare and then flamed into nothing. The Maulks stopped for a split-second and then continued the molestation. Except with a completely new strategy. Instead of widespread shooting all about the big boat this time many laser cannons aimed at the same spot on the Queens exterior. To the BEEs frightened sight, a small hole was dissolved in the massive bulkhead. The Maulks were relentless at zeroing in and enlarging the damage. Bo swung 180 degrees and fired back at the Maulk gunners, they scattered like roaches do when the light is turned on. The Queen Mary was much bigger and "Stronger" than their opponent but the quicker Maulk warbirds were elusive and apparently flown by very skilled pilots. However, the sparks and white-hot colors of the spaceships was evidence that both sides shields were weakening. Now it was a question of who would get the higher number of quality hits to the enemy, knock him out of commission, and then finish him off. Inside the Q.M. critical discussions and debate was being held about the next course of action. General Bo and the engineers made some calculations and then General Bo made a very important executive decision. The equations and his men's input carried significant creditability, but really it was more of a hunch, a gut feeling, a belief and confidence in the excellence of oneself that swayed Bo's final command. Sometimes that's how ordinary men do extraordinary things; they go against the grain and conventional measures and just do what they think will work, regardless of the push-back. Bo was going to forget maneuverers and strategy; he was just going to steer right into the belly of the beast; jump in the middle of the nest of vipers; slug it out like Ali and

Frazier in the thriller in Manilla. He was to trade shot for shot blow for blow, do or die, victory or defeat. It was a very gutsy call. He radioed UKBA with his thoughts, "Sir, delay profits us nothing. They are wearing us down with hit and run tactics. We are physically wearing down, it's been 4 straight days of battle stress and fatigue for my men, rest is impossible. Our metallic fortitude is in question. Knowing those facts, I feel it best to attack deep within enemy ranks, I plan to move immediately. I wanted to inform you before I engage the plan. If I succeed, we can all relax for a minute, if I fail, I am certain you will devise a workable strategy." UKBA, "Thanks for the vote of confidence friend. Do you have a real chance?" "My friend Angelo, I have commanded this vessel though many battles, beginning with the on-slaughter of the Red planet. My Queen is sturdy beyond specifications. I feel she has a soul and knows what is at stake. Neither one of us Sir, her or I, will let you down. Our Earth adopted families will be able to live in peace without a threat from the Red menace, I am confident of it! "Bo's prediction energized UKBA, "So be it! Go gett'em Bo. "The whole world, both the AEAR and the EAAC, was watching. The screen in the Bee scout ship had an overflow crowd. Bo powered right into the middle of the Maulk forces. He was completely surrounded. Both sides were now in range for easy point-blank shots. They were taking pot shots at the Queen, and she was scorching them. On a good strike her crystal grid would brighten and glow as the sun, and then dim to a sizzle, prepared to defend against the next charge. Multiple hits would send shock waves rippling deep into her core. But she was designed for battles like this, and the crew was drilled and well trained. She also a had a large armament package. 18 highly effective molten laser cannons, 3 in front, 3 in back, and 6 on each side. They were firing at will non-stop! This is what Bo and his courageous men wanted, they wanted to be the ones that determined the outcome, to be involved in the epic battle that would win or lose the war. These soldiers had decided a galaxy ago that their life would be forfeited so that their adopted families would live;

God-Joy's plan had worked marvelously. They were near exhaustion, but their cause and sheer will power kept them fighting. They refused to let anybody down; not their God, their planet, commander, families, or the guy fighting right beside him ...in this hell hole of a battle.

One by one the Queen was taking out individual warbirds. Each time a bird exploded cheers erupted throughout the ship. Sometimes two at once would explode from the screen, sending the crew into a short pause for jubilation. Reddish-orange fiery clouds of gases and debris filled the emptiness of space. 30-1, 29-1,28-1,25, 20 and then only 15 to one. General Bo was starting to look like a genius! Angelo Jr. "General Bo is gonna do it, he doesn't even look hurt. "The Queen did look awesome, but the screen did not reveal the carnage inside her protective casing. Enclosed within her was a living hell. Heavy as a winter cloak the thick black smoke was suffocating, roaming throughout the vessel; numerous fires were eating away at its interior, poisonous fumes wafted invisibly through the ship, sickening and sending to the infirmary those who inhaled the danger. Exploding canisters and bursting hydraulic lines flung acid burning fluids into manned positions, permanently scaring the victims. Dead, burnt bodies littered the hallways and medical beds, the action was too frantic to be more civilized with the dead and injured. Sick bay was at double capacity and that's with hundreds of injured BEEs refusing to abandon their post, not to put more burden on the next guy. They all knew this battle would be the most important thing they will ever do.

Suddenly, without a hint of a problem to the on-looking crowd, the bow of the Queen Mary burst into flames! Everybody gasped in fright! UKBA quickly contacted General BO, "BO, can you carry on, what is your condition? "BO, "Your Ultimate....Sargent," you could hear the chaos in the background. Angelo and John looked at each other, worry on their faces. Bo, "Sargent get a crew on that fire, we CAN NOT lose the back control panel! Didn't mean to be ruu.........Close around the flank, buckle down that headboard." UKBA shouted in the microphone, hoping his best all time friend could hear him, "I will see you later...keep going." John didn't know that the BEEs were created as a peaceful love, now it seemed as if they were born killers. "Hey, hey," Everyone heard Commander's Bo masculine directed voice, "Don't give up hoping' on us, we aren't done yet! "John got goosebumps. Heroism always did him that way. UKBA, "Yes, yes, of course we aren't giving up, God is with you, carry on! "Bo did feel God inside him. "Keep firing men, I'm goanna ram the Queen down their throats! "His men clapped and cheered as if they were in the lead. "C'mon, their more beat up than we are," said an encouraging Bo. But he was right. The war birds had taken a lot more shots than they were designed to, they were ready to crumble; and then one did, eliciting a tremendous eruption of cheers from the whole West! Bo, "Pour it on'em boys, their gonna start fallin' like that Earth game dominoes! "His men laughed on the inside but was too busy to do anything else but to bear down on the Maulks! They once again had hopes of victory, rest, and home. Another bird desinigrated, and another and then two at once! 11 to one, could they really pull off the greatest upset of all time? The tension and anxiety were unimaginable. Not only in the Queen, but in every good and evil heart created, including the Gods. With their superior technology just one surviving warbird could rule the world, Artis could rule the world.

Then the Maulks refocused their efforts. Instead of shooting at the bulk of the ship they concentrated on her guns. And it worked! Instead of 18 guns blasting away at the enemy suddenly there were only 9, and then just three. Kaos was furious with Peu that he hadn't done that sooner. The three back cannons on the Queen are all that was functional. But as the Maulks flew close trying to finish her off 6 more birds bit the dust. 5 to 1. Somehow the General was able to quickly jerk his pride to the starboard catching two units by surprise, 3-1. But then she stalled, everyone could tell the standard bearer for the BEE fleet was on her last leg. Angelo tuned to John, "I knew everybody on the Queen. Only the best served on her. It is the pride of the planet. I can't believe it is going out like this. We've lost the war, three birds is two to many. They will make short work of the rebellion and our families. John had never seen such a dark and saddened eye. The disappointment magnified tenfold when Queen Mary's mid-section burst into flames and started to crumble apart; Incredibly, as if she did have a heart and soul, the Queen stayed together. Kaos, "Make sure they die in agonizing pain for delaying our victory, and let the whole world see their suffering." Peu ordered the three remaining ships to move in slowly and to prolong the IMAX show as long as they safely could. The back was the most stable part of the Queen. And then there was magic! "LOOK! LOOK!. "Shouted out UKBA, his voice full of excitement. Streaming out from the rear nose cone of the Queen was three blue laser lights. "What are they, what are they," yelled John." UKBA, "Those are powerful tractor beams, the General is trying to pull the last of our enemy into the Queen. It might work, it just might work! "Intensity gripped the room. People were shouting at the screen, "You can do it...C'mon pull those %$^) burn them, burn them!" You could see the Maulk warbirds quivering and shaking, trying to break free. But closer and closer they got to Q.M. "He's gonna do it, he's, it's gonna happen." Said a most jubilant UKBA. And suddenly, quickly...all three ships bolted into the Queen! For a second the brilliant screen hurt John's eyes and he closed them, as did everyone else, but then pandemonium broke out and John opened his eyes to a junk yard of black space littered with used parts. No birds, no Queen, no more space fighting.

UKBA's scout ship was now by far the most powerful weapon in the war. A rebellion victory is possible! The success of General Bo's gutsy call cannot be overstated. Songs will be sung and poems written about Bo's leadership and his men's skill and bravery.

FINAL CHAPTER

With the help from the BEE's advanced scout ship the West routed Artis and his AEAR armies. Wherever it went UKBA brought mayhem and destruction to the enemy. His tactical command orders came down to "shoot everything that's not ours." Before attacking, war zones were evacuated of innocent civilians as best as could be done; because once unleased the unmerciful brutality of the BEE strike forces crushed anything that moved. John once asked UKBA about the savagery of the intense and constant, almost pleasurable killing, that the BEEs did to the Maulks and to the evil humans that sided with Artis.

UKBA's response was just as intense as the killing, "Young man, evil is like a burning ember, if you are fool enough to let it smolder there is no doubt that it will flame back into a rage and burn your house down, do you want your house burnt down John?, do you? "He didn't wait for an answer. "You cannot reason with, compromise, negotiate, and especially, one cannot "cure" evil. The only way to be safe and sure is to wipe it off the face of the Earth… completely. No. No. No. One does not be "nice' when confronting evil. If you do not have the stomach for it young Christlink there's a game room in the back." John had never seen UKBA's eye that mixture of deep colors before. He wasn't explaining anymore, he was angry at John's unfounded question. But he waited for an answer this time. The "I understand" answer from John was all that was needed to be said. The East, being how they are, hit every soft target they could, often killing women and children in the process. Western vigilante forces retaliated with massacres of their own. After another year of scrapping up, what started with General Bo's magnificent victory was ending with UKBA's scout ship. He wiped out the last bastion of Maulk resistance. Not one Maulk retreated or surrendered. To them they died a glorified death fighting for blood and honor. That's the best death a Maulk could pray for.

Finally, the AEAR, the Maulks, and the earthly devils and demons were defeated, a stunning victory for mankind! Thinking in wisdom and good Christian values people from the East that pleaded an oath to the constitution of the EAAC was allowed to move freely, with no punishments, just forgiveness. It sounds too good to be true but after alien abuses to every type of human there was a strong desire from all the races and creeds to have unity, acceptance, tolerance; with an understanding and agreement to make a genuine effort toward world peace and harmony. All around the world there was celebrations, parades, speeches, awards, and mostly just plain ol'e neighborhood parties! A refurbished Arlington Cemetery was the site of the official EAAC ceremony to honor the fallen. The unveiling of a statue honoring General Bo and the Queen Mary, and the funeral service for Colonel Luke was to symbolize the heroic efforts of the billions that made the ultimate sacrifice. Before attending the mid-after noon activities John and Mary had an early morning appointment with Doctor Mclean. Mary was one week overdue. A week ago, to coincide with Matthew's birthday, John and Mary decided to have a birth induction. Upon hearing the news Mat was overcome with emotion and gave the classic biblical blessing to the next generational male. Doc McClean, "Don't worry John, this is 2060, we Doctors have a firm understanding of the birth mechanism. Your baby will be born exactly the time you want it to. Like they say, wev'e come along away baby. "Doc always smiled at his own jokes; but everybody everywhere was always in a good mood now that the war was over. But John wasn't amused, this was his FIRST child. "Funny doc, your sure everything is going to be OK. This is an important baby." (Yes, it is.) Doc gave the final instructions, "With this last shot you and Mary can go to the service, take a leisurely walk back to the hospital and 12 hours later you two will be proud parents. Mary, "That sounds good to me honey. The hospital is only a mile from Arlington, we'll enjoy the sunshine together." "Right. A little healthy walk will be good for my boy." Mary, "It Could be a girl. "John gave her the puzzled look.

Never, I repeat never, has there been a female born to a Christlink, the Lord directed it that way. And the Lord made this next Christlink most special to him, a treasure, only he and MDSL knows why.

"Good, I'll give birth in this nice place under the watchful supervision of the best doctor." "Thank you. "Said the doc, and then Luke and Mary walked the short mile to the cemetery. They were assigned seats in the second row next to Pastors Donna and Simpkins, and by Reverend Radke's side. In front of them was the three men most responsible for victory, Roy, Fuller, and Matthew. Decorated Generals filled the first four rows. At rest on a freshly cut lawn was a beautiful E.A.A.C. flag draped onto a closed casket, with Luke memorable surrounding it; and 30 feet above was UKBA's scout ship holding the symbolic remains of General Bo, the Queen and his brave crew. John's plan was that after EAAC General Secretary General M. Fletcher and UKBA said some words, He and Mary would pay the proper respect, and then walk back to the hospital.

From HIS Golden Throne the Emancipator of Wisdom released MDSL and her company from their secret time freeze. MDSL continued to ramble as if nothing happened, "I know he will have some kind of trick up his sleeve; he's got those stupid Elders intimidated and his Angels are nothing but ass-kissers. He can't handle losing...that will make it all the sweeter. "Kaos, "Look, there having some kind of fancy affair, those are all the generals that opposed us, all in one location. "Kaos nearly vomited on himself by the intense anticipation of gutting his rivals. "The puny mutants that they are." Kaos, "Mother, my revenge will be blood thirsty. And I learned a truth that we can be devious with. MDSL, "What do you mean, do not keep anything from your Mother young one." Kaos, "I heard talking, and over time I made keen observations, the cheater has a pet that he prizes, his son has been charged to protect the linage and he has from the beginning; but now Mother," in all the excitement Kaos started convulsing within himself, "the newest edition is ready to pop out right into our hands." MDSL, "Be clear with me before I slit your throat!", the Mother said to her first creation. Kaos, "The fat girl with the special green eyes, the prize is in her stomach. I suggest when it comes out, we grab it and run. It will be a valuable hostage. "MDSL, "Yes, I know the "Why" of its significance. We will own it." She buffed up for a killer scream….when done she pondered to Kaos, "'Why would anyone concern themselves with the well-being of others, like the creatures of the light do. It is always best to think of yourself first and only. The stupid jerk and his sons of light do not have sense of logic or reason, they do not comprehend the desirable things; to rule others without mercy, to intimidate with fear and loathing, to use and enjoy power and authority. "Kaos, "Me too. I think we ae smart and strong enough to capture this pet right now and at the same time wreak havoc and bloodshed upon this race." Just before they arrived MDSL grabbed Peu to perform a duty, because his appearance is especially horrifying to the human weaklings. A final order from MDSL, "Send our army to destroy those machines made of flesh, they are no match for what we have. This total domination will crush any hope they might have of defeating me. I'm not Artis! "MDSL shouted, sending shock waves through those demons and devils nearby. "Bring our entire force of machinery, flesh and blood and the three servants here to the castle, and from here our whole armies are to march on this site with the world watching. I want them to see how my power and authority controls all devastation. "As they were entering Earth's lower atmosphere over D.C. the ceremony was just ending. General BO's funeral procession was starting to raise up into the blue sky, in plain view of compassionate and thankful on-lookers. Then, in glee, MDSL gave the order for Peu, who was in the new Maulk flagship, to go perform his duty.

With somber tears and patriotic feelings, accompanied by symphonic music, Bo's ship slowly lifted upward....and then BBOOMM! It blew up! Disintegrating into small bits and falling onto the stunned audience. People pushed and shoved to get out of the way of the deadly falling scraps of metal. It was a scrambled mess! John, Mat, and the spiritual hovered over Mary to protect her. John turned to comment to Angelo, but he was gone. John knew his brother wasn't a coward and guessed he was investigating the incident in stealth. The Pastors tried to comfort the panicked and all the Generals cell phones buzzed off the charts. They were informed of the worldwide destruction caused by the Army of Evil. From all the facial clues John deduced it had to be very bad, very bad. Fuller tuned to John, "It's very bad, we got to go. Trouble is on the horizon. Follow me." John didn't have to guess what the trouble was; dropping from the sky was four Hugh Maulk war birds, brand new. They landed N-S-E-W- surrounding the park releasing hundreds of Maulk soldiers, MDSL's immortals. Escape was impossible. The mere size and grossness of the Maulks caused some women to faint and other civilians to cower. Mitchell, "We must do something, I'm not going to be held prisoner. "He made his way to the edge of the crowd and dropped to his knees, hoping to get away un-noticed, as to be able to get help. But he was spotted and rat rat tat tat. No more Mitchell. Blood spattered women were either screaming or crying and then to make it worse for them a big Maulk took the butt of his rifle to Mitchell's head a few times, he didn't deserve that. Then, apparently just for the fun of it, the Maulks started randomly shooting the innocent. (Careful not to come close to the Christlink clan as they were forcefully instructed.) Then a naked "cavemen "from the Red planet relayed this message to the stunned captors, "Do not attempt to escape, it means a quicker death. The all-powerful Master of the Universe, Mother Demon Spirit Lillith, has prepared a show for you."

All the excitement and danger of this emotional happening had an adverse effect on Mary. She squeezed John's hand tight and said, "John, my water just broke. The Doc told me when that happens in this new induction method you only have about 10 minutes before the baby is born, "her eyes started to mist up, "Mary, "Darn it, I wanted to be lying in a nice hospital bed giving birth, not on a grassy knoll." "I'll help you honey, "said a visibly shaken John. "Stand back, we're the team for this, "said Pastor Simpkins, adding, "C',mon John, three servants of God are delivering your baby, what can be safer than that? "John looked at the ghastly beasts surrounding the cemetery. He had no other option. Several people put their jackets and coats on the ground for Mary to lie on. In the background there was another barrage of gunfire causing Mary to jerk her head up, "What was that?" "Just some crazies shooting off their guns, nowhere close to us," John lied to Mary, hoping she couldn't see the bloodshed. Mat, sternly looked at John, "It's hard to coral a free American spirit. "As he looked on proudly, then bent down to whisper to Mary, "Don't you worry Mary, this is a special baby meant to do great wonders. "Mary smiled, feeling Mat's warmth. From above MDSL AND kAOS/LUCIFER gleamed with satisfaction, but were also impatient, "Puny weaklings, I hat'em. "They ae a poor excuse for life." "Right, why don't they just reach in there and pull it out? What's the big deal" MDSL, "Their problem is their creator, does he know anything of worth?" Kaos, "Yes, I know. It will be so much fun to stomp human flesh into the dirt and squeeze the air from their lungs...with my bare hands I will enjoy it. "Kaos was wild eyed. They sat back and reluctantly waited for Mary to give birth. Screaming in pain Mary gave another big push, John's fingers were turning blue from her man-grip. "One more good push Mary, I can see the head now! said an overjoyed Pastor Simpkins. Mary took a big breath and exhaled with a forceful navy seal grunt. Here it is, here it is," exclaimed the man of cloth. Pastor's Donna's soothing voice calmed Mary down, "You did just fine girl, you are a mother!" Reverend Radke, "A miracle from God, I think this baby is a sign and blessing. "John, beaming, "No, he's just my boy and that's all he has to be." John bent down and kissed his sweaty wife, she flashed that Miss America smile at him, a smile he will never forget. Mat handed John a new American flag, "I was going to drape this over Luke's coffin but now this seems more appropriate. This flag has always been a symbol for life, and so is this newborn babe." Tears were streaming down Mat's cheeks. "It is fitting" said General Norris. For a moment they forgot about their dire circumstances. Then a shadow, no, a cloud, and then "That thing is as big as a mountain, "said a startled Roy, "I'm not embarrassed to say that object intimidates me. "Said Fuller, as he slid behind the pastors. "That's the single biggest thing I have ever seen!" Mat stayed speechless. A door on the visible side opened and out flew Artis, he was being levitated by Kaos. His arms and legs were spread eagle and as he floated to the ground. Then a much larger and confident Peu exited the monster ship. He stopped about 10 feet above Artis, his size dwarfing him. His terrifying appearance made some turn away from him and when he started his ferocious howling everyone had to cover their ears, most bending over in pain. Then, Lucifer started to exit the craft. It bought him pleasure that from even from a great distance his grotesque shape and appearance, couple with his trident, putrid odor, and blazing eyes, caused women to faint and men to hide. He knew the fear he invoked so he multiplied the effect by snorting out his nostrils, arching his back all the way down to his tail and raising the four-inch spikes running down his spine; he flexed his supernatural muscles and roared with jet engine intensity. The whole crowd screamed in horror and laid on the ground frozen stiff with fear. Lucifer landed first and started yelling at the people, "Before you comes the Master of the Universe, Dictator to all the living and dead. The Supreme Authority Herself, Mother Demon Spirit lillith!" Could it get any worse!? First Artis, Commander of the AEAR, then Peu, savage leader of the Maulks, then Lucifer, Ruler of hell and the devils, and now, the second most powerful force IN ALL OF CREATION! It got worse with each introduction! To make sure she had everyone's attention MDSL spit a little acidic rain down on her new slave worshippers, only enough for them to gag, cough, and to burn their eyes a beautiful color of red. She headed for the cemetary, lightning bolts and flames of fire screamed out from her fingertips. She hovered above Luke's casket and shouted, "Your God is dead! I am the one who causes all futures. It is I who must be pleasured. It all revolves around me, "she said looking up, mocking the Father "Son, do your job." she said. The events of the next few minutes IS the galactic future. Lucifer nodded over to Peu and with a thick finger directed his attention to the newborn baby. Before anybody had time to react the Red monster bullied his way to John; Peu pulled him up by his hair, the Generals and Matthew rushed to John's aid but was brushed aside by one swing of a massive forearm. With a combination of force and finesse Peu wrestled the prize away from John's gentle grasp. Peu dropped John right next to Mary, who was now on her feet demanding Peu give her baby back to her. When he started to walk away the Angelo's suddenly appeared. In a charge UKBA flew right towards Peu, and gorged him in the gut with his head sword. PEU curled over dropping the newest Christlink into Mary's waiting arms. "Let's run! "She said, adrenalin masking her pain. In a remarkable turn from fear to unbelievable courage the Generals, some officers and other on-lookers made a wedge and rammed the few Maulk soldiers blocking their escape. In Maulk language Lucifer called out to the barricading soldiers, "Do not harm the flesh, the baby must not be damaged! "John had stayed behind to help get UKBA"S three-foot sword out of PEU's innards. Before UKBA could release himself, the Hugh Lucifer walked over to them; he knocked John to the ground and with a forceful punch plunged his massive fist deep inside of Angelo's Sr. stomach. With a snort, and looking down at John with a gruesome smile, Lucifer forced his fingers up into UKBA's chest cavity. John had never heard a BEE wheeze with so much difficulty. His eye was cascading in a wild mixture of dark colors. With comparably thin arms John's mentor tried to reach up and grab Lucifer by the neck; John clearly heard the "crack" when Lucifer snapped his twig arms. It made John sick to his stomach. John jumped to his feet but got pushed back down. With a "umph" and a jerk Lucifer pulled something out of UKBA's chest and threw it in John's face; it was covered in dark green BEE blood. Angelo was having a hard time breathing, his last words to his adopted boy was "I love you son! "He heaved heavily one more time and then quit breathing, his eye went black, he was dead. Even in this time of turmoil John couldn't fight back the tears, he never been so sad his whole life. Only a scream from Mary brought him back to dim reality. He turned to see Angelo Jr. struggling with two Maulks....they were trying to steal his boy! Mat was right in the middle of the fracas. He took a handoff from Mary and started to run with the baby, as fast as HE could. After about ten small steps Mat clumsily handed the baby back to Mary, he was clutching his chest as he knelt to the ground. Angelo Jr. flew over and bent down to help his adoptive parent, the only one he ever knew besides UKBA. Mat had the strength for one last sentence, as he looked up to a loving purple eye, his last words were, "I love you son!" and then his fatal heart attack was done. It was his birthday; he was 100 years old. Because of evil his final day was full of grief and sorrow. Across the knoll Angelo's and John's eyes met, they went to each other to console each other's hurts. I'm sorry old friend," "I'm sorry for both of us. "They each walked to their blood father and grieved some more, but they did not have time to properly grieve because they heard Mary scream again and jammed themselves back into gear. They could see that Lucifer now had his prize so at top speed they went to the rescue. When Lucifer noticed them, he pointed at a fast-approaching Angelo and immediately 10 blaster carrying Maulks started shooting at John's brother and best friend. 10 killer Maulks wasn't going to miss, Angelo ducked once and that was all... splat, splat, splat! The majestic flying Angelo plopped to the dust in 1000 different pieces! Each just a glob of blood and tissue, that just one second ago he was a beautiful person. Angelo had been a playmate, a confidant, plain ol'e good buddy, a brother and friend. John felt he didn't deserve such a horrible and ghastly death. That's war. And then the horribleness continued; John tuned back to look at Mary and the baby just in time to see Lucifer slap her hard enough that she and the baby fell into his arms. John screamed in agony as he watched the monster fly away with his family. He had no options, no recourse. He could only stand there stunned. In the last two minutes he witnessed the two wisest and most beloved elders that he knew die; his best friend exploded into a sloppy mess that you don't want to look at, and now, the two most precious things in his life being taken away by the very manifestation of evil, Lucifer! After a few deep inhales John screams out with all his might, WWWWHHHHHHYYYYY!?" he called out to the heavens. People didn't even console him, what's the use? Then, more loud exclamations brought him to his senses. Look! Look!, "he heard someone yell, maybe a way to save Mary, he naively thought. A giant spacecraft from the north came quickly upon them and hovered about 500 feet above the skyline.

MDSL came out a short distance from the entrance and spoke, "Your God is dead! I am the one that causes all outcomes, it is I who must be pleasured. It all revolves around me! Slaves, follow me to finish our work." Immediately, all MDSL's evil forces stampeded from above the horizon; She pounded the Earth with a clawed foot, causing tremors to ripple throughout the region and then commanded her evil to attack. Artis's slave army, the demons and devils, and the remainder of the Maulk menace, everything that MDSL had converted from pureness to sin, marched forward to end humanity. With a gargantuan explosion of blackness, the onslaught began. A continuous roar where your ears never stop ringing. The never ceasing concussion waves caused their noses and ears to bleed, but that was minimal compared to the vast array of death that the small, frightened group witnessed. All over the Earth MDSL's forces were killing goodness. With the Earth being blasted away by death rays, mega-ton mountain busters, and everything the dark could hurl at them the Christlkink clan and friends were amazed at their survival. It was amazing and must be classified a miracle. Up above there was more than just amazement, Kaos and MDSL was pissed off! "He's trying to cover his pets with a blanket of Angels! Well soon they won't have any Earth to stand on. What then you dumbass! He sickens me!" lashes out MDSL. Tuning to Kaos she magnified her screaming, always screaming, "When they float off to space and die that it will be the end of it, I will be the victor. There will be no defending their lost effort, not when there dead." Pour it on them you stiffs!" The Christlink clan and friends were grateful to be alive but couldn't logically, by worldly reasoning, explain why or how. Pastor Simpkins wasn't taking any chances, "Everybody here is saved, right? "Radke, "If not there is never a better time than now." Roy, "Didn't you here, God is dead, he is not around any more to offer redemption; I would have, but now it is too late, I waited too long; we will lose, I am lost." John hated to see his favorite uncle like that, plus and mostly, John STILL didn't feel defeated! "Or "He beamed, "This could be the greatest comeback of all time!! "Everybody nervously laughed. Pastor Donna, "There IS a supernatural reason why we are alive." "Yes, "agreed Reverend Radke, "I believe very soon something will be revealed to us." The unbelievable calamity around them somehow intensified, as though trying to squash any hope the group was holding on to. Any picture you can imagine of an atomic catastrophe pale in comparison to this attempt at Earthly genocide. The ruin was indescribable. MDSL truly did command her evil to erase Earth from the Milky Way spiral. She told Artis to finish the (Human Fleas!). So over 200 million marching demons, devils, and willing human slaves charged forward, firing from canons, tanks and handheld guns. Above them was about 500 brand new awesome looking Maulk warbirds.

Anticipating a quick finish, the group stood closer for personal prayer and condolences. Fuller, "Roy, I always appreciated and respected your calm professionalism. You are a good soldier brother," his eyes couldn't hold back the waterfall of emotion. Norris, "Yes, we did all we could, it took supernatural aliens to defeat our human spirit." Roy, "The demon is right, all we have to do now is die. ""Why don't you shut up and see what happens," said Norris, not a relative but close trusted friend. "At the very least we are going to stand tall and die like men, "Roy straightened his back bone and scolded, "Like dignified soldiers."

From above the S.H.F. sent three more Guardian Angels to protect his favorite clan. Their survival was important to him, and it was a legal move according to the "bet' rules. Their names were Warren, Charlotte, and Neola. "Oh! Your auras are so big and beautiful, you must be full of Love," they were told. "Thank you. Our desire is to serve God." With the other Angels they formed an invisible, transparent dome covering the chosen family. The Angels did a stupendous job, the Christlinks and other servants remained unharmed, despite such catastrophic destruction raining down in close quarters. Occasionally there would be a break in the thick sulfur smelling smoke long enough for the group to get a glimpse of the nightmare. Black potholes of Earth and exploding bombs is all they could ever see. No buildings, streets or anything else resembling civilization. They stood in silence when suddenly a giant gust of wind blew the dark clouds of trouble away... far away until there was just a beautiful blue sky. "Could that be a sign? "Loudly asked John, turning to face the group. Again, they just stood in silence.

Then, un-natural strangeness began to happen. From above unseen heights came floating down a solitary figure. Closer you could tell it was a man dressed in a white robe sitting on a white stallion. As he got close enough to recognize he turned and smiled at the astonished servants. For a moment the humans could see their caretakers; it filled them with hope. The Angels smiled back at the savior. "Did you see that! "Exclaimed Pasto Simpkins, "It is Jesus, the Son of God! "Reverend thought she was saying a silent prayer, but she was actually yelling loudly, "Thank you Father for protecting us. Please lead us right now, according to your will. Amen. "Even

Roy felt upbeat, "YYYAAHHHOOOO!" He said with great enthusiasm. Then, just as quickly as their hopes had risen, they were quickly put to question; from the far background was the unmistakable sound of cannon fire. They had thought just the presence of the savior ended the strife; no, it only intensified it! The one shot was instantly followed by dozens and then hundreds of firings; the erratic screech of the approaching nosecones made it all the more dreadful. Then, miracles eclipsing the good book started! The Good Lord simply stuck out his hand and snuffed out the first incoming missel, then the next and the next and then his hands stated to blur like propellers of an airplane, and then faster they became just a swirling cloud with steaks of colors zipping in and out and all around. What could be seen by the thankful group was bombs falling harmlessly to the ground, turning into fine floating ashes the last 10 feet of flight. For a moment there was jubilation, then the group heard an enormous barrage of laser and cannon fire and the sky's zenith opened up and swarms of the new Maulk warbirds came surging to the battle. The Lord had elicited the total fury of hell. The groups non-tangible feelings of faith and belief was put to the test by visible destruction. Supernaturally the Lord's power reached every incoming sortie, not one got through, and then to the delight and rousing encouragement from the family clan, the Lord went on the offensive! He emitted colored streamers of destruction from his eyes; they shot out multiple balls of energy simultaneously zooming to, hitting and destroying every Maulk spaceship! Artis's men scrambled around trying to hide from their condemnation like scared rats. Godly power swept through the evil ranks row by row; then the righteous force added a double edge sword to His arsenal; it came from the Lord's mouth; it was a mile long and glowed with Authority. Back and forth, back and forth it went. Anything of man or machine, that the energy got close to, would spark like high voltage electricity and extinguished whatever it touched, sizzling it with a flash of crispness. The savior was making quick work of evil and sin. Then, even more. It seemed the Lord had the same feelings about evil as UKBA did. From the precious Lamb's fingertips came balls of flame, again, whatever they contacted, and they never missed a target, it was quickly brought to dust. The Lord moved forward, going beyond the horizon, and then came back. There was an eerie silence. The destruction took 7 minutes! He looked at the group, smiled again, and began to slowly ascend upward. Then appearing for the first time was the multitude of Angels that had accompanied the Master; they formed a choir, followed the Creator, singing inspirational songs of worship and praise. Jesus had saved the day!

The "BET "from ages ago, that was intended to determine which high Authority is the better Creator; and would be the Eternal Master, and whom would be the slave; the bet that started an inter-species galactic war; nearly eliminating mankind; the bet that killed both of John's families and caused the manifestation of evil, the devil, to kidnap his wife and baby and is still on the loose; the BET and the war is over.. It is another fresh beginning for Love's creations.

John, "Praise the Lord, this has been amazing. "Pastor Simpkins, Donna and Reverend Radke all expressed their own thoughts of appreciation and awe. Roy, "He sure knows how to leave an impression. Fuller, "Yes, nothing could ever top this. "They all nodded in agreement; but did so to soon.

Without warning and from all around them PEOPLE was showing themselves! A lot of people! They were spaced out surrounding the knoll, about one-person for every square yard! They were stacked together close as sardines as far as the eye could see! And still more strange; they were all dressed differently, very differently! From all ages and times people were walking around looking dazed and confused. A cave man, sailor, a sheik, minister, a little boy, a small girl; any and all types of person you can imagine. Most of them looked sick, diseased and tormented. To the intelligent survivors it looked like a representation of people from all cultures and creeds from all times since the beginning of people. It was freaky weird. Then so fast as to shock a person it instantly got pitch black!

Cause your brain to hallucinate darkness! Nobody could see the thousands, millions of people that was just there. It was too dark to see your own hand in front of your face. Roy, "What is this? I don't like it." "SSSHHH! Said Donna, "Please, I'm afraid." Pastor Simpkins, "After all that we've been through the Lord is not going to allow harm to come to us now." Fuller, "I agree, but be quiet so I can know what's going on, that's an order." "He can't really order us, "thought John to himself. Then, filling up their senses, was small red glowing splotches of what looked like fluorescent red paint dotting the surface. They were about 2 inches diameter and there were thousands, maybe millions of them; probably more in this supernatural day. Then whoosh, whoosh, whoosh, small flames shot out of the holes where the splotches were, and then out of those same holes came agonizing screams of pain! Heart wrenching noises nobody should have to hear... or worse...make! "I'm sshheeaakkkkiinngggggg, "said a terrified Roy. "So am I.," said Donna. "What should we do? "Asked Radke. Simpkins, "Just be still and have faith, I'm sure we are not in danger." With tears in his voice the man that favors righteousness says, "The Lord is separating the chafe from the wheat, and it has to be done." He lowered his head to silently pray. John, still a little bewilder but understood by the time he finished his own sentence," Those were sinners being dragged off to hell! Why didn't they just believe? "He felt like he had been punched in the stomach. Another amazement started to happen. The darkness instantly removed itself and the sky got bluer and bluer, their eyes were allowed to see a brightness they never experienced on the natural Earth. Oh, it feels so warm! "I feel at peace, I think for the very first time. "Everybody was serene. Then another incident brought them great joy. "I don't know why I didn't believe enough before to get down on my knees, just procrastinated. UUMMM." Roy was almost crying, almost. The exceptional happenings were not through. The blue sky turned to a shimmering white, yet it was not painful to look at. It should have blinded them, but it only filled them with more love than each person ever thought possible. Something again manifested in the ground.

Instead of red splotches a transparent 2-inch diameter tube shot straight up from the ground to heaven(?) It had a spiritual realm vibe to it. Each tube lasted only a few seconds but there was enough of them that you could deduce what was happening. Suddenly General Norris was gone! And then Fuller! But Roy and the others were not. It soon ended. "Wow! you were right Pastor Simpkins; the chafe is now separated from the wheat." Said Pastor Donna. Then she pointed to the charred eaten Earth in the near distance. "Look! These people have been granted a second chance, come we have work to do before it is too late, we do not know when the thief will again come in the night." The disciples started to walk to the masses. "I don't understand all those people, not after that attack; it's not possible." said Roy. John, "Well, it's there in plain view. Maybe where're not supposed to know everything, all we have to do is believe and have faith, damn easy to do after what we've been a witness to, don't you agree?"

General Roy ran the knoll to catch Pastor Simpkins. "Hey Pastor wait on me; I am ready now! Do me first ...of this new age. "The Pastor turned to the enthusiastic new believer, "You two go on, I'm going to help the General." The wide grinning Pastor hugged Roy and said, "I'm so thankful for this, you will be a tremendous Shepard, first for your family, and then all those you meet. "Now, with a sincere heart repeat these words, the same words any sinner can say now to redeem themselves.

{Holy Father, I admit I am a sinner. I want to repent. I believe that Jesus is your son and was born from the virgin mother Mary, I believe that Jesus willingly died on the cross to wash away my sins. I ask that he come into my heart now to be my Lord and Savior.}"

Roy, "MAN, what a difference, I DO feel it. "Pastor, "That's how it works. You are a new creature now. C'mon, we have others that need to hear our witness, that's how it all started in the very beginning. People shared their testimony." John went to his uncle and hugged him. As it turned out he became a crusader, a great man of God. But now he and John turned to see an alien spacecraft, it had to be. But it was of a

258

different design and looked to be of a different composite material. Plus, it was shiny brand new; it hadn't gone through battle! John walked closer and on cue an entrance ramp lowered in front of him. He stepped on its padded footer. Hesitantly at first, then a plan sprang into John's head. His uncle Roy called out to him, "Hey John be careful. What are you doing anyway? "John looked at Roy, and when he turned back to the ship a door slid open, John took a step and saw something that made him stop and catch his breath.... a lovely blue-velvety hand, with a high gloss silk look, with a thumb and four fingers, highlighted by diamond bling fingernails! John took another excited step and again hesitated, "was that Mary's perfume? "He hesitated one more time, made a decision, turned excitedly to Roy and pronounced to mankind, "I'm going to find my wife, and my son, ADAM!"

But that's the beginning of the next story!

Printed in the United States
by Baker & Taylor Publisher Services